MAN-EATERS
VOLUME 4

A collection of:
MAN-EATERS: THE CURSED, ISSUE 1-5
(*a stand-alone story arc*)
~ PLUS ~
A PATRIARCHY REPARATIONS PACKET

With Our Compliments!

CREATORS CHELSEA CAIN & LIA MITERNIQUE
WRITER CHELSEA CAIN
COVER ARTIST & GRAPHIC DESIGNER LIA MITERNIQUE
ARTISTS KATE NIEMCZYK AND LIA MITERNIQUE
COLORIST RACHELLE ROSENBERG
LETTERER JOE CARAMAGNA
SUPPLEMENTAL BACKGROUND INKER ANIA SZERSZEN
POEMS, SPELLS, REPORT & POST-IT LETTERING ELIZA FANTASTIC MOHAN
CELEBRITY HAIKU COLUMNIST EMILY POWELL
ADDITIONAL INTERIOR ART STELLA GREENVOSS
ADULT HANDWRITING MARY JO BIERIG

YOU HAVE BEEN CONTACTED BY THE MINISTRY OF TROUBLE. AWAIT FURTHER INSTRUCTIONS. ♀

PRODUCTION BY TRICIA RAMOS

IMAGE COMICS, INC. • **Robert Kirkman:** Chief Operating Officer • **Erik Larsen:** Chief Financial Officer • **Todd McFarlane:** President • **Marc Silvestri:** Chief Executive Officer • **Jim Valentino:** Vice President • **Eric Stephenson:** Publisher / Chief Creative Officer • **Nicole Lapalme:** Controller • **Leanna Caunter:** Accounting Analyst • **Sue Korpela:** Accounting & HR Manager • **Marla Eizik:** Talent Liaison • **Jeff Boison:** Director of Sales & Publishing Planning • **Lorelei Bunjes:** Director of Digital Services • **Dirk Wood:** Director of International Sales & Licensing • **Alex Cox:** Director of Direct Market Sales • **Chloe Ramos:** Book Market & Library Sales Manager • **Emilio Bautista:** Digital Sales Coordinator • **Jon Schlaffman:** Specialty Sales Coordinator • **Kat Salazar:** Director of PR & Marketing • **Drew Fitzgerald:** Marketing Content Associate • **Heather Doornink:** Production Director • **Drew Gill:** Art Director • **Hilary DiLoreto:** Print Manager • **Tricia Ramos:** Traffic Manager • **Melissa Gifford:** Content Manager • **Erika Schnatz:** Senior Production Artist • **Ryan Brewer:** Production Artist • **Deanna Phelps:** Production Artist • IMAGECOMICS.COM

CHAPTER 1

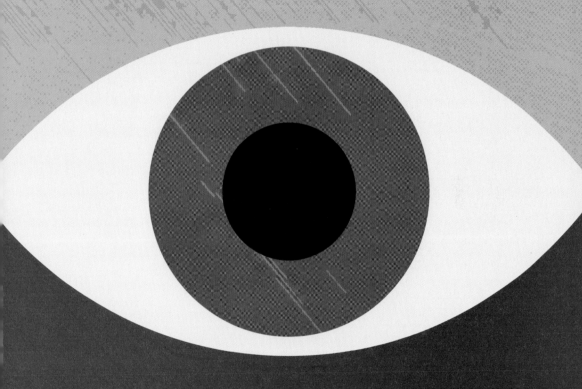

man-eaters:
THE CURSED

NO. 1

CHELSEA CAIN   LIA MITERNIQUE   KATE NIEMCZYK   RACHELLE ROSENBERG   JOE CARAMAGNA

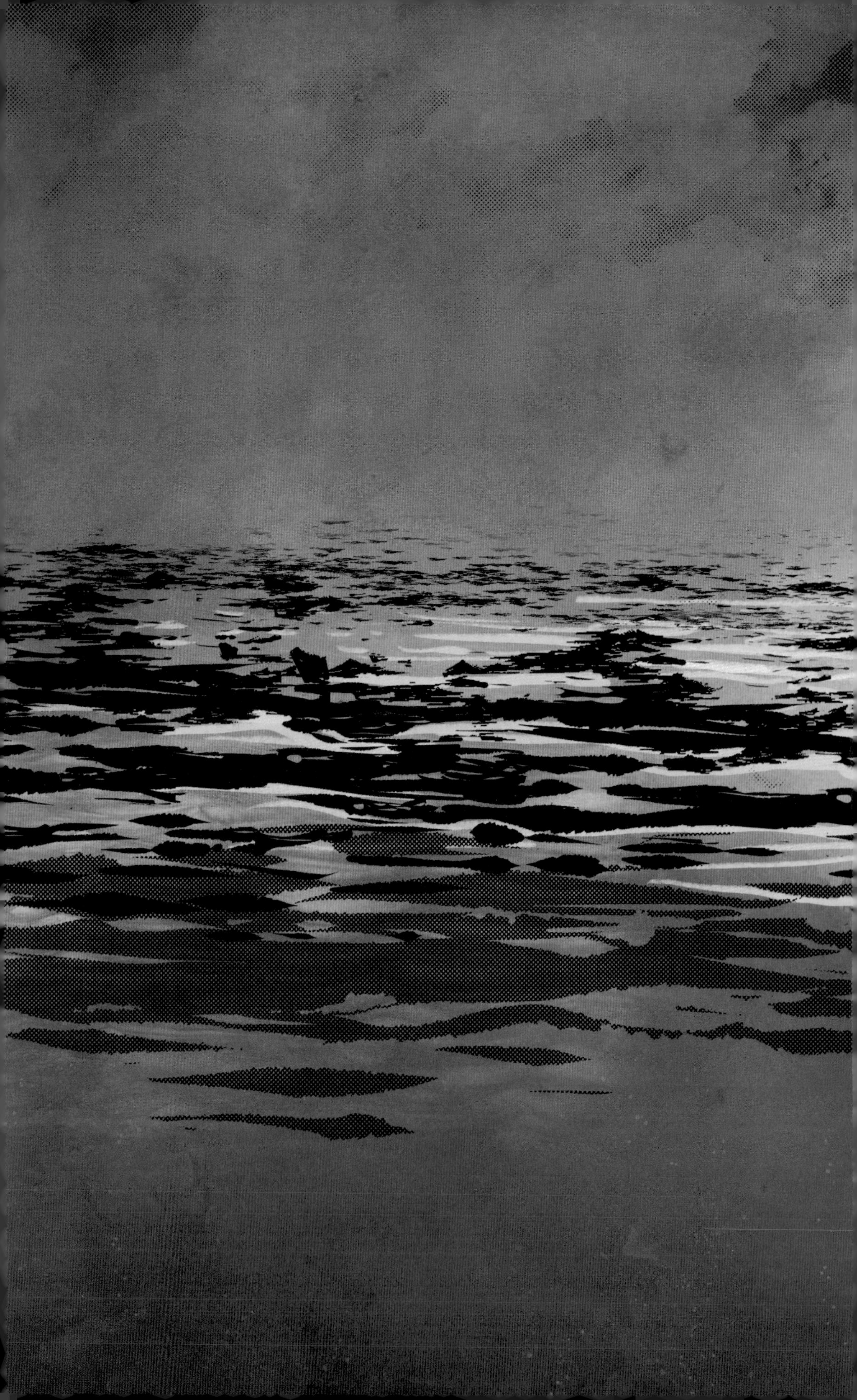

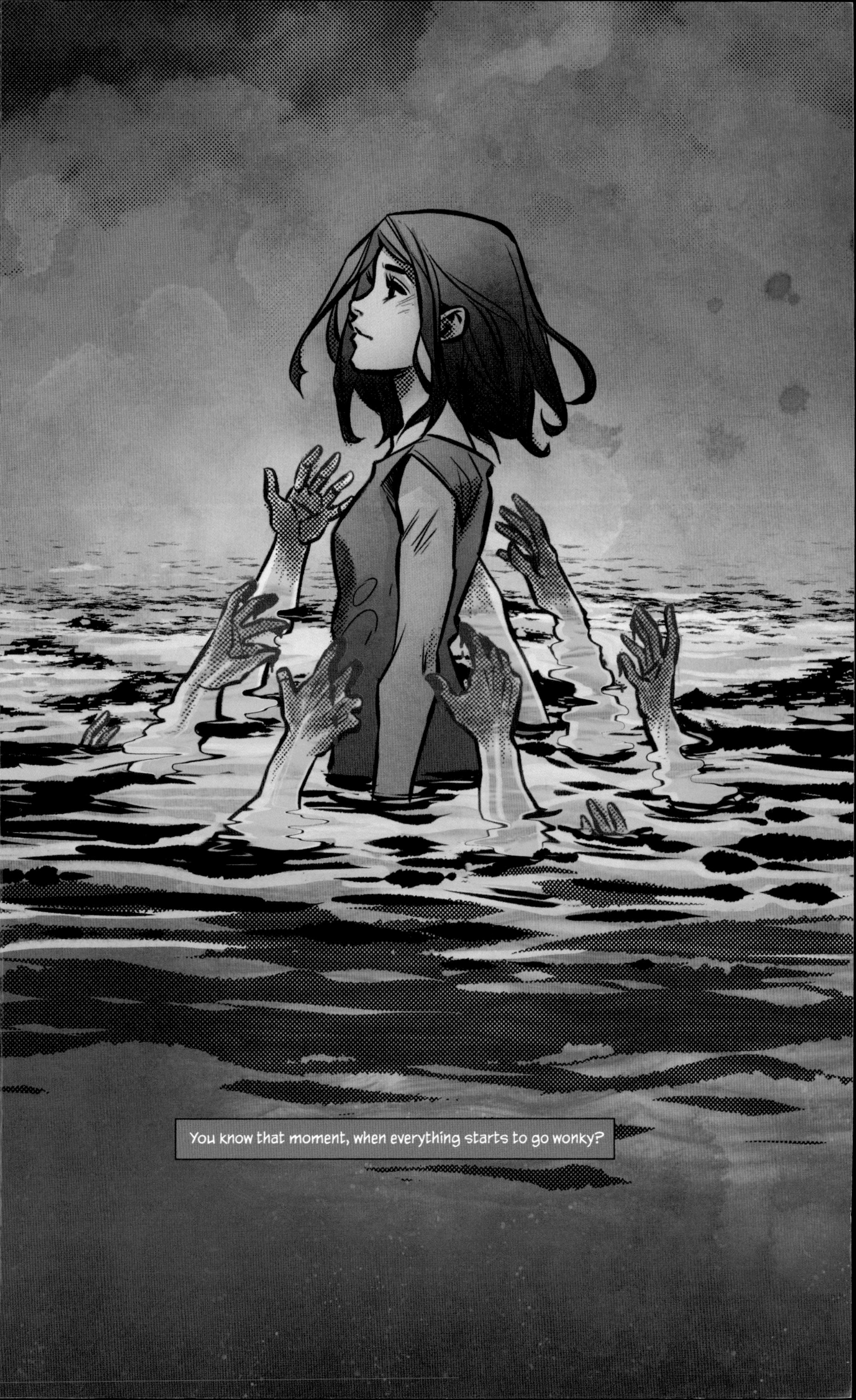
You know that moment, when everything starts to go wonky?

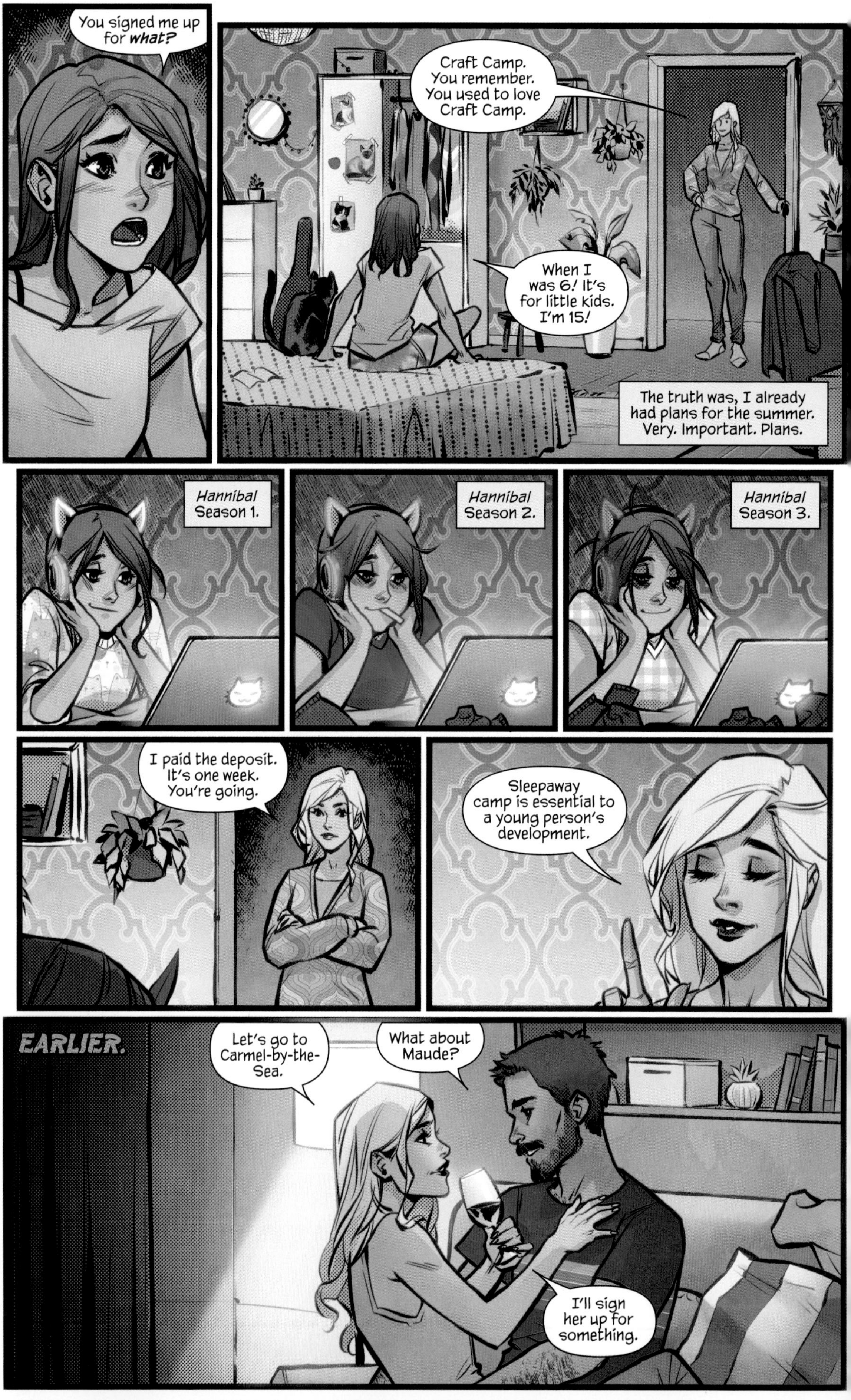

You signed me up for *what?*
Craft Camp. You remember. You used to love Craft Camp.
When I was 6! It's for little kids. I'm 15!
The truth was, I already had plans for the summer. Very. Important. Plans.
Hannibal Season 1.
Hannibal Season 2.
Hannibal Season 3.
I paid the deposit. It's one week. You're going.
Sleepaway camp is essential to a young person's development.
EARLIER.
Let's go to Carmel-by-the-Sea.
What about Maude?
I'll sign her up for something.

Romantic Carmel-by-the-Sea Cottage Getaway

★ 4.80 (85 reviews) · Carmel-by-the-Sea, California, United States

Share Save

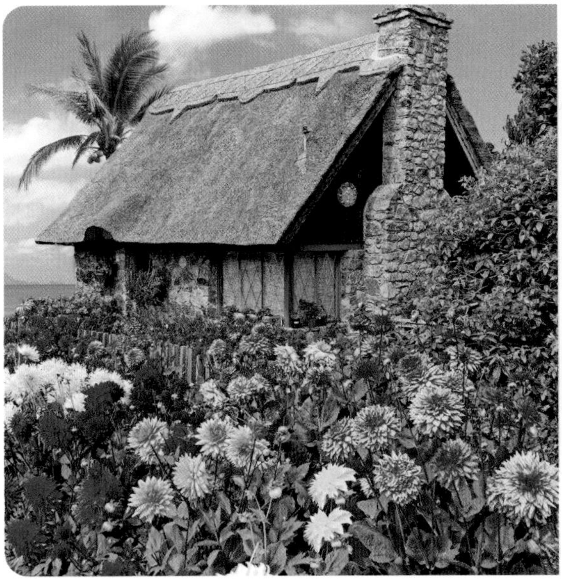

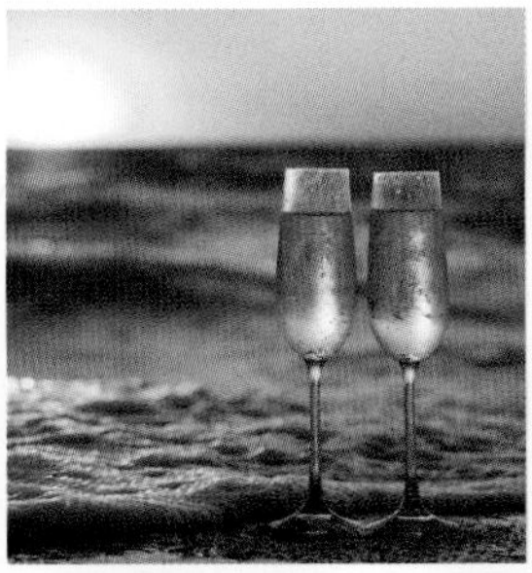

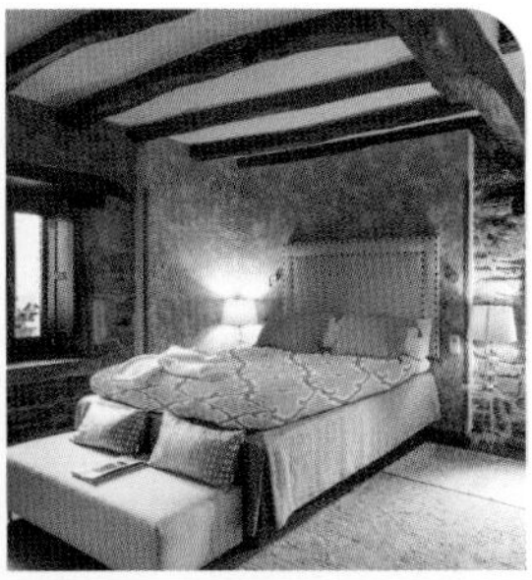

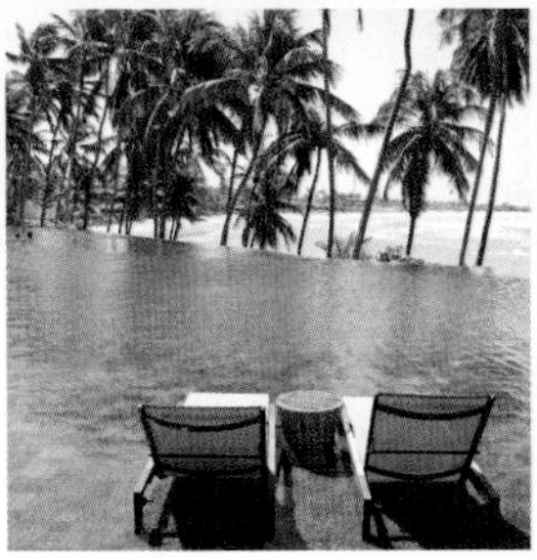

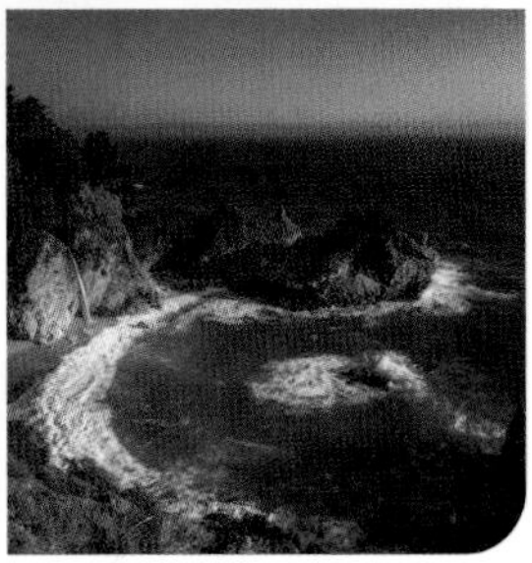

Entire house

2 guests. 1 bedroom. 1 bed. 1 bath.

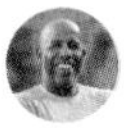

Tidy
This host committed to a 5-step enhanced cleaning process. Learn more

Super spot
90% of recent guests gave the location a 5-star rating.

Friendly check-in
90% of recent guests gave the check-in process a 5-star rating.

Free cancellation for 48 hours
After that, cancel before 4:00 PM and get a 50% refund, minus the first night and service fee.
Get details

Things to know
The host doesn't allow pets, parties, or smoking. Get details

Your dream come true

Perfect for couples! This classic Carmel-by-the-Sea fairytale bungalow offers easy access to the beach, as well as an outdoor seating area. Partial Ocean View. Walking distance to galleries, wine bar, and boutiques. Revive your relationship with a weekend at this charming rustic home.

Everything you want

The entire cottage will be yours to enjoy, along with access to a meditation garden and private hot tub. (Nearby pool is available for an hourly rate.)

It's all fine, don't worry

A valid credit card is required at check-in to cover hot tub chlorination fee. Your room charge and taxes will be paid prior to your arrival. Taxes are 11.795%, and a nightly $2 gardening fee. A historical zone fee ($30 + tax or $33.54 total) will also be charged to your account. No on-street parking. No pets. No children.

Amenities

Free parking on premises	Carbon monoxide alarm	Essentials	First aid kit
Pool	Meditation garden	Birdbath	Hot tub
TV	Wifi	Fireplace	
Heating	Breakfast	Smoke alarm	

$225 / night ★ 4.80 (85 reviews)

CHECK-IN	CHECKOUT
07/03	07/10

GUESTS
2 guests

Reserve

You won't be charged yet

$225 x 7 nights	$1,575
Cleaning fee	$75
Service fee	$233
Occupancy taxes and fees	$25
Total	**$1,908**

This is a bargain gem. Stephen's place is usually fully booked.

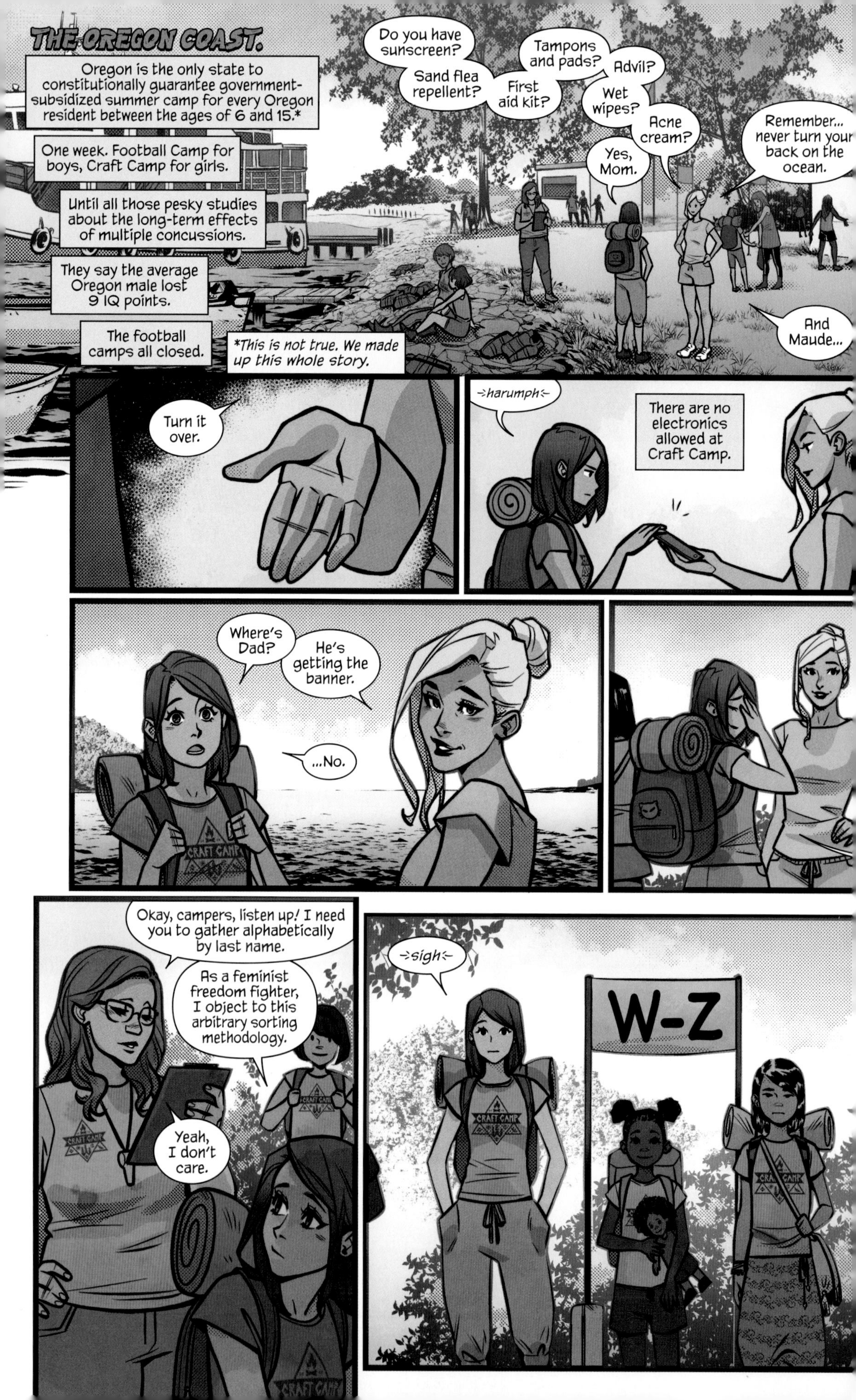
THE OREGON COAST.
Oregon is the only state to constitutionally guarantee government-subsidized summer camp for every Oregon resident between the ages of 6 and 15.*
One week. Football Camp for boys, Craft Camp for girls.
Until all those pesky studies about the long-term effects of multiple concussions.
They say the average Oregon male lost 9 IQ points.
The football camps all closed.
*This is not true. We made up this whole story.
Do you have sunscreen?
Sand flea repellent?
First aid kit?
Tampons and pads?
Advil?
Wet wipes?
Acne cream?
Yes, Mom.
Remember... never turn your back on the ocean.
And Maude...
Turn it over.
harumph
There are no electronics allowed at Craft Camp.
Where's Dad?
He's getting the banner.
...No.
CRAFT CAMP
Okay, campers, listen up! I need you to gather alphabetically by last name.
As a feminist freedom fighter, I object to this arbitrary sorting methodology.
Yeah, I don't care.
sigh
W-Z

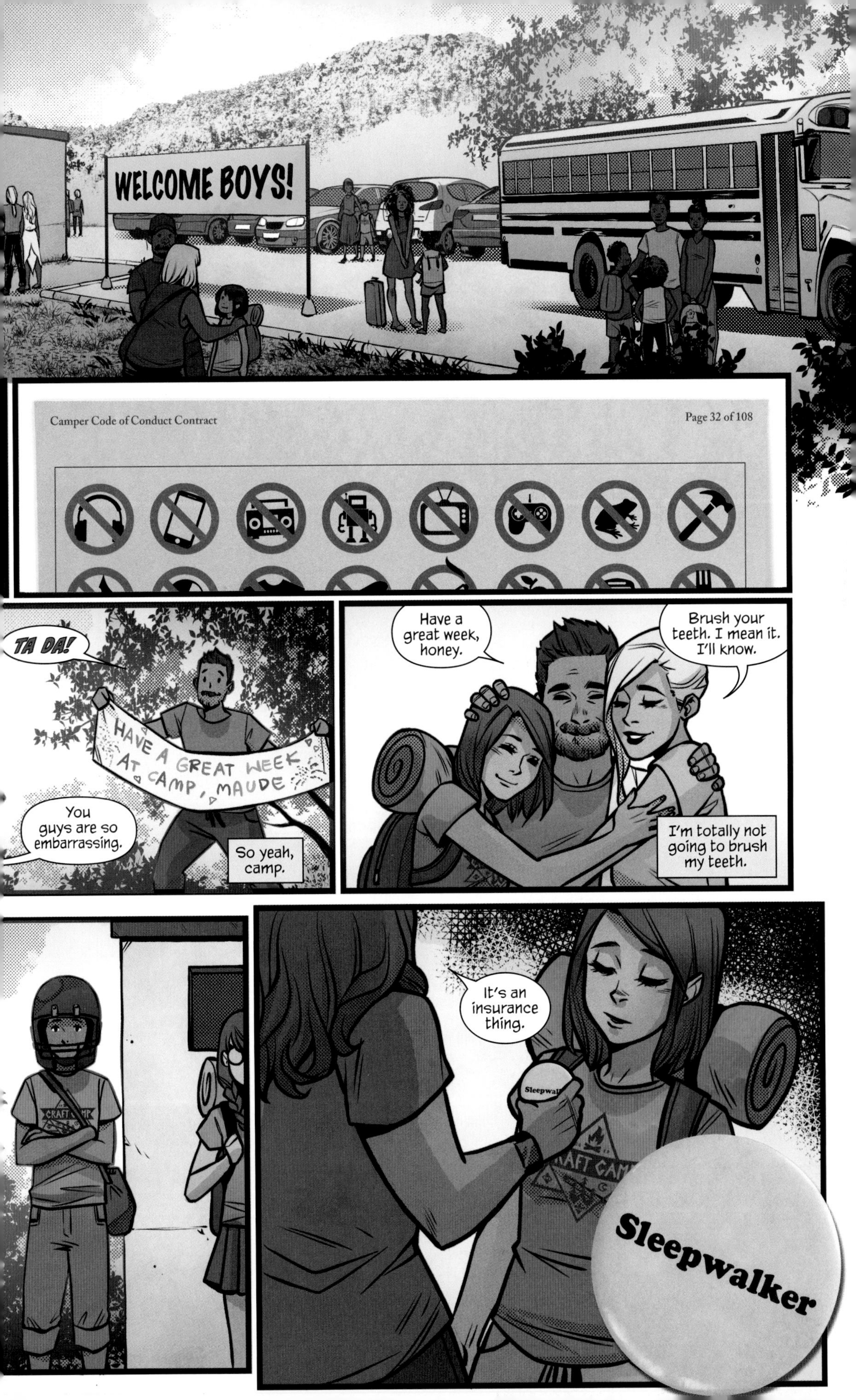
WELCOME BOYS!
Camper Code of Conduct Contract
Page 32 of 108
TA DA!
HAVE A GREAT WEEK AT CAMP, MAUDE
You guys are so embarrassing.
So yeah, camp.
Have a great week, honey.
Brush your teeth. I mean it. I'll know.
I'm totally not going to brush my teeth.
It's an insurance thing.
Sleepwalker
Sleepwalker

CO ED

CRAFT CAMP

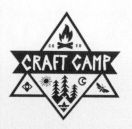

SUMMER CAMP REGISTRATION FORM

Camper's Name: Maude W. Is registrant a returning camper? (Y) N

Pronouns: She/Her Age: 15

City of Residence: Portland, OR

Parent/Guardian: Jo W. Relationship: Mother

Will you be vacationing while your child is at camp? (Y) N Destination: Carmel-by-the-Sea

To help us provide the best care possible, please answer the following questions (use additional paper if needed)

Is the/your camper allergic to any of the following: (check all that apply)

☐ mint	☐ goldenseal	☐ cow's tongue	☐ pinecones	☐ bluejay eggs
☐ garlic	☐ lemon zest	☐ graveyard dirt	☒ marigolds	☐ chalk
☐ sage	☐ chanterelles	☐ thyme	☐ frankincense	☐ volcanic ash
☐ sandalwood	☐ honey	☐ Venus flytraps	☐ cashews	☐ wheat
☒ moss	☐ blackthorn	☐ dew	☐ jezebel root	☐ peanut butter

Has the camper ever transformed into a werepanther? (Y) N *If Yes, how long has it been since their last episode?* ______

Please check any of the below that apply to your camper:

☐ gluten intolerant	☐ clumsy	☐ unvaccinated	☐ panic attacks
☒ sleepwalker	☐ picky eater	☐ easily startled	☐ contagious rash
☐ hyperactive	☐ dog allergy	☐ bed wetter	☐ dyslexic
☐ left-handed	☐ lice	☐ menstruating	☐ socially awkward

Should we be aware of any other conditions that might affect your camper's ability to participate in camp activities? (Y) N

If Yes, please explain. Maude is afraid of hammocks

IDENTIFYING CHARACTERISTICS

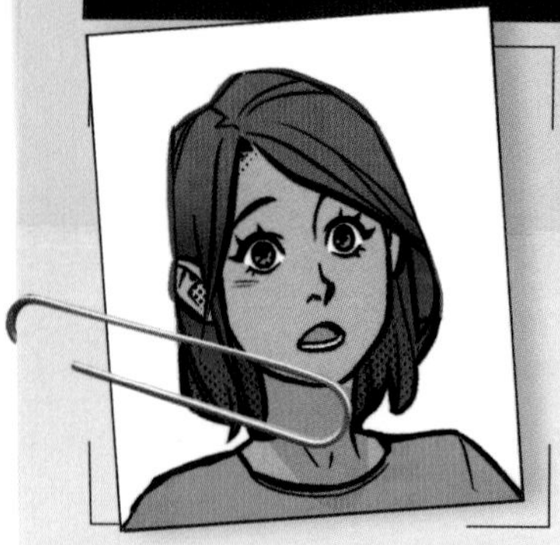

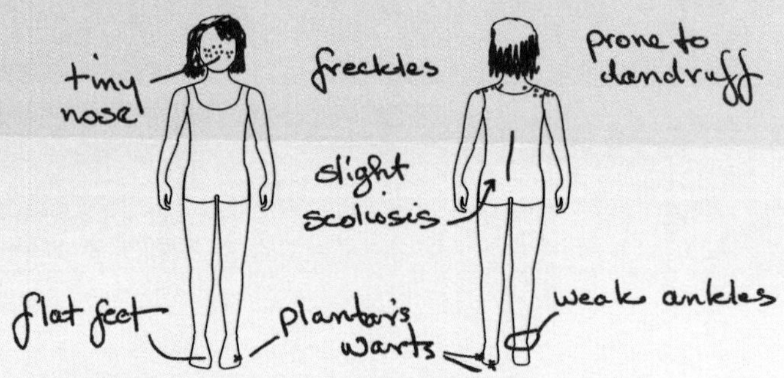
tiny nose
freckles
prone to dandruff
slight scoliosis
flat feet
plantar's warts
weak ankles

LEFT HAND | **RIGHT HAND**

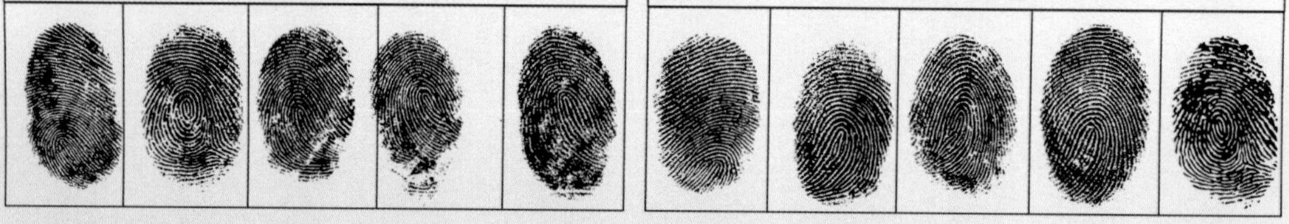

Do you agree to all terms and conditions listed on the Craft Camp website? (Y) N

SIGNATURE: Jo W. DATE: 6/26

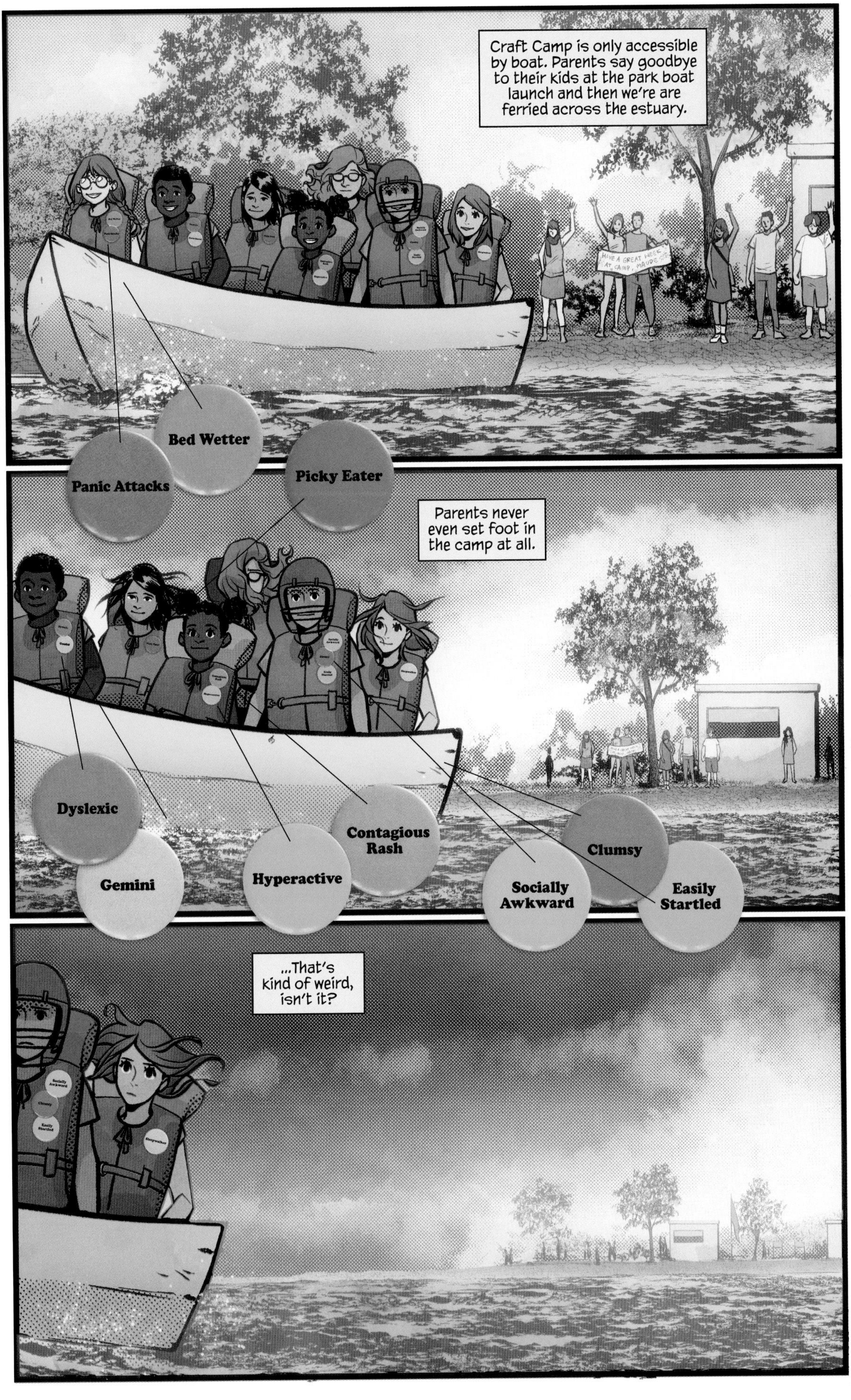
Craft Camp is only accessible by boat. Parents say goodbye to their kids at the park boat launch and then we're are ferried across the estuary.
HAVE A GREAT WEEK AT CAMP, MAUDE
Bed Wetter
Panic Attacks
Picky Eater
Parents never even set foot in the camp at all.
Dyslexic
Gemini
Hyperactive
Contagious Rash
Clumsy
Socially Awkward
Easily Startled
...That's kind of weird, isn't it?

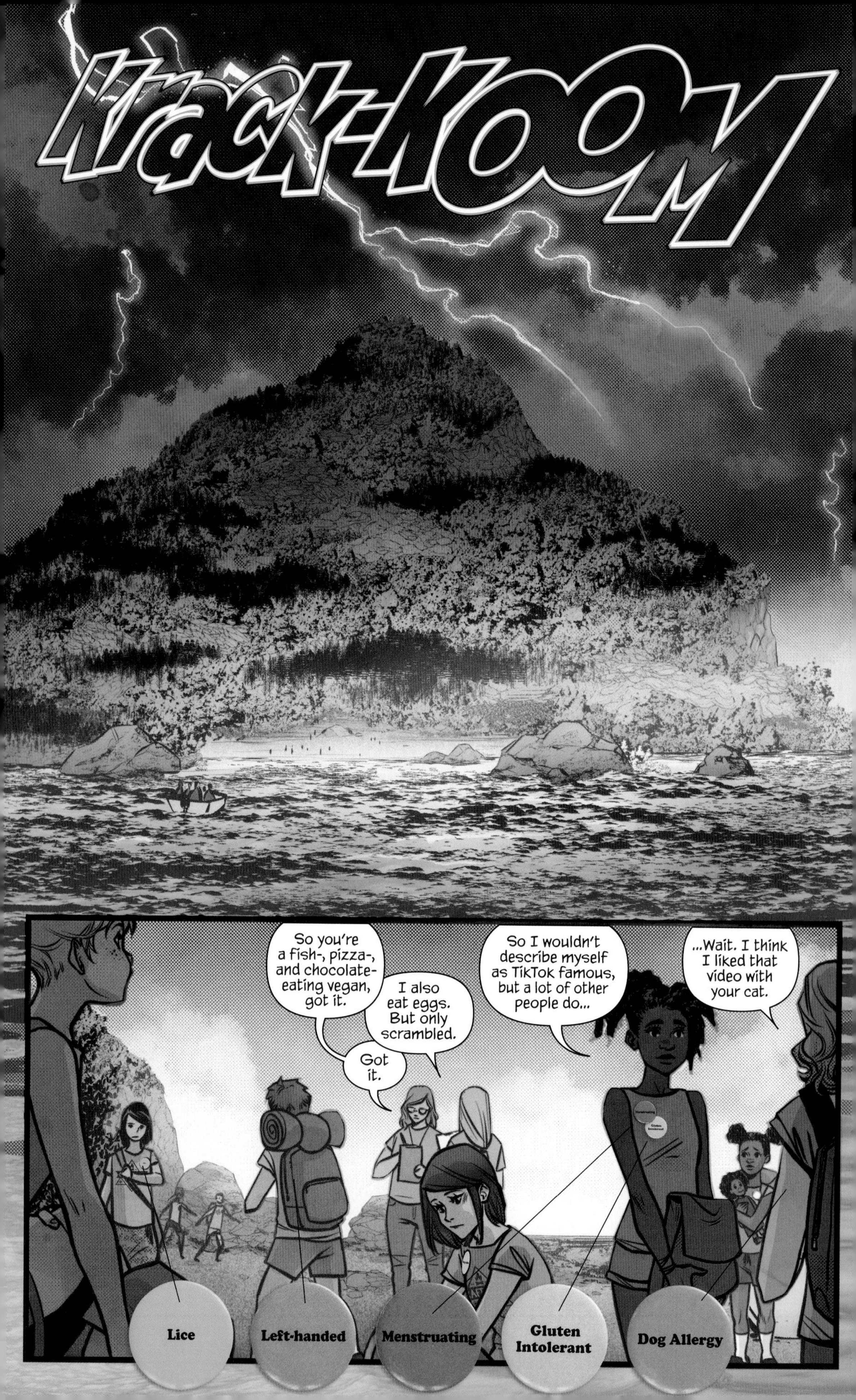

KRACK-KOOM
So you're a fish-, pizza-, and chocolate-eating vegan, got it.
I also eat eggs. But only scrambled.
Got it.
So I wouldn't describe myself as TikTok famous, but a lot of other people do...
...Wait. I think I liked that video with your cat.
Lice
Left-handed
Menstruating
Gluten Intolerant
Dog Allergy

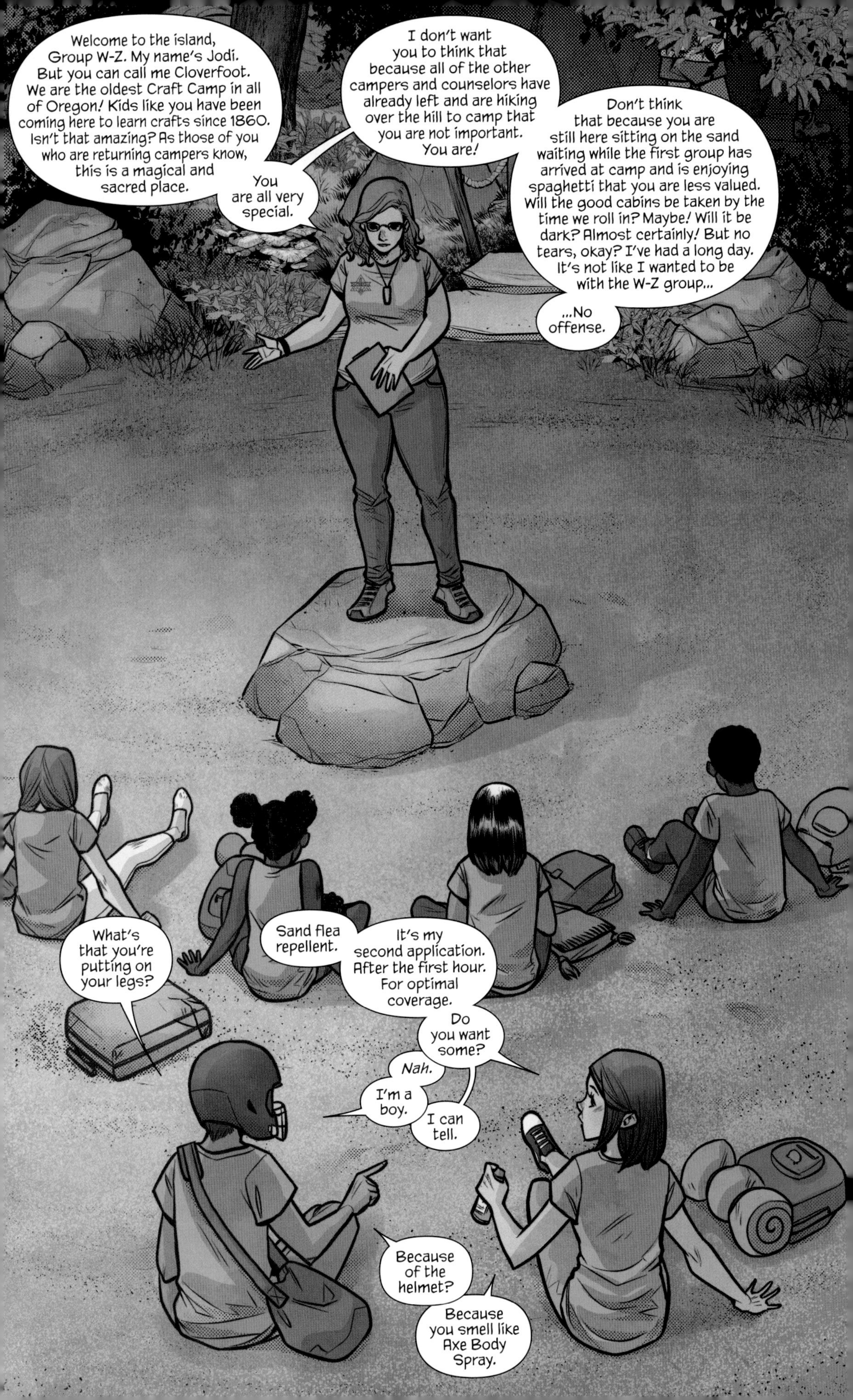
Welcome to the island, Group W-Z. My name's Jodi. But you can call me Cloverfoot. We are the oldest Craft Camp in all of Oregon! Kids like you have been coming here to learn crafts since 1860. Isn't that amazing? As those of you who are returning campers know, this is a magical and sacred place.
You are all very special.
I don't want you to think that because all of the other campers and counselors have already left and are hiking over the hill to camp that you are not important. You are!
Don't think that because you are still here sitting on the sand waiting while the first group has arrived at camp and is enjoying spaghetti that you are less valued. Will the good cabins be taken by the time we roll in? Maybe! Will it be dark? Almost certainly! But no tears, okay? I've had a long day. It's not like I wanted to be with the W-Z group...
...No offense.
What's that you're putting on your legs?
Sand flea repellent.
It's my second application. After the first hour. For optimal coverage.
Do you want some?
Nah.
I'm a boy.
I can tell.
Because of the helmet?
Because you smell like Axe Body Spray.

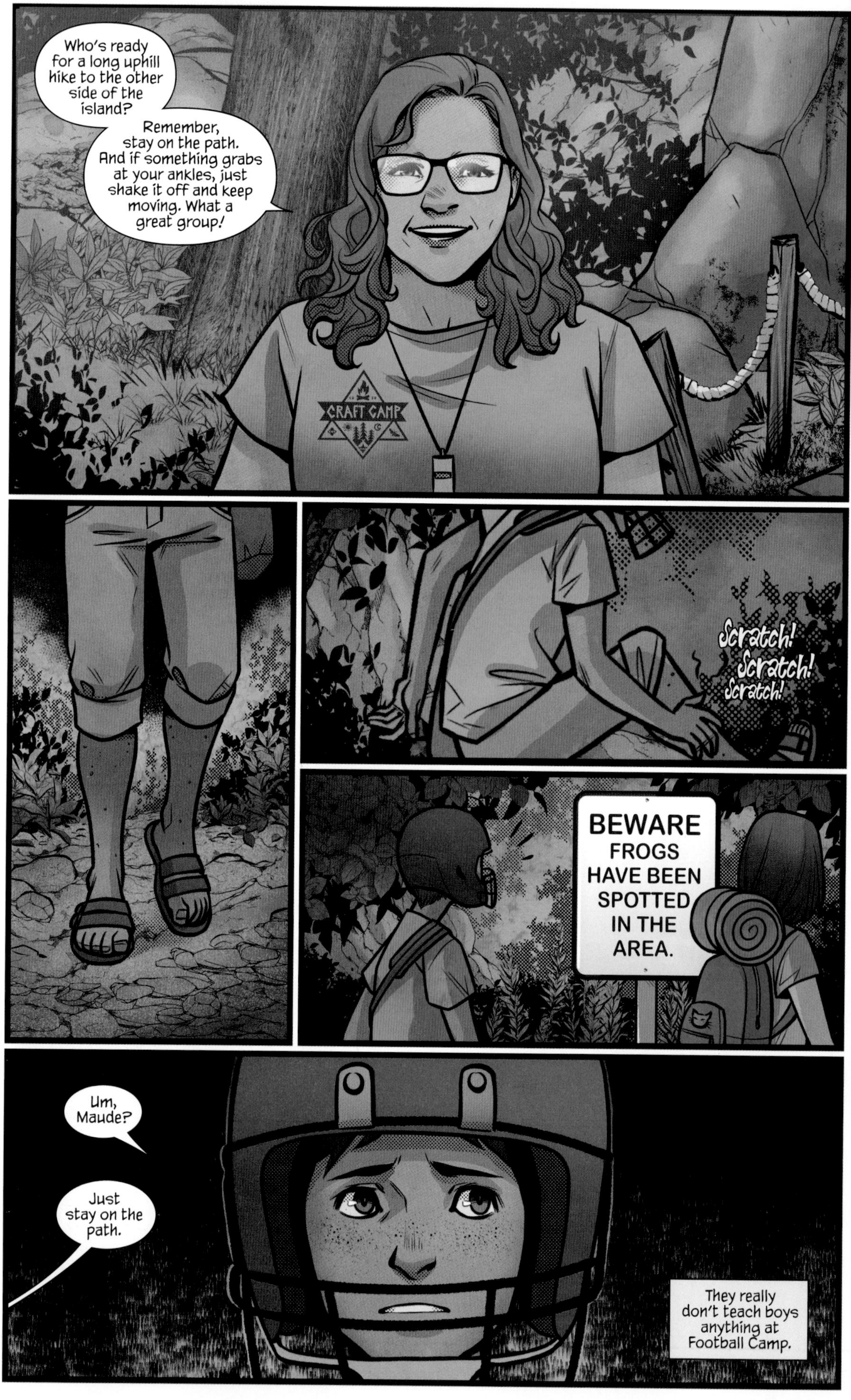
Who's ready for a long uphill hike to the other side of the island?
Remember, stay on the path. And if something grabs at your ankles, just shake it off and keep moving. What a great group!
CRAFT CAMP
Scratch! Scratch! Scratch!
BEWARE FROGS HAVE BEEN SPOTTED IN THE AREA.
Um, Maude?
Just stay on the path.
They really don't teach boys anything at Football Camp.

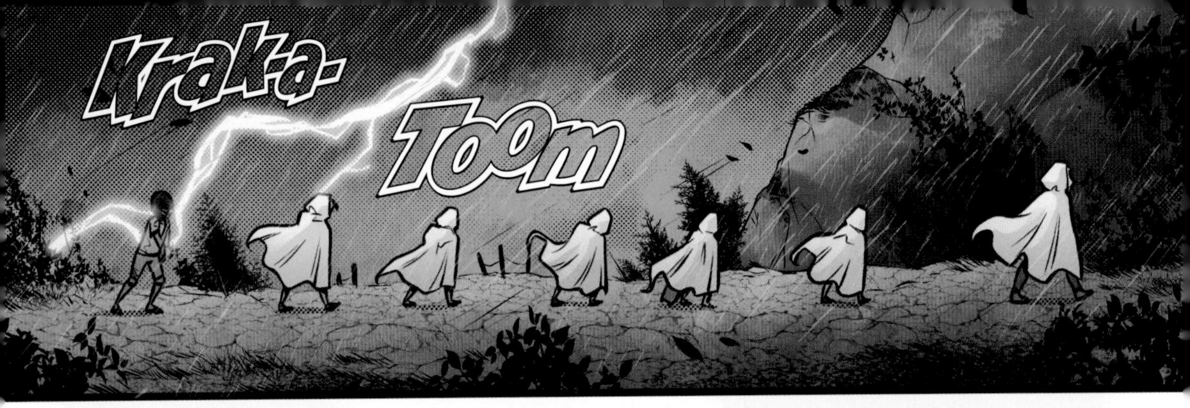
Kraka-
Toom

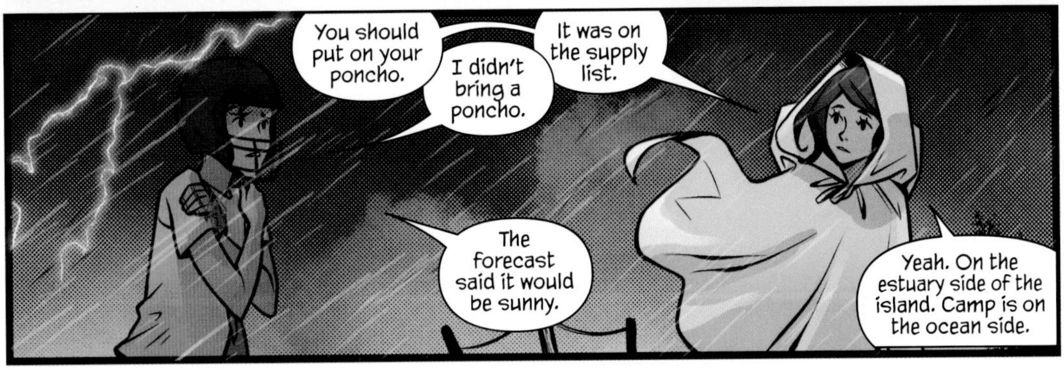
You should put on your poncho.
I didn't bring a poncho.
It was on the supply list.
The forecast said it would be sunny.
Yeah. On the estuary side of the island. Camp is on the ocean side.

Five-day forecast

Estuary side

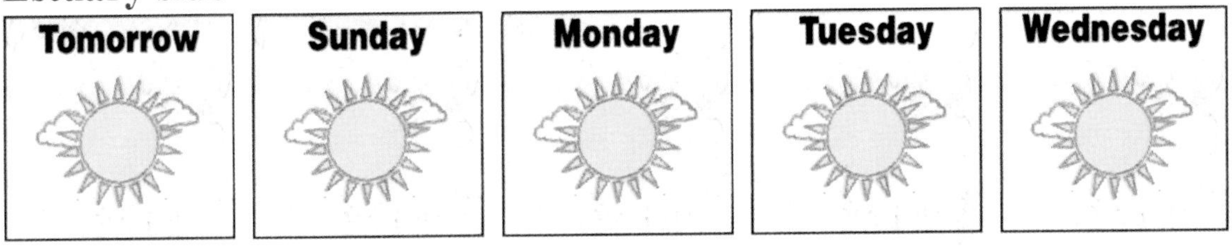
Tomorrow
Sunday
Monday
Tuesday
Wednesday

Ocean side

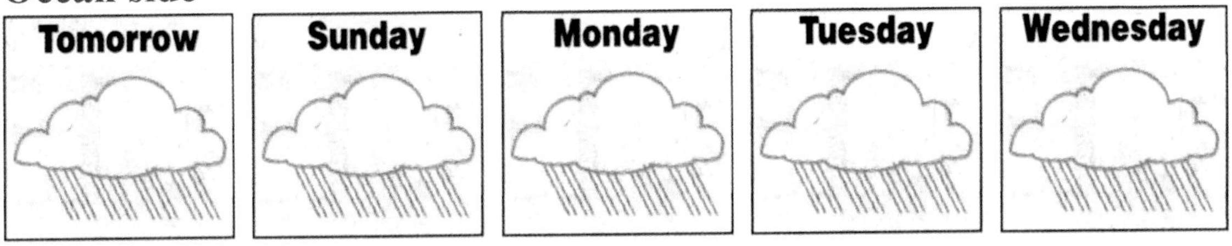
Tomorrow
Sunday
Monday
Tuesday
Wednesday

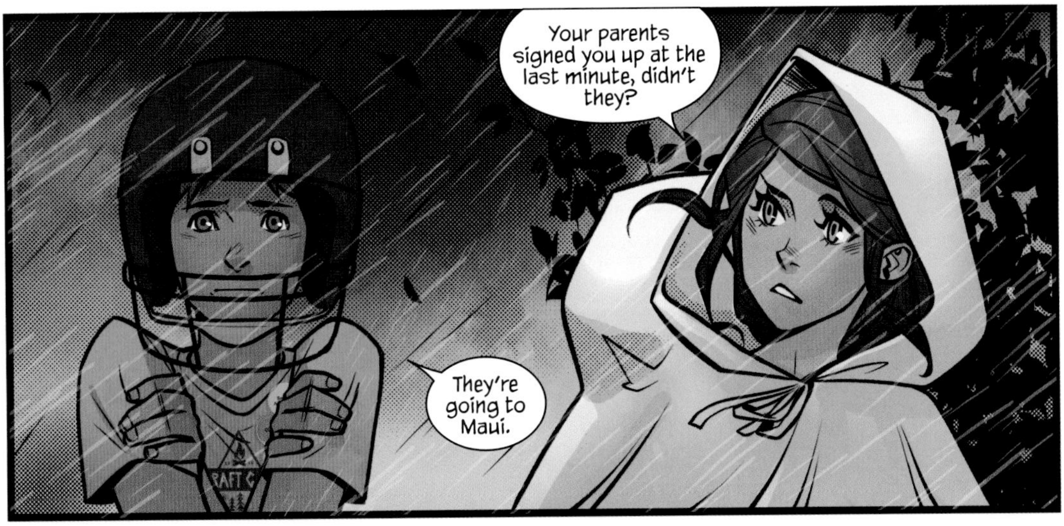
Your parents signed you up at the last minute, didn't they?
They're going to Maui.

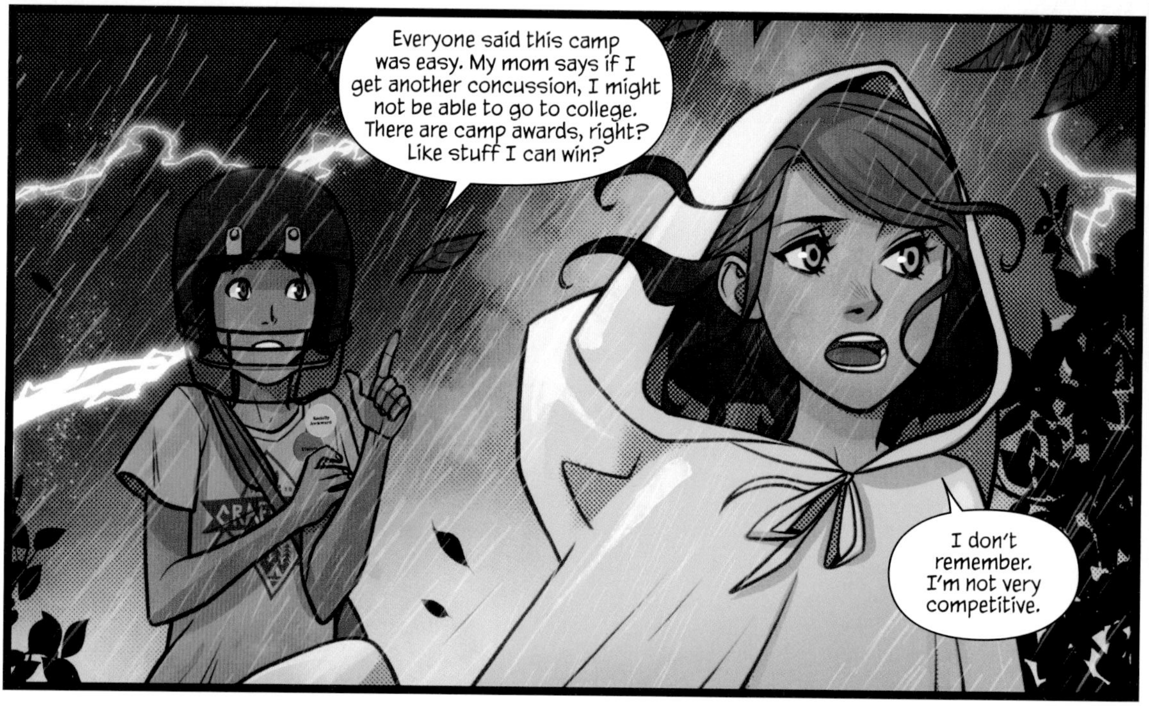
Everyone said this camp was easy. My mom says if I get another concussion, I might not be able to go to college. There are camp awards, right? Like stuff I can win?
I don't remember. I'm not very competitive.

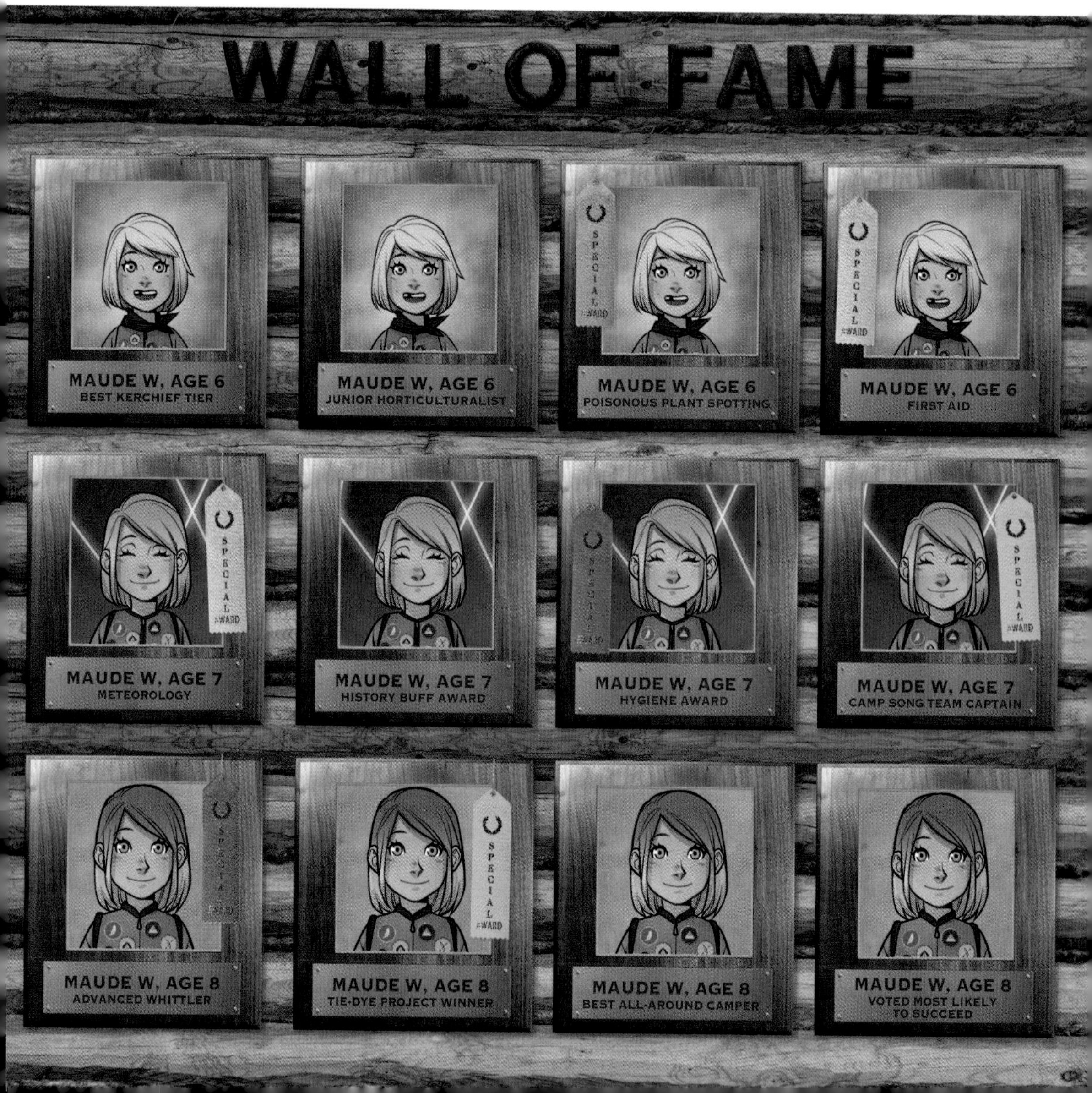
WALL OF FAME
MAUDE W, AGE 6 BEST KERCHIEF TIER
MAUDE W, AGE 6 JUNIOR HORTICULTURALIST
MAUDE W, AGE 6 POISONOUS PLANT SPOTTING
MAUDE W, AGE 6 FIRST AID
MAUDE W, AGE 7 METEOROLOGY
MAUDE W, AGE 7 HISTORY BUFF AWARD
MAUDE W, AGE 7 HYGIENE AWARD
MAUDE W, AGE 7 CAMP SONG TEAM CAPTAIN
MAUDE W, AGE 8 ADVANCED WHITTLER
MAUDE W, AGE 8 TIE-DYE PROJECT WINNER
MAUDE W, AGE 8 BEST ALL-AROUND CAMPER
MAUDE W, AGE 8 VOTED MOST LIKELY TO SUCCEED

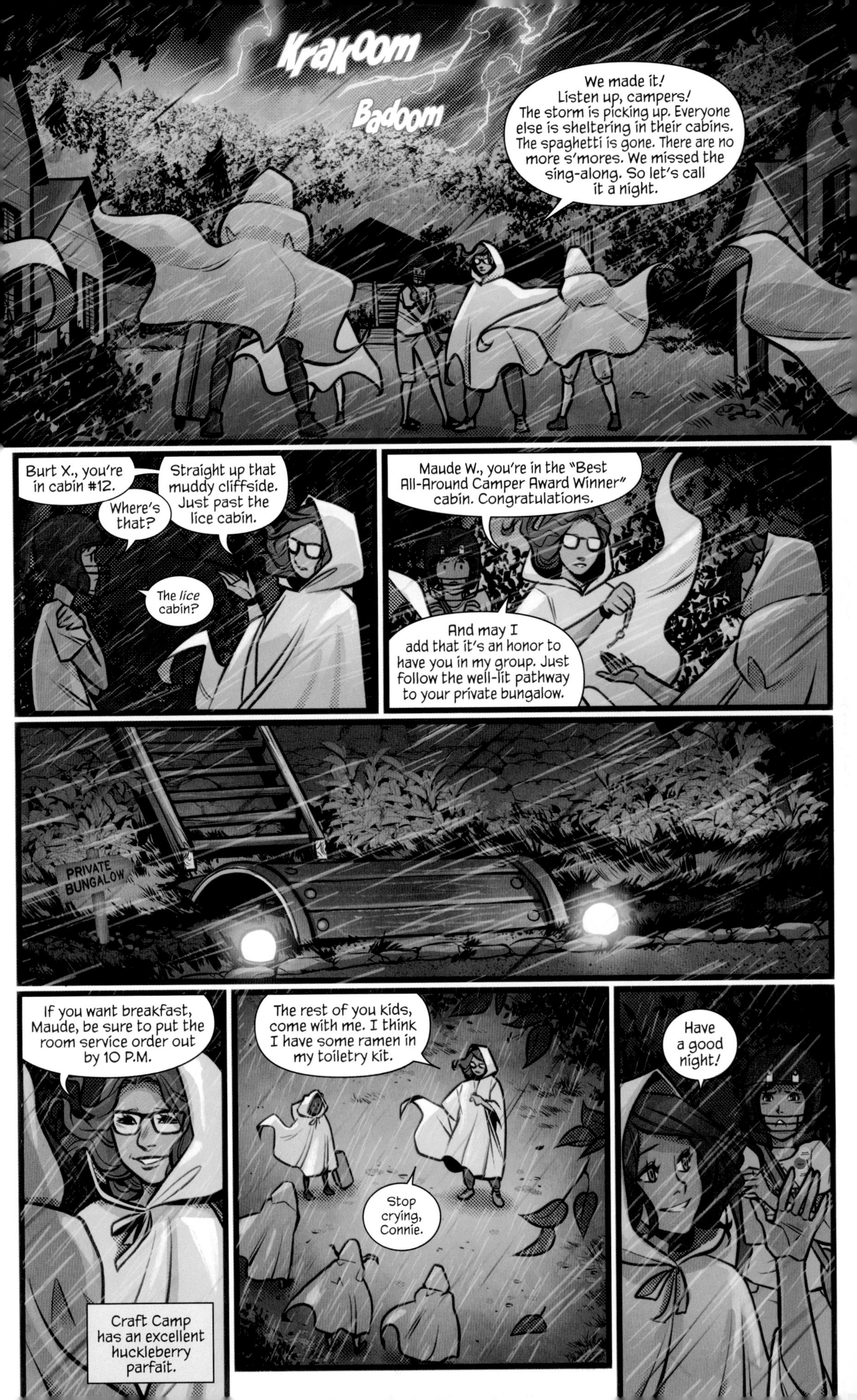
KRAKOOM
BADOOM
We made it! Listen up, campers! The storm is picking up. Everyone else is sheltering in their cabins. The spaghetti is gone. There are no more s'mores. We missed the sing-along. So let's call it a night.
Burt X., you're in cabin #12.
Where's that?
Straight up that muddy cliffside. Just past the lice cabin.
The *lice* cabin?
Maude W., you're in the "Best All-Around Camper Award Winner" cabin. Congratulations.
And may I add that it's an honor to have you in my group. Just follow the well-lit pathway to your private bungalow.
PRIVATE BUNGALOW
If you want breakfast, Maude, be sure to put the room service order out by 10 P.M.
Craft Camp has an excellent huckleberry parfait.
The rest of you kids, come with me. I think I have some ramen in my toiletry kit.
Stop crying, Connie.
Have a good night!

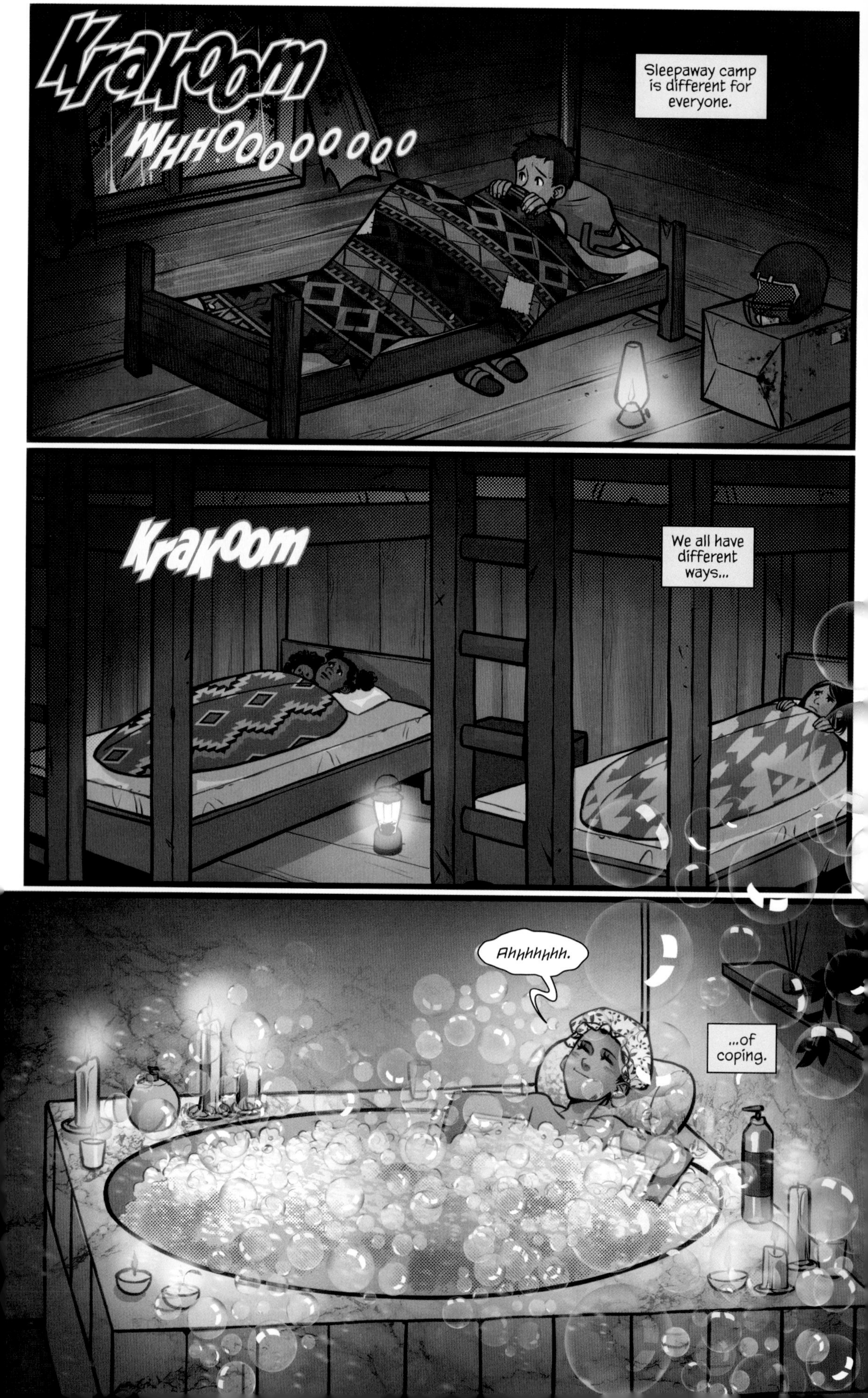
KRAKOOM
WHHOOOOOOOO
Sleepaway camp is different for everyone.
KRAKOOM
We all have different ways...
Ahhhhhhh.
...of coping.

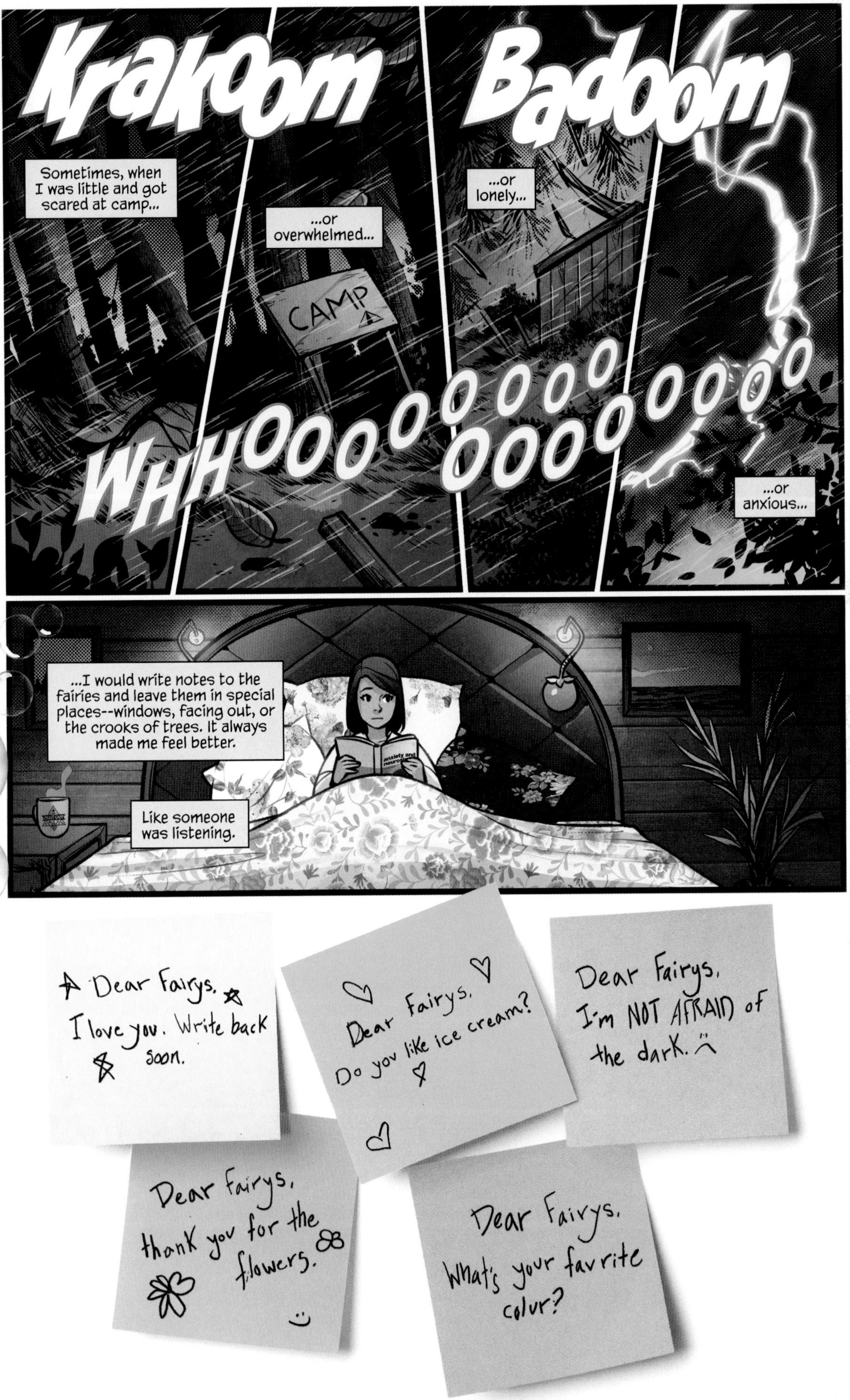
Krakoom
Sometimes, when I was little and got scared at camp...
...or overwhelmed...
CAMP
Badoom
...or lonely...
WHHOOOOOOOOOOOOOOOO
...or anxious...
...I would write notes to the fairies and leave them in special places--windows, facing out, or the crooks of trees. It always made me feel better.
Like someone was listening.
Dear Fairys. I love you. Write back soon.
Dear Fairys. Do you like ice cream?
Dear Fairys. I'm NOT AFRAID of the dark.
Dear Fairys, thank you for the flowers.
Dear Fairys. What's your favrite colur?

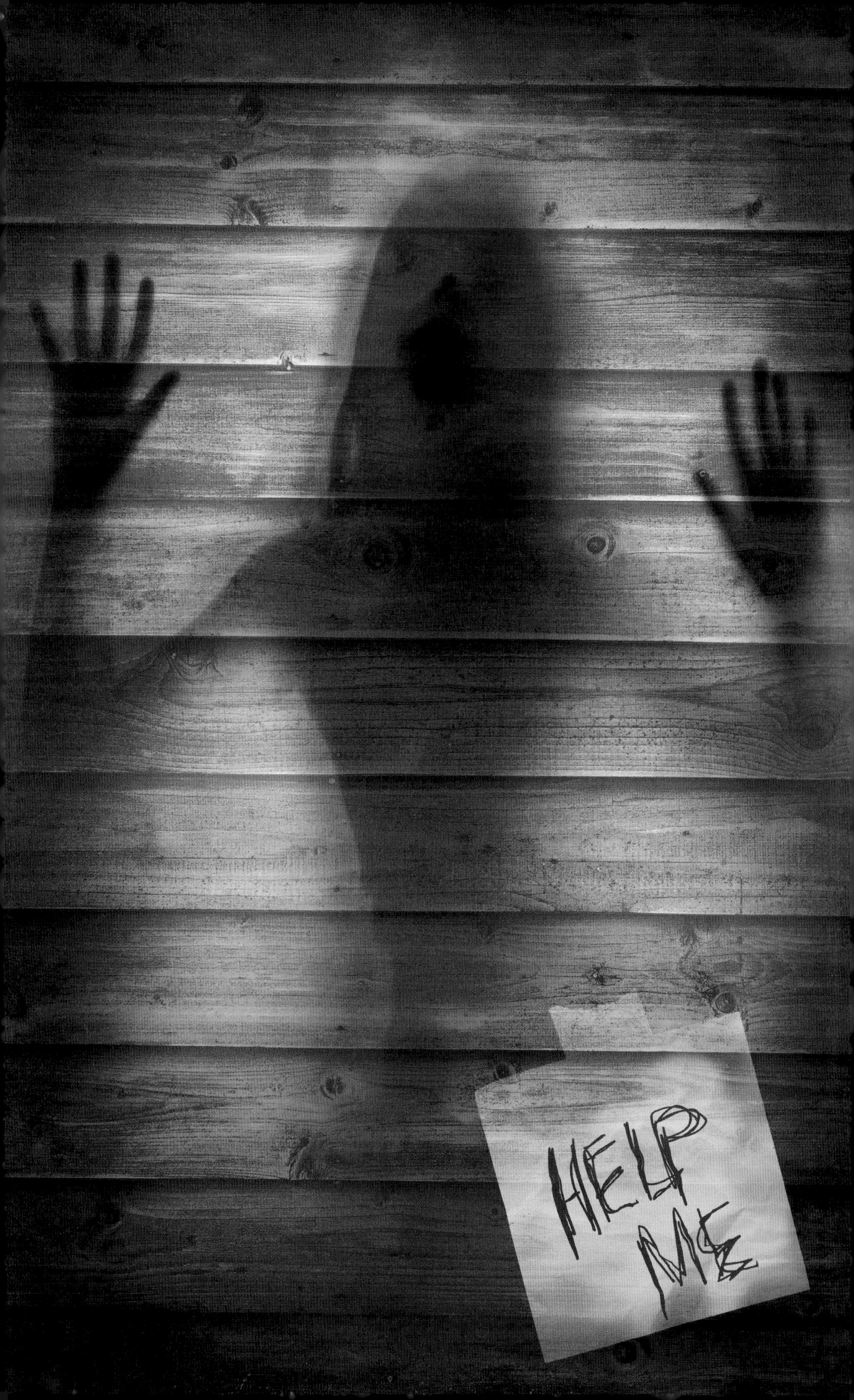
HELP
ME

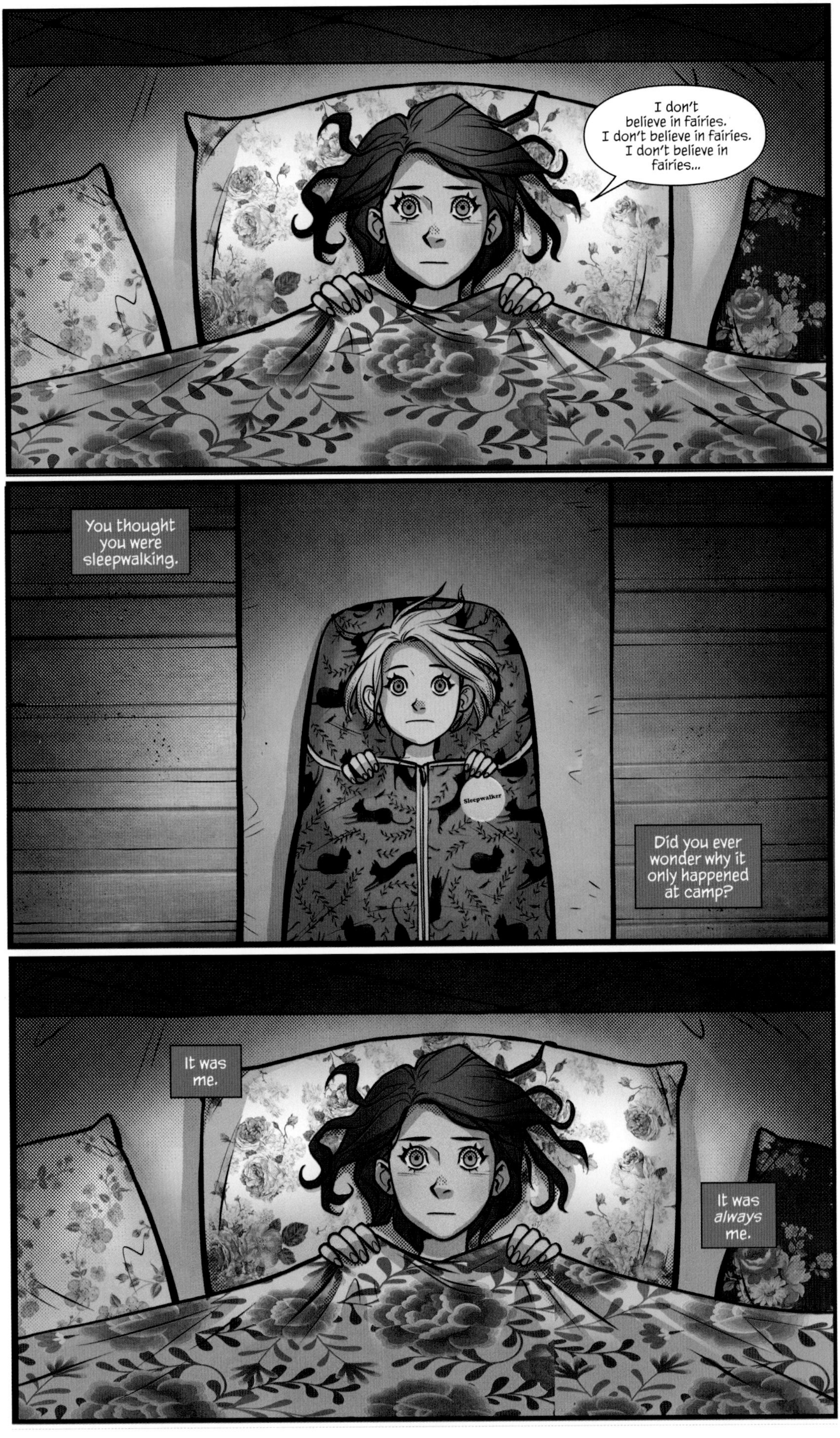
I don't believe in fairies. I don't believe in fairies. I don't believe in fairies...
You thought you were sleepwalking.
Sleepwalker
Did you ever wonder why it only happened at camp?
It was me.
It was *always* me.

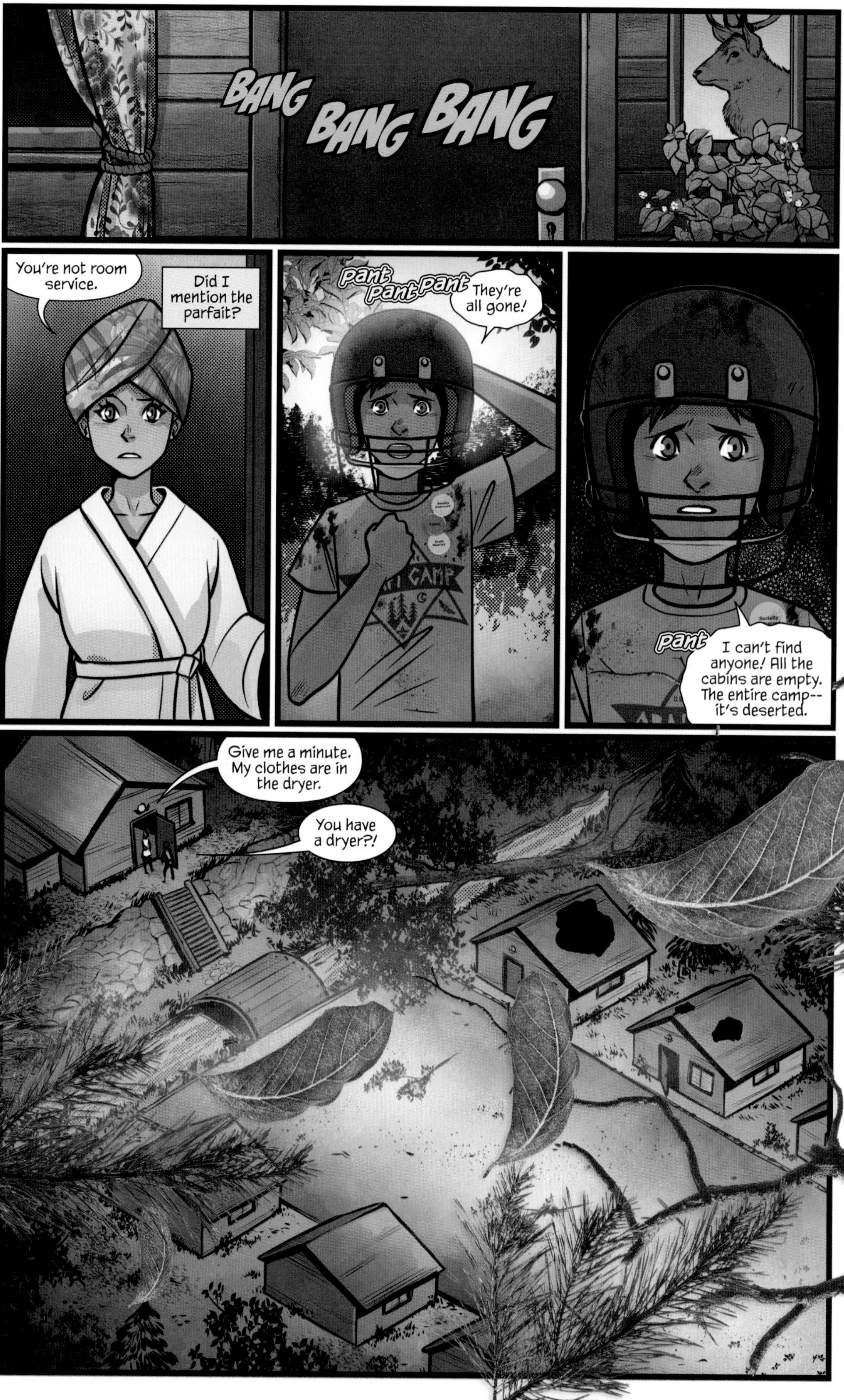
BANG BANG BANG
You're not room service.
Did I mention the parfait?
Pant Pant Pant
They're all gone!
Pant
I can't find anyone! All the cabins are empty. The entire camp-- it's deserted.
Give me a minute. My clothes are in the dryer.
You have a dryer?!

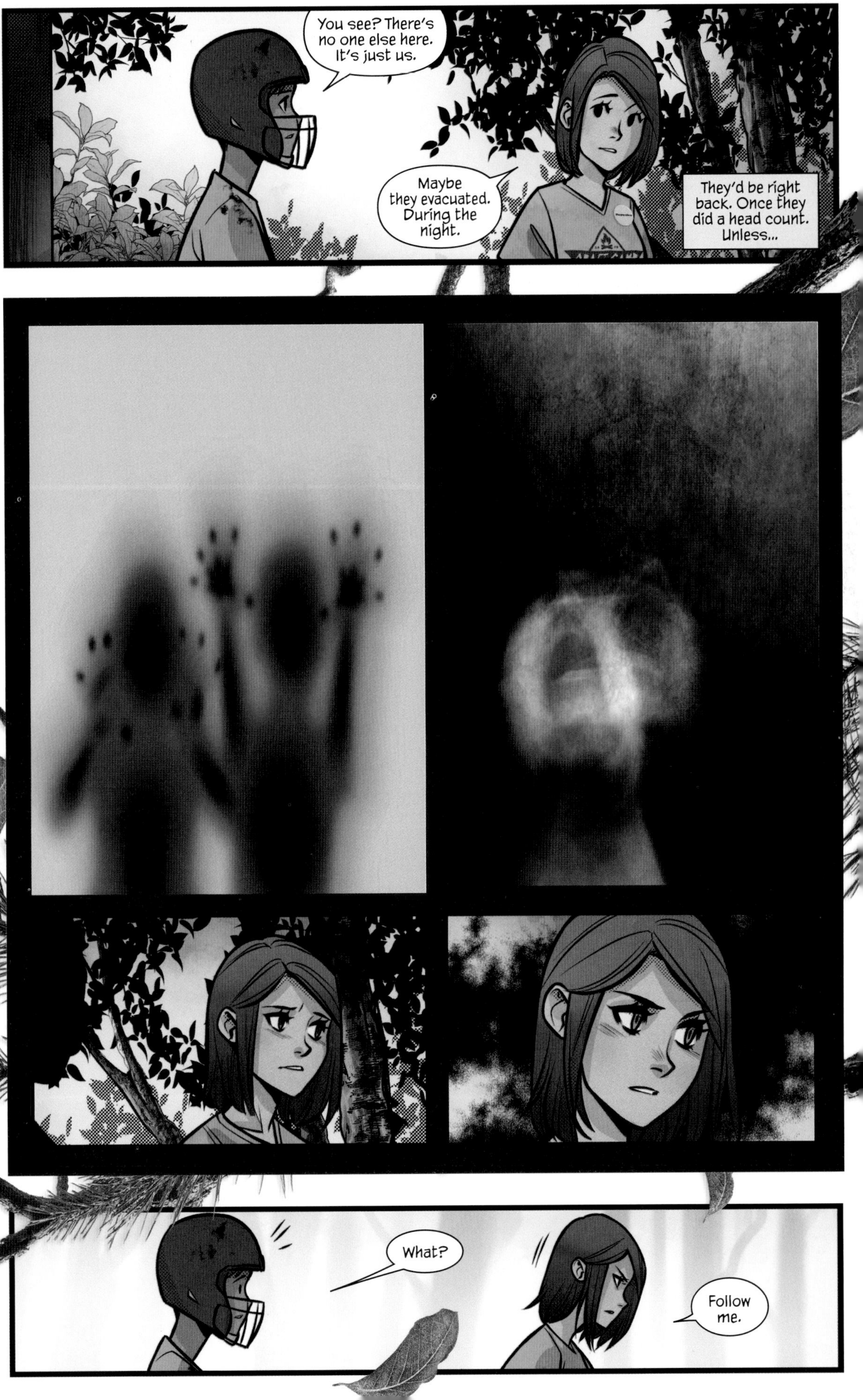
You see? There's no one else here. It's just us.
Maybe they evacuated. During the night.
They'd be right back. Once they did a head count. Unless...
What?
Follow me.

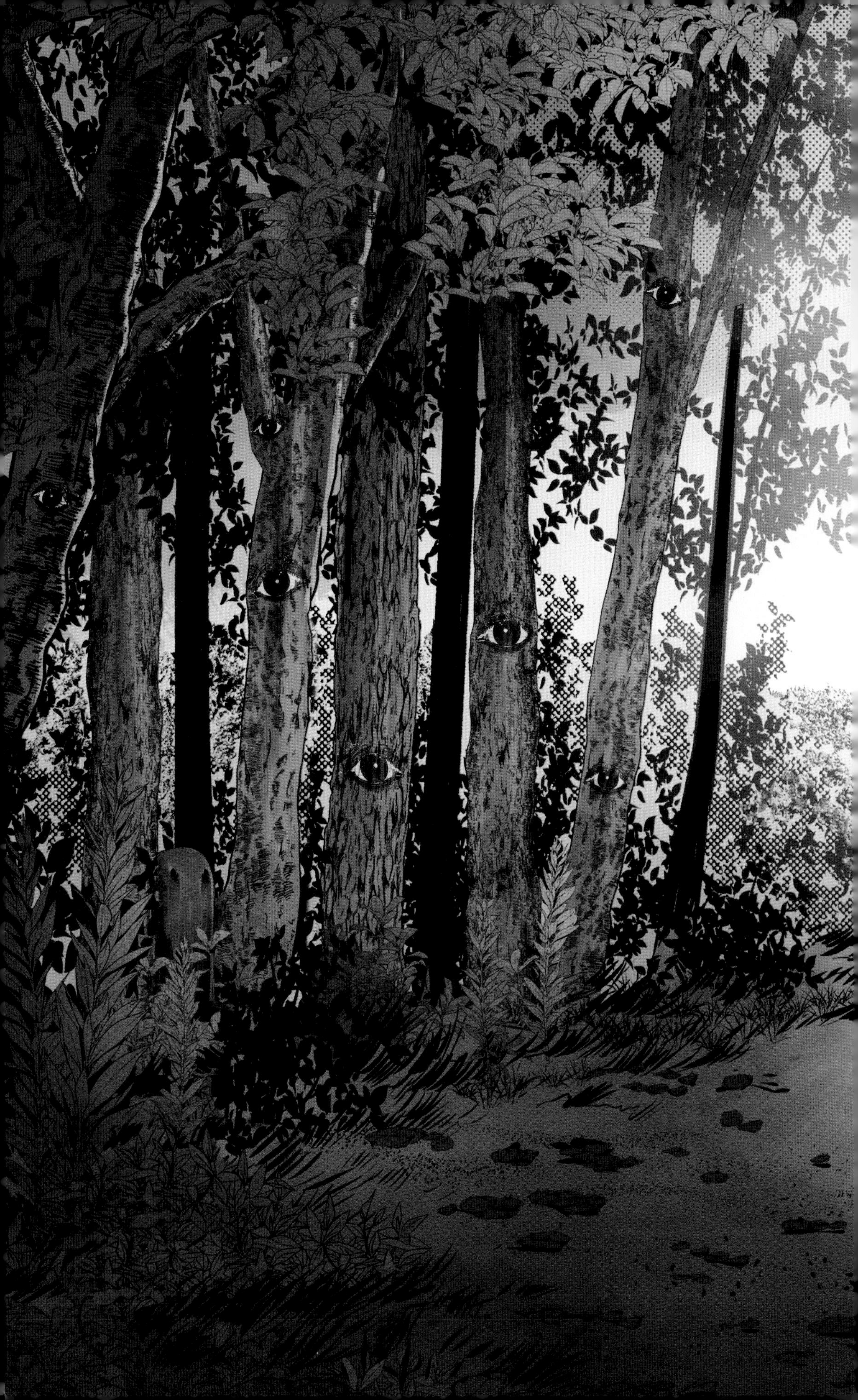

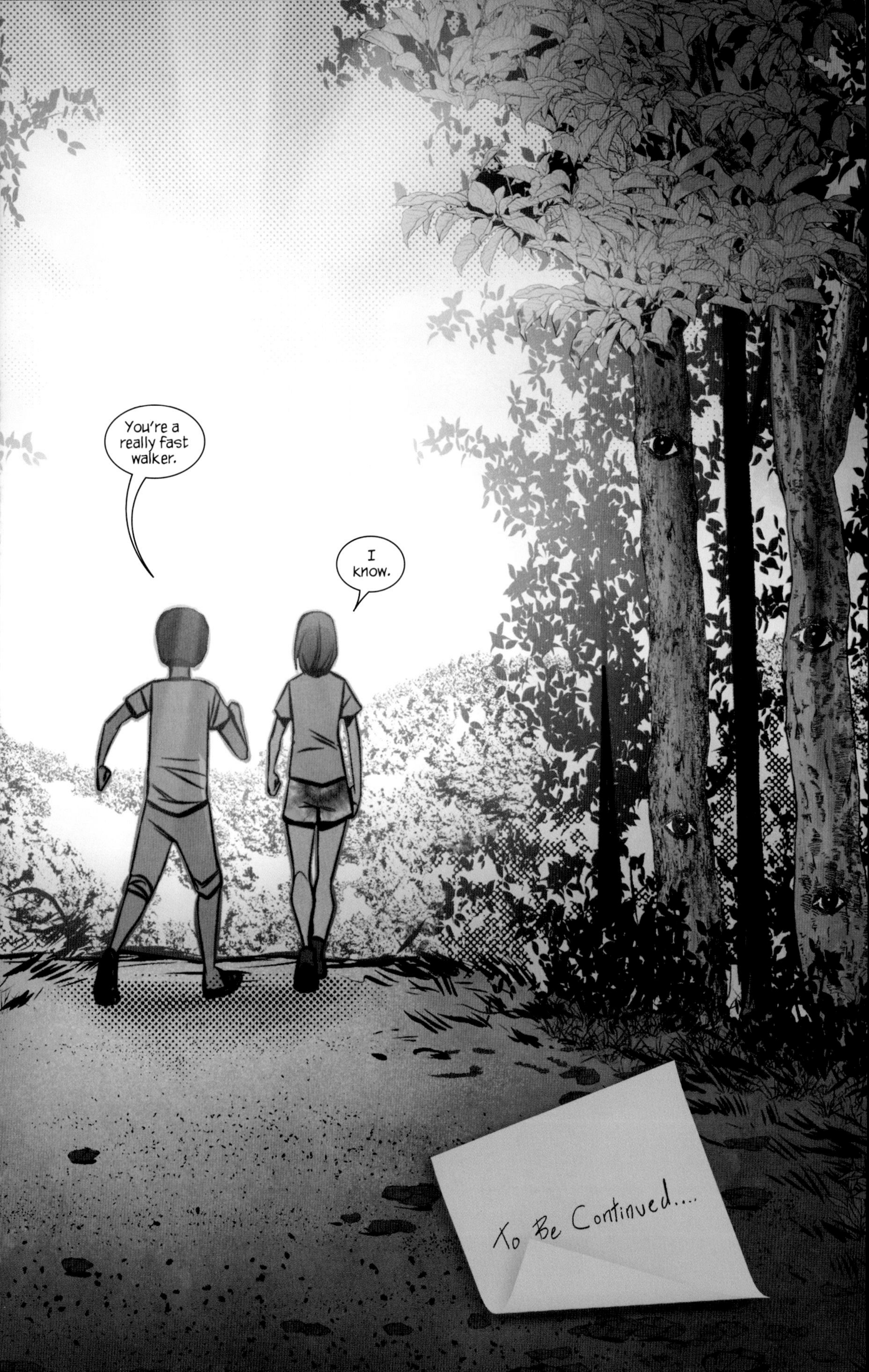
You're a really fast walker.
I know.
To Be Continued...

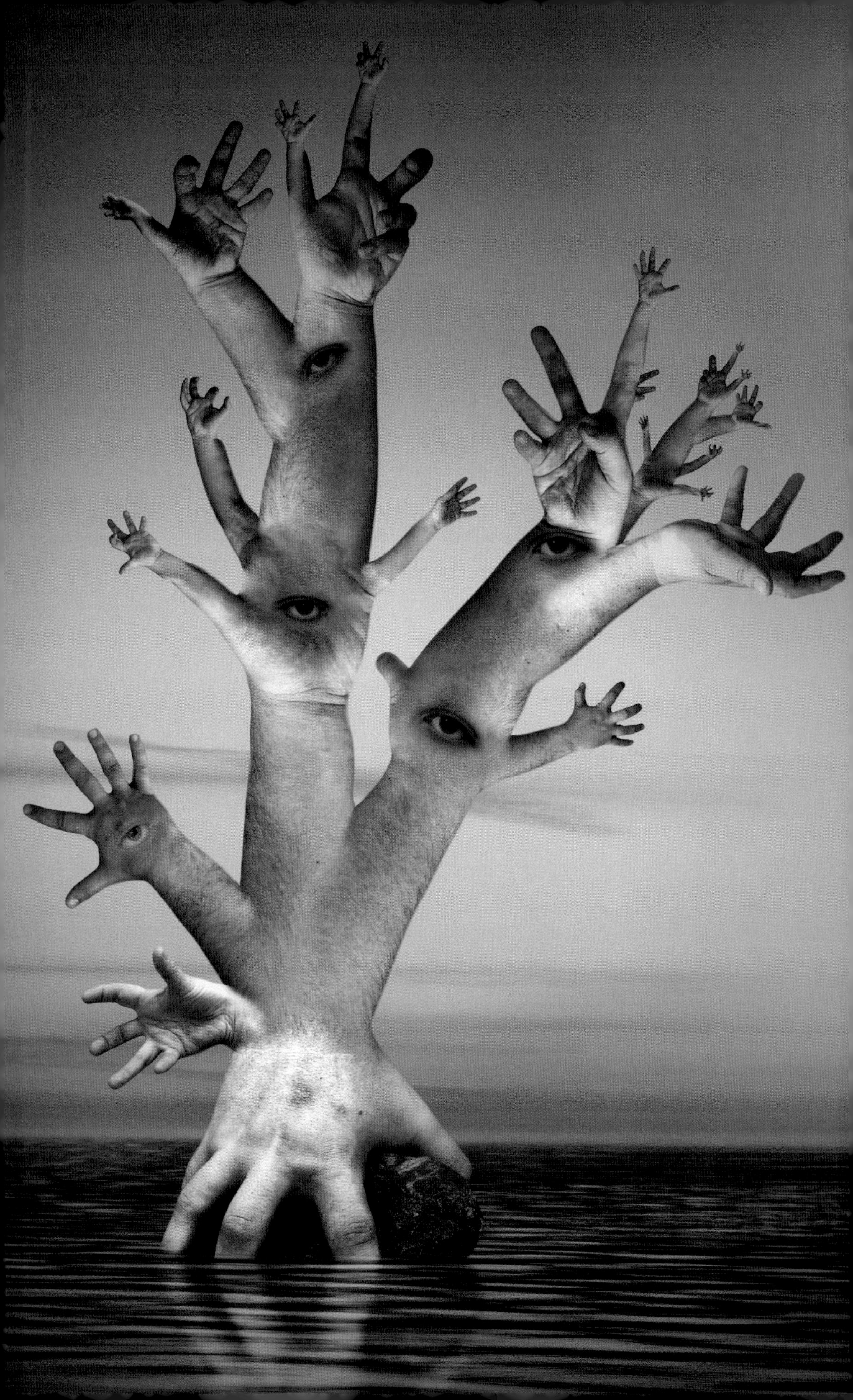

Dear Ten Richest Men:

by Eliza Fantastic Mohan (age 16)

Are you haunted?
By the screams
and the cries of the
unfortunate lives
I wish to speak of babies born in
broken homes
but how can i know
when columns and balconies are all I've ever known
Smooth walls i drip down in
absence
Pages i flip
through
feathers holding me in the sheet of
night
When monsters come,
wave a hand and
all bursts into flight
How can a child of paper and opinion
raised on phones and freedom
Speak for the ones who fight for scraps of skin and
throw it all away for one single win
Then how can the men who corrupt and ruin
Sitting on their thrones of broken backs
and stacks
of stocks
and rot
Speak for the victims of past mistakes
The very backs you break
Innocent of crime but you throw away the key
Lose themselves in indignity
Frequently.
You lie and twist in wishes made by the
bedside
Prayers brought to you for even a crumb of the cakes
you make
I hope your eyes are hollow and bruised
I hope your ties are knotted loose
I hope your fingers shake under marble tabletops
I hope you don't think you really make a change
When you sprinkle chances into the hands of the ones you know will praise
And show up on tv crying to the god that is you
Is that what it is?
I almost don't care if you're evil
or confused
If you hate what you were and like what
you do
Or you walked on severed paychecks down a yellow brick road
To get where you were going
And never turned back or looked down never let yourself frown
I don't care if you read the websites telling you you don't deserve it
I care if you'll change if you shed your skin and hide-
Or finally crack your footstools upright

Haiku
by Emily Powell (age 16)

Every year I leave
I can feel them all staring.
They all know my name.

MAKE YOUR OWN

SIDE A

Sleepwalker

Clumsy

Socially Awkward

Contagious Rash

Hyperactive

Bed Wetter

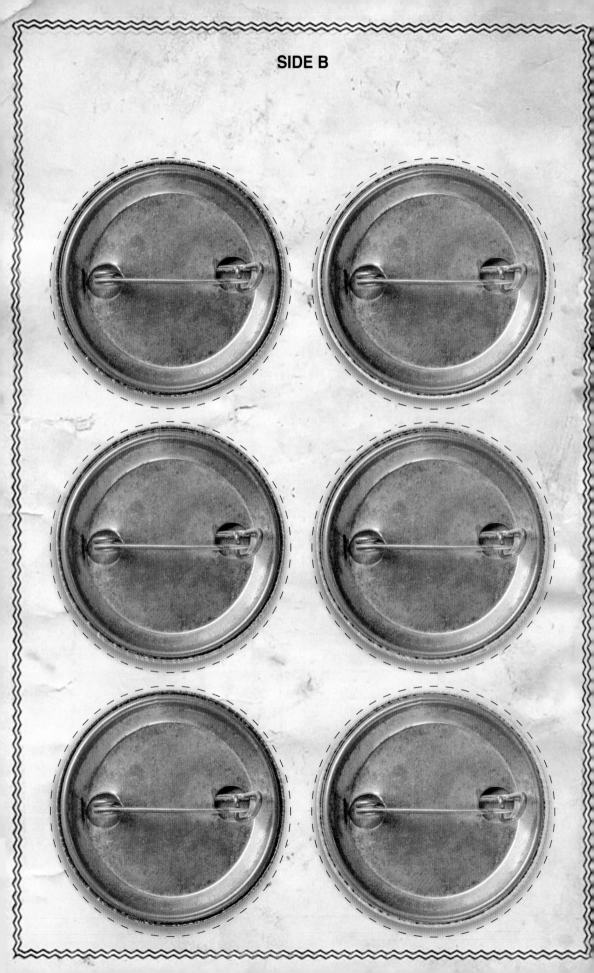

SIDE B

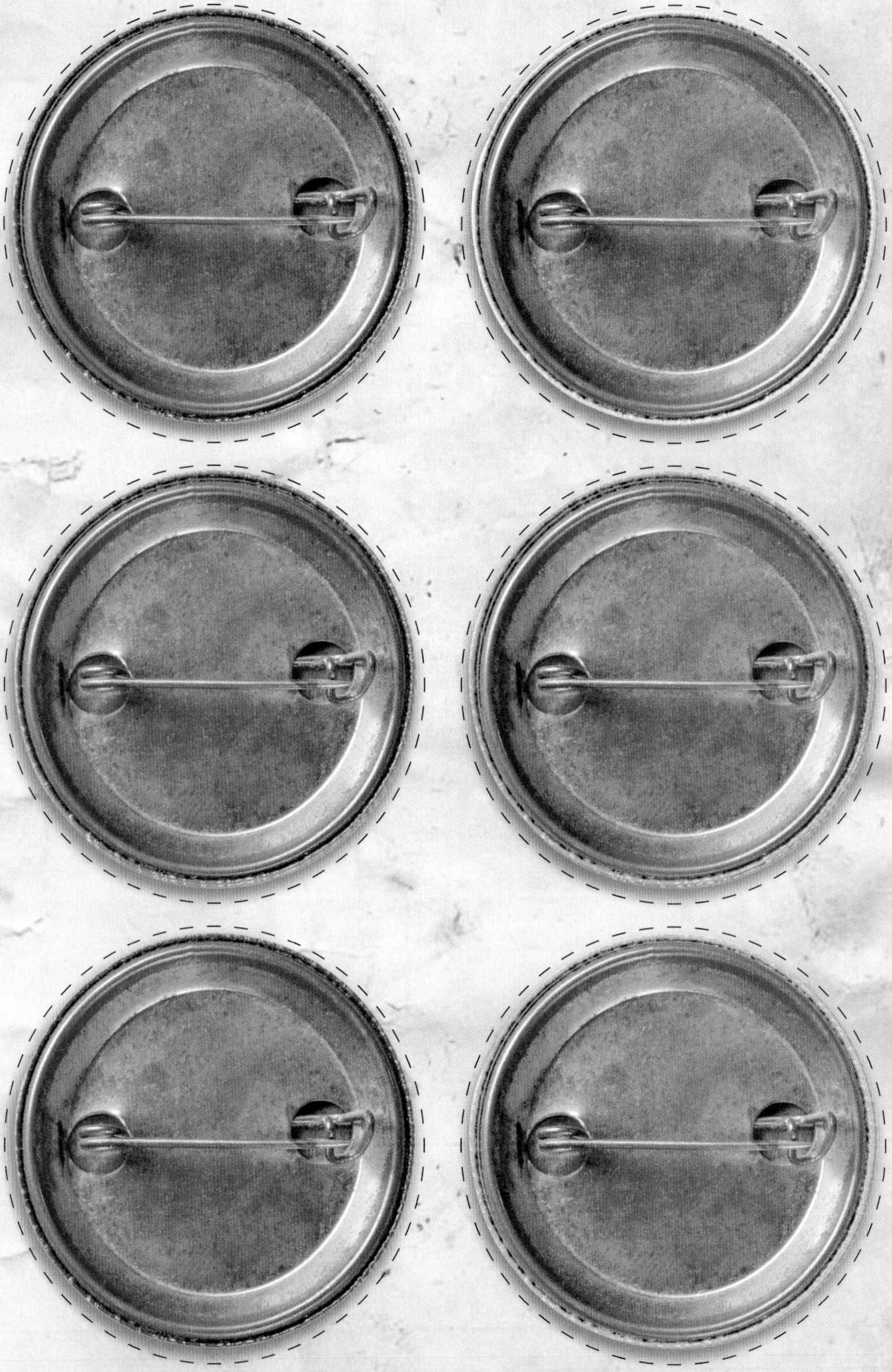

MINISTRY OF
TROUBLE

CREDITS: ISSUE #1

CREATORS CHELSEA CAIN & LIA MITERNIQUE
WRITER CHELSEA CAIN
COVER ARTIST & GRAPHIC DESIGNER LIA MITERNIQUE
ARTISTS KATE NIEMCZYK AND LIA MITERNIQUE
COLORIST RACHELLE ROSENBERG
LETTERER JOE CARAMAGNA
POEM & POST-IT LETTERING ELIZA FANTASTIC MOHAN
HAIKU EMILY POWELL
ADDITIONAL INTERIOR ART STELLA GREENVOSS

YOU HAVE BEEN CONTACTED BY THE MINISTRY OF TROUBLE. AWAIT FURTHER INSTRUCTIONS.

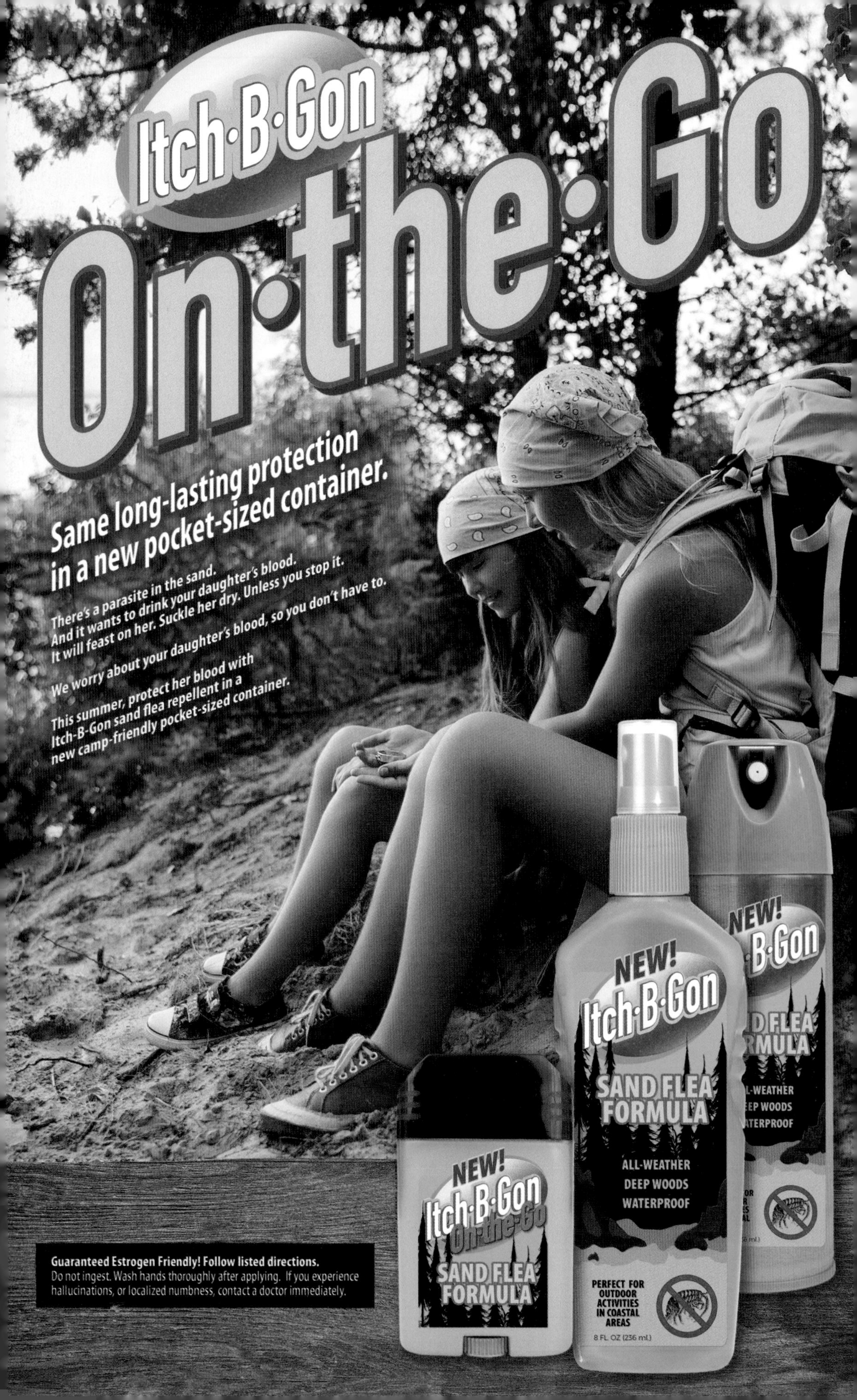
Itch·B·Gon
On·the·Go
Same long-lasting protection in a new pocket-sized container.
There's a parasite in the sand.
And it wants to drink your daughter's blood.
It will feast on her. Suckle her dry. Unless you stop it.
We worry about your daughter's blood, so you don't have to.
This summer, protect her blood with Itch-B-Gon sand flea repellent in a new camp-friendly pocket-sized container.
Guaranteed Estrogen Friendly! Follow listed directions.
Do not ingest. Wash hands thoroughly after applying. If you experience hallucinations, or localized numbness, contact a doctor immediately.
NEW!
Itch·B·Gon
On·the·Go
SAND FLEA FORMULA
NEW!
Itch·B·Gon
SAND FLEA FORMULA
ALL-WEATHER
DEEP WOODS
WATERPROOF
PERFECT FOR OUTDOOR ACTIVITIES IN COASTAL AREAS
8 FL OZ (236 ml)
NEW!

[Issue 1, Cover B]

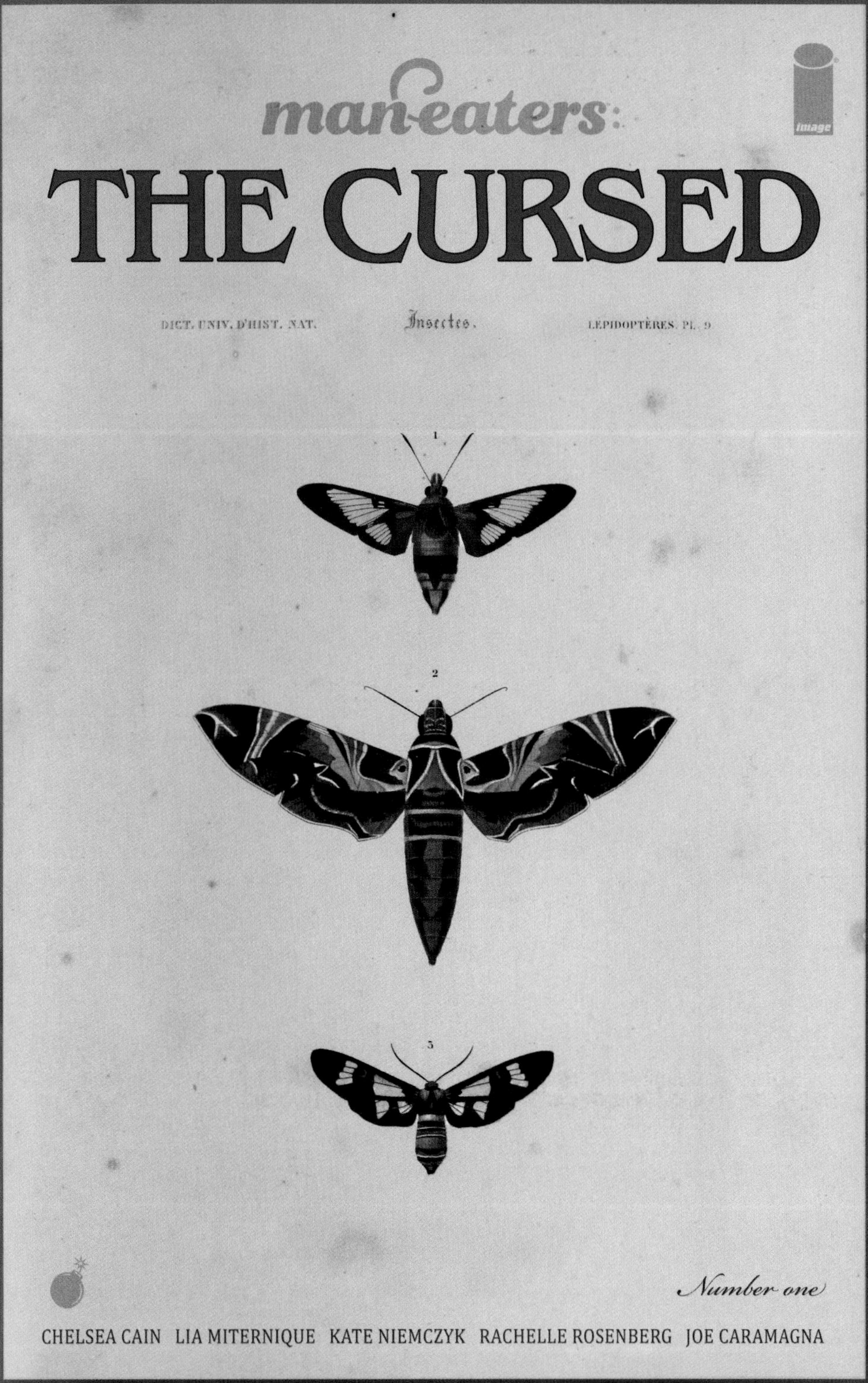

man-eaters:
THE CURSED
DICT. UNIV. D'HIST. NAT.
Insectes.
LEPIDOPTÈRES. PL. 9
1
2
3
Number one
CHELSEA CAIN LIA MITERNIQUE KATE NIEMCZYK RACHELLE ROSENBERG JOE CARAMAGNA

CHAPTER 2

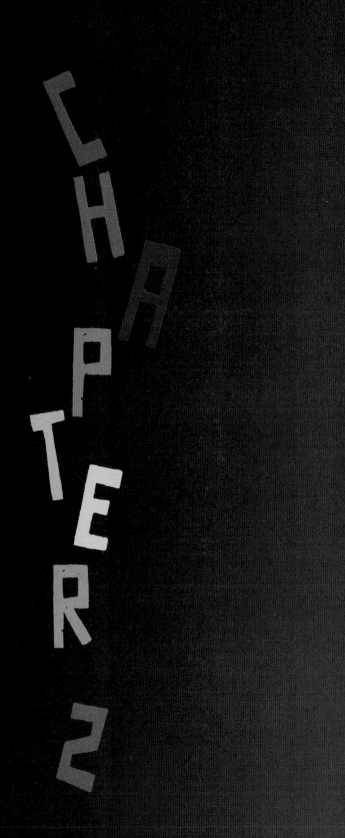

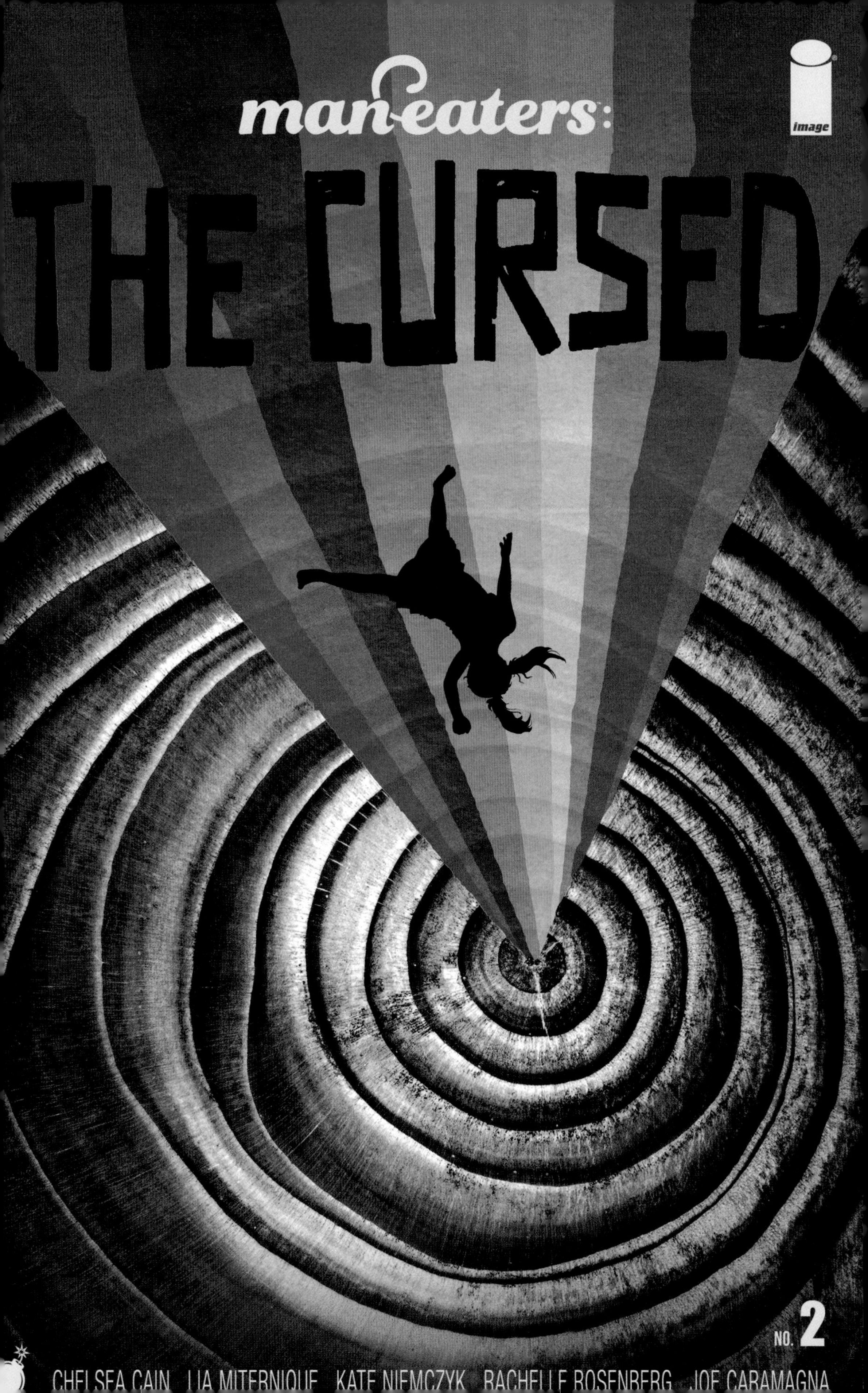
man-eaters:
THE CURSED
image
NO. 2
CHELSEA CAIN LIA MITERNIQUE KATE NIEMCZYK RACHELLE ROSENBERG JOE CARAMAGNA

WHAT HAPPENED IN "MAN-EATERS: THE CURSED" #1?

THE TEEN

Maude has to go on
a journey.

THE PARENTS

Maude's parents book a
romantic getaway to Carmel-
by-the-Sea.

THE RETREAT

Meanwhile, Maude is
sent to Craft Camp.

THE STRANGER

Maude is sorted alphabetically,
by last name, into the "W-Z"
cohort. She meets another
teen named Burt.

THE CHILDREN

Four younger campers are
also in the "W-Z" cohort.
But they're little kids,
and we don't pay much
attention to them.

THE ISLAND

Craft Camp is on an island off
the Oregon coast. It is entirely
isolated. No wifi, no cell
service. You get the picture.
Beware of the frogs.

THE STORM

A storm damages the camp.

THE MORNING

Maude sleeps late and wakes
up rested and refreshed. Burt
shows up at Maude's door.
He is not well rested.

THE VANISHING

The counselors and other
campers have vanished
overnight! Maude and Burt
are seemingly on their own.

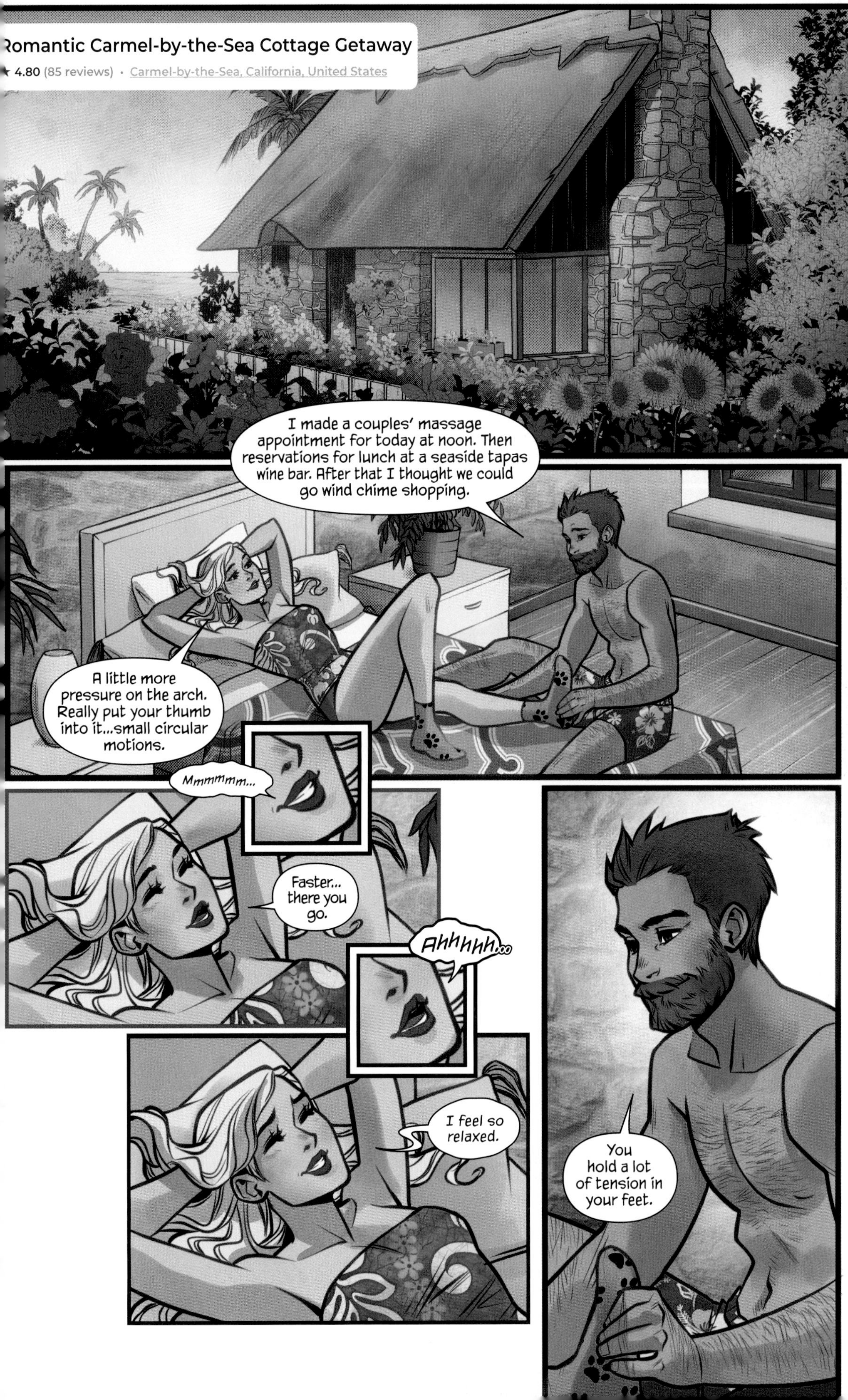
Romantic Carmel-by-the-Sea Cottage Getaway
4.80 (85 reviews) • Carmel-by-the-Sea, California, United States
I made a couples' massage appointment for today at noon. Then reservations for lunch at a seaside tapas wine bar. After that I thought we could go wind chime shopping.
A little more pressure on the arch. Really put your thumb into it...small circular motions.
Mmmmmm...
Faster... there you go.
Ahhhhh...
I feel so relaxed.
You hold a lot of tension in your feet.

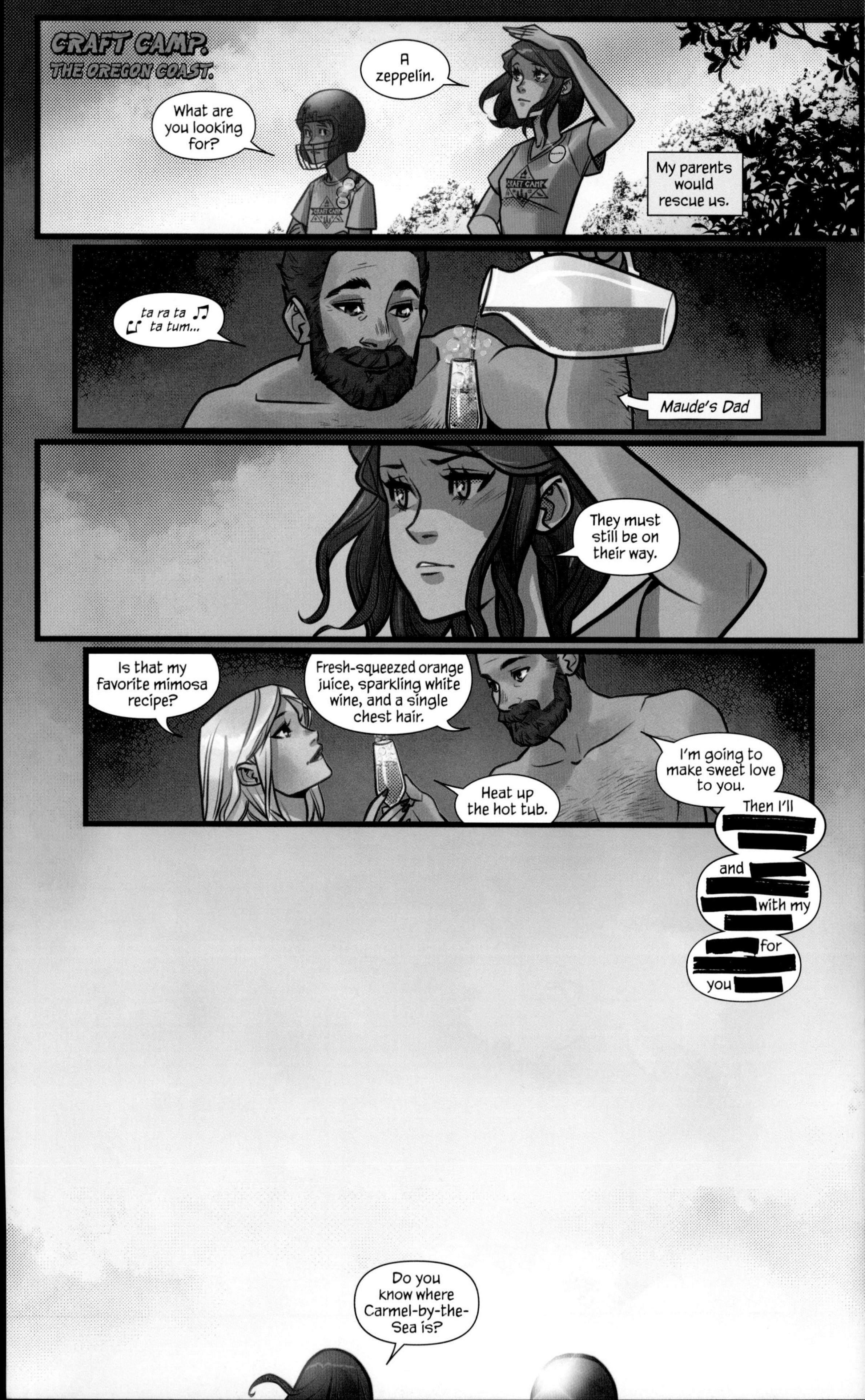
CRAFT CAMP.
THE OREGON COAST.
What are you looking for?
A zeppelin.
My parents would rescue us.
ta ra ta ta tum...
Maude's Dad
They must still be on their way.
Is that my favorite mimosa recipe?
Fresh-squeezed orange juice, sparkling white wine, and a single chest hair.
Heat up the hot tub.
I'm going to make sweet love to you.
Then I'll [redacted] and [redacted] with my [redacted] for [redacted] you [redacted]
Do you know where Carmel-by-the-Sea is?

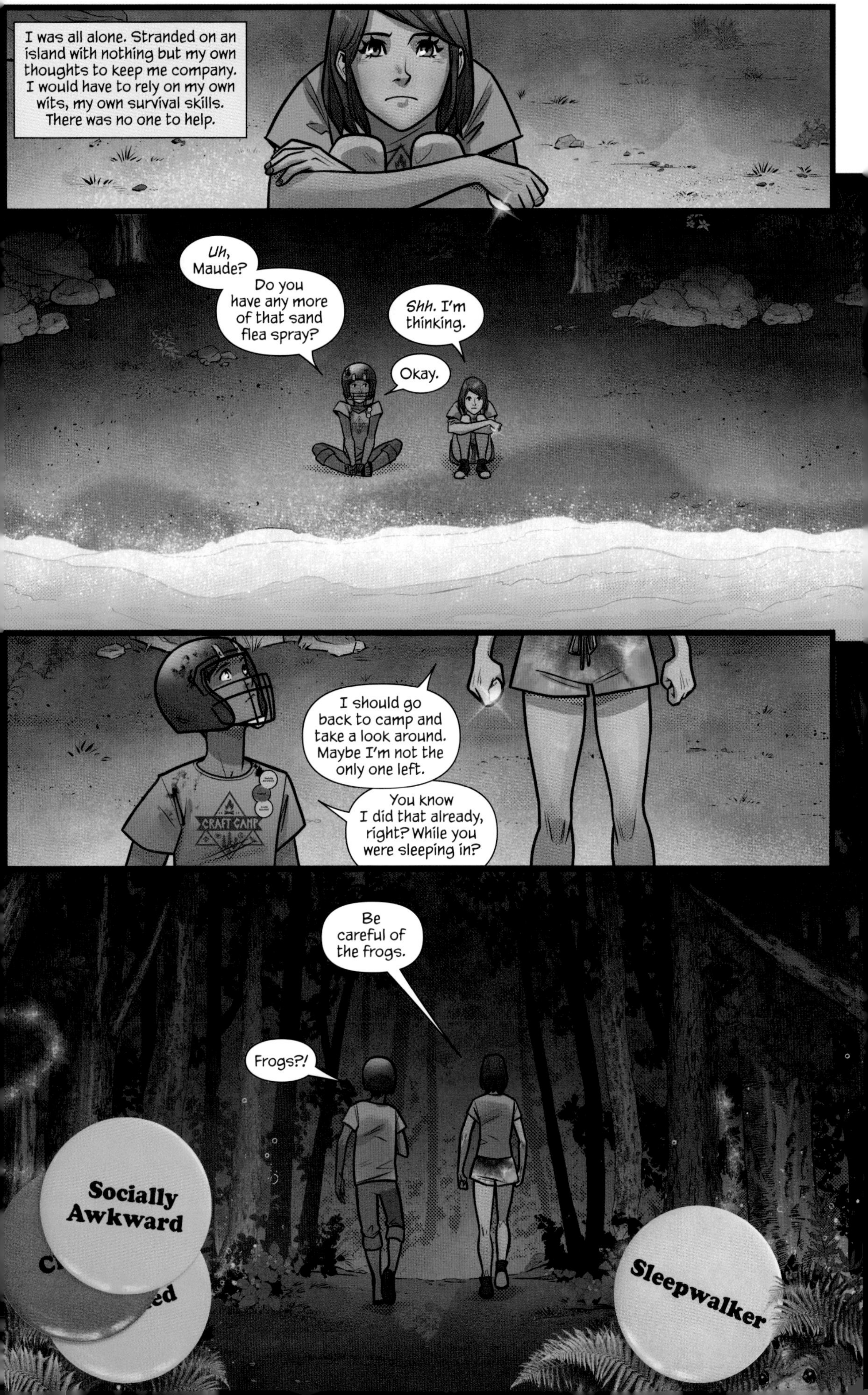
I was all alone. Stranded on an island with nothing but my own thoughts to keep me company. I would have to rely on my own wits, my own survival skills. There was no one to help.
Uh, Maude?
Do you have any more of that sand flea spray?
Shh. I'm thinking.
Okay.
I should go back to camp and take a look around. Maybe I'm not the only one left.
You know I did that already, right? While you were sleeping in?
CRAFT CAMP
Be careful of the frogs.
Frogs?!
Socially Awkward
Sleepwalker

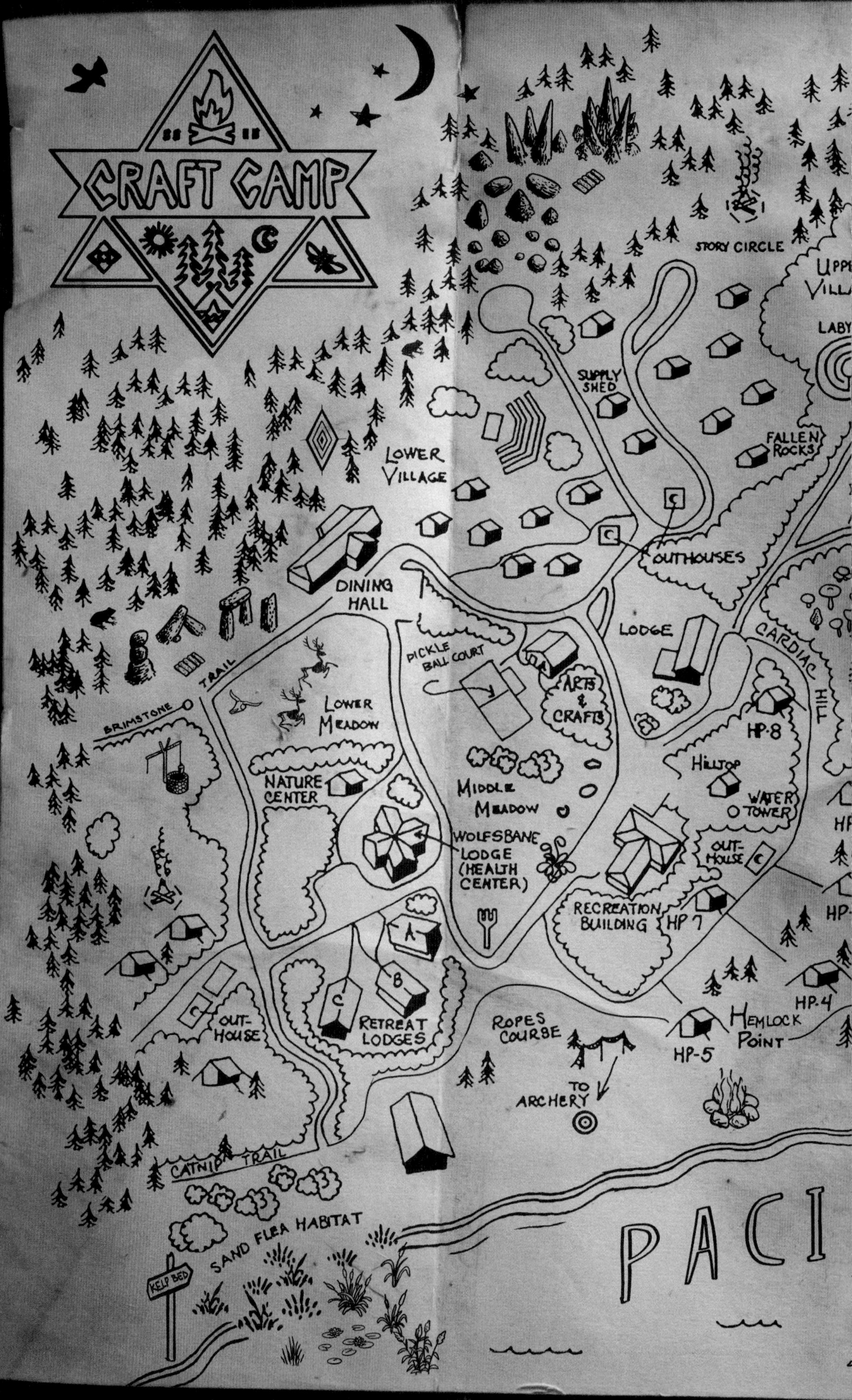
CRAFT CAMP
STORY CIRCLE
UPP
VILLA
LABY
SUPPLY SHED
FALLEN ROCKS
LOWER VILLAGE
OUTHOUSES
DINING HALL
LODGE
CARDIAC HILL
PICKLE BALL COURT
ARTS & CRAFTS
HP-8
BRIMSTONE
TRAIL
LOWER MEADOW
HILLTOP
WATER TOWER
NATURE CENTER
MIDDLE MEADOW
WOLFSBANE LODGE (HEALTH CENTER)
OUT-HOUSE
RECREATION BUILDING
HP 7
OUT-HOUSE
RETREAT LODGES
ROPES COURSE
HEMLOCK POINT
HP-5
HP-4
TO ARCHERY
CATNIP TRAIL
SAND FLEA HABITAT
KELP BED
PACI

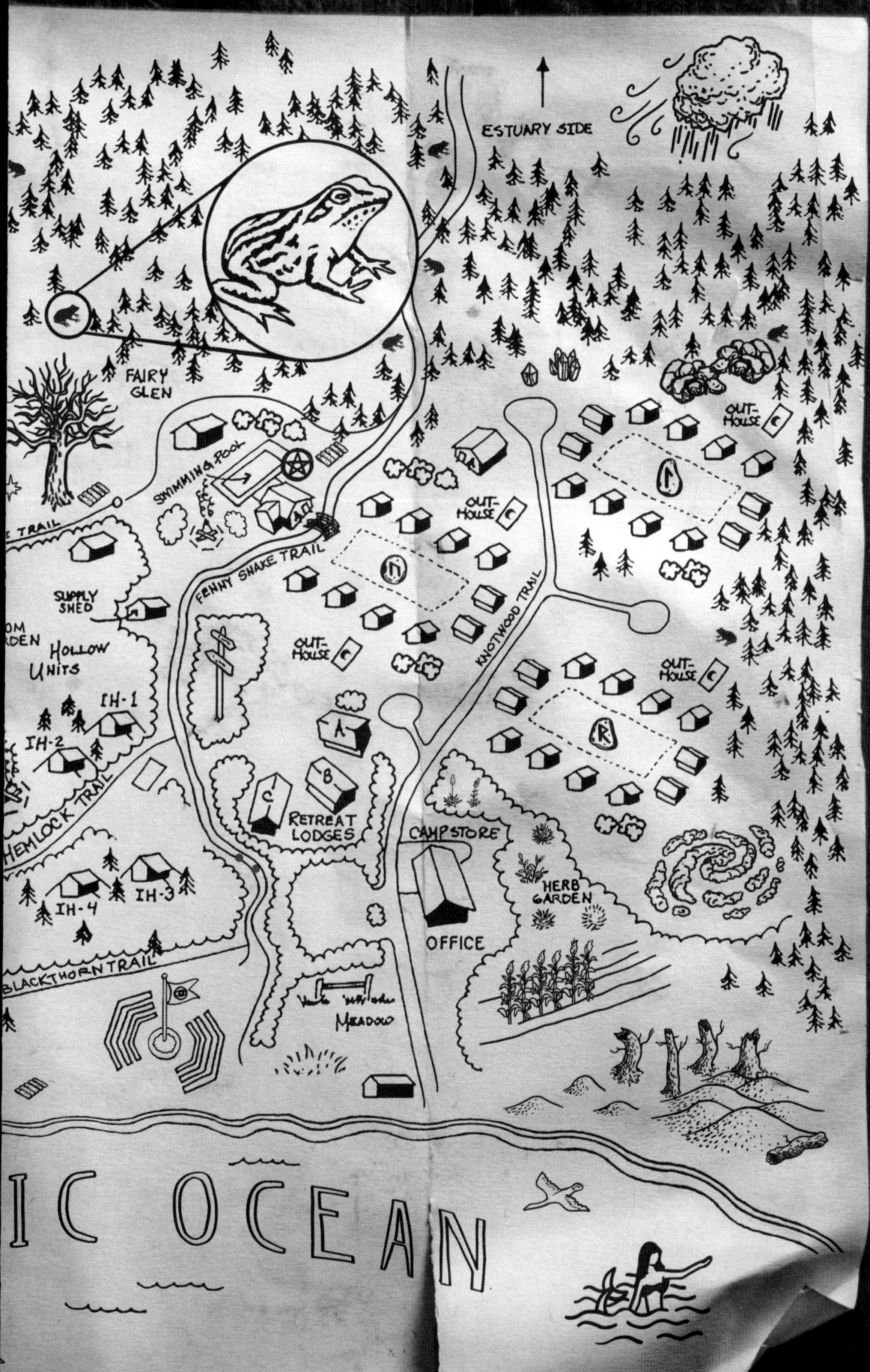
ESTUARY SIDE
FAIRY GLEN
SWIMMING POOL
FENNY SNAKE TRAIL
OUT-HOUSE
SUPPLY SHED
HOLLOW UNITS
IH-1
IH-2
IH-3
IH-4
HEMLOCK TRAIL
KNOTWOOD TRAIL
RETREAT LODGES
A
B
C
CAMPSTORE
OFFICE
HERB GARDEN
BLACKTHORN TRAIL
MEADOW
IC OCEAN

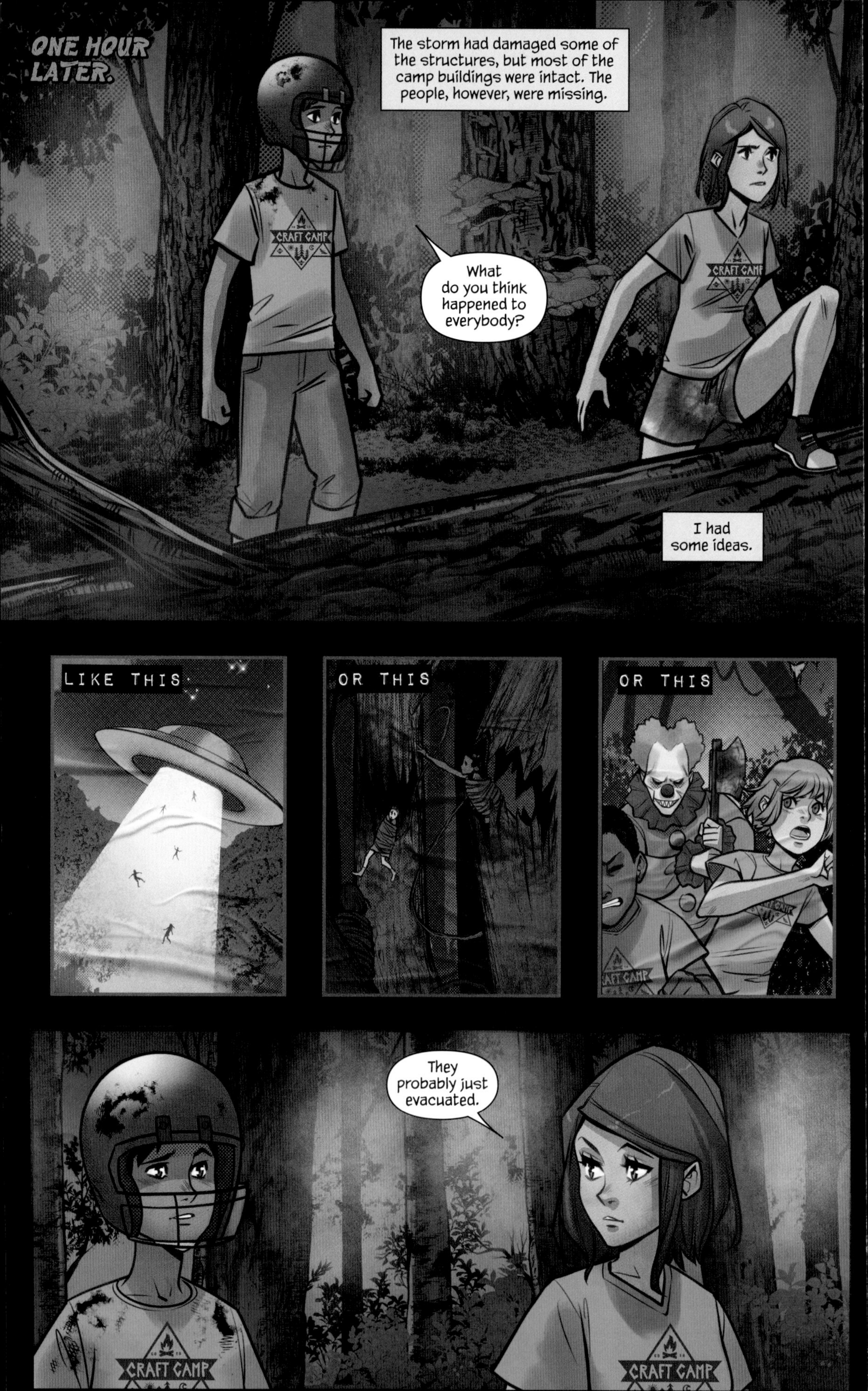
ONE HOUR LATER.
The storm had damaged some of the structures, but most of the camp buildings were intact. The people, however, were missing.
CRAFT CAMP
CRAFT CAMP
What do you think happened to everybody?
I had some ideas.
LIKE THIS
OR THIS
OR THIS
They probably just evacuated.
CRAFT CAMP
CRAFT CAMP

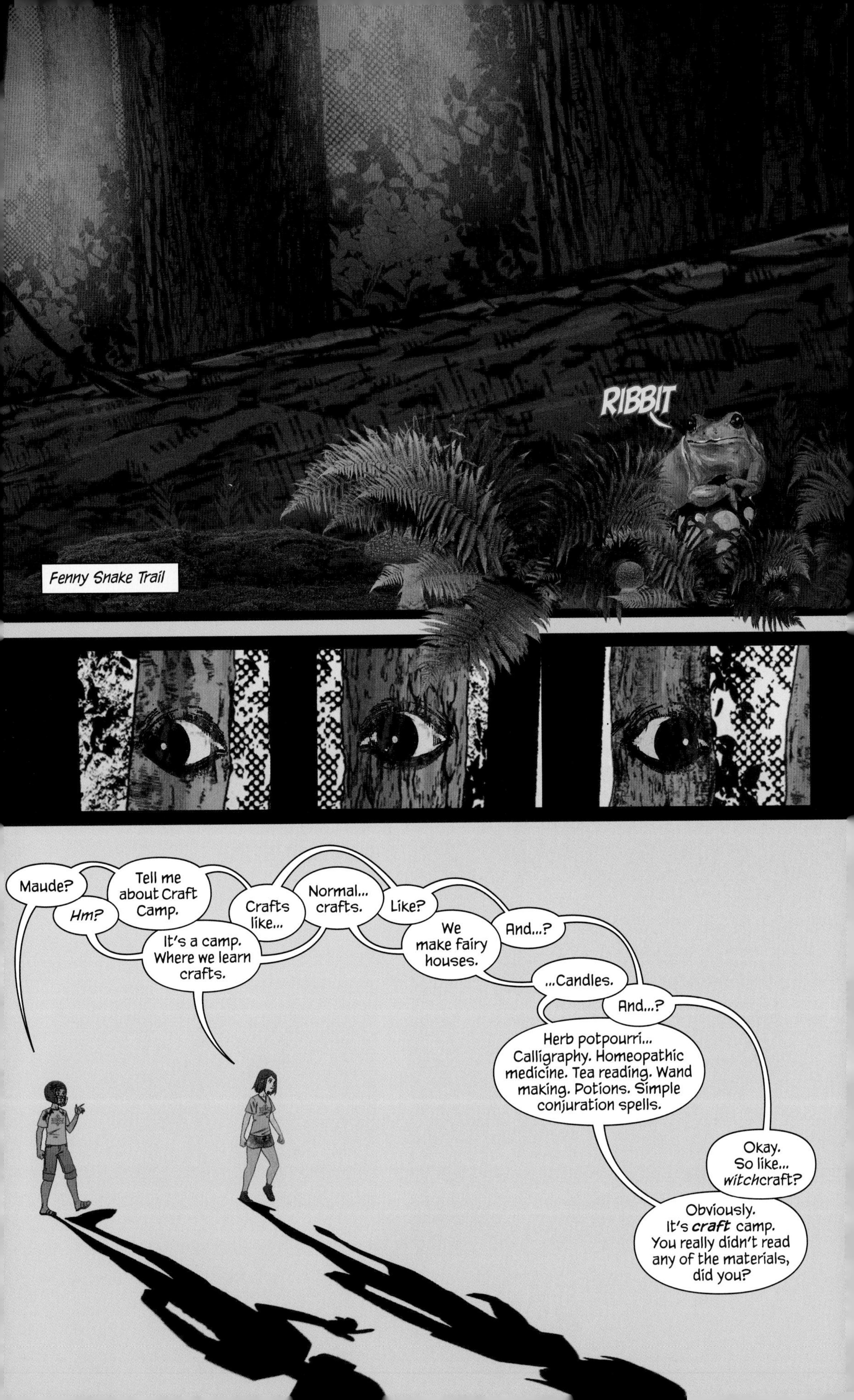
RIBBIT
Fenny Snake Trail
Maude?
Hm?
Tell me about Craft Camp.
It's a camp. Where we learn crafts.
Crafts like...
Normal... crafts.
Like?
We make fairy houses.
And...?
...Candles.
And...?
Herb potpourri... Calligraphy. Homeopathic medicine. Tea reading. Wand making. Potions. Simple conjuration spells.
Okay. So like... *witch*craft?
Obviously. It's ***craft*** camp. You really didn't read any of the materials, did you?

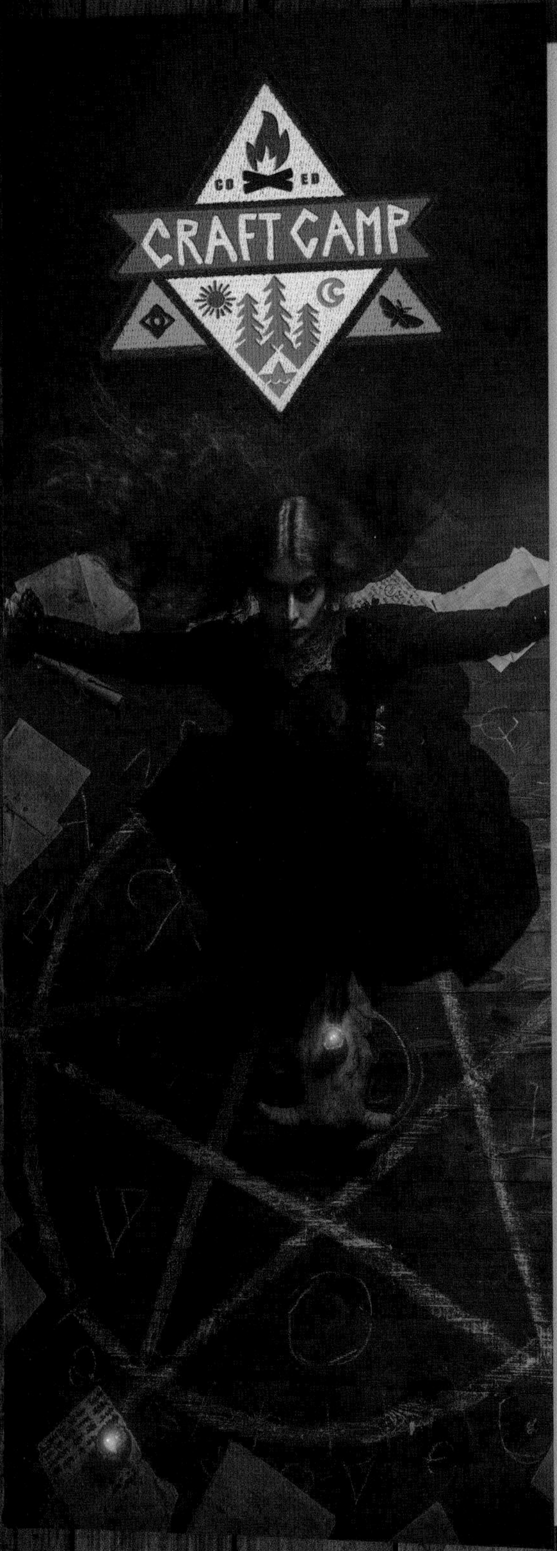
CO ED
CRAFT CAMP

CAMPER

NAME ______________________

PRONOUNS ______________ AGE ______

ADDRESS ______________________

CONTACT NUMBER ______________________

EMERGENCY CONTACT ______________________

SHIRT SIZE

☐ XS ☐ S ☐ M ☐ L ☐ XL ☐ XXL

SHIRT STYLE

- ☐ t-shirt crew neck (short sleeve)
- ☐ t-shirt v-neck (short sleeve)
- ☐ t-shirt crew neck (long sleeve)
- ☐ t-shirt v-neck (long sleeve)
- ☐ polo shirt
- ☐ tank top
- ☐ halter top
- ☐ hoodie (full zip)
- ☐ hoodie (pull over)
- ☐ sweatshirt

OUTERWEAR

- ☐ windbreaker
- ☐ parka
- ☐ fleece

CASH ONLY. NO CHECKS PLEASE.

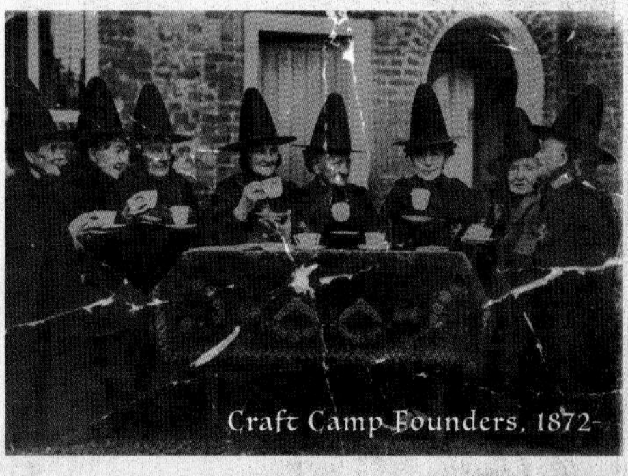

Craft Camp Founders, 1872

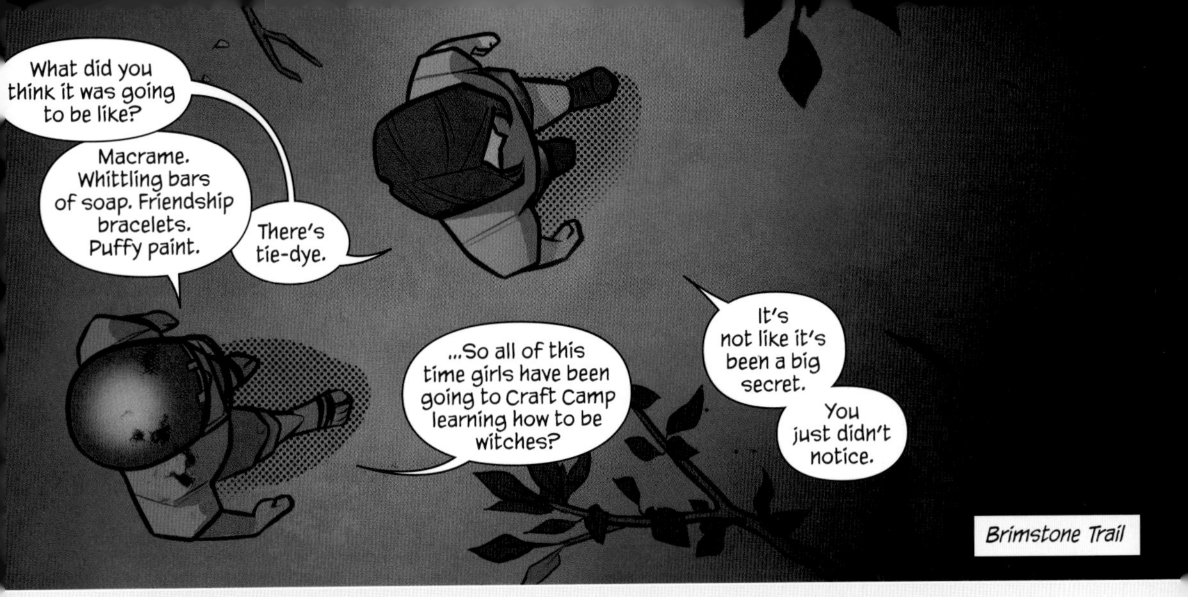
What did you think it was going to be like?
Macrame. Whittling bars of soap. Friendship bracelets. Puffy paint.
There's tie-dye.
...So all of this time girls have been going to Craft Camp learning how to be witches?
It's not like it's been a big secret.
You just didn't notice.
Brimstone Trail

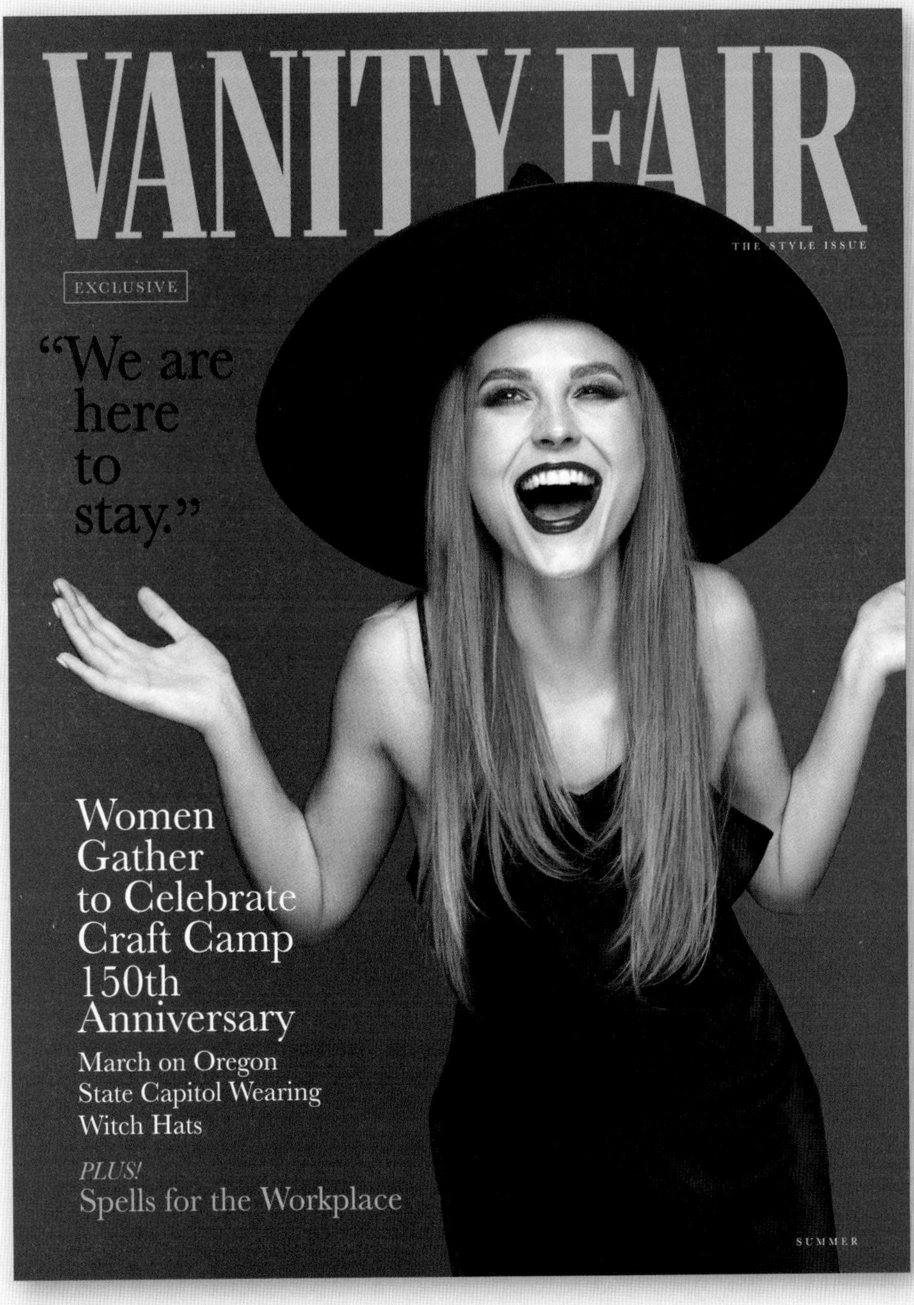
VANITY FAIR
THE STYLE ISSUE
EXCLUSIVE
"We are here to stay."
Women Gather to Celebrate Craft Camp 150th Anniversary
March on Oregon State Capitol Wearing Witch Hats
PLUS!
Spells for the Workplace
SUMMER

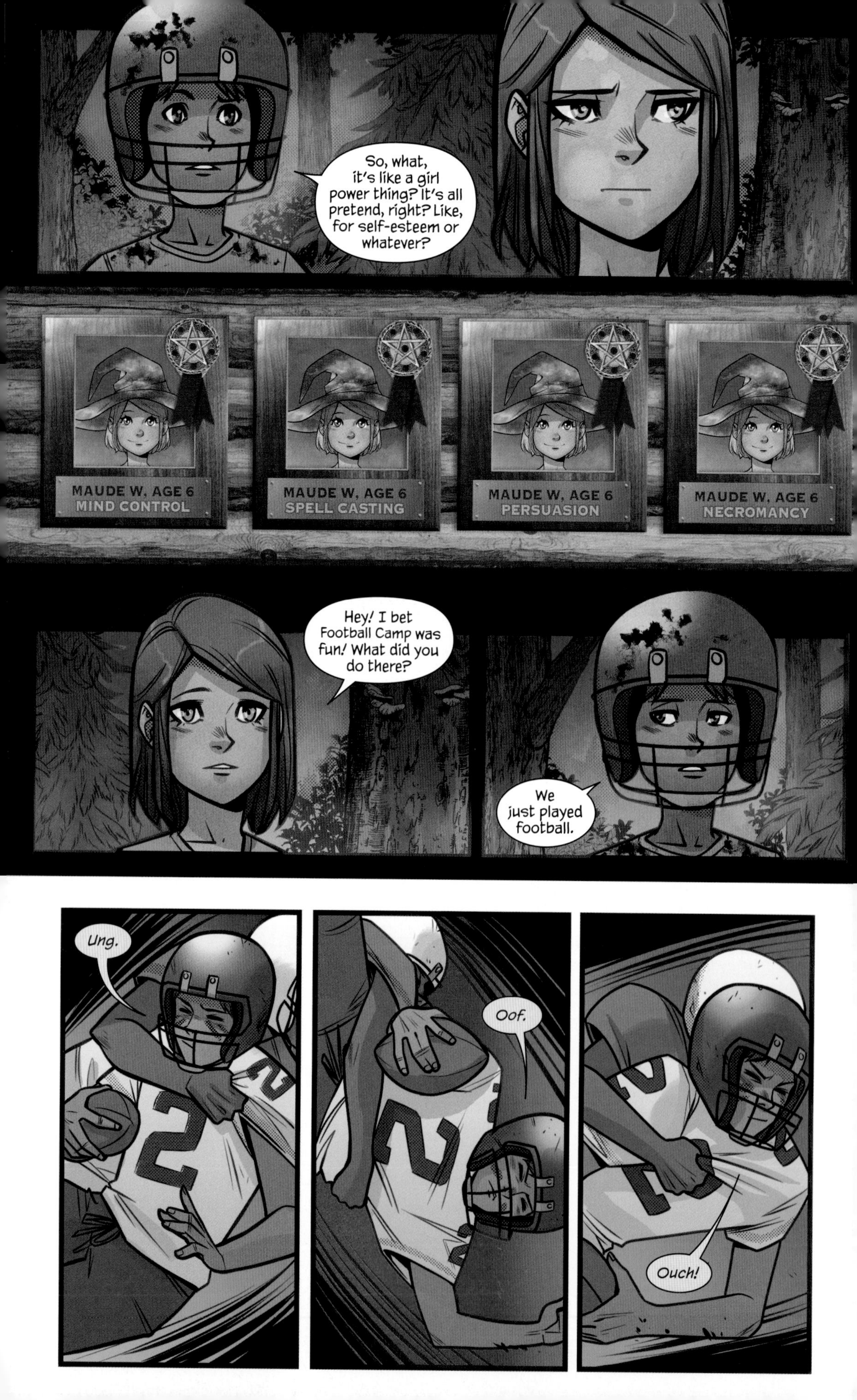
So, what, it's like a girl power thing? It's all pretend, right? Like, for self-esteem or whatever?
MAUDE W, AGE 6
MIND CONTROL
MAUDE W, AGE 6
SPELL CASTING
MAUDE W, AGE 6
PERSUASION
MAUDE W, AGE 6
NECROMANCY
Hey! I bet Football Camp was fun! What did you do there?
We just played football.
Ung.
Oof.
Ouch!

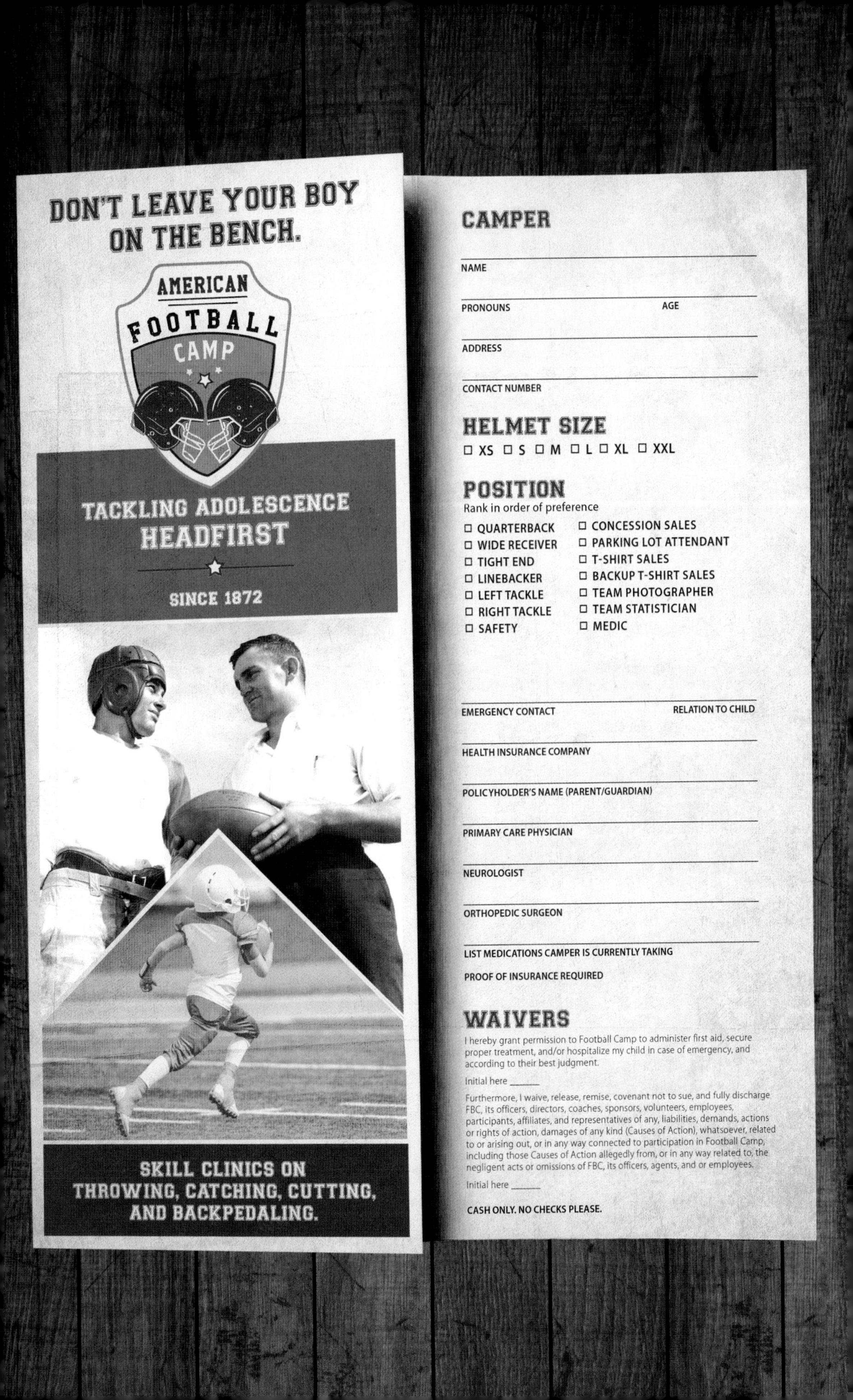

DON'T LEAVE YOUR BOY ON THE BENCH.

AMERICAN
FOOTBALL
CAMP

TACKLING ADOLESCENCE HEADFIRST

SINCE 1872

SKILL CLINICS ON THROWING, CATCHING, CUTTING, AND BACKPEDALING.

CAMPER

NAME ______

PRONOUNS ______ AGE ______

ADDRESS ______

CONTACT NUMBER ______

HELMET SIZE

☐ XS ☐ S ☐ M ☐ L ☐ XL ☐ XXL

POSITION

Rank in order of preference

- ☐ QUARTERBACK
- ☐ WIDE RECEIVER
- ☐ TIGHT END
- ☐ LINEBACKER
- ☐ LEFT TACKLE
- ☐ RIGHT TACKLE
- ☐ SAFETY
- ☐ CONCESSION SALES
- ☐ PARKING LOT ATTENDANT
- ☐ T-SHIRT SALES
- ☐ BACKUP T-SHIRT SALES
- ☐ TEAM PHOTOGRAPHER
- ☐ TEAM STATISTICIAN
- ☐ MEDIC

EMERGENCY CONTACT ______ RELATION TO CHILD ______

HEALTH INSURANCE COMPANY ______

POLICYHOLDER'S NAME (PARENT/GUARDIAN) ______

PRIMARY CARE PHYSICIAN ______

NEUROLOGIST ______

ORTHOPEDIC SURGEON ______

LIST MEDICATIONS CAMPER IS CURRENTLY TAKING ______

PROOF OF INSURANCE REQUIRED

WAIVERS

I hereby grant permission to Football Camp to administer first aid, secure proper treatment, and/or hospitalize my child in case of emergency, and according to their best judgment.

Initial here ______

Furthermore, I waive, release, remise, covenant not to sue, and fully discharge FBC, its officers, directors, coaches, sponsors, volunteers, employees, participants, affiliates, and representatives of any, liabilities, demands, actions or rights of action, damages of any kind (Causes of Action), whatsoever, related to or arising out, or in any way connected to participation in Football Camp, including those Causes of Action allegedly from, or in any way related to, the negligent acts or omissions of FBC, its officers, agents, and or employees.

Initial here ______

CASH ONLY. NO CHECKS PLEASE.

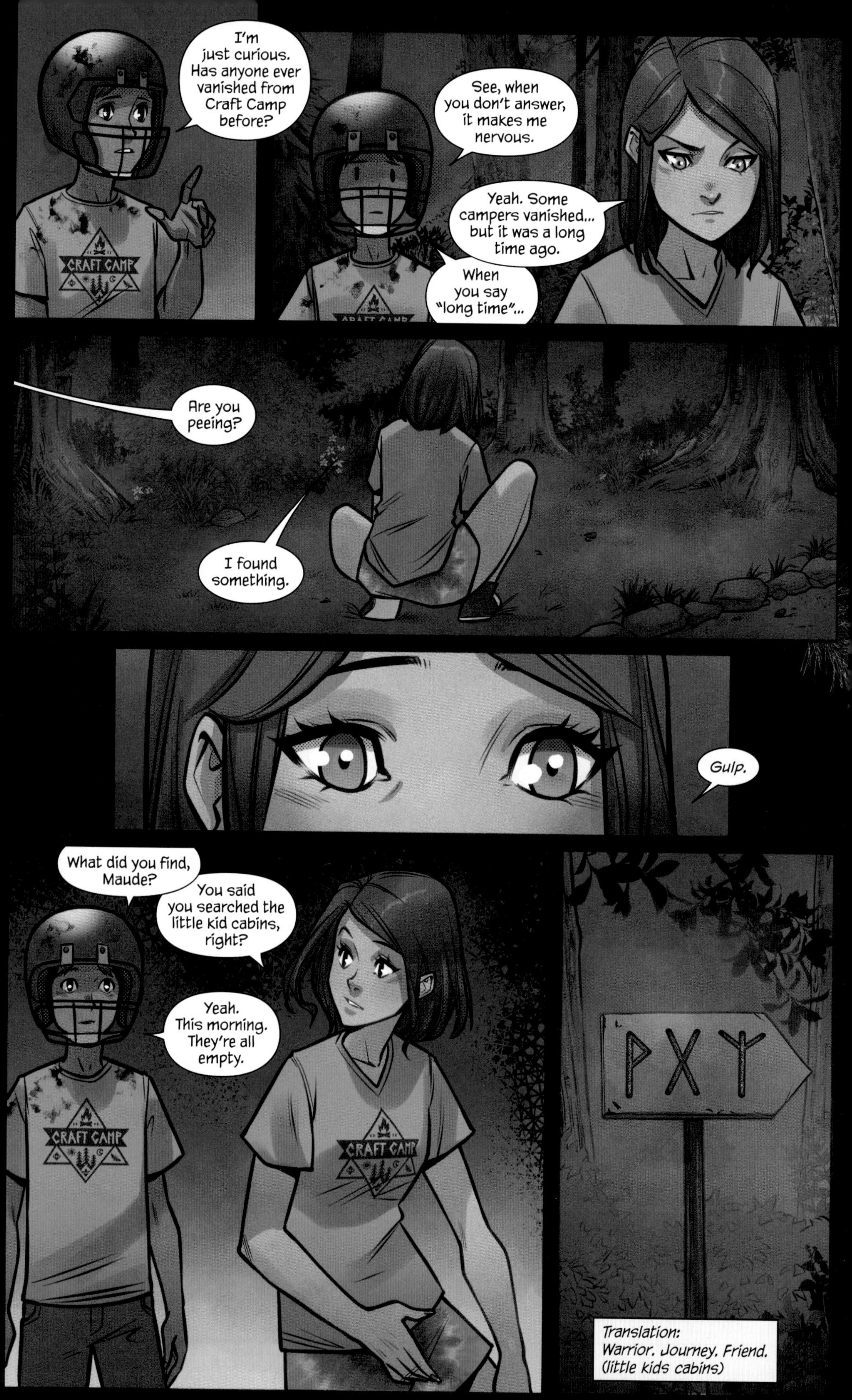
I'm just curious. Has anyone ever vanished from Craft Camp before?
See, when you don't answer, it makes me nervous.
Yeah. Some campers vanished... but it was a long time ago.
When you say "long time"...
CRAFT CAMP
Are you peeing?
I found something.
Gulp.
What did you find, Maude?
You said you searched the little kid cabins, right?
Yeah. This morning. They're all empty.
CRAFT CAMP
CRAFT CAMP
Translation:
Warrior. Journey. Friend.
(little kids cabins)

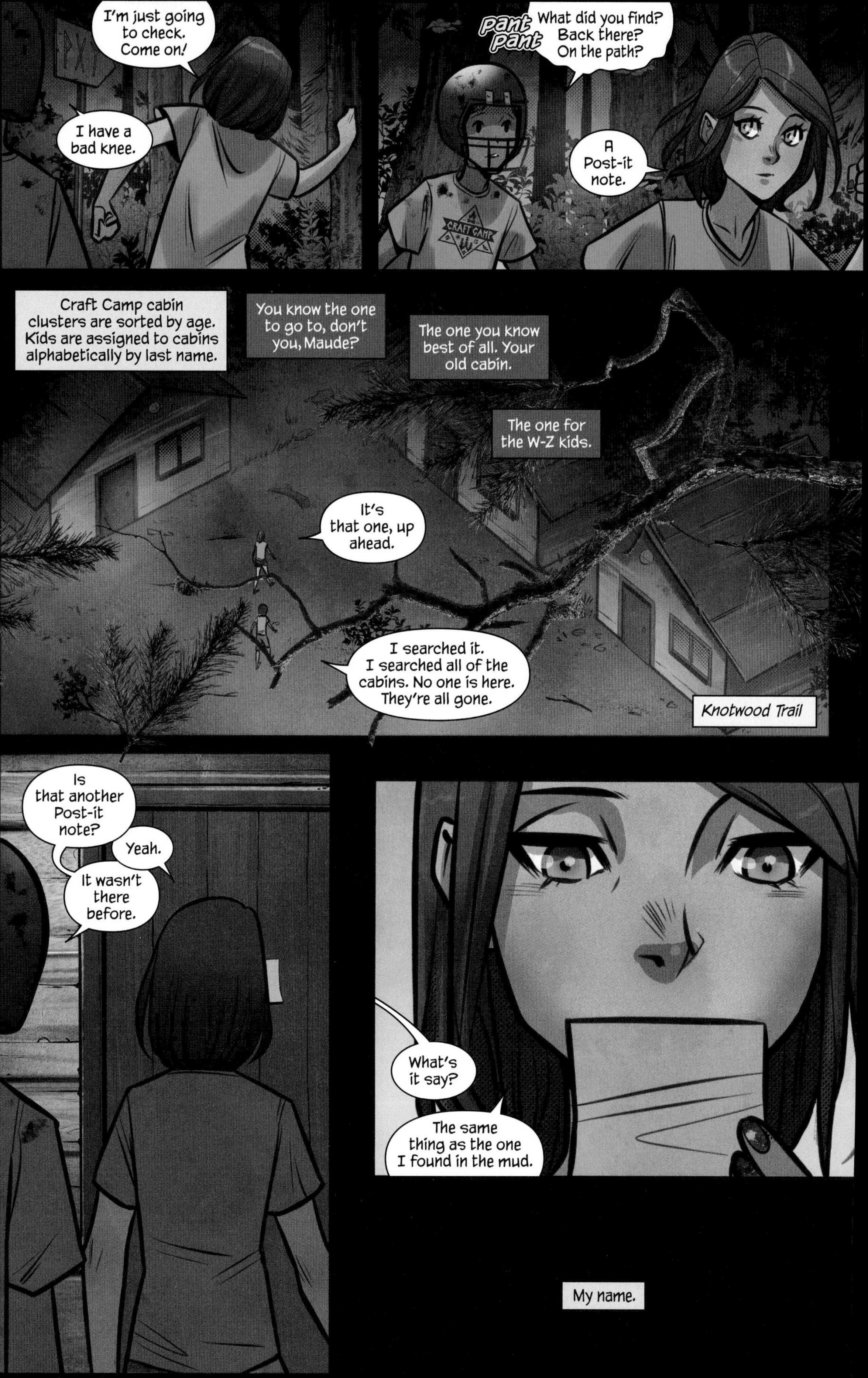
I'm just going to check. Come on!
I have a bad knee.
Pant Pant
What did you find? Back there? On the path?
A Post-it note.
Craft Camp cabin clusters are sorted by age. Kids are assigned to cabins alphabetically by last name.
You know the one to go to, don't you, Maude?
The one you know best of all. Your old cabin.
The one for the W-Z kids.
It's that one, up ahead.
I searched it. I searched all of the cabins. No one is here. They're all gone.
Knotwood Trail
Is that another Post-it note?
Yeah.
It wasn't there before.
What's it say?
The same thing as the one I found in the mud.
My name.

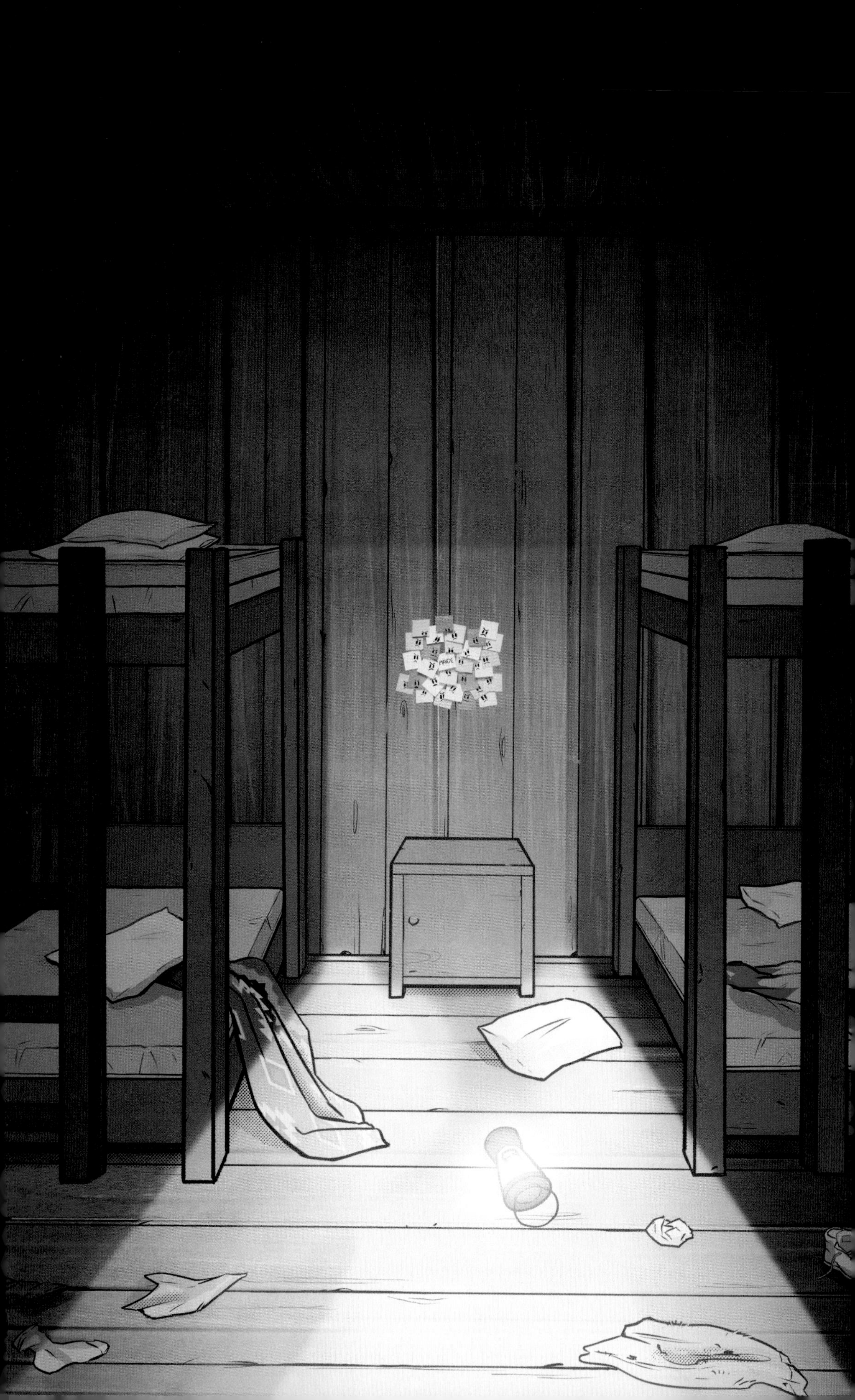

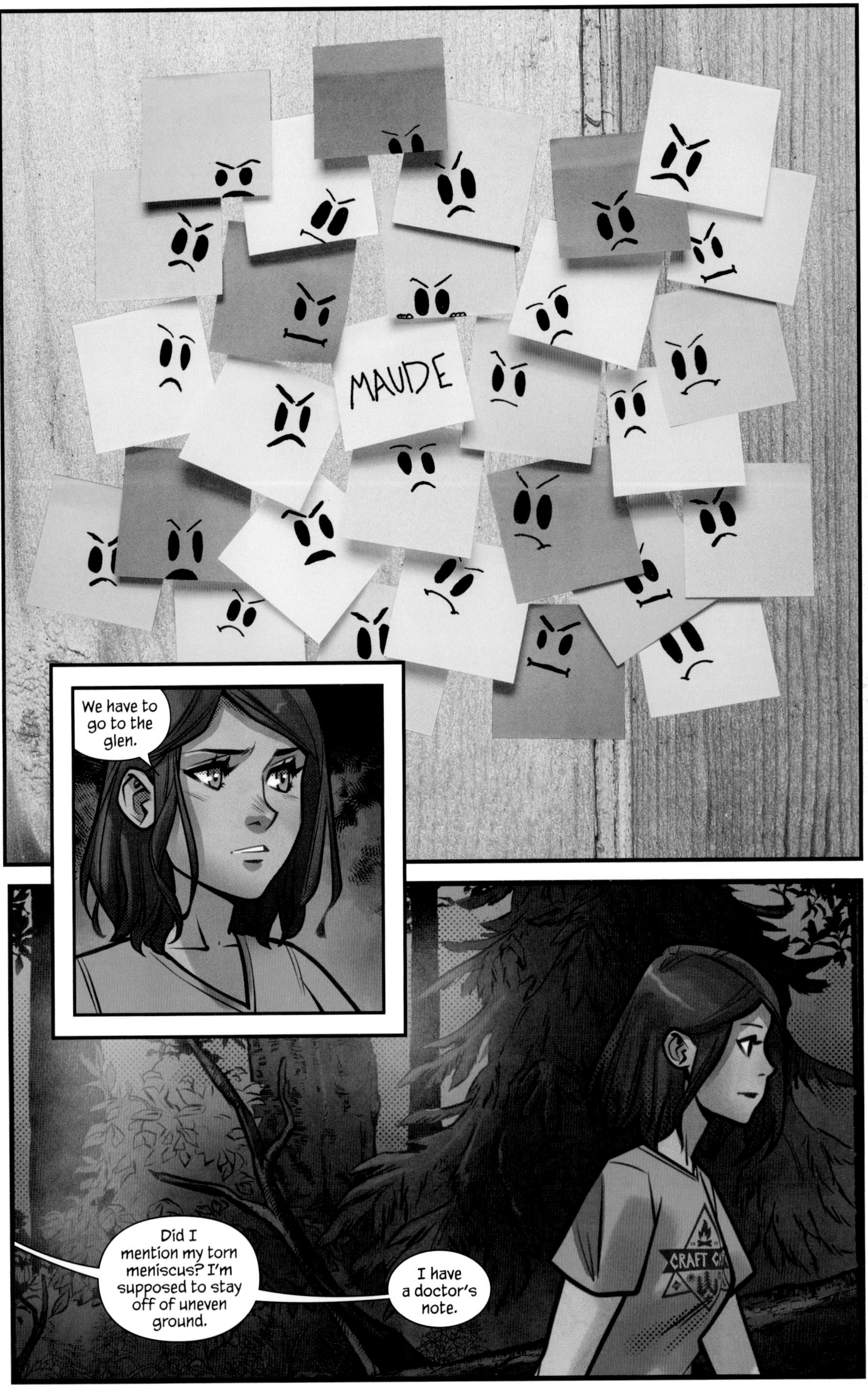
MAUDE
We have to go to the glen.
Did I mention my torn meniscus? I'm supposed to stay off of uneven ground.
I have a doctor's note.
CRAFT CA

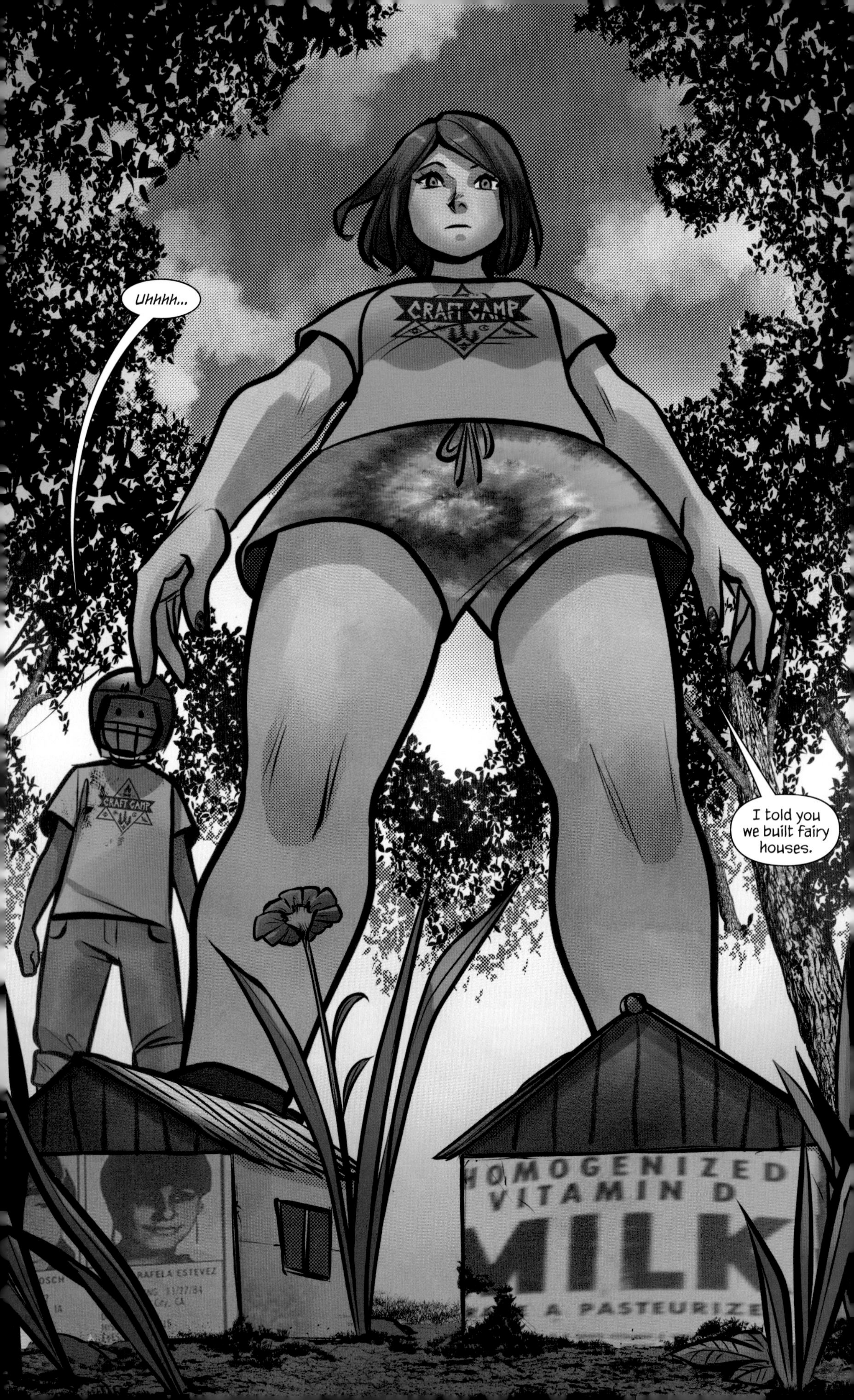
Uhhhh...
CRAFT CAMP
CRAFT CAMP
I told you we built fairy houses.
HOMOGENIZED
VITAMIN D
MILK
A PASTEURIZE

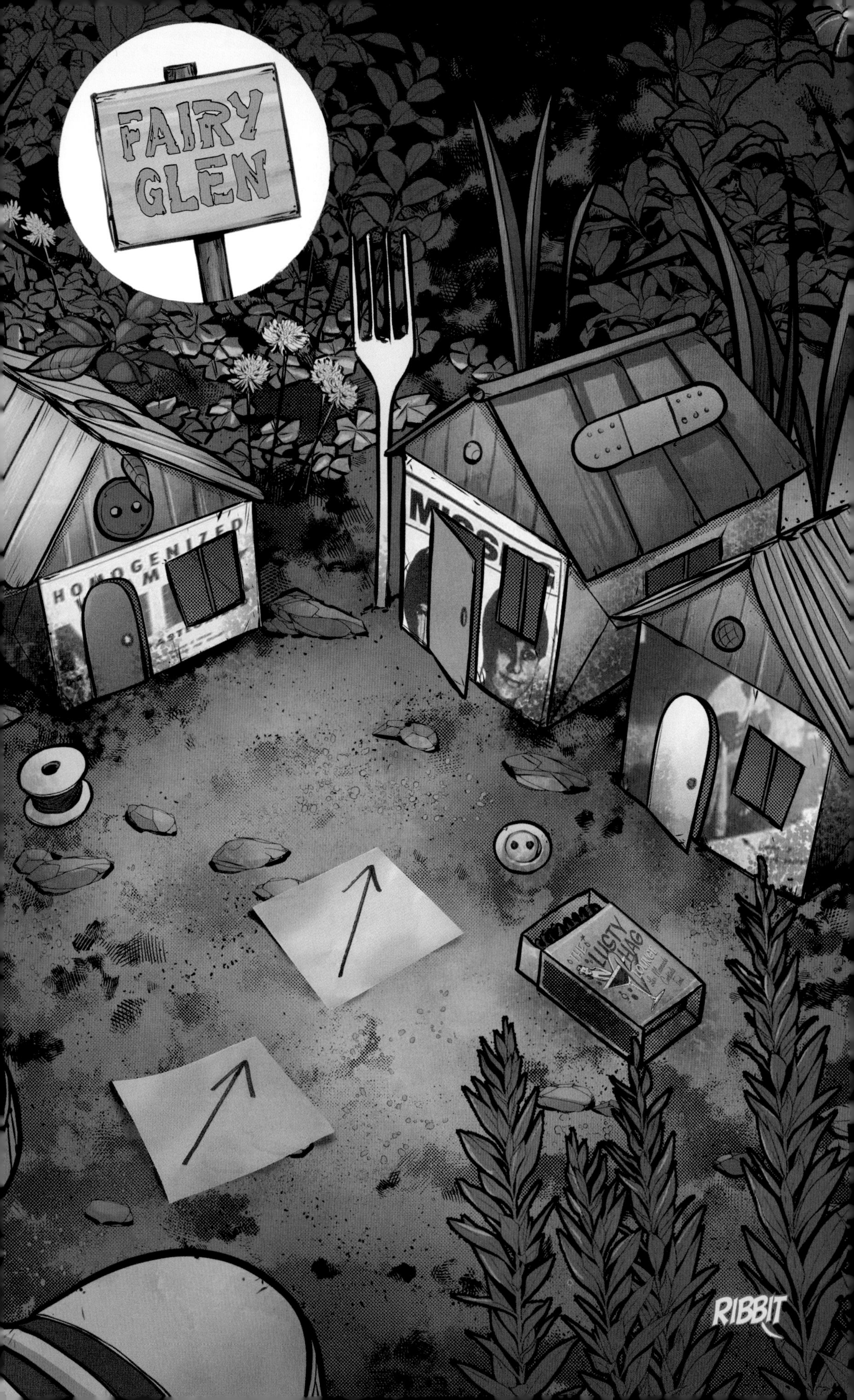
FAIRY GLEN
HOMOGENIZED
THE LUSTY HAG LOUNGE
RIBBIT

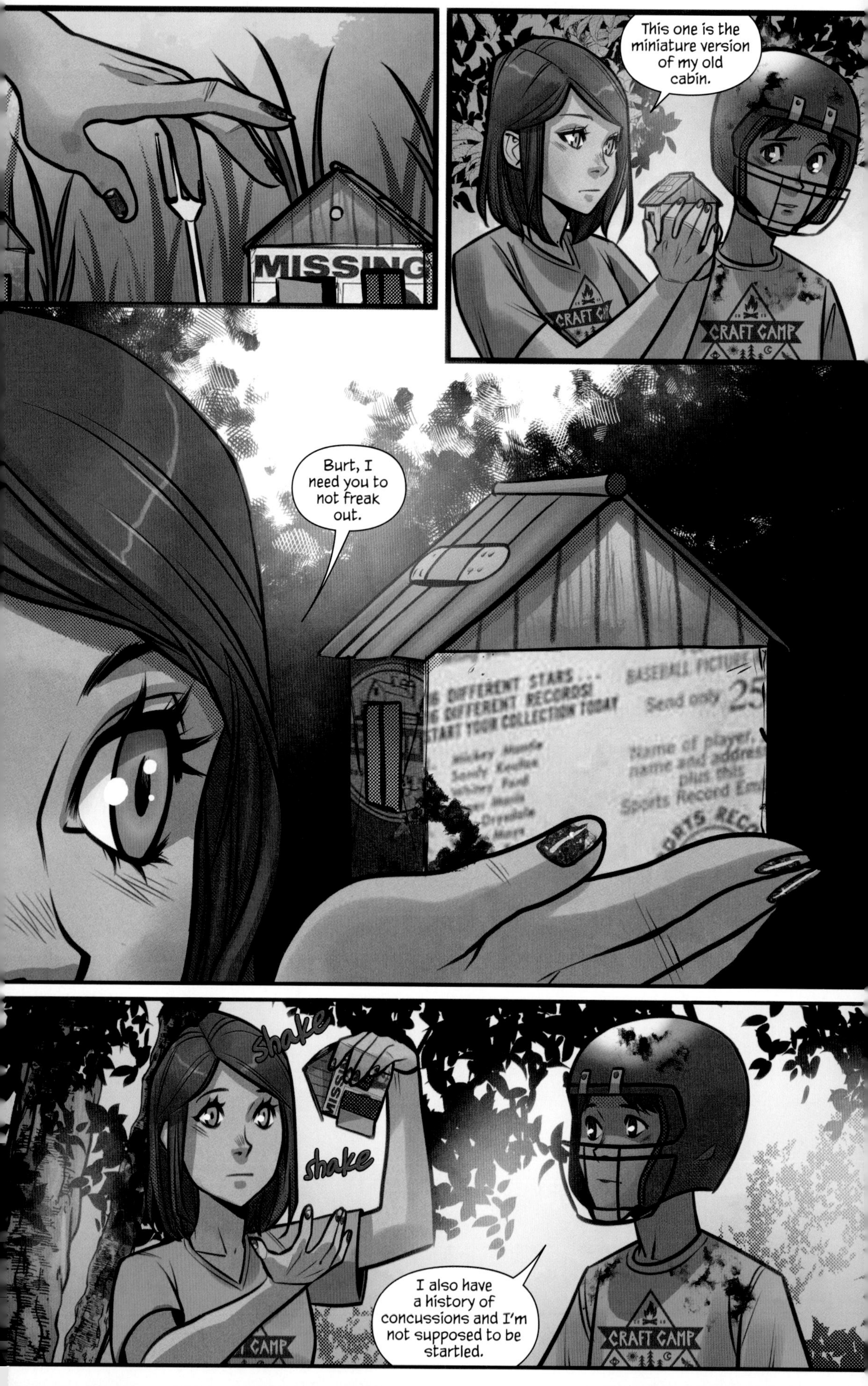

MISSING
This one is the miniature version of my old cabin.
CRAFT CAMP
CRAFT CAMP
Burt, I need you to not freak out.
DIFFERENT STARS...
DIFFERENT RECORDS!
START YOUR COLLECTION TODAY
BASEBALL PICTURE
Send only 25
Mickey Mantle
Sandy Koufax
Whitey Ford
shake
shake
I also have a history of concussions and I'm not supposed to be startled.
CRAFT CAMP
CRAFT CAMP

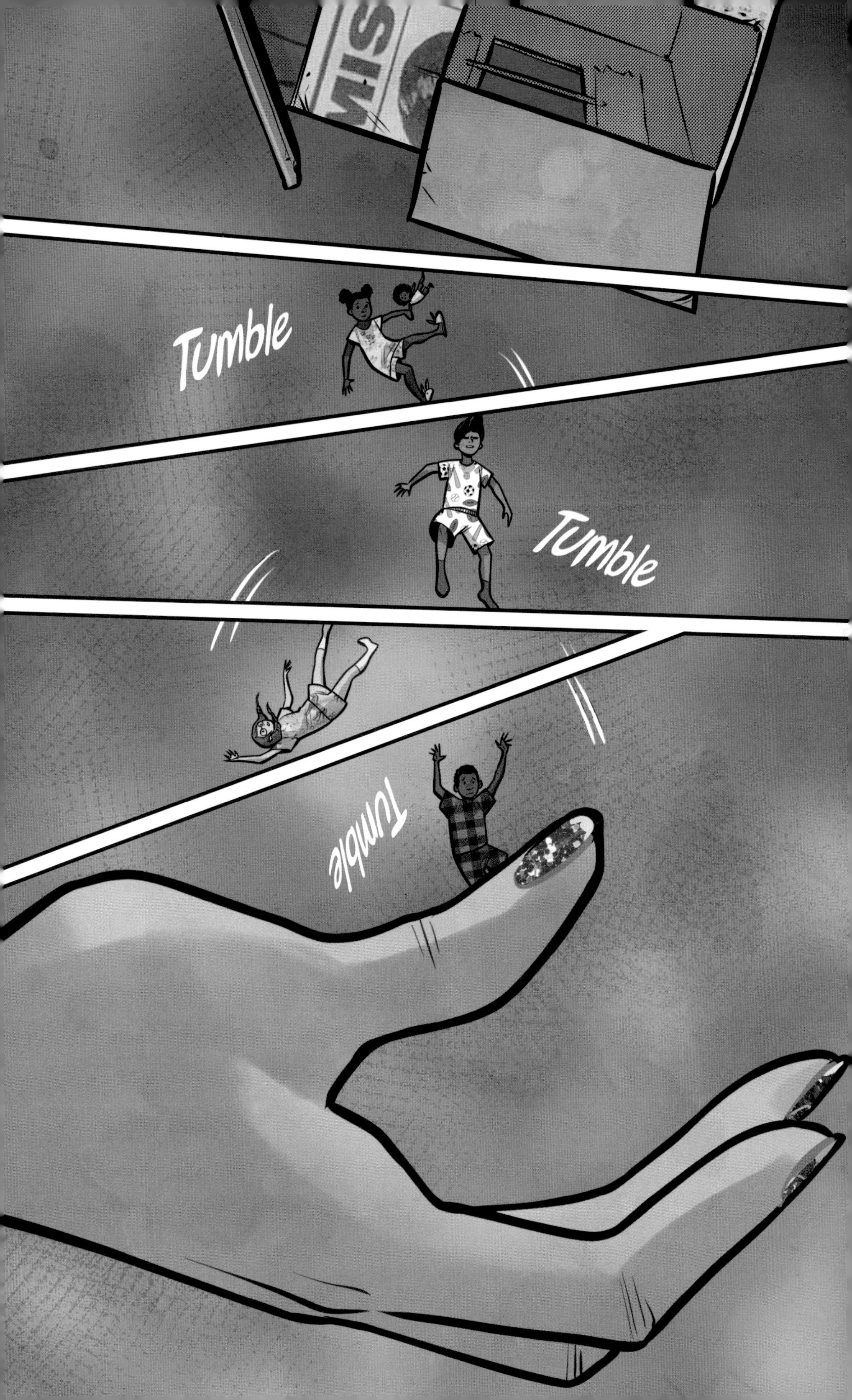
Tumble
Tumble
Tumble

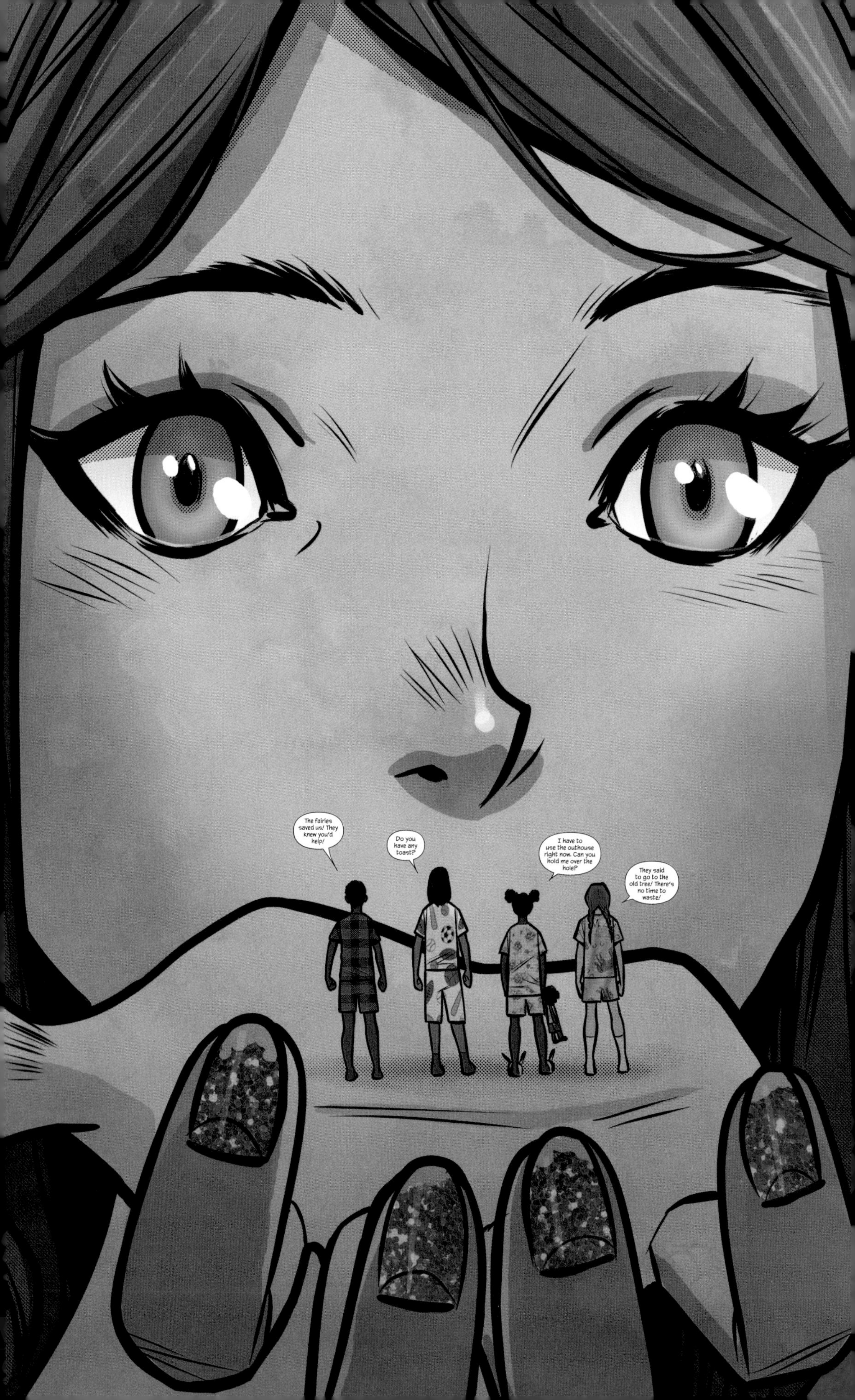
The fairies saved us! They knew you'd help!
Do you have any toast?
I have to use the outhouse right now. Can you hold me over the hole?
They said to go to the old tree! There's no time to waste!

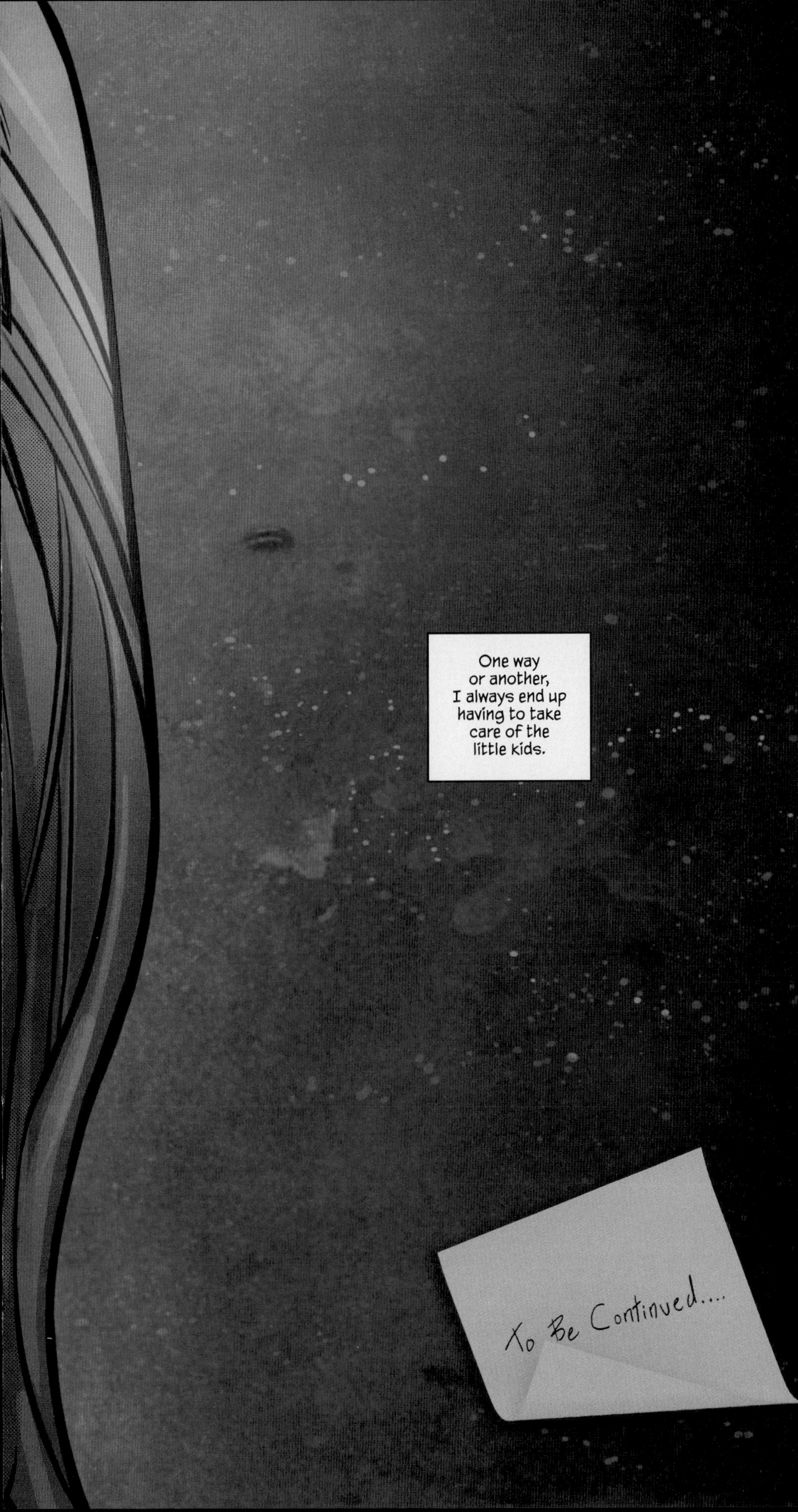
One way or another, I always end up having to take care of the little kids.
To Be Continued....

5,928 days

by Eliza Fantastic Mohan (age 16)

The clock struck twelve as my mother confessed
twisting
curling
worries
of the various skins I shed
Her eyes spoke of a little blonde girl
Hair platinum
and irises a summer's sky
I told her what I tell myself
on the sunny June days
When I see her in mirrors
and I forget my place

For as long as I live
I will never love as strong
as I do
for the little blonde girl

She is the tear I shed
when I miss what I
will someday leave behind

She is the gleam in my eye
when I know who I am
And the smile in my pain
when I know I'm not there yet

She's an organ beating
in my bruised chest
A ring around the tree roots
reaching west
She is all of my pain
hope sorrow
and love
Wrapped in the yesterdays of the girl
I always was

I am 5928 days old,
This body has breathed since 2004.
I slept walked into the woods at nine-years-old
And every second since
has been a blessing
& curse
I am the blonde girl lit like a halo
Who wore neon shirts
whose favorite color was teal
I am the one in the corgi themed clothes
Before insecurity crept in and took her hold
I am the 13-year-old with the side shaved to the skull
And the remnants of the bubble that popped
too soon
I am 14-years-old and rising from ruin
with bright pink hair and crumbs of foundation
Friends by her side and fractures slowing healing
And
I am the freshmen
surrounded by smoke and decay
Threatened by rib cages and blackened lungs
Secondhand smoke tried to drown me young
In all the worlds I breathed
perhaps this was the real one
I am the sophomore
stuck in her room
grown out forest fairy hair and bookshelf reinvigorated
I am the one
who cries to phoebe bridgers
wishing she could reshape the rubber of her skull
I am the one
who laughs in the faces of those who wish me ill will
I am wise
and broken
and stronger than ever
I smile to my demons
and second guess the angels
And as long as I live I'll never forget
the girl in the dress
who lived so I could regret
And I hope beyond hope that those who come next
Provide me the same tender immortality
As the Ones in my chest.

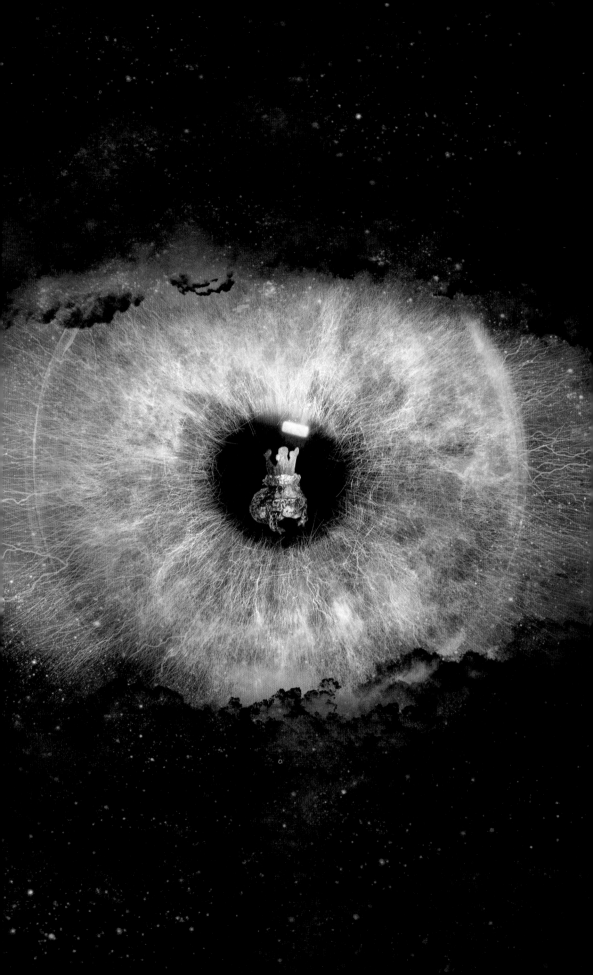

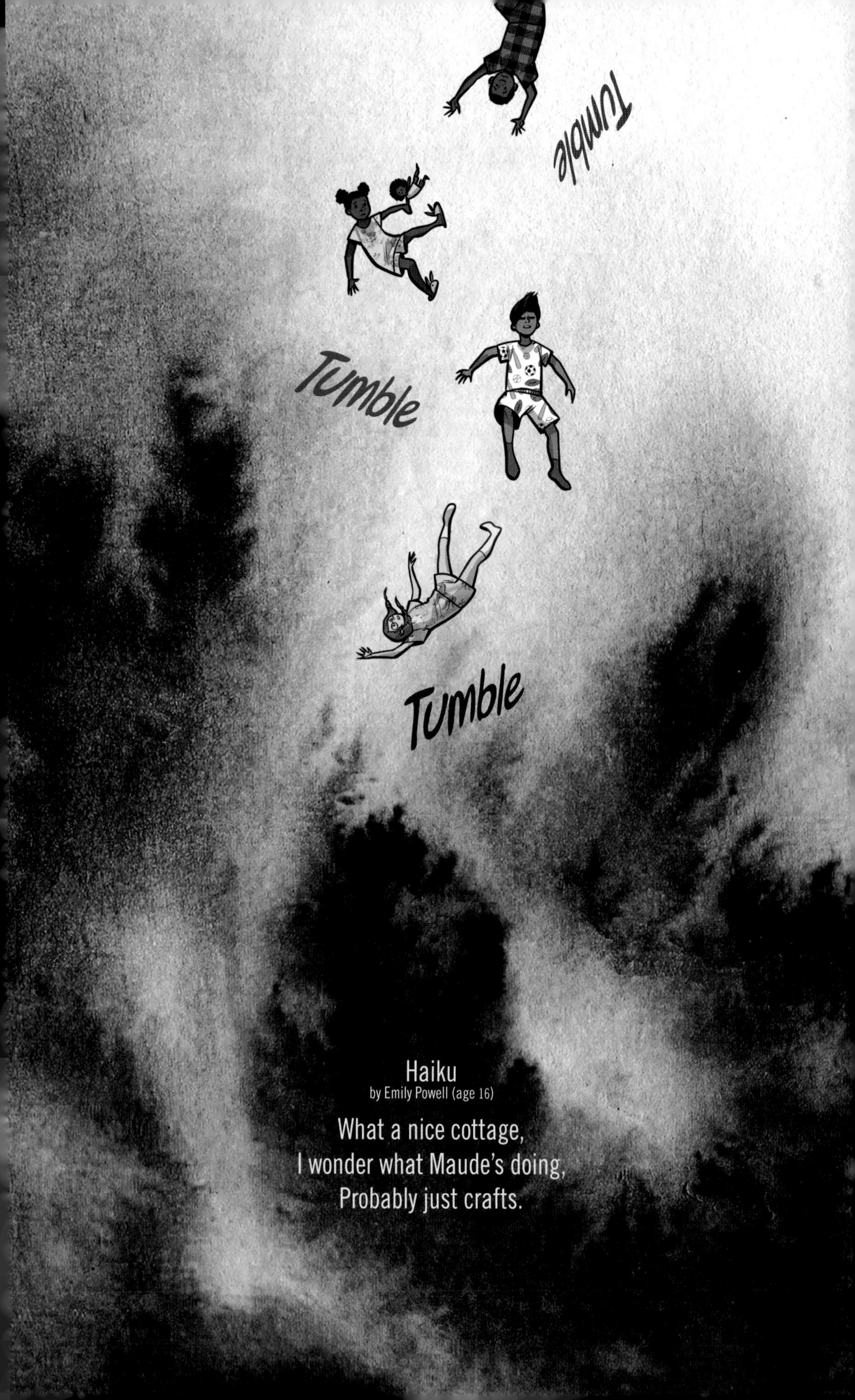
Tumble
Tumble
Tumble

Haiku

by Emily Powell (age 16)

What a nice cottage,
I wonder what Maude's doing,
Probably just crafts.

Cut along dotted line. Punch out hole at top. Lace with orange string. (Fro

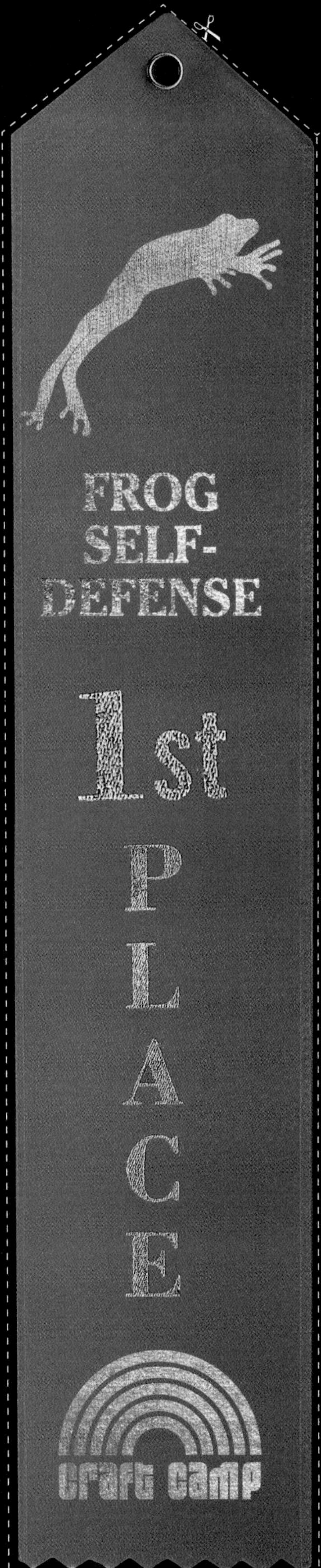
FROG SELF-DEFENSE
1st PLACE
craft camp

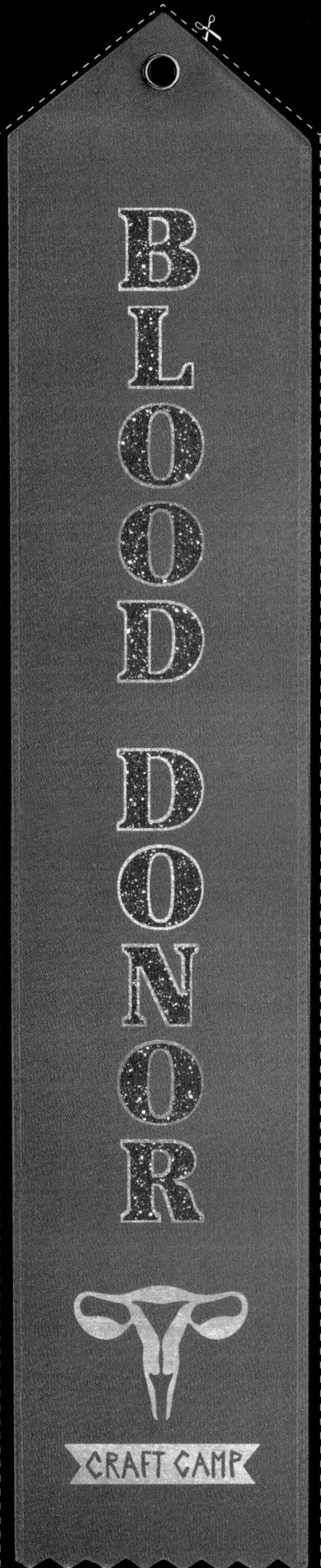
BLOOD DONOR
CRAFT CAMP

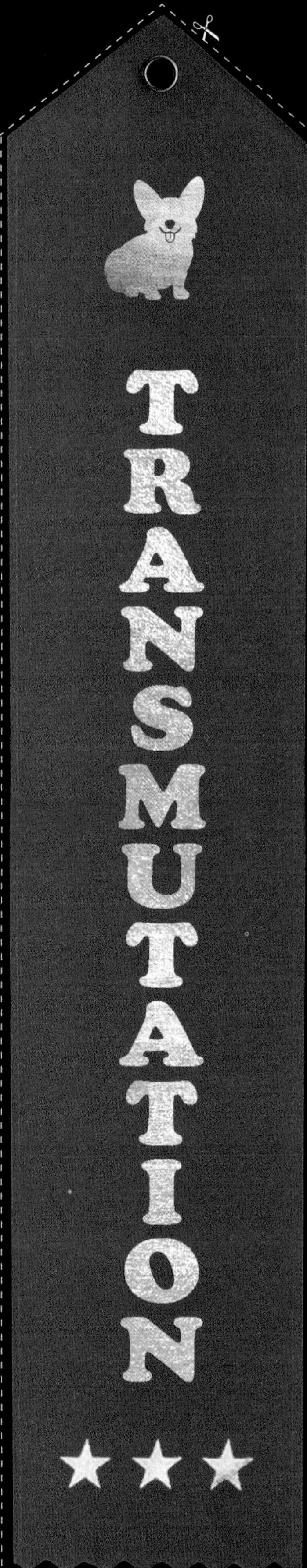
TRANSMUTATION

(BACK)

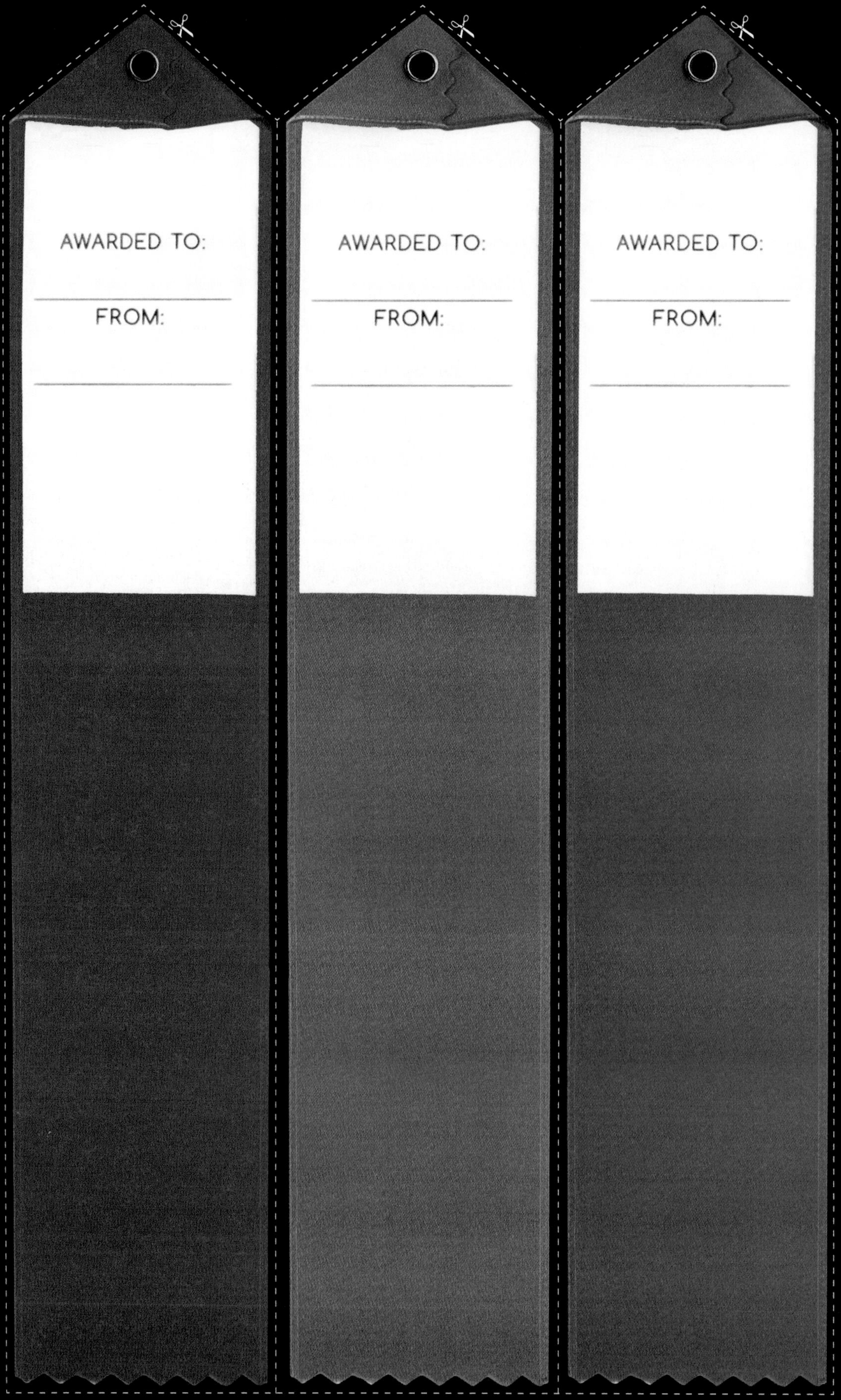
AWARDED TO:
FROM:
AWARDED TO:
FROM:
AWARDED TO:
FROM:

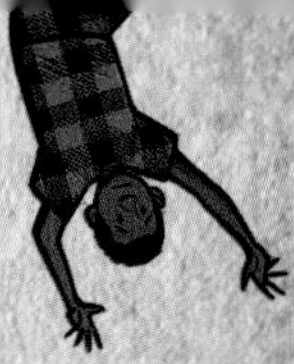

MINISTRY OF
TROUBLE

CREDITS: ISSUE #2

CREATORS CHELSEA CAIN & LIA MITERNIQUE
WRITER CHELSEA CAIN
COVER ARTIST & GRAPHIC DESIGNER LIA MITERNIQUE
ARTISTS KATE NIEMCZYK AND LIA MITERNIQUE
COLORIST RACHELLE ROSENBERG
LETTERER JOE CARAMAGNA
SUPPLEMENTAL BACKGROUND INKER ANIA SZERSZEN
POEM & POST-IT LETTERING ELIZA FANTASTIC MOHAN
HAIKU EMILY POWELL
ADDITIONAL INTERIOR ART STELLA GREENVOSS

YOU HAVE BEEN CONTACTED BY THE MINISTRY OF TROUBLE. AWAIT FURTHER INSTRUCTIONS. ☿

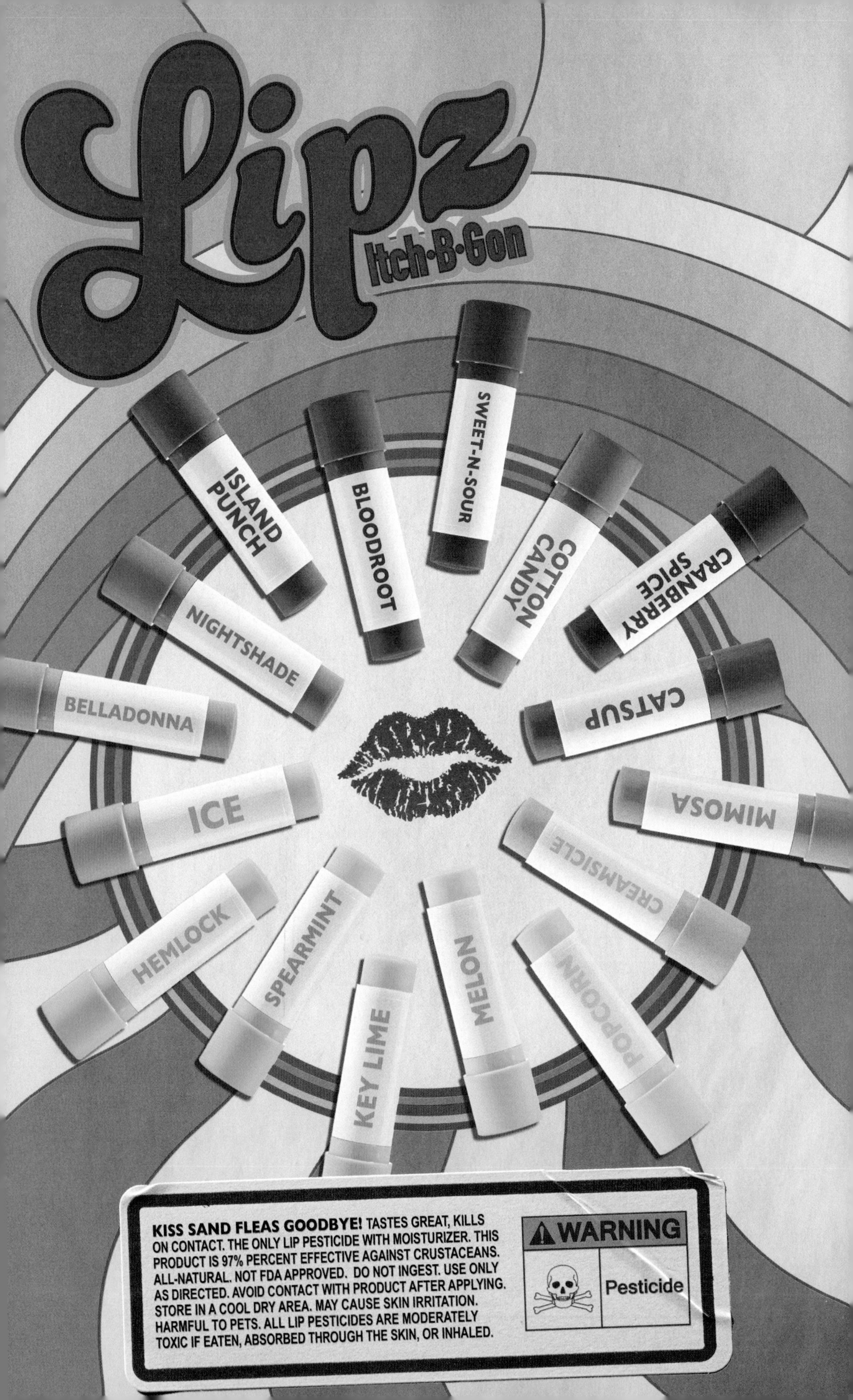
Lipz
Itch-B-Gon
SWEET-N-SOUR
ISLAND PUNCH
BLOODROOT
COTTON CANDY
CRANBERRY SPICE
NIGHTSHADE
BELLADONNA
CATSUP
ICE
MIMOSA
CREAMSICLE
HEMLOCK
SPEARMINT
MELON
POPCORN
KEY LIME
KISS SAND FLEAS GOODBYE! TASTES GREAT, KILLS ON CONTACT. THE ONLY LIP PESTICIDE WITH MOISTURIZER. THIS PRODUCT IS 97% PERCENT EFFECTIVE AGAINST CRUSTACEANS. ALL-NATURAL. NOT FDA APPROVED. DO NOT INGEST. USE ONLY AS DIRECTED. AVOID CONTACT WITH PRODUCT AFTER APPLYING. STORE IN A COOL DRY AREA. MAY CAUSE SKIN IRRITATION. HARMFUL TO PETS. ALL LIP PESTICIDES ARE MODERATELY TOXIC IF EATEN, ABSORBED THROUGH THE SKIN, OR INHALED.
WARNING
Pesticide

[Issue 2, Cover B]

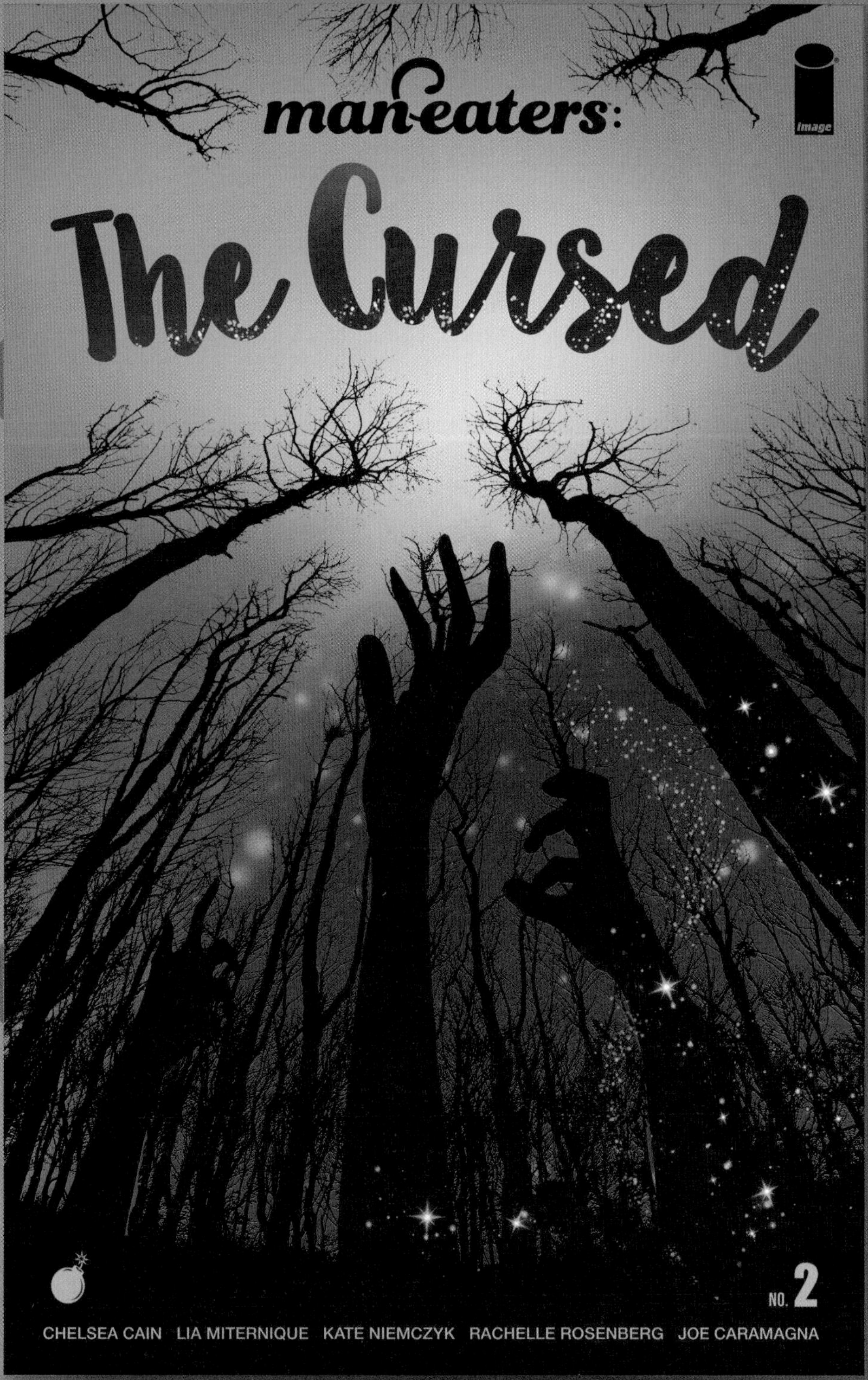
man-eaters:
The Cursed
image
NO. 2
CHELSEA CAIN LIA MITERNIQUE KATE NIEMCZYK RACHELLE ROSENBERG JOE CARAMAGNA

CHAPTER 3

MAN-EATERS: THE CURSED

WITCHCRAFT FOR CHILDREN

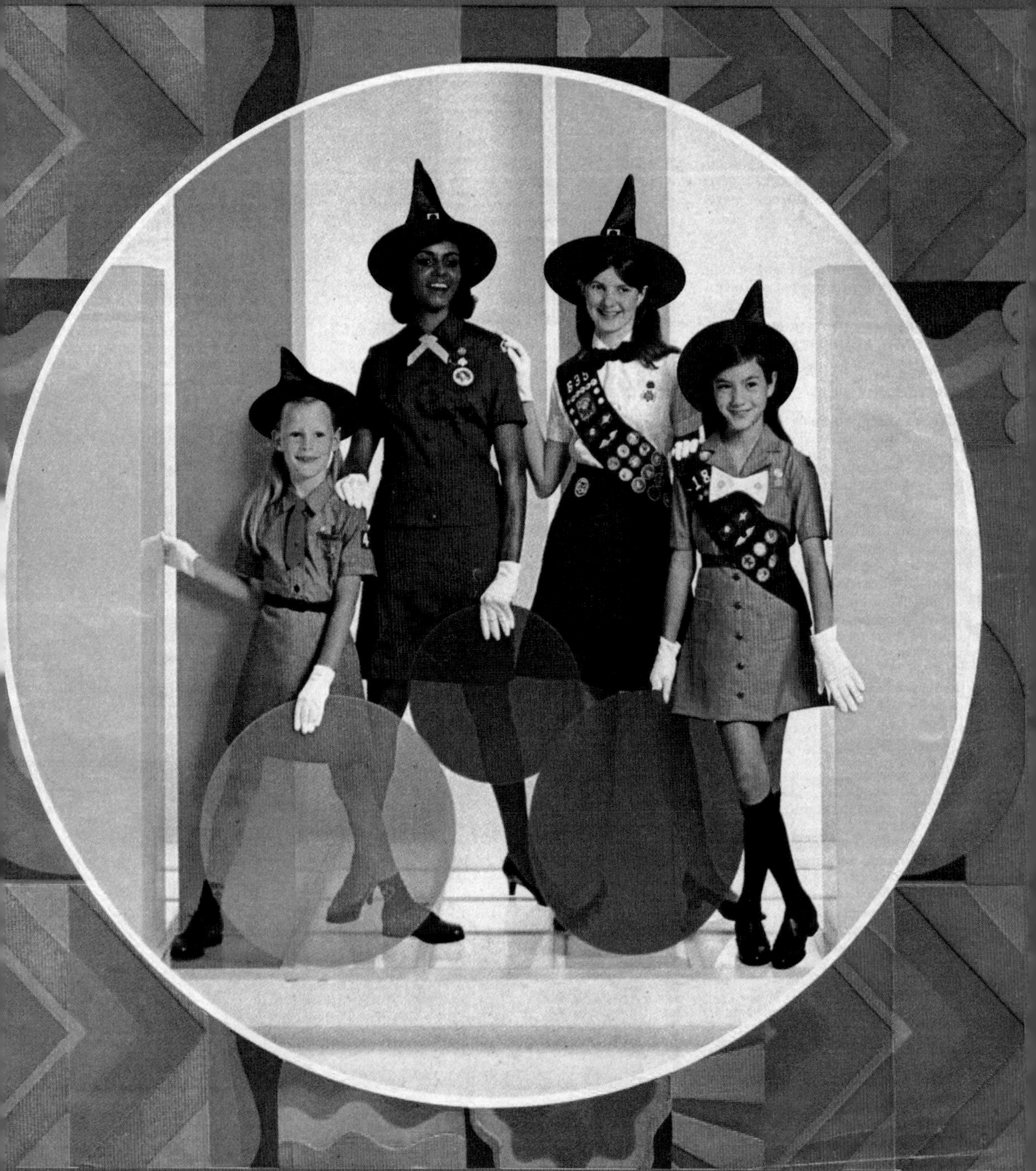

CHELSEA CAIN LIA MITERNIQUE

NO. 3

craft camp

1983

Dear Camper: J0   ,

Enclosed is a complimentary issue of Witchcraft for Children.

Welcome back to Craft Camp! You are confirmed for session 4.

Your cabin assignment is: ᚱ ᚼ ᚠ

We are looking forward to a summer full of witchcraft, friends, and fun.

Lice
All campers are required to undergo a lice check upon arrival. Parents
should carefully inspect children's heads for lice at least two weeks
prior to sending them to camp, and again within 48 hours prior to camp.
Any lice infestation should then be treated. As lice are immune to all
known spells, any camper with lice will be sent home.

Activities
Activities will include — but not be limited to — swimming, tide pooling,
archery, demonology, transmutation, blood magik, and windsurfing.

Camp Store
Don't forget to bring your camp bucks to spend at the Camp Store. We're
excited to introduce new merchandise, including Craft Camp pint glasses,
zipper hoodies, and sigil key chains. Pre-order your Craft Camp Feminine
Hygiene products while supplies last!

Camp Forms
Do you turn into a werepanther when you menstruate? Please make sure
you fill out the appropriate forms so counselors can take appropriate
precautions.

Transportation
Please let us know if you are planning on arriving via bus, zeppelin, or
car.

Craft Camp is committed to promoting magic through innovative instruction
and positive reinforcement.

- Cloverfoot

Cloverfoot

Lead Camp Counselor
Craft Camp [OR #1]

Witchcraft for Children

1983 Vol. 9, No. 3

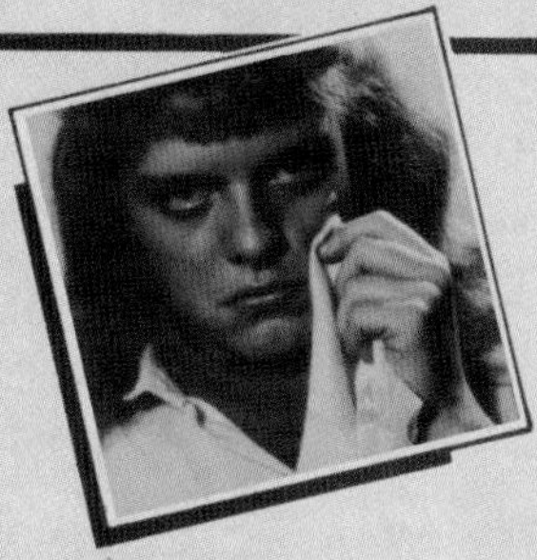
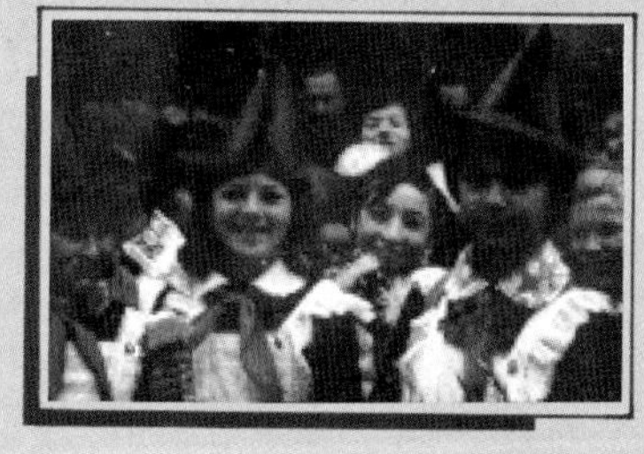
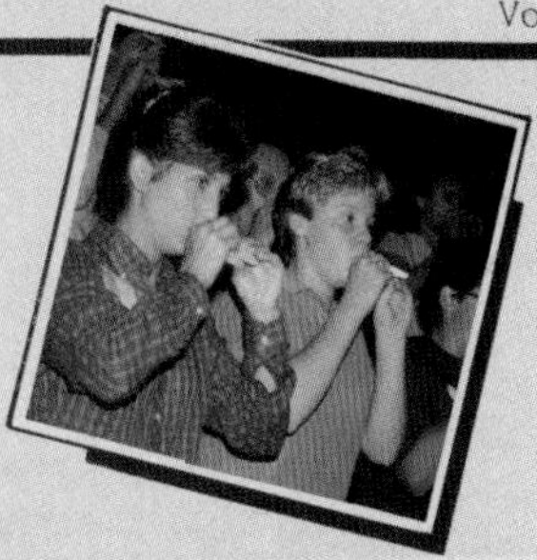

FEATURES

REGULARS

SPECIALS

WfC

Mailbag

Witchcraft for Children

SPREADING THE GOOD WORD SINCE 1692

CREATORS
Chelsea Cain & Lia Miternique

WRITER
Chelsea Cain

COVER ARTIST
GRAPHIC DESIGNER
Lia Miternique

SPELL WRITER/
ACTIVITIES DIRECTOR
Eliza Fantastic Mohan

SUPPLEMENTAL ART
Stella Greenvoss

HAIKU
Emily Powell

MINISTRY OF
TROUBLE

YOU HAVE BEEN CONTACTED BY THE MINISTRY OF TROUBLE. AWAIT FURTHER INSTRUCTIONS.

PRODUCTION BY
DEANNA PHELPS & TRICIA RAMOS

CONTROVERSY

For the past few months I've been telling my friends about your magazine, saying that it's one of the best new witch periodicals — make that THE best. As a teenager I'm bombarded with new witch magazines every week, and most of them, while well-intentioned, simply don't seem any different from any other. I opened my first issue of your magazine expecting more of the same, but I was very pleased to find it well-written and well-thought-out.

It is obvious that you cover controversial subjects, and challenge the kids you serve with real-life situations. You offer us facts, and leave it to us to make up our own minds. I will continue to recommend your magazine to everyone I know.

Hail Satan.

Kelsey
Staten Island

THAT SHOCKING COVER

Dear WFC,

I was shocked and offended by the cover of your April issue showing a boy and his dog. Bestiality is a real problem here in rural America, and normalizing boy-canine relationships can only lead to uncomfortable situations. Do better.

Anonymous
Des Moines, IA

P.S. Keep up the good work!

SMITING

Dear WFC,

I am twelve, and I would like to smite my mother's boyfriend and my gymnastics coach. I have limited access to spell ingredients and materials. I have a little money. Is ordering a voodoo doll a good investment?

Name Withheld
Evanston, IL

MISSING SISTER

Dear WFC,

My sister has been missing for over a year. She disappeared at Craft Camp (session 6) at the Oregon Coast. I have heard rumors that other campers have vanished at this camp? This could be an interesting investigative piece. Maybe some of your other readers have missing relatives? Please help. Also I really enjoy your articles on eyeliner.

Yours,

Julie
Renton, WA

SATAN'S LI'L HELPERS

Dear editors,

I think it's important to point out a significant error in the "facts" presented in your article entitled "Dark Magic for Middle Schoolers" from the April 1982 issue. You reported that the Kansas City school board voted against granting "after school club" status to the KC branch of Satan's Li'l Helpers (grade 6). In fact this club was approved unanimously. We support every child's spiritual journey. I'm proud to say that our Li'l Helper troop has 43 active members and works tirelessly to spread the word of our Dark Lord through choral performances at local retirement homes and pediatric wards.

Gregory
Kansas City

Editor's Note: You are correct. We regret the error.

WORDCRAFT

Dear Haiku Columnist,

I love your haikus. You are my favorite thing about this magazine, which frankly is not very good. My mom says I can't make a living writing haikus. I want to grow up to be just like you!

Aspiring Poet
Portland, Oregon

PATRIARCHY ANXIETY

Dear Editors,

I am interested in protection spells against the Patriarchy? Can you help? I am interested in Banishing and Warding.

Yours,

Carol S.
Iowa City, IA

Editor's Note: Please review our feature in this issue — DOES THE PATRIARCHY MAKE YOU CRY? It includes several excellent anti-patriarchy spells. Banishing is a more specific spell than warding, and a useful form of defensive magic. Warding is a gentler defensive magic option that is used in a more general manner.

Over 250,000 sold!

Best Selling Devotionals for Witches

by Timothy Johnson

If I'm So Good At Magic, Why Can't I Get My Locker Open?

91 short pagan devotionals dealing with panic and how to forgive yourself, and other teen issues. Includes searching questions, and Book of Shadows references. $4.95

Why Do They Keep Burning Us at the Stake?
Timothy Johnson
If I'm So Good At Magic, Why Can't I Get My Locker Open?
Menstrual Tree and Other High Places

Why Do They Keep Burning Us at the Stake?

Concrete easy-to-understand answers on basic witch doctrines such as free will, rationality, and decision-making. Cartoon illustrations add impact. 91 chapters. Includes thought provoking questions and paper dolls.

Climbing the Menstrual Tree and other High Places

These 91 pagan devotionals address working through fear, rock music, menstruation, and other issues pertinent to teens. $4.95

At your bookstore or

Spellbound Publishers
a division of Itch-B-Gon

Add $1 for mail orders

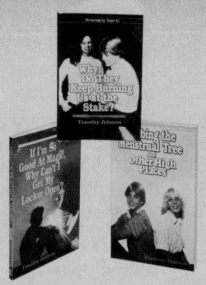

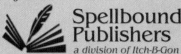

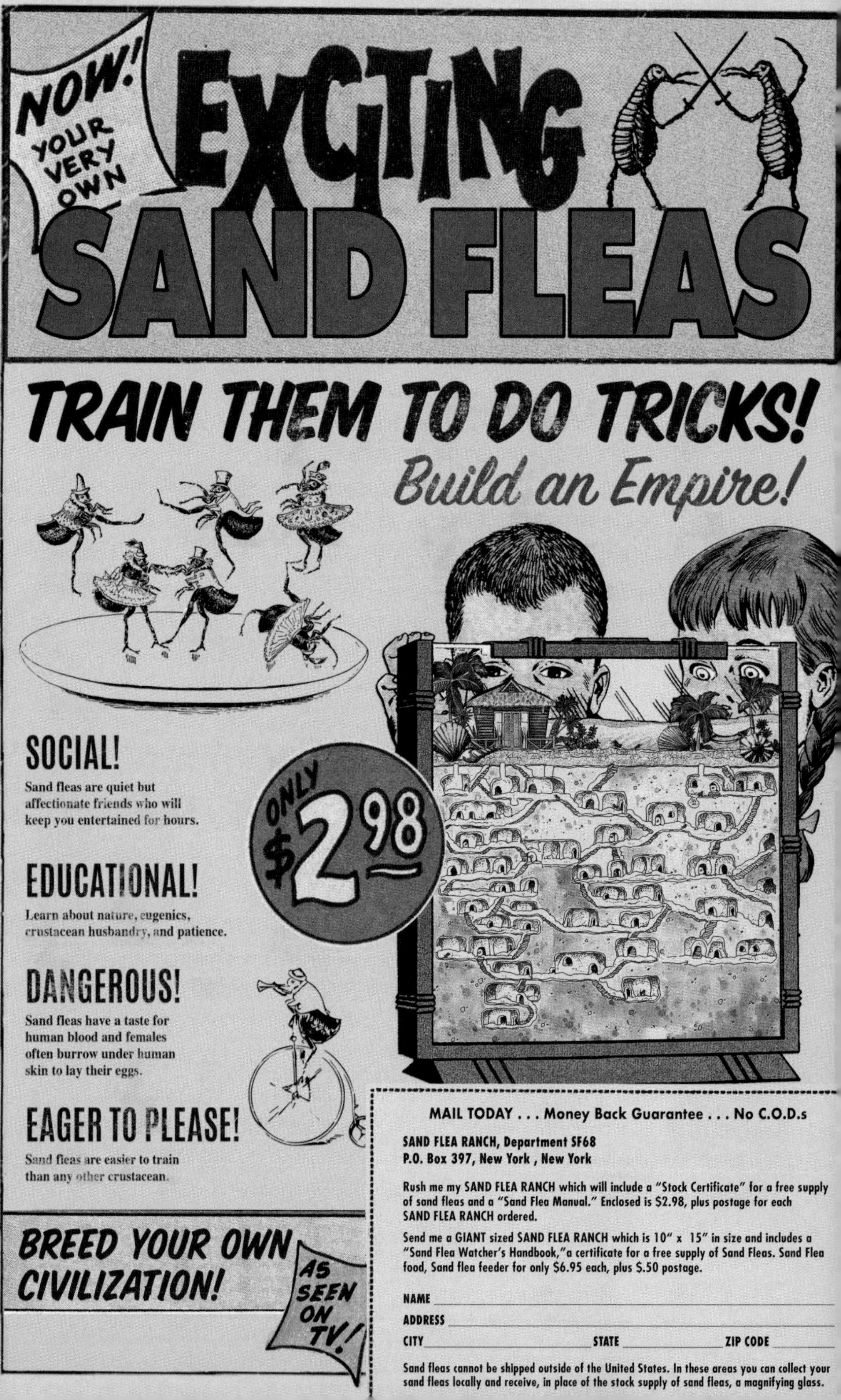
NOW! YOUR VERY OWN
EXCITING SAND FLEAS
TRAIN THEM TO DO TRICKS!
Build an Empire!
SOCIAL!
Sand fleas are quiet but affectionate friends who will keep you entertained for hours.
EDUCATIONAL!
Learn about nature, eugenics, crustacean husbandry, and patience.
DANGEROUS!
Sand fleas have a taste for human blood and females often burrow under human skin to lay their eggs.
EAGER TO PLEASE!
Sand fleas are easier to train than any other crustacean.
ONLY $2.98
BREED YOUR OWN CIVILIZATION!
AS SEEN ON TV!
MAIL TODAY . . . Money Back Guarantee . . . No C.O.D.s
SAND FLEA RANCH, Department SF68
P.O. Box 397, New York , New York
Rush me my SAND FLEA RANCH which will include a "Stock Certificate" for a free supply of sand fleas and a "Sand Flea Manual." Enclosed is $2.98, plus postage for each SAND FLEA RANCH ordered.
Send me a GIANT sized SAND FLEA RANCH which is 10" x 15" in size and includes a "Sand Flea Watcher's Handbook," a certificate for a free supply of Sand Fleas. Sand Flea food, Sand flea feeder for only $6.95 each, plus $.50 postage.
NAME
ADDRESS
CITY STATE ZIP CODE
Sand fleas cannot be shipped outside of the United States. In these areas you can collect your sand fleas locally and receive, in place of the stock supply of sand fleas, a magnifying glass.

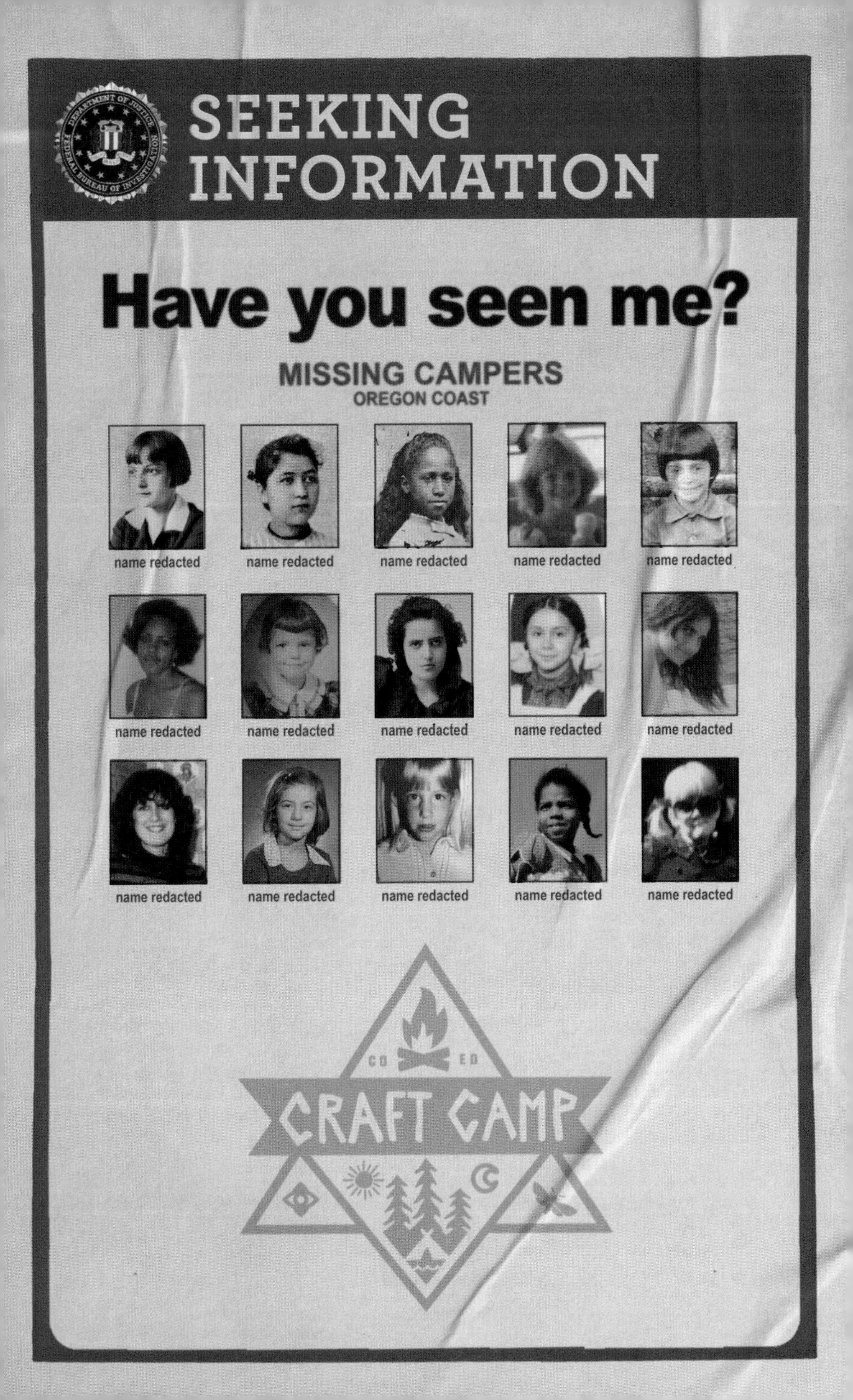
DEPARTMENT OF JUSTICE
FEDERAL BUREAU OF INVESTIGATION
SEEKING INFORMATION
Have you seen me?
MISSING CAMPERS
OREGON COAST
name redacted
name redacted
name redacted
name redacted
name redacted
name redacted
name redacted
name redacted
name redacted
name redacted
name redacted
name redacted
name redacted
name redacted
name redacted
CO ED
CRAFT CAMP

Does the Patriarchy

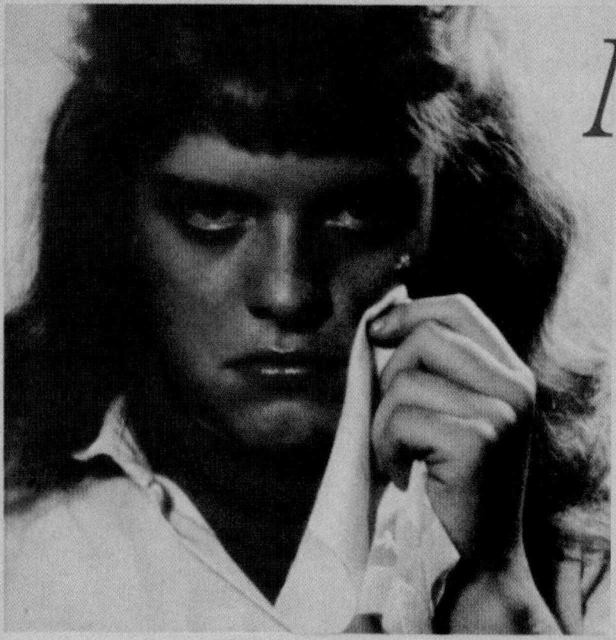

Most of us came into the world crying. Some of us still find ourselves doubled over, tears spilling from our eyes. Why?

It's unavoidable. The world is really, really shitty. And if you cry because of it, well hey, you're human.

But there are downsides to shedding tears. It can be dehydrating.

Turn that frown upside down by recycling your tears into potent potions of protection and revenge.

Spell of Emotional Release

- Write the cause for your emotional distress down on a piece of paper. Let your tears fall onto the paper, preferably until the ink blurs together.
- Create a circle of salt in a neat consistent line around you on the floor.
- Cross your legs in front of you and take three deep breaths.
- SCREAM AT THE TOP OF YOUR LUNGS. This spell ensures that you will not be heard. Expel your anguish.

Spell of Jerk Annihilation

- Combine one tear from the Wronged and one tear from the Accused in a small jar.
- Add a sprinkle of black salt (for protection) and a clear quartz (for concentration).
- Write your preferred form of vengeance onto a leaf, burn the leaf, and sprinkle the leaf's ashes into the jar.
- Close the jar and seal it with melted black wax. Wait for effects.

House Plant Healing Spell

- Find a sunny and fulfilling place for your dying plant.
- Collect and place as many smoky quartz, black tourmaline, clear quartz, amethyst, and any other crystal with healing properties in a tight circle around your plant.
- Spray your plant's leaves with rosemary tear water (five parts rosemary water; one part tears) in a clockwise circle while channeling your love for this plant and the joy it brings you.

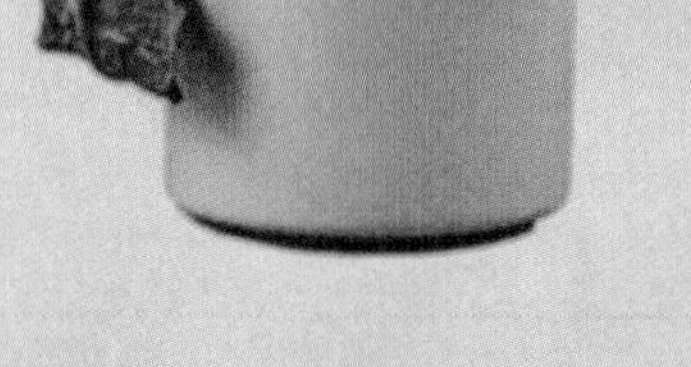

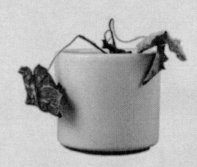

Make You Cry?

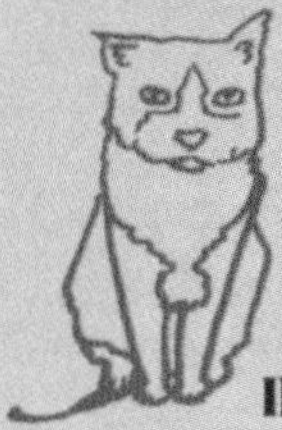

Potion for... INVISIBLE CAT!

- Mix three tablespoons of milk, one generous pinch of lavender, a few pinches of rosemary, and a teaspoon of honey into a small bowl.
- Add one rose quartz crystal and meditate on your connection with your cat while breathing deeply.
- Strain the liquid from the bowl and place near your cat. Your cat should be drawn to this potion, and after drinking it will be invisible to everyone but you for 12-14 hours.

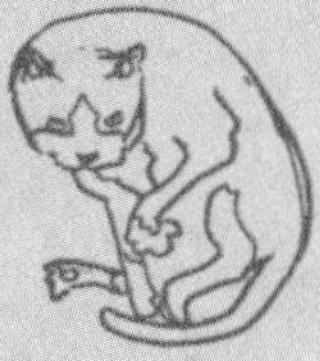

Potion of Bad Friend Banishment

- Pour a juice of your choice (or water, if necessary) into any cup.
- Sprinkle 1-2 pinches of salt (for protection) into the cup, and mix with your finger.
- Blink 1-3 tears into the cup, stir, and let sit under the full moon for at least five hours.
- In the morning, drink the potion in one sip. Your urge to see your bad friend will vanish (until the next full moon).

Potion of Perception

- Put rosemary, sage, and one tear into a small spray bottle containing witch hazel. Mix thoroughly.
- Add smoky quartz and then shake vigorously.
- Write your intention (Would like to be perceived "more" by strangers, or "less"?) on a leaf, shred the leaf, and place into the spray bottle. Shake again.
- Meditate on your intention, then spray potion on your face before bed and then again in the morning.

Spell of Memorization

- Find a small talisman/charm and place it in front of you.
- Then trace a salt circle around yourself and whatever physical paper you wish to memorize (no more than five pages). Dampen each page with your tears.
- Breathe deeply.
- Read the pages aloud and let the words sink into the charm in your hand.
- Now whenever you are touching the charm, you will have the necessary information memorized.

Libro Amnesia

- If a book makes you cry, harvest three tears and wipe them onto the last page. Rip the page out and shred it. Drop the torn pieces into a small jar along with a piece of black tourmaline and seal the jar with white wax. Now you can experience the book again, for the first time.

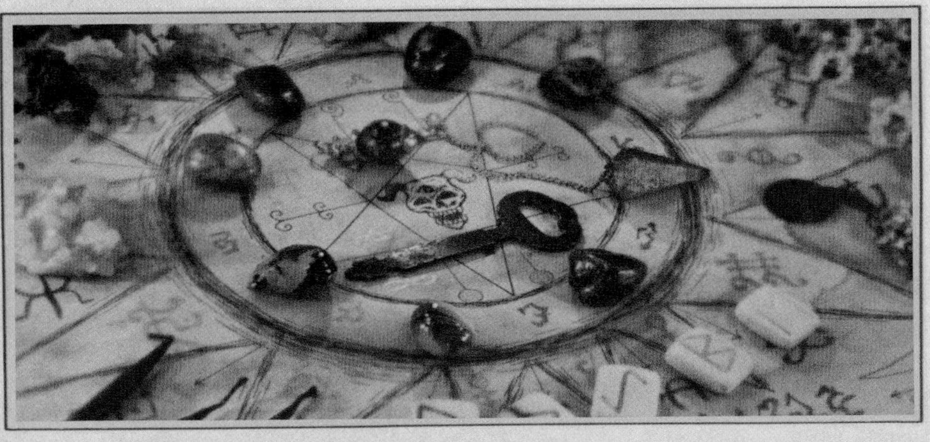

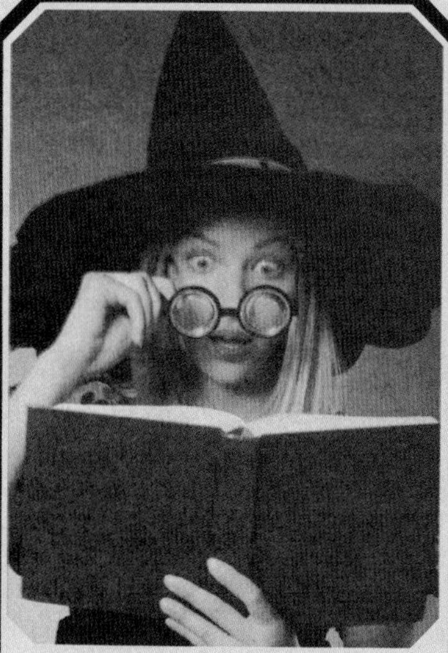

Yes, there is financial help.

Southeast Witch College has scholarships available to superior students. If your high school grade average is 3.5 or better, you are eligible to apply for one of our $1,000.00 scholarships. Other scholarships and grants-in-aid are also available for other evidence of ability, talent and leadership.

SO aspire to a degree – Bachelor of Arts, Science or Crafts – with a major in Witchcraft and General Studies.

Such degree programs at Southeast Witch College include concentration in special areas of professional witchcraft as well as liberal arts. Bachelor of Transmutation and Associate of Science degrees are also offered.

Study in an accredited program on a beautiful campus. Attend small classes, and enjoy individual, caring attention.

Southeast Witch College

is a neopaganism institution
In our 87th year of Service

Tell me more about Southeast Witch College

Name ____________________

Address ____________________

____

City ____________________

State ____________ Zip ____________

☐ Please include information about scholarships.

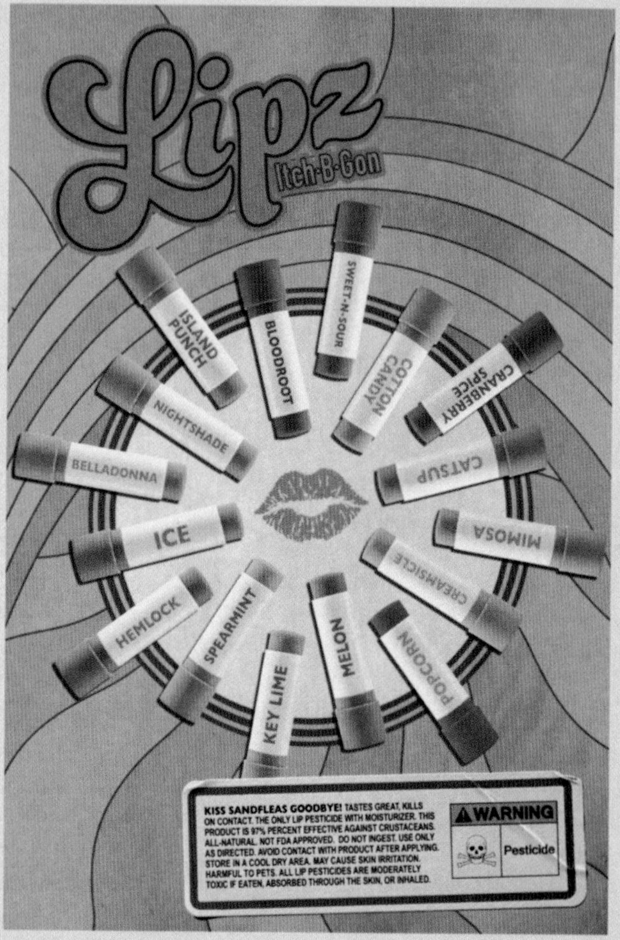
Lipz
Itch-B-Gon
SWEET-N-SOUR
BLOODROOT
ISLAND PUNCH
COTTON CANDY
CRANBERRY SPICE
NIGHTSHADE
BELLADONNA
CATSUP
ICE
MIMOSA
CREAMSICLE
HEMLOCK
SPEARMINT
MELON
POPCORN
KEY LIME
KISS SANDFLEAS GOODBYE! TASTES GREAT, KILLS ON CONTACT. THE ONLY LIP PESTICIDE WITH MOISTURIZER. THIS PRODUCT IS 97% PERCENT EFFECTIVE AGAINST CRUSTACEANS. ALL-NATURAL. NOT FDA APPROVED. DO NOT INGEST. USE ONLY AS DIRECTED. AVOID CONTACT WITH PRODUCT AFTER APPLYING. STORE IN A COOL DRY AREA. MAY CAUSE SKIN IRRITATION. HARMFUL TO PETS. ALL LIP PESTICIDES ARE MODERATELY TOXIC IF EATEN, ABSORBED THROUGH THE SKIN, OR INHALED.
WARNING
Pesticide

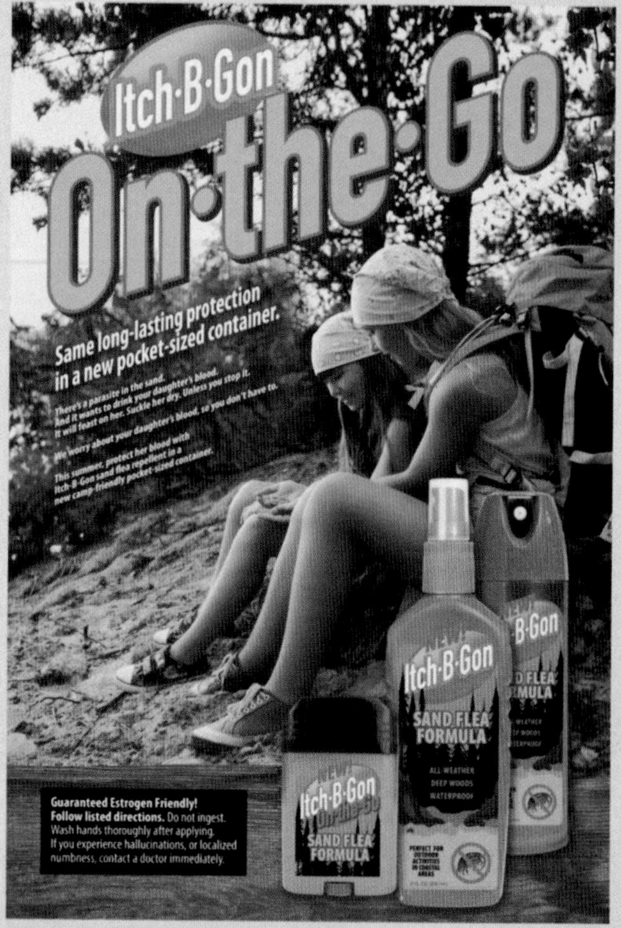
Itch·B·Gon
On·the·Go
Same long-lasting protection in a new pocket-sized container.
There's a parasite in the sand. And it wants to drink your daughter's blood. It will feast on her. Suckle her dry. Unless you stop it.
We worry about your daughter's blood, so you don't have to.
This summer, protect her blood with Itch-B-Gon sand flea repellent in a new camp-friendly pocket-sized container.
Guaranteed Estrogen Friendly!
Follow listed directions. Do not ingest. Wash hands thoroughly after applying. If you experience hallucinations, or localized numbness, contact a doctor immediately.
Itch·B·Gon
SAND FLEA FORMULA
ALL-WEATHER
DEEP WOODS
WATERPROOF
Itch·B·Gon
SAND FLEA FORMULA

W·I·T·C·H SPECTACULAR

VIDEO PREVIEW

Your group can experience the sights, sounds and excitement of a spectacular summer event for witch youth.

Perhaps your coven has considered participating in this summer's Witch Youth Jamboree in Orlando, Florida, June 24-26, or the National Witch Youth Congress, July 22-25, at Estes Park, Colorado. Here's your chance to preview these big events via a special audio-visual presentation at your gathering.

Your coven can schedule a showing of a color video show or a slide-and-sound presentation. You may choose between shows on the Witch Youth Jamboree and National Witch Youth Congress.

In the Jamboree show you'll get a preview of the seminars, workshops, concerts and special events at the big event. And you'll get a peek at some of the other dazzling attractions in the Orlando area.

With the Congress show you'll see scenes from last year's Congress. And you'll preview this year's big concerts, workshops, seminars, jubilations and youth choir competition. You'll also see views of possible side trips in Colorado: Rocky Mountain National Park, Great Sand Dunes, Colorado River rafting and more.

For the video show, you'll need a VHS or Beta playback unit and TV set. For the slide presentation, you'll need a Kodak Carousel slide projector and a cassette tape player.

To schedule either show, supply preferred and alternate show date. Also, supply the show format desired: video cassette (VHS or Beta), or slide-and-sound. Include $10 for video, $15 for slides to cover handling and first-class postage both ways. Your show date will be confirmed by letter.

SHOW RESERVATION REQUEST

Please reserve the following show for our group:

Witch Youth Jamboree (Fla.)
☐ VHS   ☐ Beta   ☐ Slides-Cassette

National Witch Youth Congress (Colo.)
☐ VHS   ☐ Beta   ☐ Slides-Cassette

Preferred show date: _____

Preferred show date: _____

Enclosed: ☐ $10 for video show   ☐ $15 for slide show

Name _____

Coven _____

Address _____

City _____ State _____ Zip _____

WfC Events, Box 666, Portland, OR 79205

WfC EVENTS

NEOPAGANISM REPORT CARD

Grade How Well Your Coven Supports You

Here's your chance to evaluate your coven support system. How effectively does your coven help you reach your objectives?

Next month many of the nation's youth coven leaders will meet together in Estes Park, Colorado, for a WFC-sponsored National Youth Summit meeting. At this three-day event, the leaders will get to know each other better, swap notes and brush up on administrative management and youth coven leadership techniques.

We've set aside a period to introduce the results of several important WFC research projects involving sand flea habitat in coastal wetlands.

This is where you come in. By completing the following report card you'll help your coven leader clarify areas of strength and weakness for his or her future planning and development.

Your confidential responses and grades will be added with others from your coven to make a composite grade in each category.

Take a few minutes now to grade your coven.

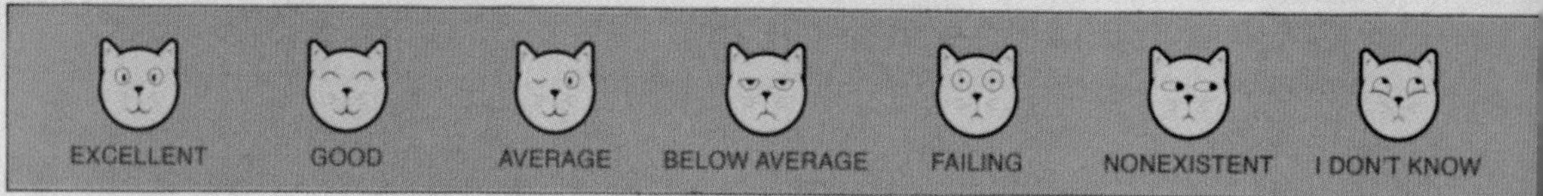
EXCELLENT
GOOD
AVERAGE
BELOW AVERAGE
FAILING
NONEXISTENT
I DON'T KNOW

Coven name: ______________________________

Coven location: ______________________________

Area	Grade	Comment
youth coven programming materials		
help in finding camp counselor jobs		
covenstead facilities		
sabbat safe spaces		
fundraising activities		
transportation		
hammock safety		
national coven youth gatherings		
district or regional youth gatherings *(i.e., retreats, rallies, conventions, conferences, concerts, craft camps)*		
ritual curriculum		
festival decorations		
frog defense		

What's the best thing your coven does for you?

What could your coven do to help you most?

What's one thing you'd like to change about your coven?

What's one thing you'd like to tell your coven leader?

Raise money
for Craft Camp
at **50¢** will raise **$300 PLUS**

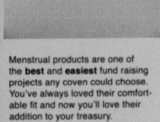

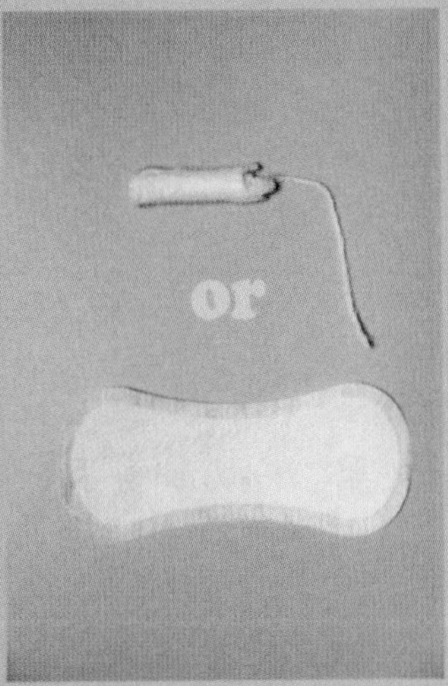

or

CRAFT CAMP menstrual pads

CONTENTS: 4

CRAFT CAMP tampons

CONTENTS: 4

Menstrual products are one of the **best** and **easiest** fund raising projects any coven could choose. You've always loved their comfortable fit and now you'll love their addition to your treasury.

Tampons are a favorite 50-cent fund raiser. There are 60 packs to a case. You earn $11 per case **PLUS** you will receive one bonus case for each 20 cases you order and pay for within 30 days of receipt of your order.

Plus Special Offer of 1 free case worth $30 just for choosing our company!

We prepay all freight charges on 38 cases or more. However you may order as few as 25 cases and the freight will be added to your order. (Orders less than 38 cases shipped when available.)

PROFIT SCHEDULE
If You Order	You Can Earn
20 cs.	$335.00
50 cs.	$640.00
100 cs.	$1,280.00
200 cs.	$2,530.00

**WITCHCRAFT FUNDRAISERS COMPANY
A DIVISION OF ITCH-B-GON
BOX 666, Portland, OR 79205**

**TOLL FREE # 1-800-555-7557
Alabama call collect 793-7031**

Free T-Shirt
Each member who sells 3 cases of Menstrual Products will receive our specially designed T-Shirt...ABSOLUTELY FREE (a $5.00 value) ask for details.

**FOR RUSH ORDERS
CALL TOLL FREE
1-800-555-7557**
ALABAMA CALL COLLECT 793-7031

Please send us _____ cases tampons [Wt. 1.48 oz.]
_____ cases menstrual pads [Wt. 1.48 oz.]
Minimum order—25 cs. when available. Freight charges will be added to your order.

Name of Group_____ Number of Members_____

School/Coven _____ Phone (   )_____

Person Ordering_____ Age_____

Shipping Address_____

City_____ State_____ Zip_____

Adult Sponsor_____ Phone (   )_____

Sponsor's Signature_____ Date of Campaign_____

No returns accepted. Weight and prices subject to change. Net 30 days.
Terms: 30 days from receipt of merchandise or your scheduled sales date, whichever is later. To qualify for Bonus Cases and Cash Rebate, simply make payment in full within 30 days after you receive your order. All orders subject to approval. Offer subject to change.

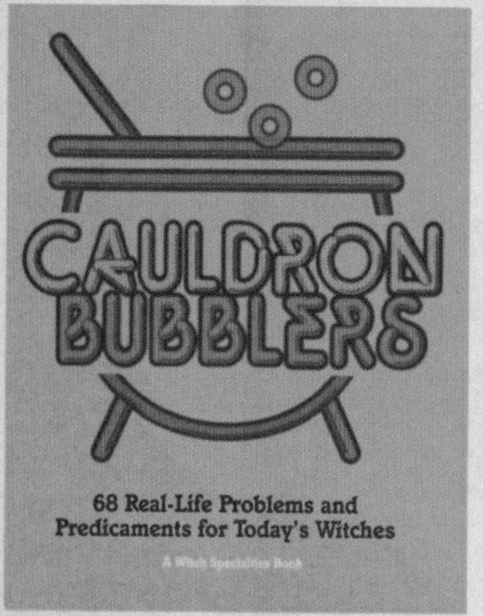
CAULDRON
BUBBLERS
68 Real-Life Problems and
Predicaments for Today's Witches

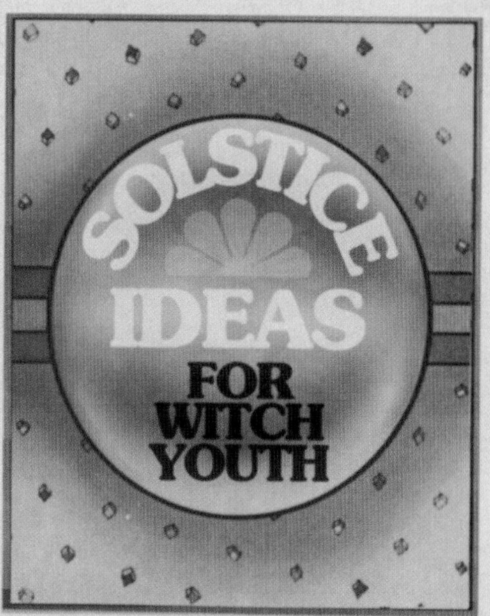
SOLSTICE
IDEAS
FOR
WITCH
YOUTH

Is Your Coven Learning How To Be Bored?

CAULDRON BUBBLERS can change all that!

CAULDRON BUBBLERS is an exciting new book that will get your youth coven excited about learning.

CAULDRON BUBBLERS contains 68 short real-life situations that closely resemble situations encountered by young people every day. As your youth coven members struggle with the issues in each scenario, they will be forced to make some difficult choices and apply their understanding of rituals and conjuring.

CAULDRON BUBBLERS creates an atmosphere that promotes witch spiritual growth through key questions, and includes spell references for each of the 68 strategies.

If you have been looking for a new way to get your youth coven excited, **CAULDRON BUBBLERS** is just what you need!

The Book Every Witch Has Been Waiting For

SOLSTICE IDEAS FOR WITCH YOUTH is the world's largest collection of great ideas for solstice celebrations. You'll find hundreds of solstice activities and decorating ideas that you can use for parties, socials, special events, youth meetings, special programs, service projects, and cauldron circles. Make your Sabbat one to remember…with **SOLSTICE IDEAS FOR WITCH YOUTH.**

Please Send Me

________ **CAULDRON BUBBLERS BOOK(S)**
Leaders Edition ($6.95)

________ **CAULDRON BUBBLERS BOOK(S)**
Student Edition ($4.95)

________ **SOLSTICE IDEAS FOR WITCH YOUTH** ($6.95 each)

SPECIAL OFFER! Send a check and deduct 15% from total cost!

☐ Check provided (Deduct 15%) for $ ____________

☐ Bill me (add 85¢ billing charge)

Name ______________________________

Address ______________________________

City ________________ State ______ Zip ______

Coven Specialties c/o Itch-B-Gon Box 666 Portland OR 79205

WITCH YOUTH
Jamboree

Orlando, Florida   June 24-26, 1983

PLAN NOW TO BRING YOUR COVEN

Headquarters will be the new
Orange County Convention
Center in Orlando

Please send my free brochure on Witchcraft for Children
Magazine's 1983 Witch Youth Jamboree.

FREE COLOR
BROCHURE
(Please print)

Name_____
Coven_____ Address_____ City_____ State _____ Zip _____

1983 Witch Youth Jamboree
PO Box 666
Portland, OR 79205

YOUTH COVEN IDEA BANK

QUALITY RESOURCES FROM

Witchcraft for Children

BOOKS

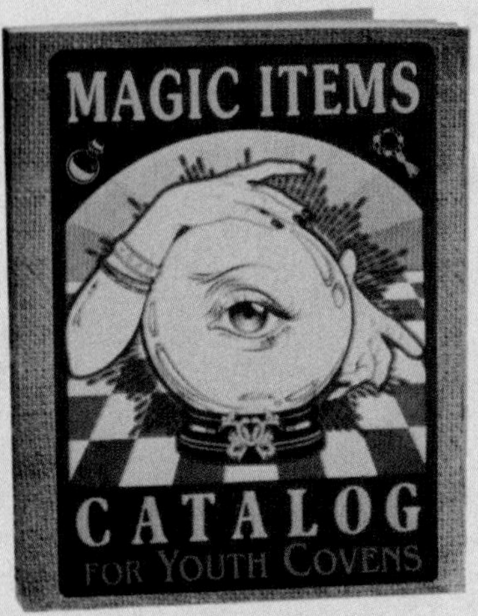

MAGIC ITEMS
CATALOG
FOR YOUTH COVENS

MAGIC ITEMS CATALOG FOR YOUTH COVENS

You'll find charmed items such as burlap, dandelions, handkerchiefs, tea bags, balloons, old filmstrips, slides, comic strips, and countless other common objects, available at rock-bottom prices. Plus, new ideas are offered for leadership, development, parents, guest speakers, retreats, creative worship, multimedia, games, and many more areas.

All Magic Items are practical, inexpensive and simple to reproduce and adapt.

$14.95

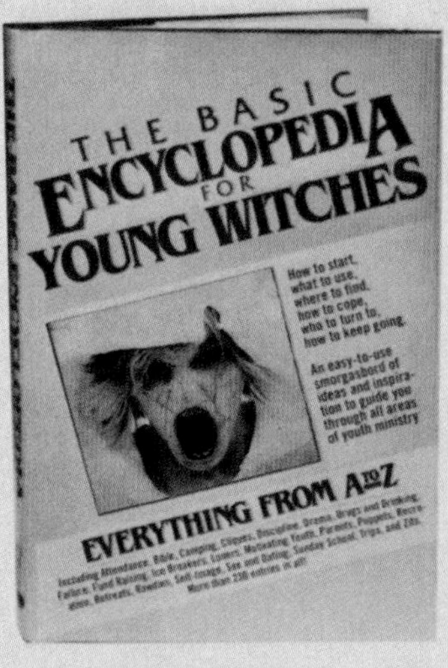

THE BASIC
ENCYCLOPEDIA
FOR
YOUNG WITCHES
How to start, what to use, where to find, how to cope, who to turn to, how to keep going.
An easy-to-use smorgasbord of ideas and inspiration to guide you through all areas of youth ministry
EVERYTHING FROM A to Z

THE BASIC ENCYCLOPEDIA FOR YOUNG WITCHES

This resource is an authority on more than 230 different topics. Use it as you would any encyclopedia — when a problem or question arises in your coven, simply pick up this book and turn to the topic of concern. You'll find answers, ideas, encouragement and inspiration.

It's all here — attendance, cliques, discipline, drinking, failure, music, parents, retreats, rowdies, sex and dating, suicide, zits, and much, much more.

Hardbound, $15.95

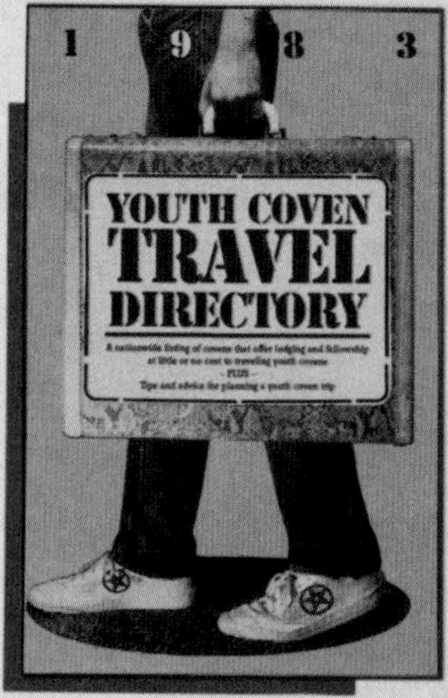

1 9 8 3
YOUTH COVEN
TRAVEL
DIRECTORY

1983 YOUTH COVEN TRAVEL DIRECTORY

With this handy book, your traveling coven can get free lodging all across the country.

Here's a nationwide listing of facilities that offer lodging and sistership to traveling covens at little or no cost.

By the way, this edition's listings more than double the 1981-82 edition, with no change in price.

Many hosts will organize local covens to meet with your coven for sistership and a tour of the local area. Some hosts will even prepare meals for you. Most will allow you to use their kitchens.

$7.95

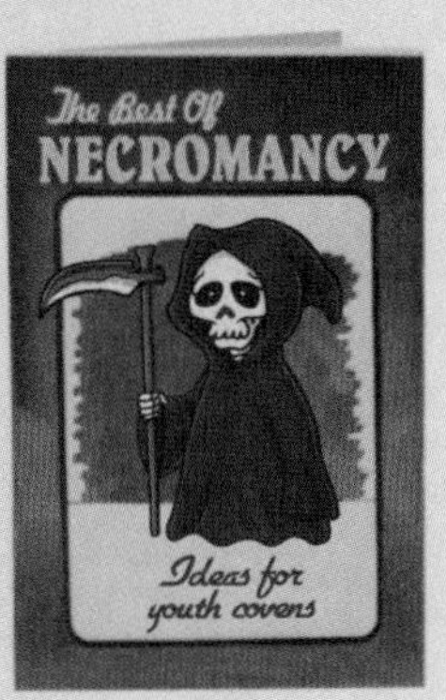
The Best Of
NECROMANCY
Ideas for youth covens

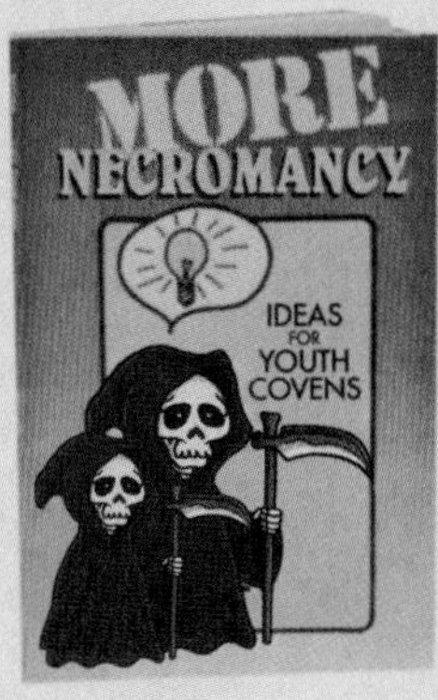
MORE
NECROMANCY
IDEAS FOR YOUTH COVENS

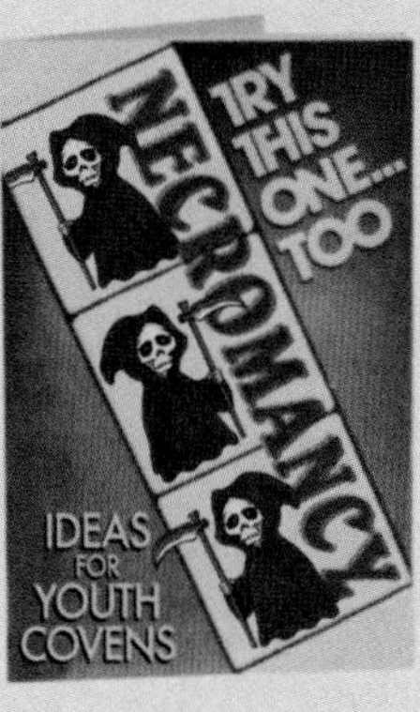
TRY THIS ONE... TOO
NECROMANCY
IDEAS FOR YOUTH COVENS

NECROMANCY: TRY THIS ONE...TOO

The third book in our hugely popular NECROMANCY series, this book includes ready-to-use necromancy ideas contributed by youth covens from all over the country.

- THE BEST OF NECROMANCY
- MORE NECROMANCY IDEAS FOR YOUTH COVENS
- NECROMANCY: TRY THIS ONE...TOO

$5.95 or $15.95 for all 3

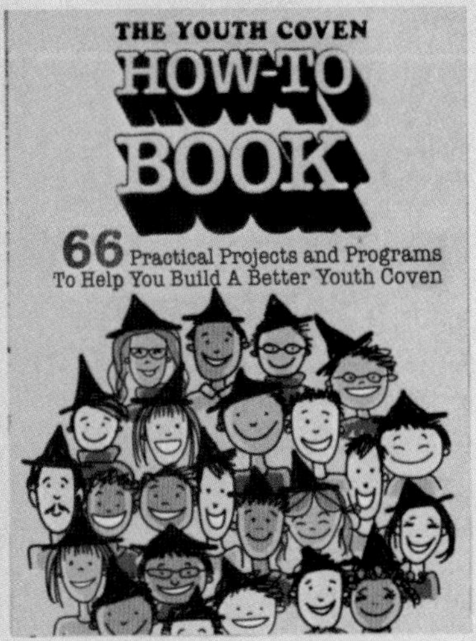
THE YOUTH COVEN
HOW-TO
BOOK
66 Practical Projects and Programs
To Help You Build A Better Youth Coven

THE YOUTH COVEN HOW-TO BOOK

A practical collection of 66 youth coven projects and programs that have appeared in WITCHCRAFT FOR CHILDREN Magazine over the past 290 years. Including: puffy paint, puppetry, building attendance, discussions, finding good sponsors, simulation games, group newsletters, ice breakers, building unity, role plays, banner-making, buying and recycling a bus, backpacking, paper dolls, leadership models, retreats, cauldron circles, world hunger projects, workcamping, multimedia, sand tray work, fundraisers, witch concerts, canoe trips, cliques, obnoxious members, burn-out.

$14.95

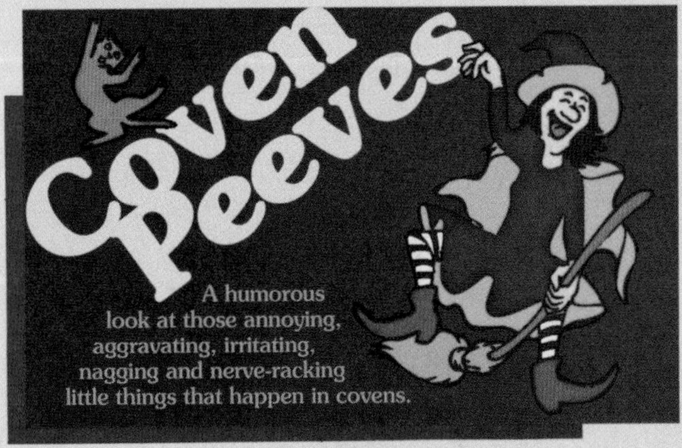
Coven Peeves
A humorous look at those annoying, aggravating, irritating, nagging and nerve-racking little things that happen in covens.

COVEN PEEVES

A light-hearted collection of those aggravating, irritating, nagging and nerve-racking little things that happen in covens. You'll laugh at things like high priestesses who sound like Julia Child, muddy auras, spilled potions, digital watches beeping during silent salt circles, silly coven slogans, and scores more. Humorously illustrated throughout.

$3.95

AT YOUR WITCHCRAFT BOOKSTORE OR ORDER DIRECT:

SPECIAL PACKAGE DEAL:

___All 8 books – $69.95 (save $5.65)

___Magic Items Catalog For Youth Covens . . . $14.95
___The Basic Encyclopedia For Young Witches $15.95
___1983 Youth Coven Travel Directory $7.95
___The Best Of Necromancy $5.95
___More Necromancy. $5.95
___Necromancy...Too $5.95
___Necromancy...all 3 books $15.95
___The Youth Coven How-To Book $14.95
___Coven Peeves $3.95

Total amount $__________

☐ Check enclosed *(free postage and handling)*
☐ Bill me *(add $2 postage and handling)*

(Please print)
Name ____________________
Address ____________________
City ____________ State ____ Zip ____

(NOTE: Colorado residents add 3% tax)

GUARANTEE: You must be completely satisfied of return books within 15 days for a refund of the price of the books.

WfC Books
Box 666
Portland, OR 79205

The *Only* Book You'll Ever Need

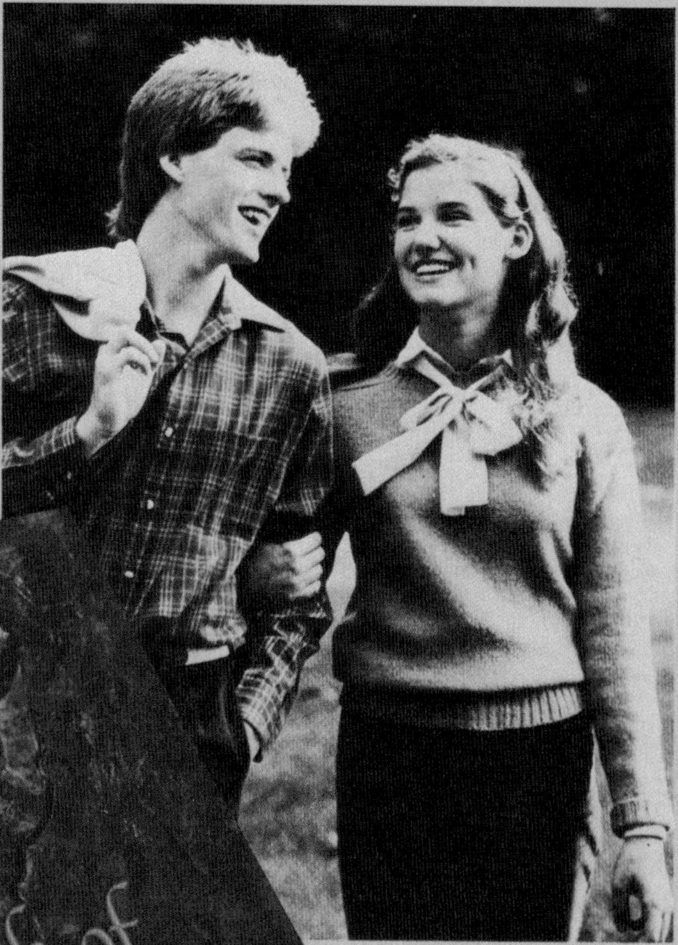

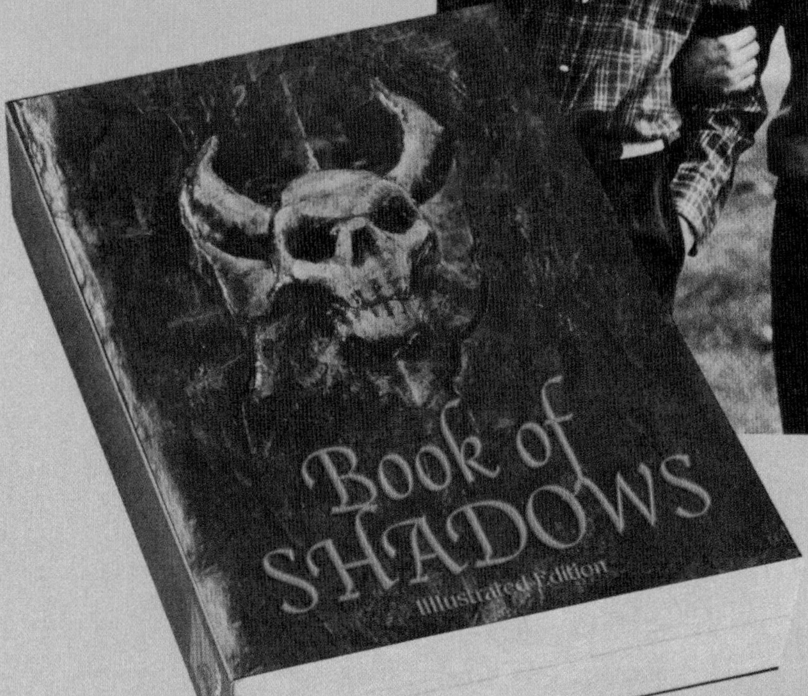
Book of
SHADOWS
Illustrated Edition

Brings Understanding To *Life*

Sometimes it seems that growing up gets more complicated every day. Questions arise that don't have easy answers. Problems grow larger before solutions can be found.

Here's a book that speaks directly to you about the questions and problems in your life... The *Book of Shadows*, the illustrated edition of The *Big Book of Shadows* for today's teens.

The *Book of Shadows* will help uncomplicate things that may trouble you. It reads the way you speak today, letting the message of Witchcraft come through to you directly and powerfully. The *Book of Shadows* introduces each section with a few paragraphs of timely thoughts. Written with your questions in mind, it will help bring understanding to life.

Available in kivar, hardback, and Catholic editions.

Youth Publishing
A Division of Itch-B-Gon

Mail this STAMP and get a Double Album of GREAT WITCH SONGS - FREE

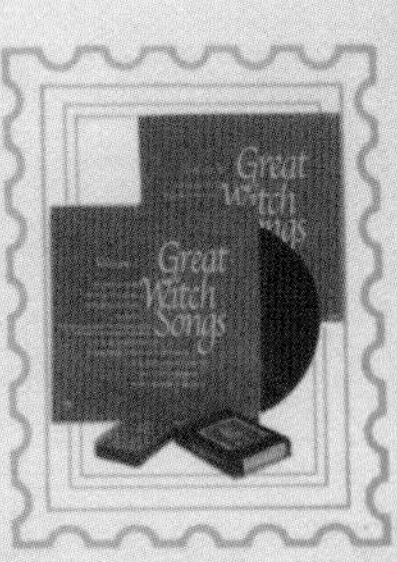

Great Witch Songs

Traditional! Contemporary! Hymns! Gospel!

Now...WITCH MUSIC for all the family!

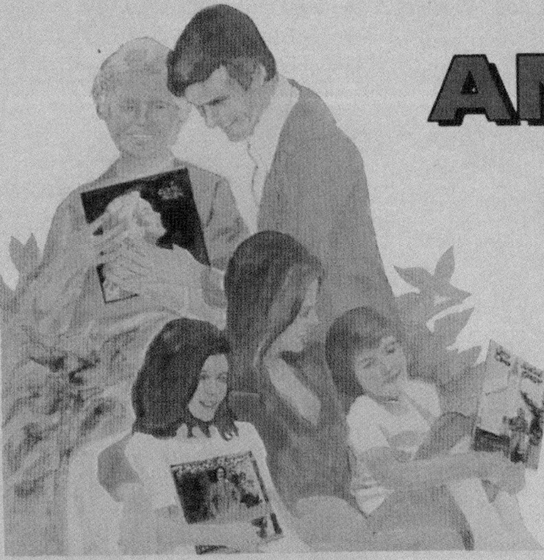

ANY 4 RECORDS OR TAPES for only $1.00

with trial membership in the Witch Record and Tape Club

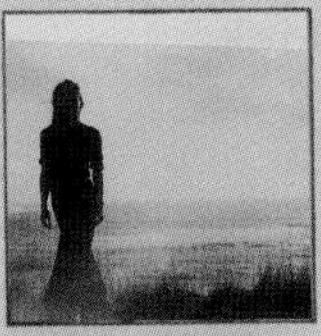

ONLY THE DARK LORD · 4027 · The Best · Sweet Love Of The Dark Lord · Train To Glory · Thank You Dark Lord · Greater Is He · 5 more

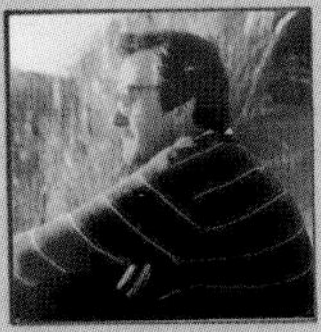

NEW AGE · 6697 · I Love A Lonely Day · Fat Baby · I Have Decided · El Fuerte · Got To Let It Go · 5 more

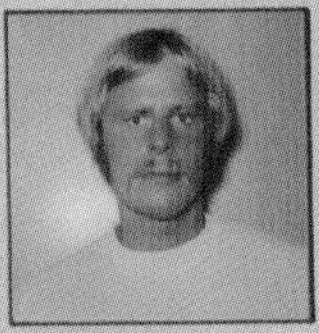

PRECIOUS DARK LORD · 6702 · What A Friend · In The Garden · How Great Thou Art · Rock of Ages · The Old Rugged Broom

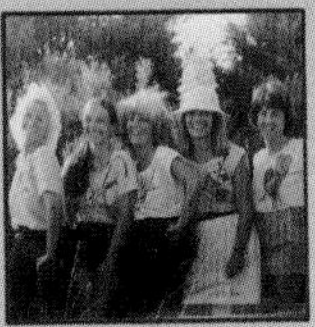

MIRACLE · 6705 · Born Again · Hey Dark Lord · Would They Love Him Down In Shreveport · Satan You're a Friend · 7 more

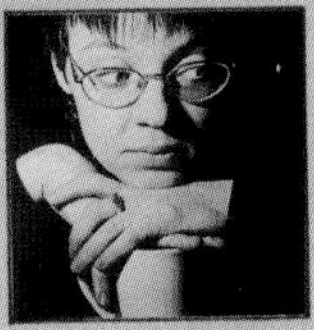

FOR EVERY MAN · 6654 · The Dark Lord Drawing Me · Thank You · Run To The Battle · Back In The Furnace · 6 more

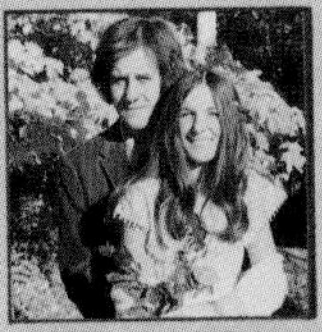

PRIORITY · 4017 · I'd Rather Believe In You · Any Good Time At All · Pieces · See Ye First · 5 more

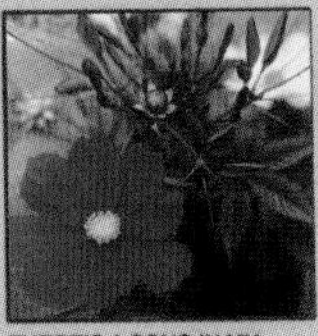

THERE'S A SONG IN MY HEART · 8858 · Amazing Grace · His Hands · The Dark Lord Paid It All · Leavin' On My Mind · 8 more

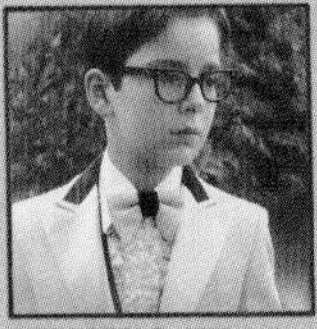

REFLECTIONS · 8852 · Little By Little · He Is Risen · Depend On Me · How Much Longer · We Are The Reason · 5 more

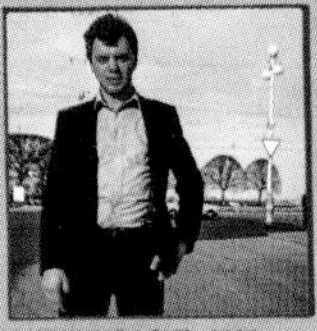

UNFAILING LOVE · 8867 · Bind Us Together · I Love My Satan · All The Glory · The Dark Lord's Prayer · How I Love You Lord · 5 more

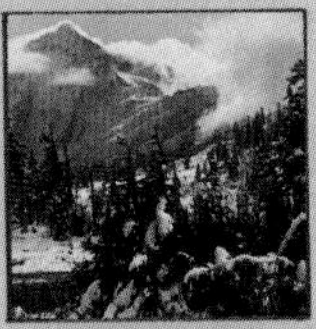

HEED THE CALL · 4011 · Overcomer · Praise The Dark Lord · Oh Buddha · He Didn't Lift Us Up To Let Us Down · 7 more

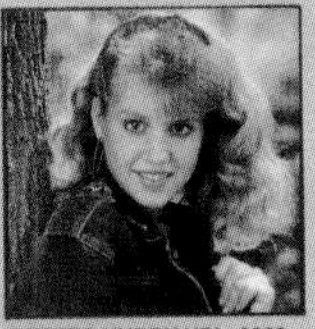

BETTER HURRY UP! · 9860 · We're Almost Home · Better Hurry Up · Set Another Place At The Table · 7 more

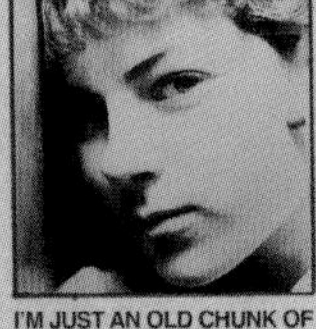

I'M JUST AN OLD CHUNK OF COAL (BUT I'M GONNA BE A DIAMOND SOME DAY) · 9874 · The Great Reward · Down By The Riverside · Wait For The Light To Shine · 6 more

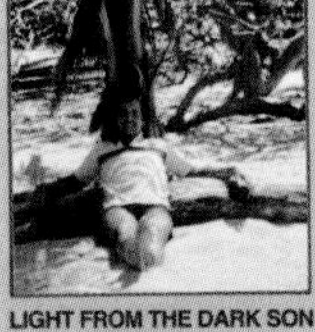

LIGHT FROM THE DARK SON · 0088 · (DOUBLE ALBUM) · Since I Met The Dark Lord · Perfect Will · Just a Spell Away · Losers And Winners · Sandy Point · 14 more

MAIL THIS GIFT CERTIFICATE

YES, please rush me the 4 recordings I've selected for only $1.00 plus a small charge for shipping and handling along with GREAT WITCH SONGS—mine FREE as a bonus. If not thoroughly delighted with my selections, I can return them within 10 days and you will cancel all charges. Otherwise, I will begin my trial membership in the' Witch Record and Tape Club and buy 5 more records or tapes in the next 2 years at regular club prices. A small charge will be added to each shipment for postage and handling. The bonus recordings are mine to keep FREE.

Print Name________________

Address________________

City__________ State__________ Zip__________

Keep GREAT WITCH SONGS —FREE (even if you cancel)

*Texas residents add 5% sales tax. WRT-39

FREE BONUS: GREAT WITCH SONGS

8839 & 8843

Send my selections on:
- ☐ Stereo records
- ☐ Stereo 8-track tapes
- ☐ Stereo cassettes

I prefer the following kind of recordings:
- ☐ Traditional
- ☐ Contemporary
- ☐ Gospel

AFFIX STAMP HERE FOR FREE BONUS ALBUMS

6-5-24-1.00

Rush me these 4 selections (enter code numbers only)

Allow 4-6 weeks for delivery. 6173

Haiku Corner

by celebrity haiku columnist EMILY POWELL!

At first I was scared,
Being a witch ain't easy,
But it's so worth it.

Magic can be hard,
It takes practice and patience,
And lots of mistakes.

Come here my witches,
And I will teach you my tricks,
There's so much to learn.

A unicorn's hair,
The toenail of a dragon,
Makes a cool potion.

Witches keep secrets,
Sometimes this is difficult,
Let me teach you how:

First: Always be vague.
Second: Maintain eye contact.
Third: Sometimes just run.

(also)

When conducting spells,
Read all the instructions first,
Trust me on this one.

Show that you care...

REMEMBER THE WOMEN WHO BURNED in Sterling Silver or 14K Gold

Show that you care with this beautifully crafted and comfortable-to-wear WITCH REMEMBRANCE Medallion. Wear it yourself or give it to a friend or relative.

- **Only $19.95 in Sterling Silver. $59.95 in 14K Gold.**
- **More than 2 inches in circumference.**
- **Florentine finish.**
- **Rushed to you first class, insured.**
- **Attractively gift-boxed.**
- **Sterling Silver or 14K Gold chain with every medallion.**

SPECIAL OFFER FOR READERS OF THIS MAGAZINE:

Buy a Sterling Silver WITCH REMEMBRANCE Medallion @ $29.95 and get a second for only $14.95. Chain included. Buy a 14K Gold Medallion @$59.95 and get a second 14K Gold Witch Remembrance Medallion for only $29.95! Chain included.

ONLY

$19.95

"Witch Remembrance Medallion"

The symbol of the living world and the ever lasting power of the Dark Lord.

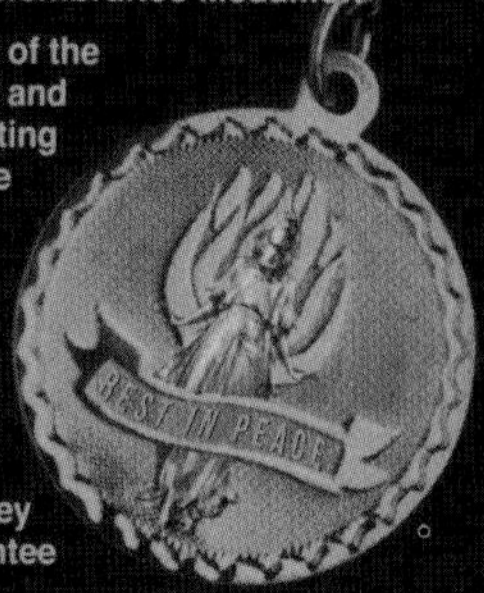
REST IN PEACE

Enlarged to show detail

15 day money back guarantee

Rush my Witch Remembrance Medallion(s) and chain(s) as checked below.

____Sterling Silver Medallions @ $19.95 each plus $2.00 postage and holding

____14K Gold Medallions @ $59.95 each plus $2.00 postage and handling.

I have also included $ ________ for the SPECIAL OFFER for readers of this magazine. NY and NJ residents add appropriate sales tax.

Or change my credit card. ____Mastercard. _____Visa.

Account # ______________________

Expires ______________________

Your Name ______________________

Address ______________________

City ______________________ State ___ Zip ____

Mail to: **Witchcraft Designs** Box 666, Portland, OR 97219

NO POSTAGE NECESSARY IF MAILED IN THE UNITED STATES

BUSINESS REPLY CARD

FIRST CLASS PERMIT NO. 4

POSTAGE WILL BE PAID BY ADDRESSEE

The Witch Record and Tape Club

A Division of Itch-B-Gon
PO Box 666
Portland, OR 79205

Bishop Puts Your Future First!

DON'T COMPROMISE ACADEMIC QUALITY OR WITCH COMMITMENT

IN YOUR CAREER PREPARATION

You prefer a Witch College, but your goals seem to require study at a secular university.

Take a look at Bishop, a distinctive Witch College with four-year degree programs in engineering, business, accounting, computer science, education, aviation, and communcication, along with the traditional liberal arts and sciences, and pre-medical, pre-law, and pre-witchcraft studies.

Call us now! 800-123-1000 collect or send this coupon to:

Bishop College
Portland, OR 79205

As a Bishop graduate you will be well prepared for a challenging career and for effective Witch living.

Don't settle for less!

 People learning in Witchcraft Perspective

Bishop College admits students of any race, color, sex, religion, handicap, and national or ethnic origin.

Please send me information about Bishop:

area/phone

name

zip

street address

state

grad. year

city

city

coven

high school

major fields of interest

BY CHELSEA S. CAIN

REMEMBERING THE LOST GIRLS OF CRAFT CAMP

Whether you use kazoos, balloons, traditional chanting, or theater, you and your young people can create memorable vigils.

Exciting, interesting, totally-involving. Dead-girl vigils can become part of your youth coven program. What makes dead-girl vigils so thrilling? The term suggests that things happen, new things come to be, a new situation is created – in people, among people, in the world. But can dead girls be FUN?

Yes! With the right glitter bombs and mylar. Keep reading to learn how you can make the most of your dead-girl-vigils.

continued

Young people bring something special to worship by their weakness, their acceptance, their restlessness, their trust and their forgiveness.

THE BASIC INGREDIENT

The first thing that makes dead-girl vigils successful for any coven (including the full moon congregations) is the action of the High Priestess. Special things happen when we concentrate more on Magic than on ourselves and when we leave space and time for Magic to work and time for the Rage-Against-the-Patriarchy to move through our bodies.

You can expect great things to happen at any type of rage-against-the-patriarchy event, whether it's an hour-long service or just five minutes at the beginning of a meeting. Plan carefully as if that time of communication with your rage is the most important time of the whole week– and it may be just that!

As you begin that act of rage, concentrate completely on what you are doing and on the One with whom you are meeting. And don't rush from one thing to another. Chant every spell and offer every charm with total concentration and listening as if you expect an answer right then and there. Read every passage of the Book of Shadows as if you were expecting it to speak to you personally.

INVOLVEMENT IS KEY

Vigils that involve all forms of expression and all forms of black magic are exciting and compelling. Have that new member who plays in the school band offer a trumpet prelude. Use the drummer to support the group's spells. Invite the flute player to prepare a quiet accompaniment for whisper-chanting. Be ready to involve dancers (perhaps a simple bit of choreography for the Dark Lord's Prayer), actors (perhaps reading the story of the Salem Witch Trials with simple staging), poets (perhaps offering a series of haikus about real feelings we share) and artists (perhaps show the group's artistic expressions of joy, loneliness or hunger, as a visual prayer) in simple or elaborate ways, like say, in a fucking comic book.

CREATIVE WORSHIP IS BASED ON REAL EXPERIENCES

Dead-Girl vigils cannot be "religious routine" that's set apart from the stuff that goes on in our lives and in the world. Some of the most significant times of black magic any of us can remember were when we responded with others to a common crisis: when a group member was hurt seriously in an accident, when we discovered that a friend was addicted to drugs, when someone's father or mother died, or a girl went missing. Let the regular worships take up such experiences of spells and charms. Also share reasons for happiness, such as acceptance at college, the finding of work for the summer, completion of a group project, good things that happen in the world.

WICCA IS WHENEVER AND WHEREVER IT MEETS US

Magic may move us to praise, prayer and commitment in places other than the pentagram.
- On a hilltop to chant about nature, or about the surrounding towns and neighborhoods.
- At a shopping mall, huddling together in the parking lot, chanting about the way we spend money, and for the people who work in the stores.
- On a sidewalk outside a hospital, considering the ways we respond to our own illnesses and the illnesses of others, praying for sick people and for the those who minister to them.
- In the city park, sitting on the grass, praying for those who travel through your town, for those who have no home except the park, for those who play there and for the Dark Lord's mission to all these people.
- In a shut-in's home without fanfare or elaborate plans.

Try worshipping in various places around the coven steads: around the altar, in the spell loft, in the salt circle, around the cauldron or scattered around the meadow for silent prayer.

NATIONAL
WITCHCRAFT
YOUTH CONGRESS

JULY 22-25, 1983 • ESTES PARK, COLORADO

Bring your coven to the greatest
witchcraft youth event ever planned!

CONCERTS

Manny Jet

Bobby Grant

Steve Mellancamp

Leonard Katz

WORKSHOPS

WORKSHOPS CONDUCTED
DAILY, LED BY THE
NATION'S TOP WITCHCRAFT
RESOURCE PEOPLE.

YOUTH CHOIR CONTEST

FREE COLOR BROCHURE

Please send my free color brochure on the 1983 Congress.

Name _____

Coven _____

Address _____

City _____ State _____ Zip _____

**National Witchcraft Youth Congress, WfC Magazine, Box
666, Portland, OR 79205**

RECREATION

COME TO THE SCENIC CENTER OF THE SOUTH—

CHATTANOOGA; TENNESSEE

AND VOLUNTEER TO PLANT MENSTRUAL TREES FOR THE PEOPLE OF THE INNER-CITY!

Adopt-a-Curb-Strip Workcamp Scheduled for June 19-26, 1983

Clip and mail to:

MR. DOUG CHURCHILL, Director
Youth Coven Charities, Inc.
BOX 666
Chattanooga, TN 73401

- -

I want to learn more about the Adopt-a-Curb-Strip Workcamp,
June 19-26, 1983, in Chattanooga.

☐ Send me information about the summer program;

☐ Put me on the mailing list of Youth Coven Charities, Inc.

Name _____

Address _____

City _____ State _____ Zip _____

This is an invitation to join with youth coven from
across the nation in a mission to plant menstrual
tree saplings in needy inner-city areas.

Did you know that many urban areas do not have
ANY menstrual trees?

Come to Chattanooga, and join us in this unique
experiment to nurture the future. Remember the
Dark Lord's words, "She who hath seeded, hath
grown."

WHERE TO START

Hurrah for you if you're ready to host a dead-girl vigil. But don't worry if you're not quite sure where to begin. Here are six first-step suggestions.

1. Don't try it alone. It takes a group to plan a coven experience. Get with interested young people (or adult decision makers). You've got this!

2. As a group, list the different parts of a coven experience as you know it (for instance, chanting, spell-casting, necromancy). If you wish, describe what's happening in your coven's present worship services (what types of songs, who chants, type of spells, etc.).

3. Have everyone read this article. Discuss it. What ideas does this article ignite?

4. Look again at the parts of worship you listed. What are different, yet effective things you can do in one or more of these areas to make worship more meaningful for everyone? What are ways to draw upon the gifts of people in your congregation?

5. Pray. The Dark Lord has no limits in his creativity.

6. Try it.

Chelsea S. Cain is an associate Professor of Witchcraft at Bishop College.

A Touching Dead-Girl Service

A Dead Girl Service is a special time. Flowers and balloons are special things too. Here's a way to combine these special things for a special Dead Girl service.

The service opens at daybreak with each member reading his or her own brief "Memory of the Dead Girl". The opening spell should be a vibrant one – to get everybody's blood flowing. Then the group enters into a section of the worship called "Giving Joy to Our Dark Lord." Each person in attendance is given a half-pint milk carton filled with dirt.

Then, everyone walks to a table and picks out a flower seed. Next, one member of the group gives a short reading on the theme of rebirth. The worshippers are invited to plant their seeds in their containers using provided craft sticks and water. Their new plant is theirs to keep.

The symbolism of the box of dirt and seed is then explained. "This is symbolic of new life from death. A plant/flower has died so that seeds could be produced to bring new life again. The seeds bring forth flowers which add beauty to the immediate world: they will also serve as a reminder of the Dead Girl."

During the planting of the seeds, keep the mood light so participants don't worry about being proper and rigid as they poke their seeds into the dirt. Everyone is urged to help one another. Some people plant an extra carton to take to a shut-in or relative. The worship participants are urged to harvest the seeds from the new plant in the fall and save them for the next dead-girl vigil. And the multiplication effect of the many seeds from the one seed also gives symbolic representation of the power of the early church spreading the word of the Dark Lord.

Next, the service moves to a section called "Receiving Joy in Our Vaginas." This is the communion experience. Brief spells are chanted, including the Dark Lord's Prayer. Then communion is celebrated, offering the participants their choice of the common menstrual cup or individual cups. Bake several loaves of bread for the service.

The final section of the worship is called "Sending Joy to the Clitoris". A young person offers a reading, pointing out the seeds and how their potential has enhanced the immediate surroundings. And, the worshippers have nourished themselves through the eucharist. The reading goes on to point out that Wicca as a faith is based upon community, and the community encompasses the world.

Then, each worshipper is given a 3 x 5 card with small hole punches in it, a pencil, and a helium-filled balloon. Everyone is encouraged to write a message on the card that they would like to share with the Dead Girl. This may be a thought, a feeling, an emotion, a spell, anything. The cards are then tied to a string on the helium-filled balloons.

Everyone holds on to his or her balloon as the closing spell is chanted. ("Pass It On" is a good spell here.) During the chanting the people are invited to release at random their message-carrying balloons. They're told, "when the Dark Lord moves you, then release the balloon." This develops into a very moving moment. Imagine messages of joy for the world being carried aloft by multicolored balloons into the brilliance of the Dead Girl dawn sky!

A simple salt circle closes the service. Then, everyone is invited to a breakfast of rolls, coffee, tea and hot chocolate.

FREE LODGING

FOR YOUR TRAVELING YOUTH COVEN, ALL OVER THE USA

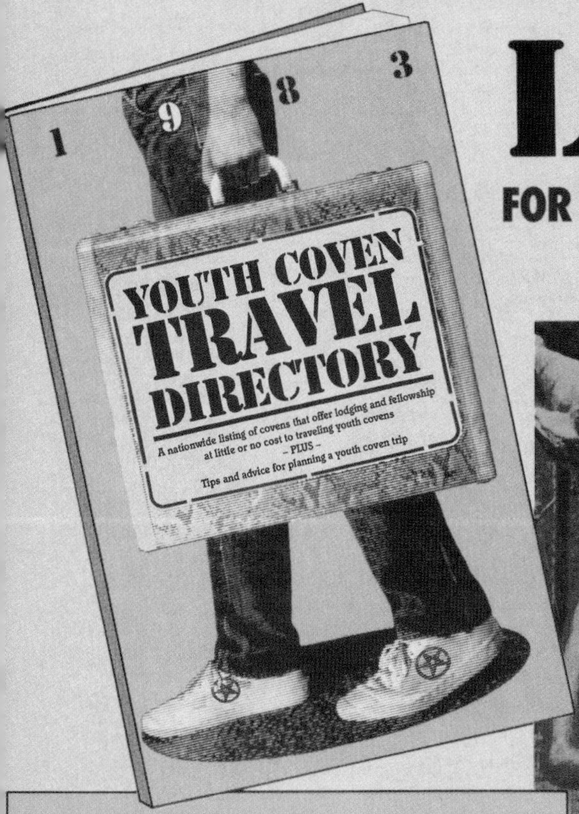
1 9 8 3
YOUTH COVEN
TRAVEL
DIRECTORY
A nationwide listing of covens that offer lodging and fellowship at little or no cost to traveling youth covens
– PLUS –
Tips and advice for planning a youth coven trip

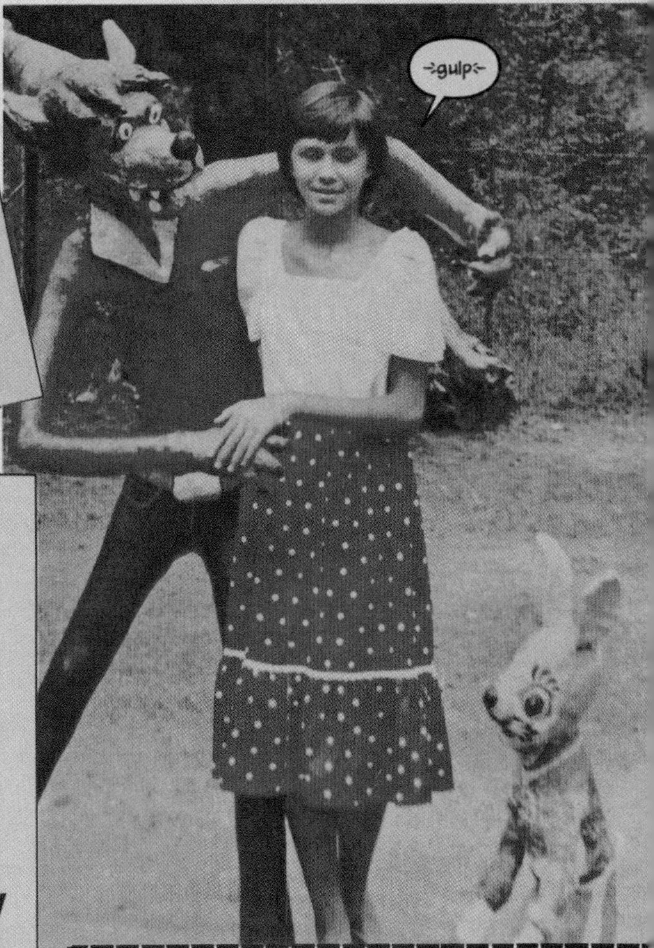
~gulp~

Your group can save hundreds of dollars on your next trip. The 1983 Youth Coven Travel Directory lists camps and other facilities that offer your coven lodging at little or no cost.

HOW TO USE THE DIRECTORY

Simply decide where you want to go, look up that area in the listing and contact the host camps. You bring sleeping bags or bedding. Some camps will arrange lodging in members' homes. Some facilities have beds and showers. Most camps offer use of their canteen. And most host groups are happy to meet with your coven for meals, worship, recreation, etc.

New Features of the 1983 Directory

- "Travel Tips for Youth Covens." This section offers practical, complete advice for efficient trip planning, authored by WfC magazine editor and veteran youth coven travel leader.
- More listings. This edition has more than twice as many listings as the previous edition. The cost to you, however, is the same as the previous edition.

Bargain Travel

At $7.95, the **1983 Directory** is a bargain. Even if you use the **Directory** just once you'll more than save the cost of the book.

At your Witchcraft bookstore or order direct:

We enclose $________ for ________ copy(ies) of 1983 Youth Coven Travel Directory. $7.95 each, postpaid.

Enclose check with order.

Name ____________________

Address ____________________

City ____________ State ____ Zip ____

WfC
BOOKS

Box 666, Portland, OR 79205

CRAFT CAMP SUMMER ACTIVITIES

JUNE — SCHEDULE

HAPPY SOLSTICE

(The letters S · U · N · D · A · Y run down the SUNDAY column as a decorative heading.)

SUNDAY	MONDAY	TUESDAY	WEDNESDAY	THURSDAY	FRIDAY	SATURDAY
(HAPPY SOLSTICE graphics)	 				**1** CAT APPRECIATION DAY	**2**
3	**4** Archery First campfire journaling	**5** Forest art class Spell jar crafting Book of shadows binding	**6** Herb collecting walk Cabin cleaning Deity studies Evening salt circle	**7** Shadow work (16+) Journaling Challenge course	**8** Tide pooling Cleansing rituals Night time beach walk	**9**
10	**11** Monday manifestations/ journaling Archery Hiking	**12** Board game night Fancy dinner Spell jars	**13** Cabin cleaning Overnight (spot tbd) Herb-collecting	**14** Journaling Trail mapping Deity studies	**15** Reading time Cooking class Beach activities (water is 12+)	**16**
17	**18** Monday manifestations/ journaling Archery Hiking	**19** Stargazing Hiking Scavenger hunt	**20** HOLIDAY	**21** Journaling Field day Spell jars	**22** Animal behavior lessons Cleansing cabins Reading time	**23**
24	**25** Monday manifestations/ journaling Archery Camp wide mafia game	**26** Activism studies :) Hiking Beach day	**27** Cabin cleaning Last overnight Arts + crafts	**28** Journaling Spell jars Lunar meditation	**29** Bottling memories Meditations Last campfire	**30**
	Transfiguration lessons Archery Making spells with glitter					

RECREATION DEPARTMENT

Message from the Dark Lord

We'd really like to hear what you think about the "new" WFC Magazine. Do articles in this issue meet your needs as a youth coven leader? What else would you like to see? How well do your young people like the special youth pullout section? Does it hold their interests and meet their needs? How well did it work as a youth coven development tool?

We want to hear from you even if you don't like the changes. What can we do to make WFC Magazine better meet your personal and youth coven needs?

We'll listen carefully to what you have to say.

Take a few seconds now to jot your thoughts in the space below. (Use an extra sheet of paper if you need it.)

Send your message to:
Message WFC Magazine
Box 666
Portland, OR 79205

TO SUBSCRIBE, fill in your name and address, indicate the length of subscription you prefer, and mail.

☐ 2 years, Leader's Edition, $35.
☐ 1 year, Leader's Edition, $18.50.
☐ BULK RATE. Start ______ Leader's Edition one-year subscriptions at $14 each (minimum 4 to one address).
☐ Send ______ Members Only subscriptions at $4 each (minimum 6).

Name ______
Address ______
City ______
State ______ Zip ______

Mail to:
Witchcraft for Children
Box 666
Portland, OR 79205

☐ Check enclosed
☐ Bill me
☐ New
☐ Renewal

MOVING?
ATTACH MAILING LABEL HERE

upcoming in
WfC

HOW TO LEAD GREAT DISCUSSIONS

WHERE KIDS ARE SEXUALLY

A STUDY ON FEAR

BUILDING ON JUNIOR HIGHERS' UNIQUE TRAITS

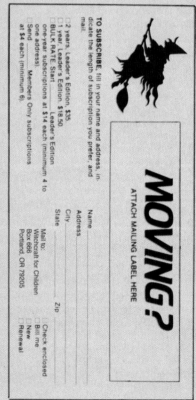

YOUR SWEAT & BLOOD

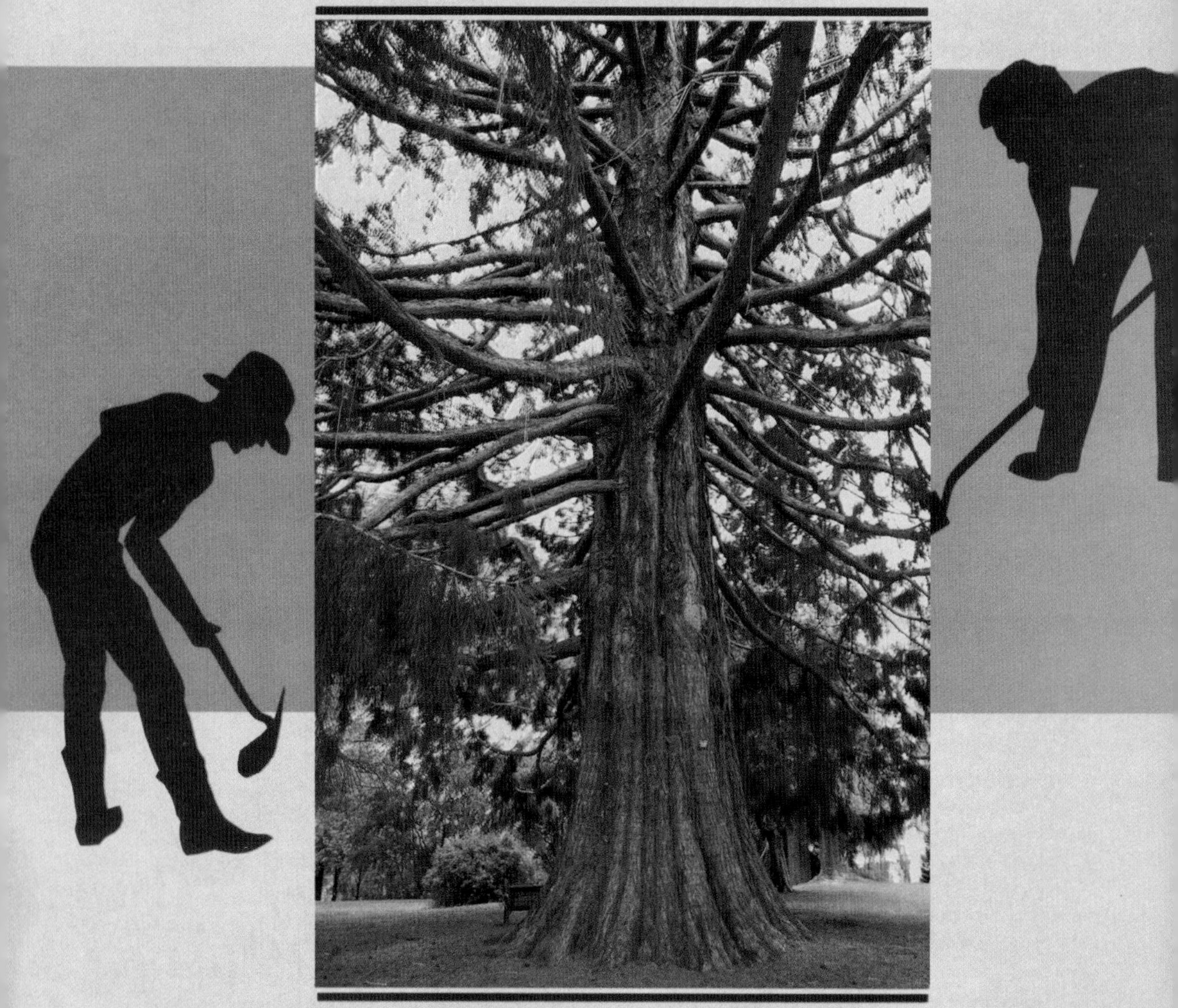

APPALACHIAN MOUNTAIN MENSTRUAL WORKCAMP

Winfield, West Virginia

July 10-16, 1983

Set in the lush, forested mountains of Putnam County, West Virginia, this menstrual workcamp will focus on feeding the trees in the hills and "hollers." Experience the poverty of the Appalachia mountains, while enjoying the outdoors.

Don't forget your ITCH-B-GON American dog tick repellent.

ROCKY MOUNTAIN MENSTRUAL WORKCAMP

Alamosa, Colorado

July 10-16, 1983

Surrounded by distant mountain peaks and national forests, the San Luis Valley suffers from an arid climate and many of the area's older menstrual trees are suffering. This workcamp will focus on clearing debris around the old trees, and providing palliative care. Knowledge of Spanish a plus.

Don't forget your ITCH-B-GON Rocky Mountain wood tick repellent!

BLUE RIDGE MOUNTAIN MENSTRUAL WORKCAMP

Burnsville, North Carolina

July 31-August 6, 1983

Lush green mountains, open meadows and fast-flowing streams - North Carolina features some of the most scenic poverty in the U.S.A. This area's old menstrual trees are located deep in forested areas and this workcamp will focus on identifying them and tagging them for future care.

Don't forget your ITCH-B-GON black-legged deer tick repellent!

OREGON COAST MENSTRUAL WORKCAMP

Otis, Oregon

August 7-13, 1983

The Oregon coast boasts some of the oldest menstrual trees in North America, including the historic Old Tree, located at the Original Craft Camp (a designated National Historic Site). This teen-plus workcamp will focus on gentle care and blood donation. The camp is equipped with outhouses and other supplies.

Don't forget your ITCH-B-GON sand flea repellent!

CAN SAVE A TREE

WfC Magazine's Child

WORKCAMPS

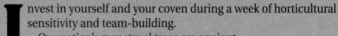

Invest in yourself and your coven during a week of horticultural sensitivity and team-building.

Our nation's menstrual trees are ancient.

Their roots connect them.

You'll combat loneliness, frustration, rejection and fear of frogs as you care for menstrual trees ravaged by years of exposure to wind and rain. You'll see the power of magic. You'll create life-long friendships.

Can't attend? You can still help. Fill out the coupon below and send it in along with a used feminine hygiene product in a sealed Ziploc bag. Questions? Call Lia at (555) 666-1212.

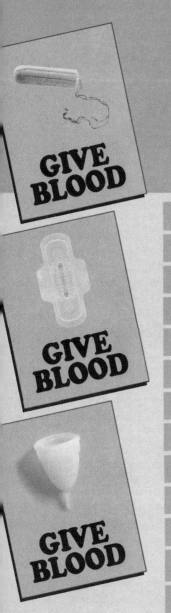

GIVE BLOOD

GIVE BLOOD

GIVE BLOOD

☐ I am enclosing a used menstrual product to support WFC's 1983 workcamps.

In order for us to best allocate this donation, please check a following box, so that we can best estimate the age of the donation.

☐ this blood is bright red.
☐ this blood is brown.
☐ this blood is black.

Name _____

Coven _____

Address _____

City _____ State ____ Zip _____

WfC
BOOKS

Box 666, Portland, OR 79205

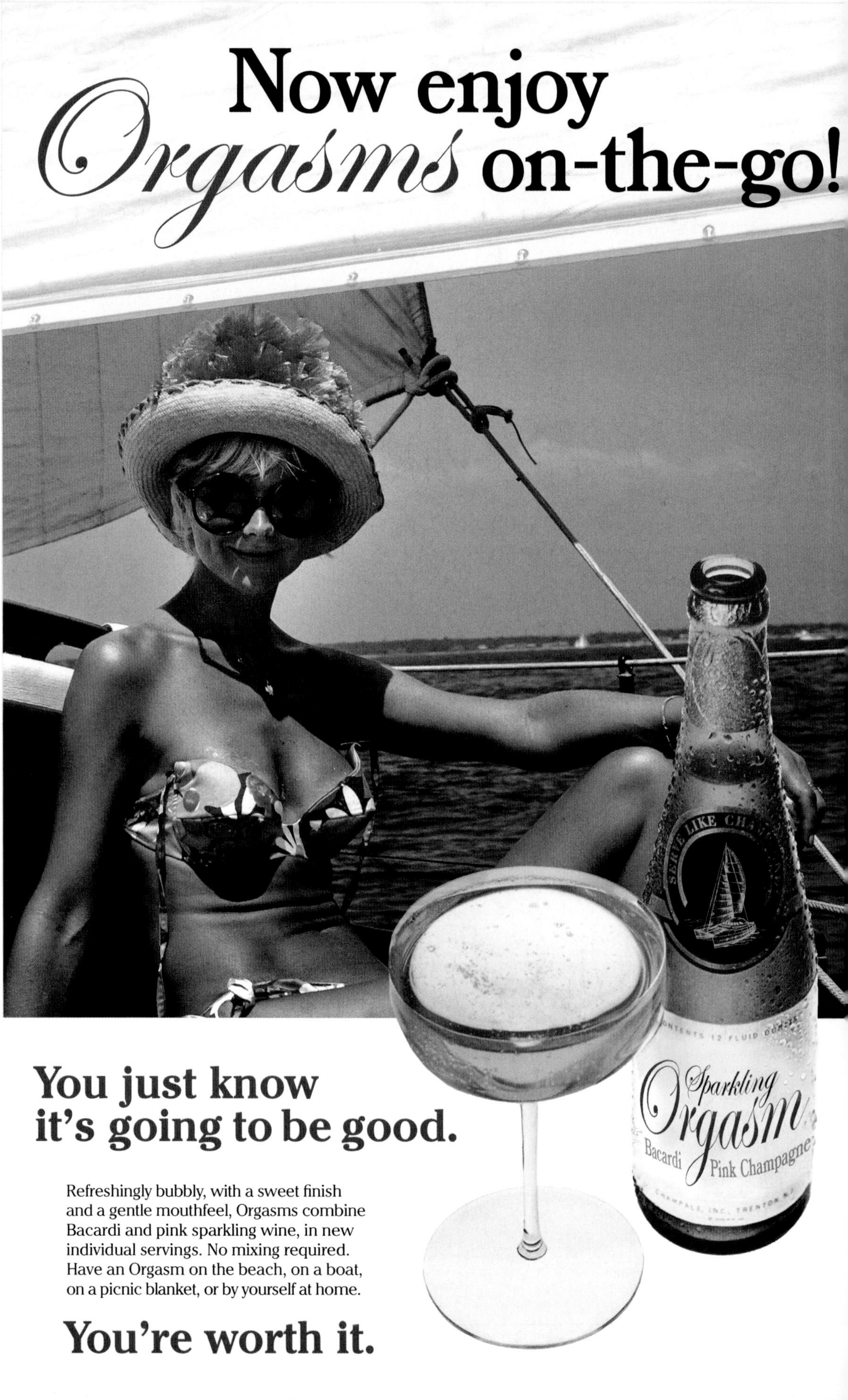
Now enjoy Orgasms on-the-go!
Sparkling Orgasm
Bacardi Pink Champagne
You just know it's going to be good.
Refreshingly bubbly, with a sweet finish and a gentle mouthfeel, Orgasms combine Bacardi and pink sparkling wine, in new individual servings. No mixing required. Have an Orgasm on the beach, on a boat, on a picnic blanket, or by yourself at home.
You're worth it.

[Issue 3, Cover B]

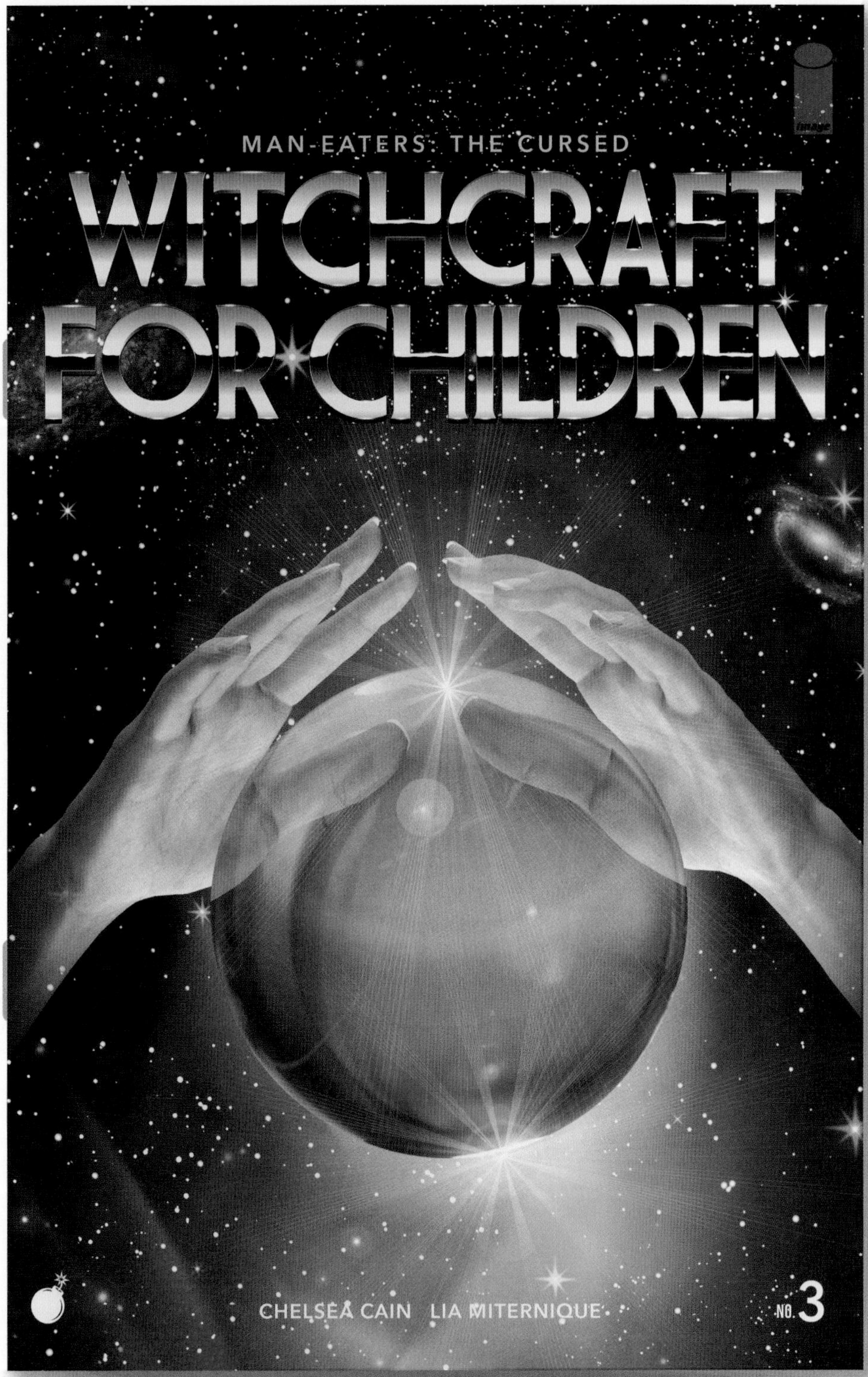

CHAPTER

4

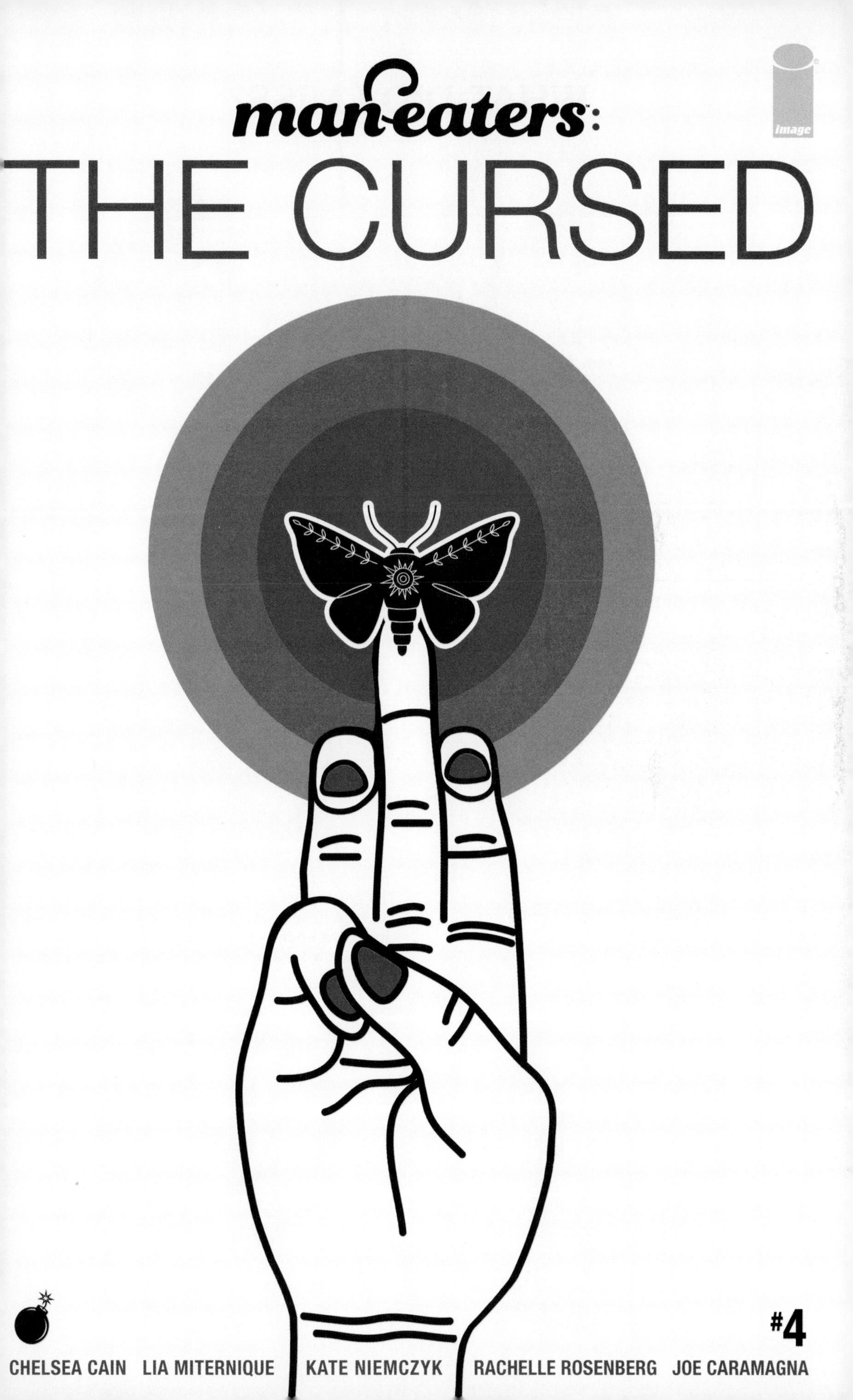
man-eaters:
THE CURSED
image
#4
CHELSEA CAIN LIA MITERNIQUE KATE NIEMCZYK RACHELLE ROSENBERG JOE CARAMAGNA

WHAT DID I MISS?

Maude, age 15, went to Craft Camp, located on an island off the Oregon Coast.

Craft Camp is actually "witchcraft camp." Maude attended as a small child and is kind of a legend. "Best All-Around Camper" three years in a row.

Now Maude has a problem.

The counselors and other campers have vanished. Except for a strange boy named Burt. And four junior campers – now peanut-sized – rescued by Maude from a fairy house she built years ago.

There is no wifi or cell service at Craft Camp. And no way off the island. They are stranded.

It's up to Maude to figure out how to save the little kids. She has a plan.

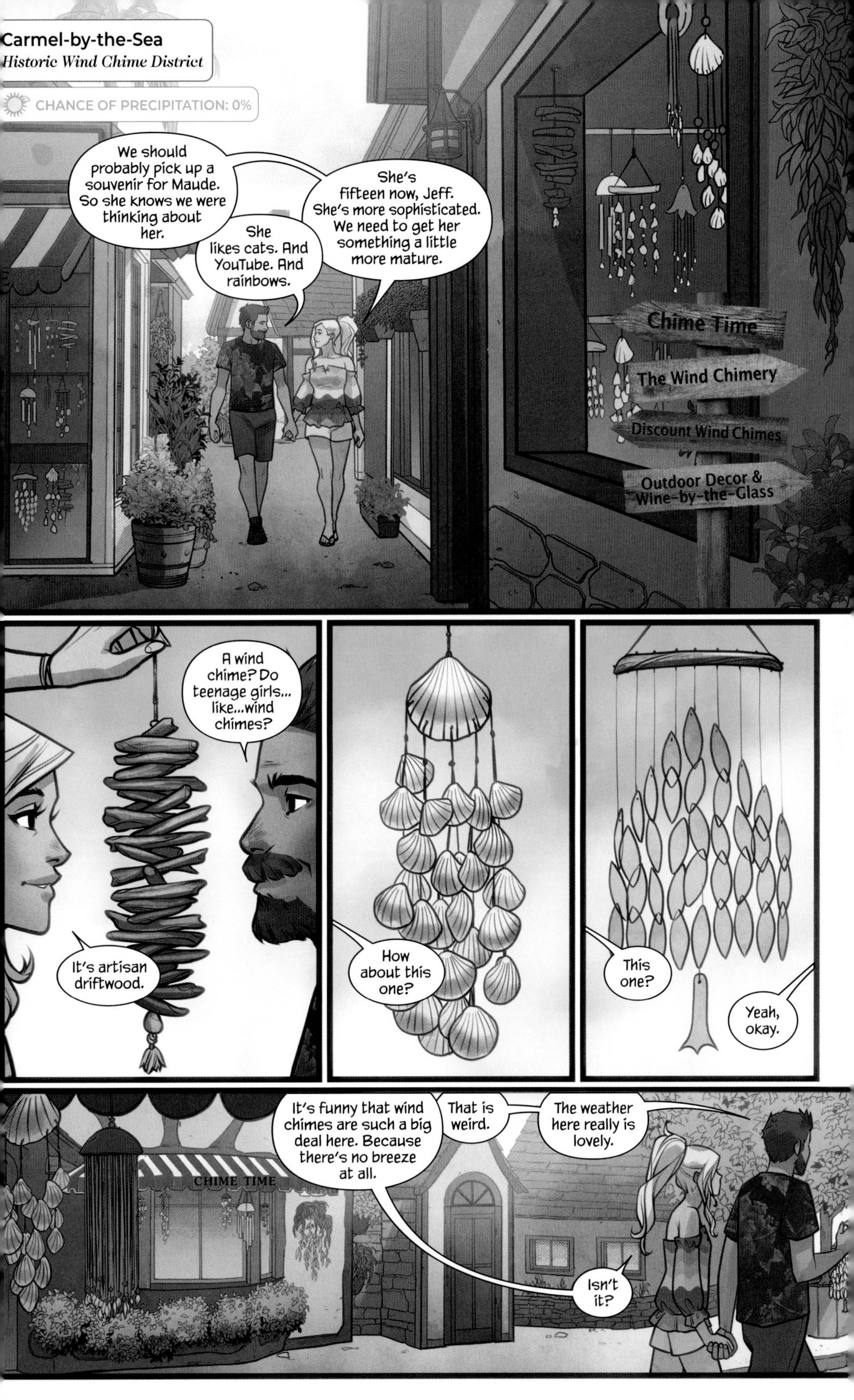
Carmel-by-the-Sea
Historic Wind Chime District
CHANCE OF PRECIPITATION: 0%
We should probably pick up a souvenir for Maude. So she knows we were thinking about her.
She likes cats. And YouTube. And rainbows.
She's fifteen now, Jeff. She's more sophisticated. We need to get her something a little more mature.
Chime Time
The Wind Chimery
Discount Wind Chimes
Outdoor Decor & Wine-by-the-Glass
A wind chime? Do teenage girls... like...wind chimes?
It's artisan driftwood.
How about this one?
This one?
Yeah, okay.
CHIME TIME
It's funny that wind chimes are such a big deal here. Because there's no breeze at all.
That is weird.
The weather here really is lovely.
Isn't it?

Transmutation

Ingredients:
2 pinches of mycorrhiza (should be fresh)

Chew 25 times or until mycorrhiza is thoroughly lubricated with saliva. Mycorrhiza is activated by the lingual lipase enzyme secreted by the acinar cells of the sublingual gland.

The mycorrhiza is ready when it transforms into a glitter-like substance.

Transmutation Reversal

Ingredients:
2 pinches of mycorrhiza (should be fresh)

Chew 25 times or until mycorrhiza is thoroughly lubricated with saliva. Mycorrhiza is activated by the lingual lipase enzyme secreted by the acinar cells of the sublingual gland.

The mycorrhiza is ready when it transforms into a glitter-like substance.

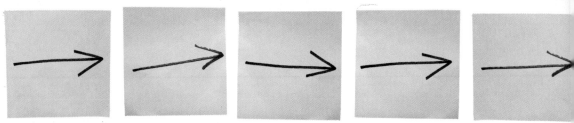

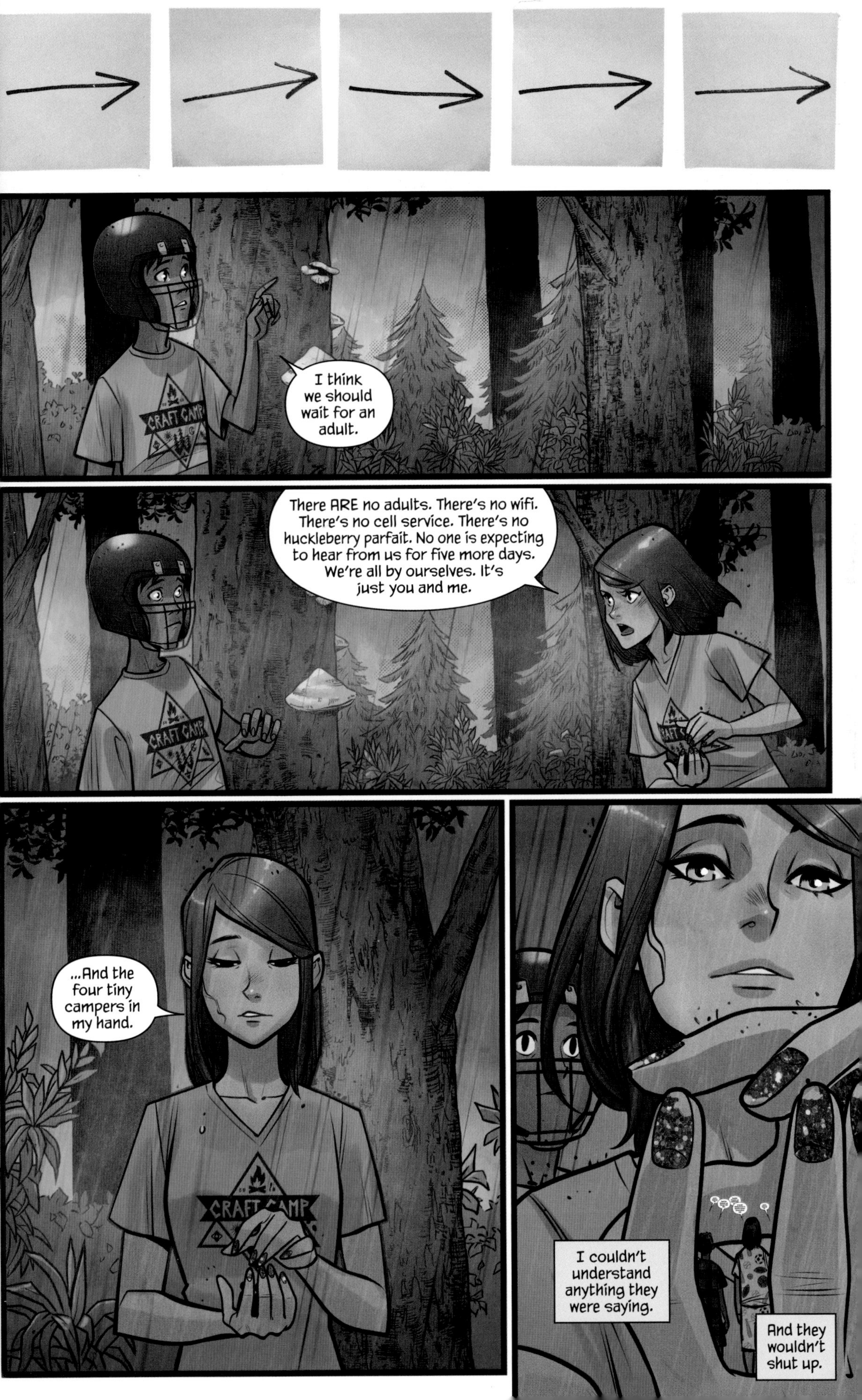
I think we should wait for an adult.
There ARE no adults. There's no wifi. There's no cell service. There's no huckleberry parfait. No one is expecting to hear from us for five more days. We're all by ourselves. It's just you and me.
...And the four tiny campers in my hand.
I couldn't understand anything they were saying.
And they wouldn't shut up.

Transmutation: lesson 1

The transmutation school of magic consists of spells that change the physical properties of a creature, object, or condition.

Size shifting is a beginner transmutation spell.

Little | Big

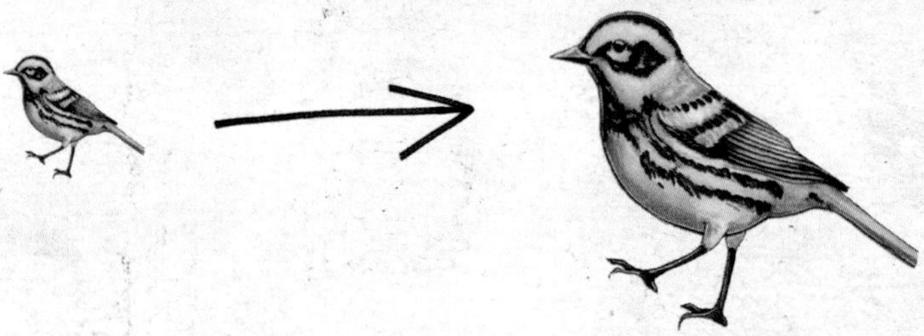

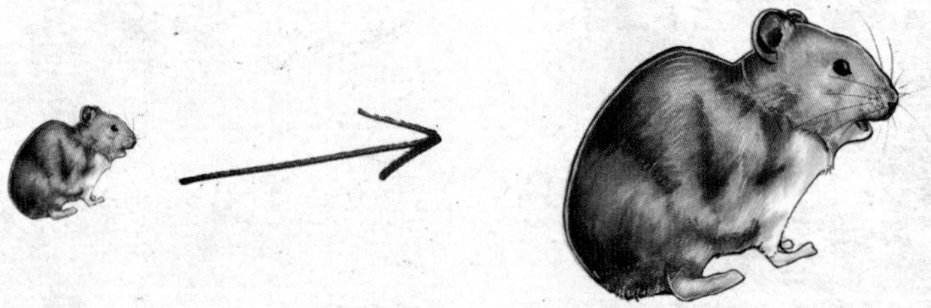

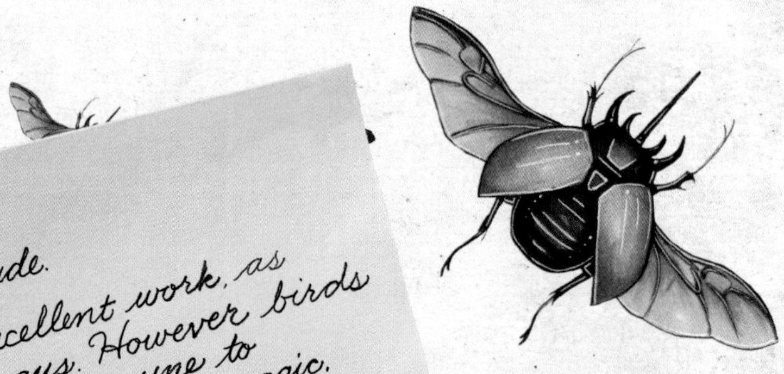

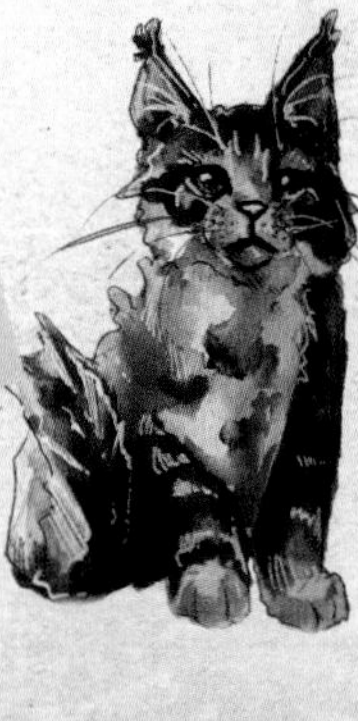

Maude.
Excellent work, as always. However birds are immune to transmutation magic. Please see me during office hours.

B+

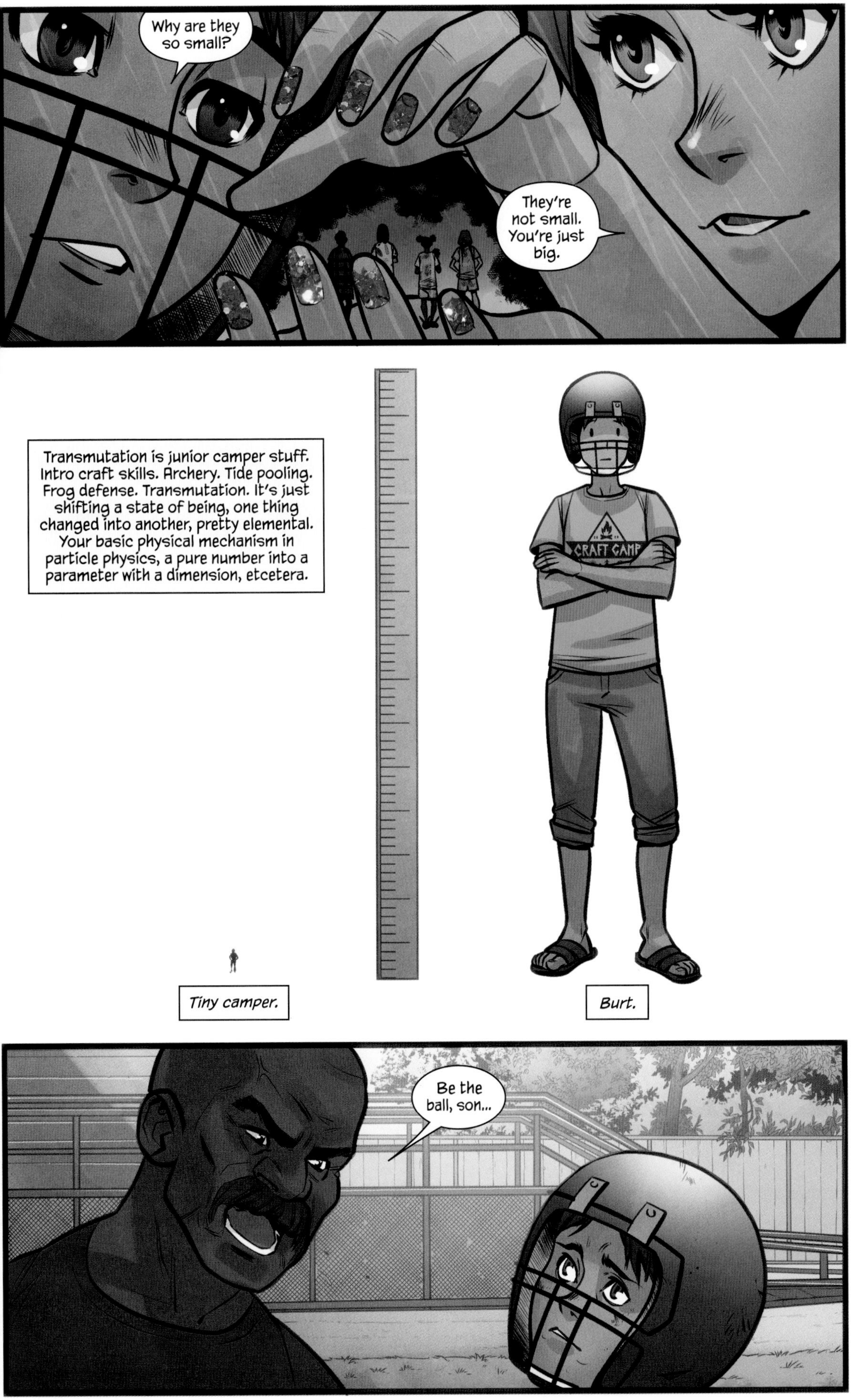
Why are they so small?
They're not small. You're just big.
Transmutation is junior camper stuff. Intro craft skills. Archery. Tide pooling. Frog defense. Transmutation. It's just shifting a state of being, one thing changed into another, pretty elemental. Your basic physical mechanism in particle physics, a pure number into a parameter with a dimension, etcetera.
CRAFT CAMP
Tiny camper.
Burt.
Be the ball, son...

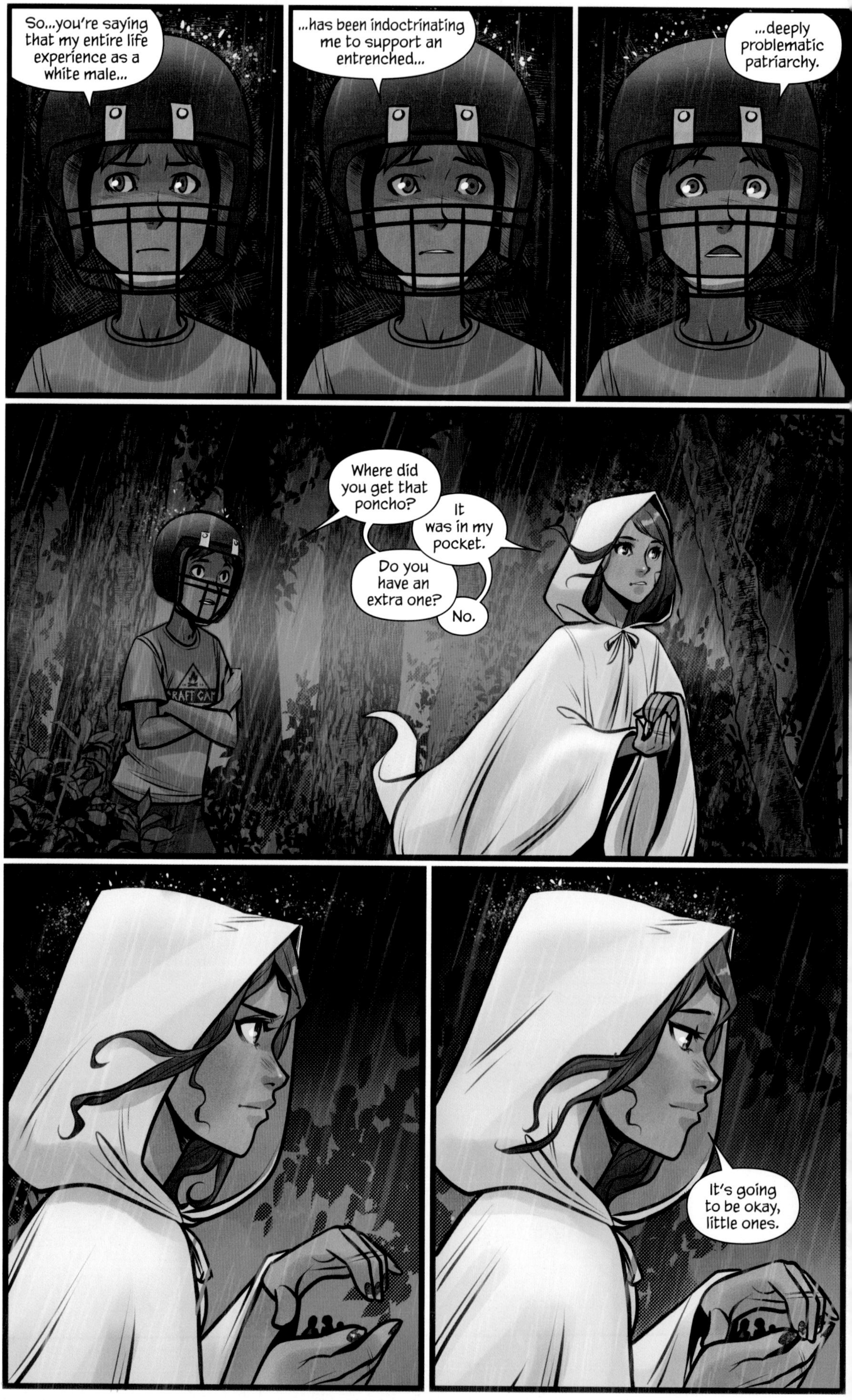

So...you're saying that my entire life experience as a white male...
...has been indoctrinating me to support an entrenched...
...deeply problematic patriarchy.
Where did you get that poncho?
It was in my pocket.
Do you have an extra one?
No.
It's going to be okay, little ones.

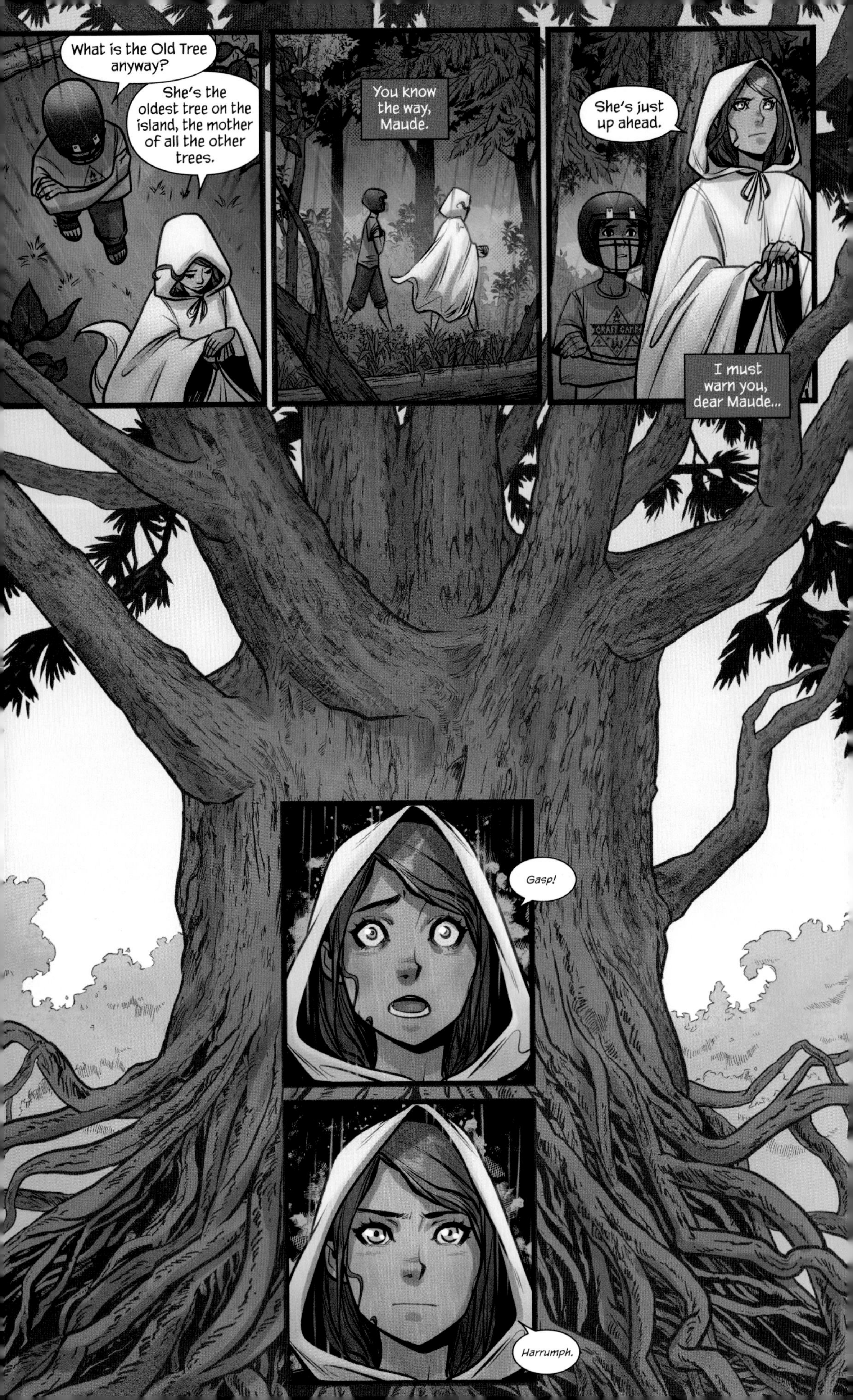
What is the Old Tree anyway?
She's the oldest tree on the island, the mother of all the other trees.
You know the way, Maude.
She's just up ahead.
I must warn you, dear Maude...
Gasp!
Harrumph.

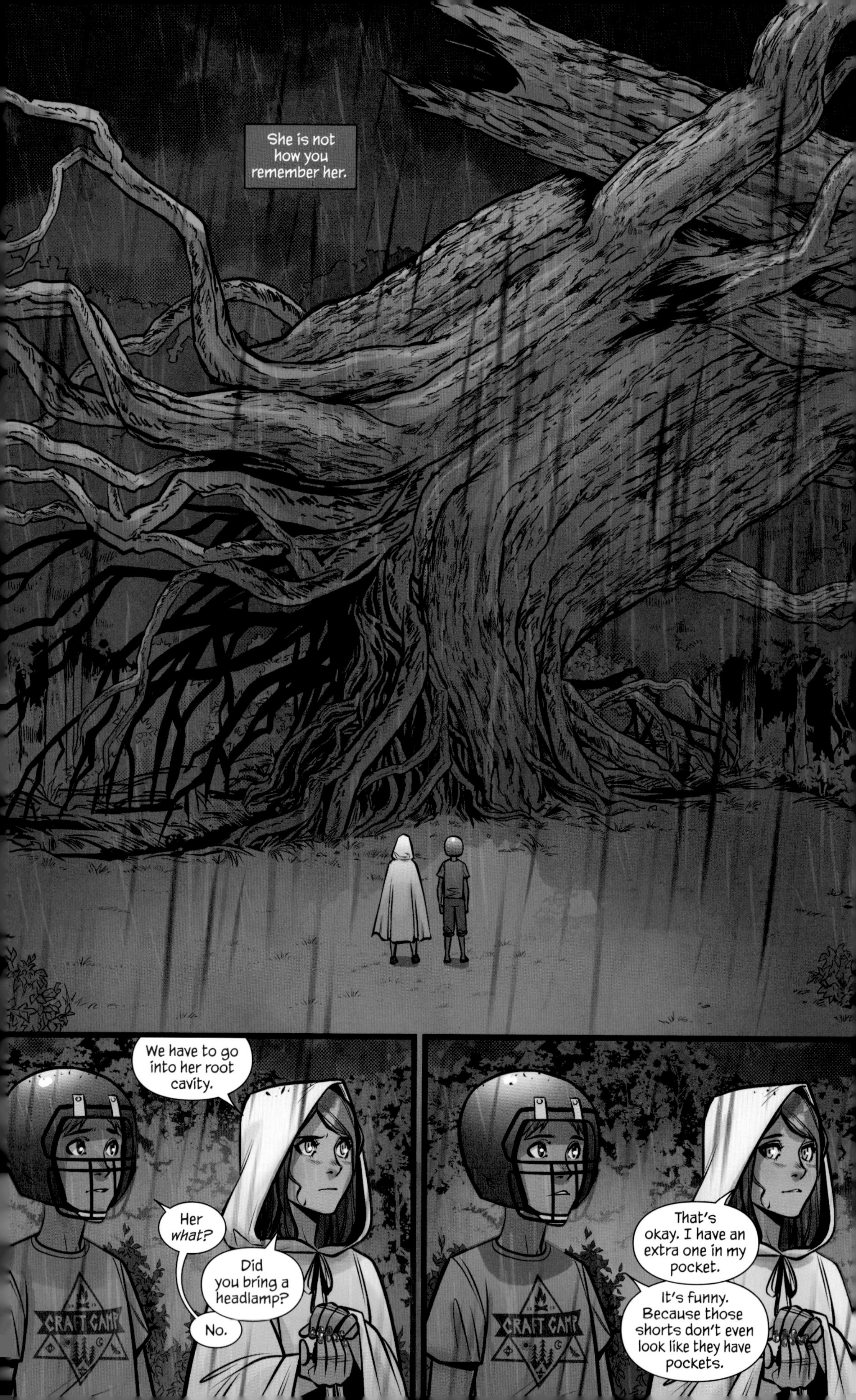
She is not how you remember her.
We have to go into her root cavity.
Her *what?*
Did you bring a headlamp?
No.
CRAFT CAMP
That's okay. I have an extra one in my pocket.
It's funny. Because those shorts don't even look like they have pockets.
CRAFT CAMP

The Tie-Dye Cargo Camp Short-Short

Innovative, stain-resistant tactical camp gear for girls on the go.

Our Tie-Dye Cargo Camp Short-Short features nine hidden pockets that will help you keep your camp supplies organized and secure. Breathable. Lightweight. Quick-dry. Low-friction performance. Wrinkle-resistant. 4-way stretch. UPF 50+. Slash-resistant double panel pocket protection. Drawstring waistband. Pre-washed for added comfort. Also available in paisley, pinstripe, and gingham.

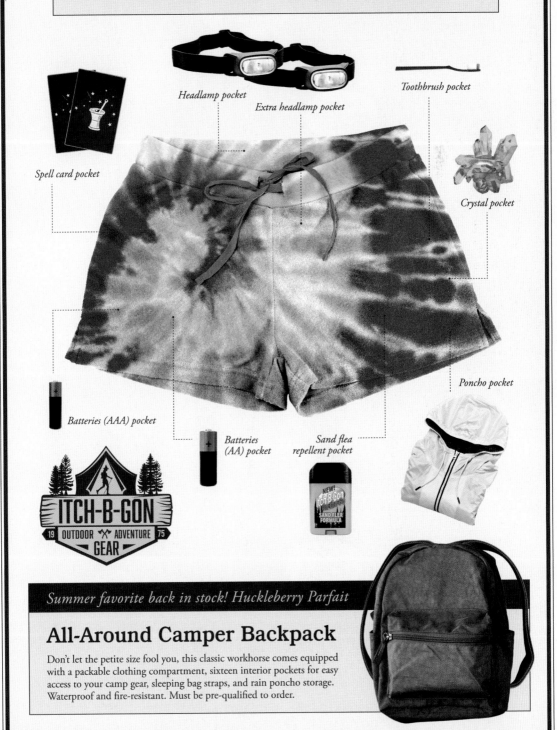

Headlamp pocket
Extra headlamp pocket
Toothbrush pocket
Spell card pocket
Crystal pocket
Poncho pocket
Batteries (AAA) pocket
Batteries (AA) pocket
Sand flea repellent pocket
NEW!
Itch-B-Gon
SAND FLEA FORMULA

ITCH-B-GON
19 OUTDOOR ADVENTURE 75
GEAR

Summer favorite back in stock! Huckleberry Parfait

All-Around Camper Backpack

Don't let the petite size fool you, this classic workhorse comes equipped with a packable clothing compartment, sixteen interior pockets for easy access to your camp gear, sleeping bag straps, and rain poncho storage. Waterproof and fire-resistant. Must be pre-qualified to order.

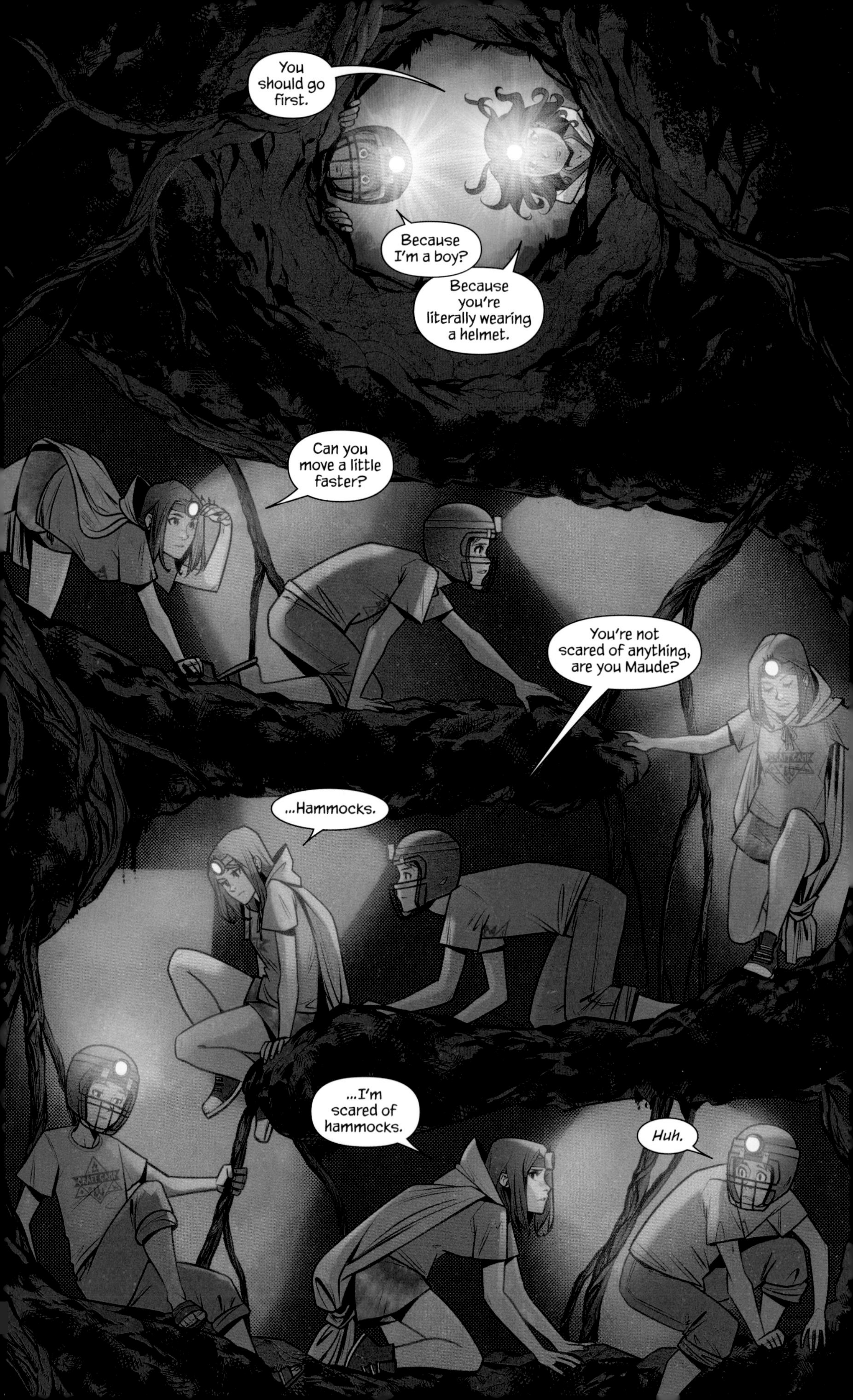
You should go first.
Because I'm a boy?
Because you're literally wearing a helmet.
Can you move a little faster?
You're not scared of anything, are you Maude?
...Hammocks.
...I'm scared of hammocks.
Huh.

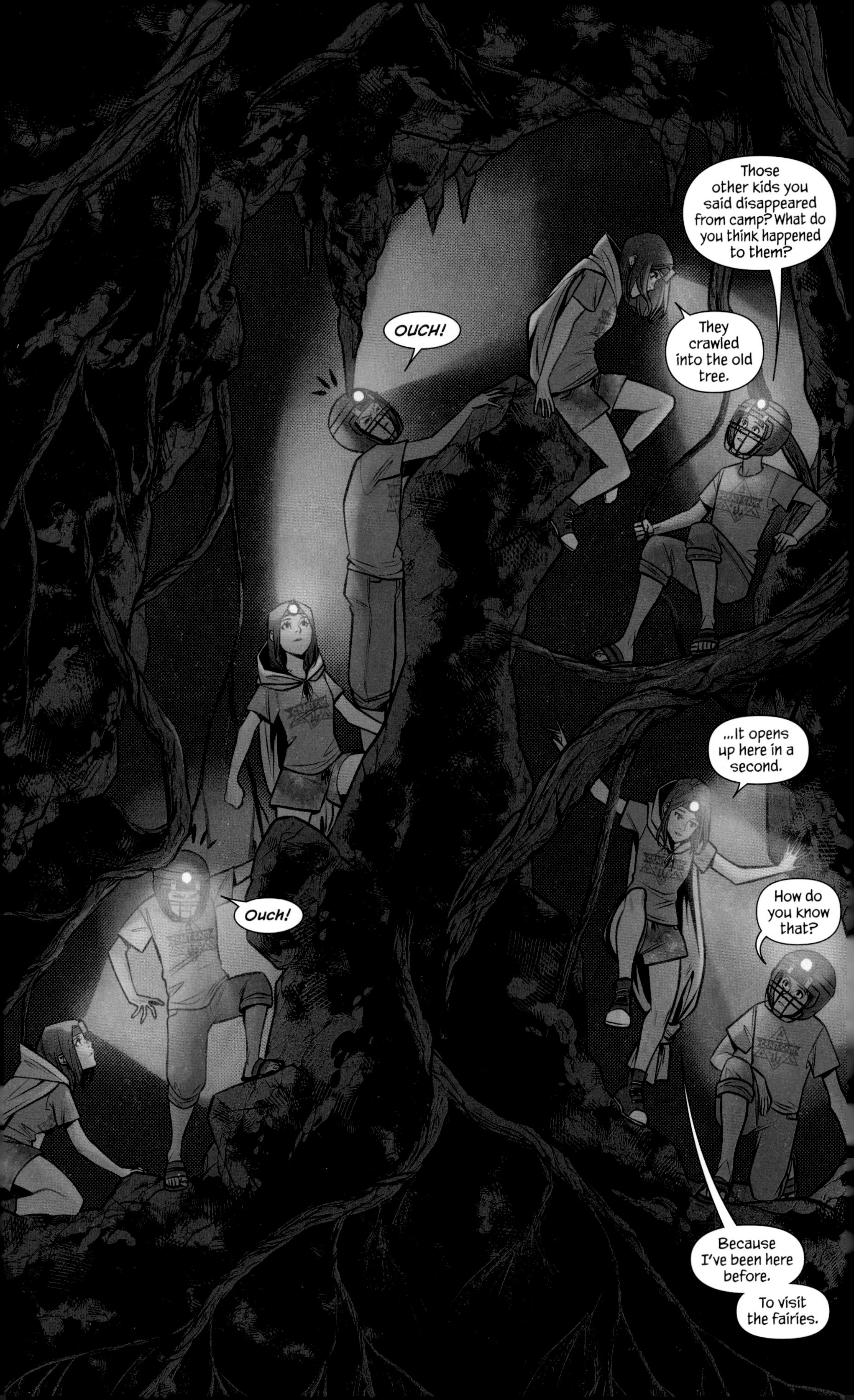
Those other kids you said disappeared from camp? What do you think happened to them?
They crawled into the old tree.
OUCH!
Ouch!
...It opens up here in a second.
How do you know that?
Because I've been here before.
To visit the fairies.

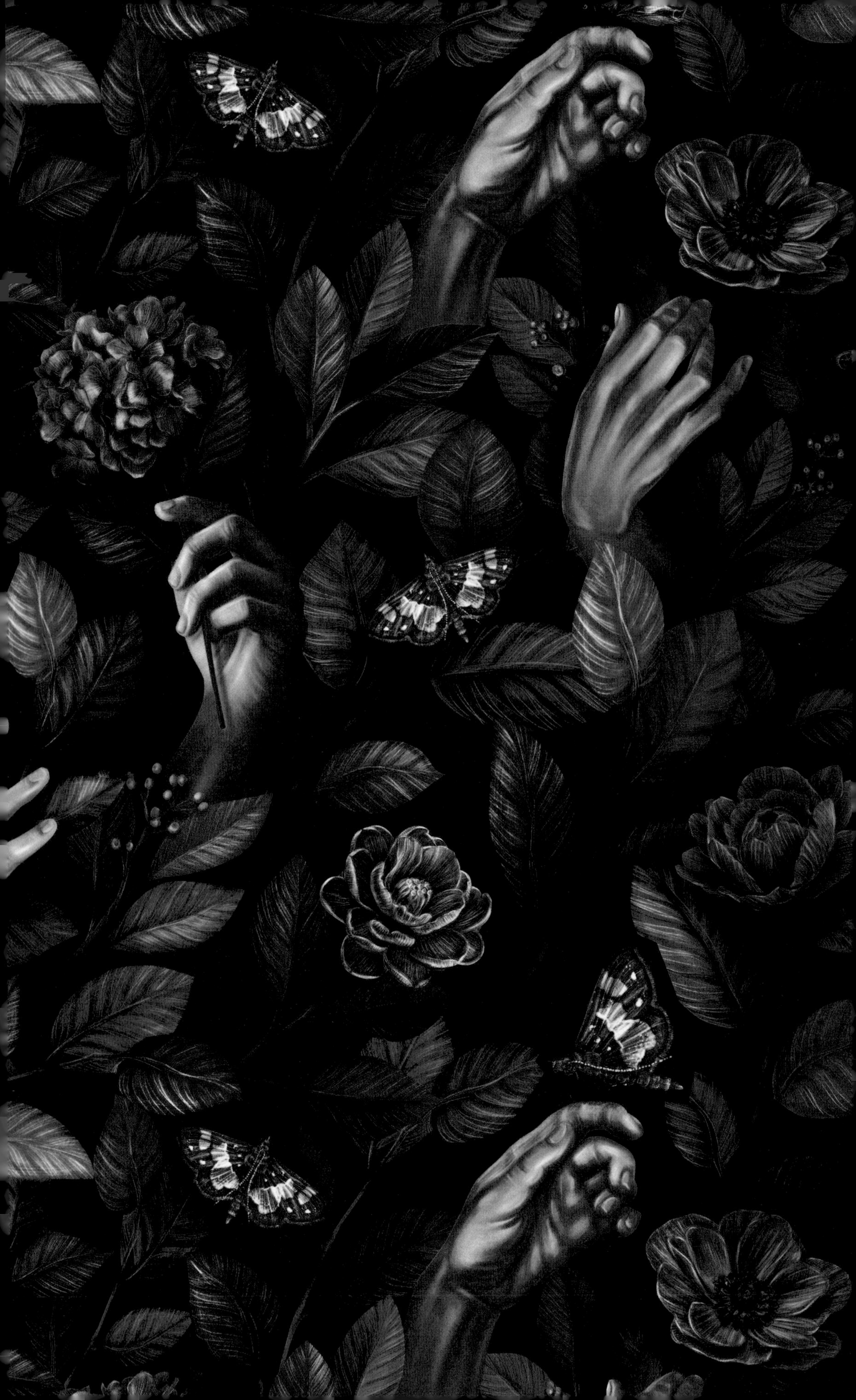

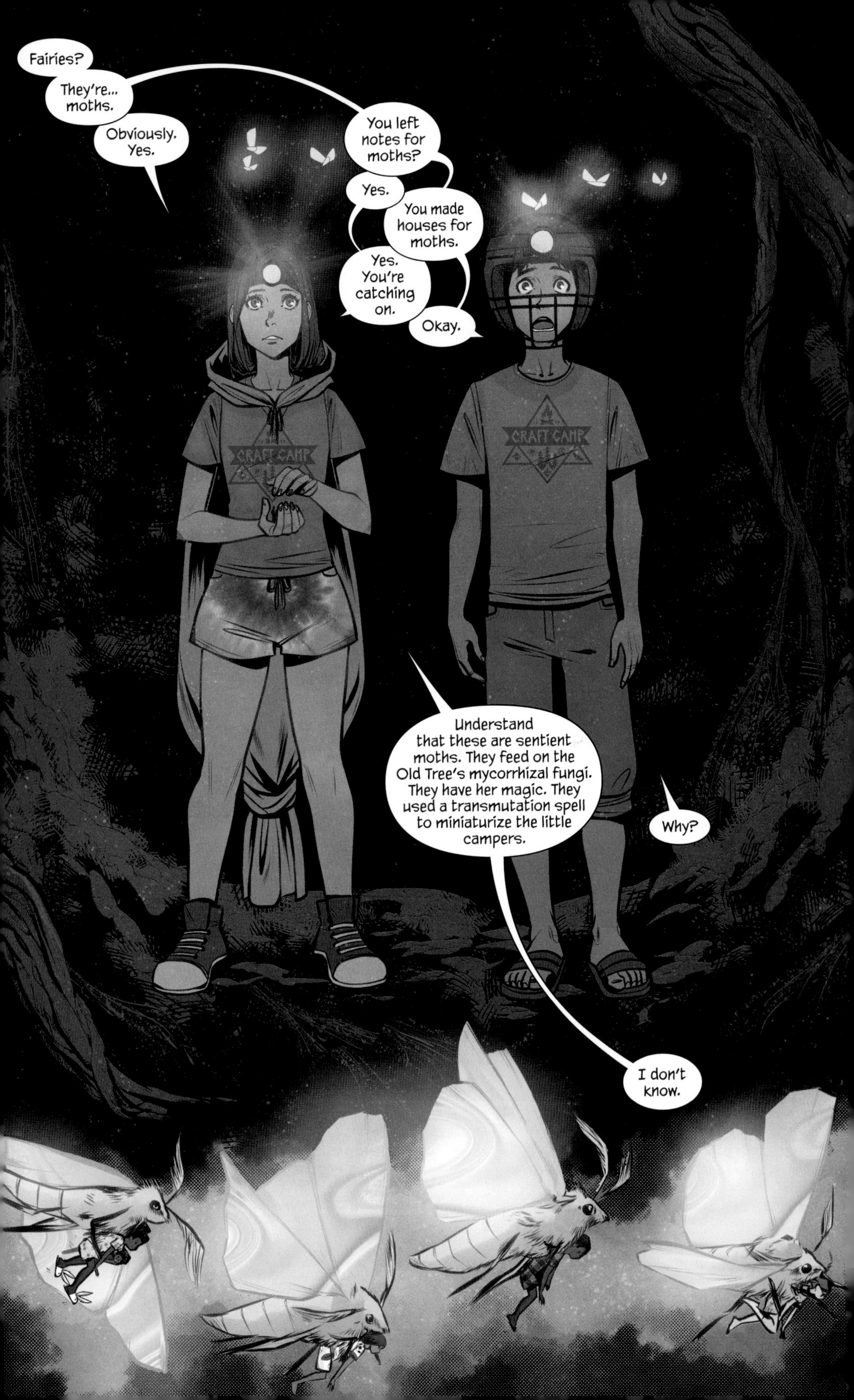
Fairies?
They're... moths.
Obviously. Yes.
You left notes for moths?
Yes.
You made houses for moths.
Yes. You're catching on.
Okay.
CRAFT CAMP
CRAFT CAMP
Understand that these are sentient moths. They feed on the Old Tree's mycorrhizal fungi. They have her magic. They used a transmutation spell to miniaturize the little campers.
Why?
I don't know.

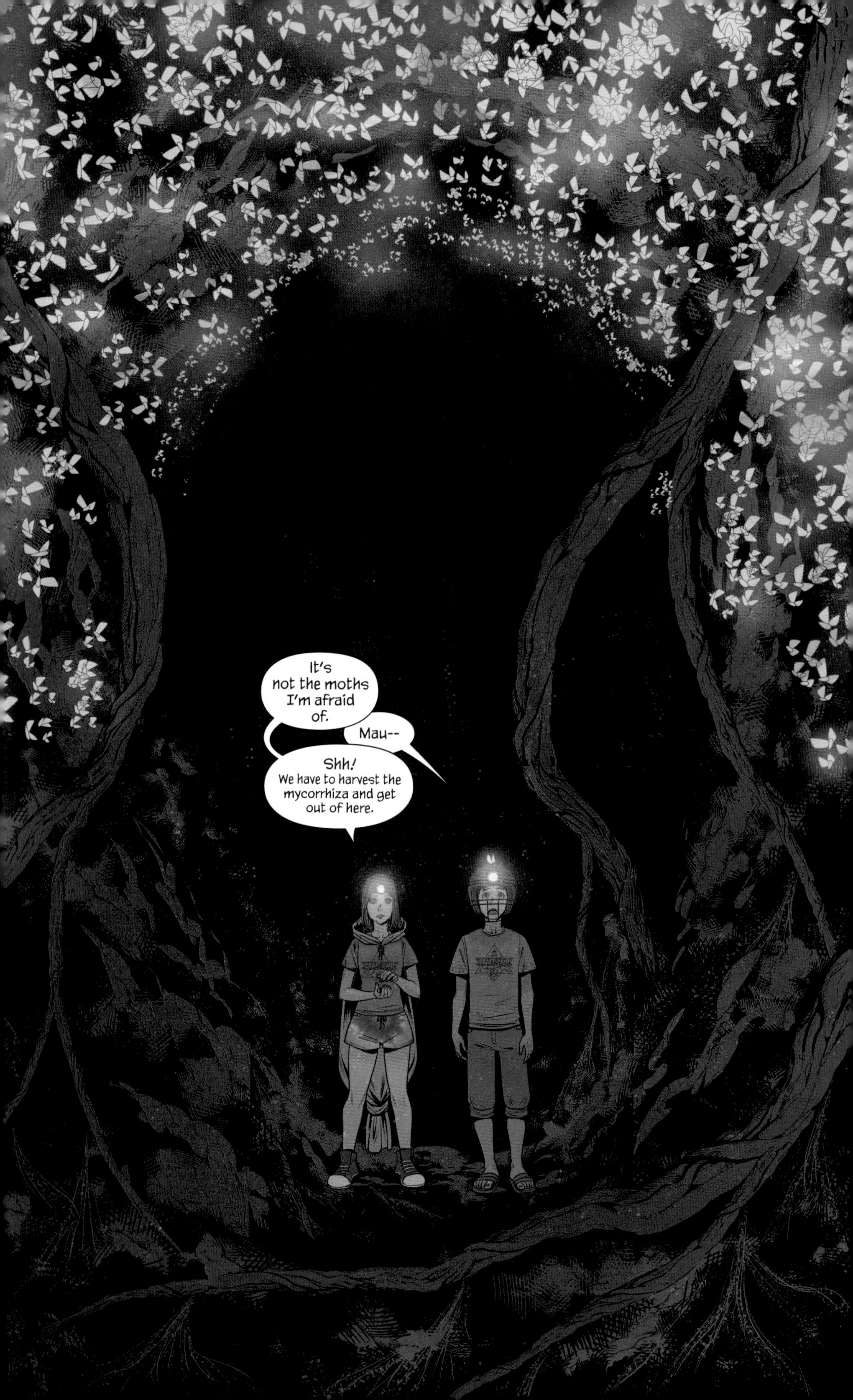
It's not the moths I'm afraid of.
Mau--
Shh! We have to harvest the mycorrhiza and get out of here.

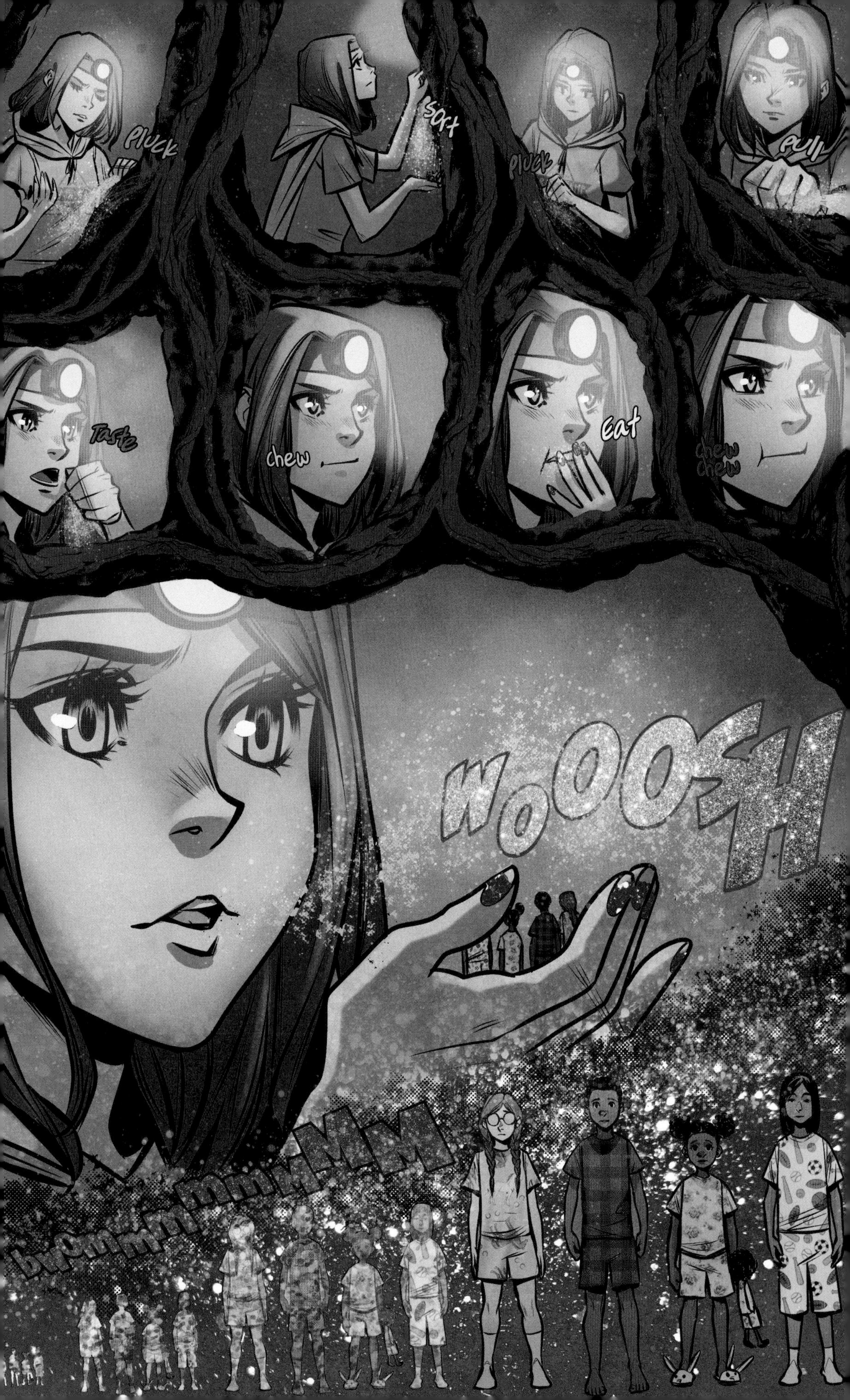
Pluck
Sort
Pluck
Pull
Taste
chew
Eat
chew chew
WOOOOSH

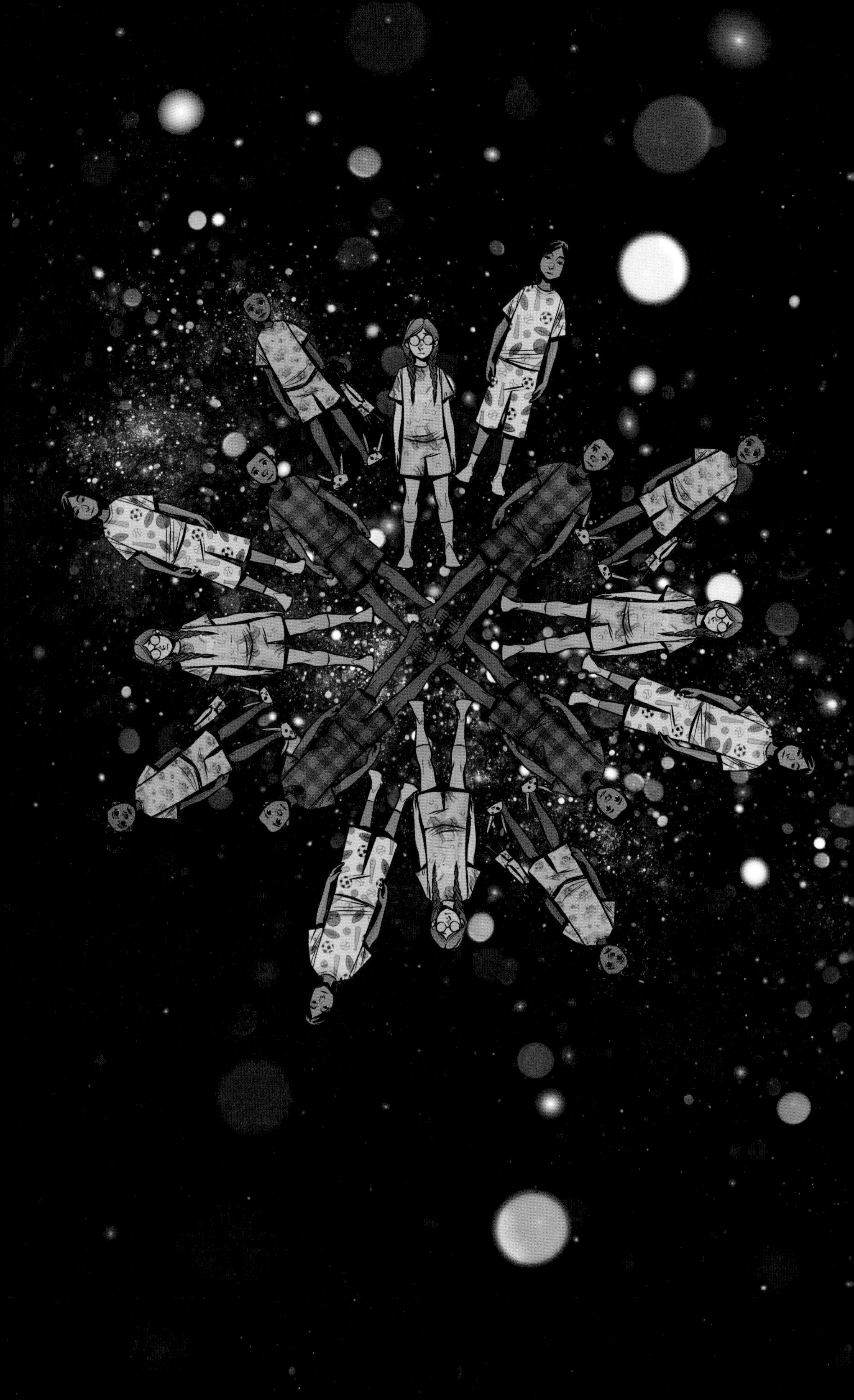

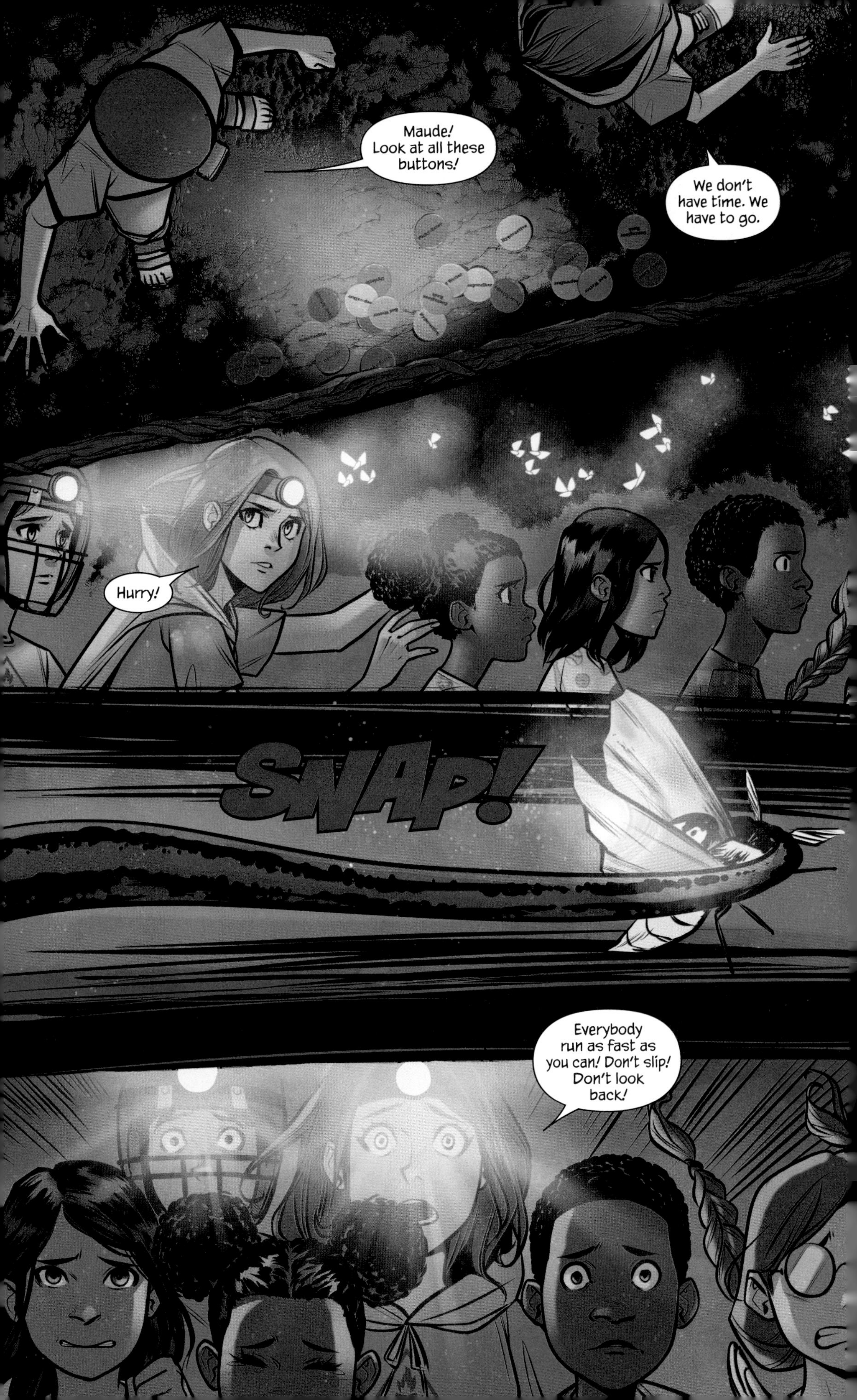
Maude! Look at all these buttons!
We don't have time. We have to go.
Hurry!
SNAP!
Everybody run as fast as you can! Don't slip! Don't look back!

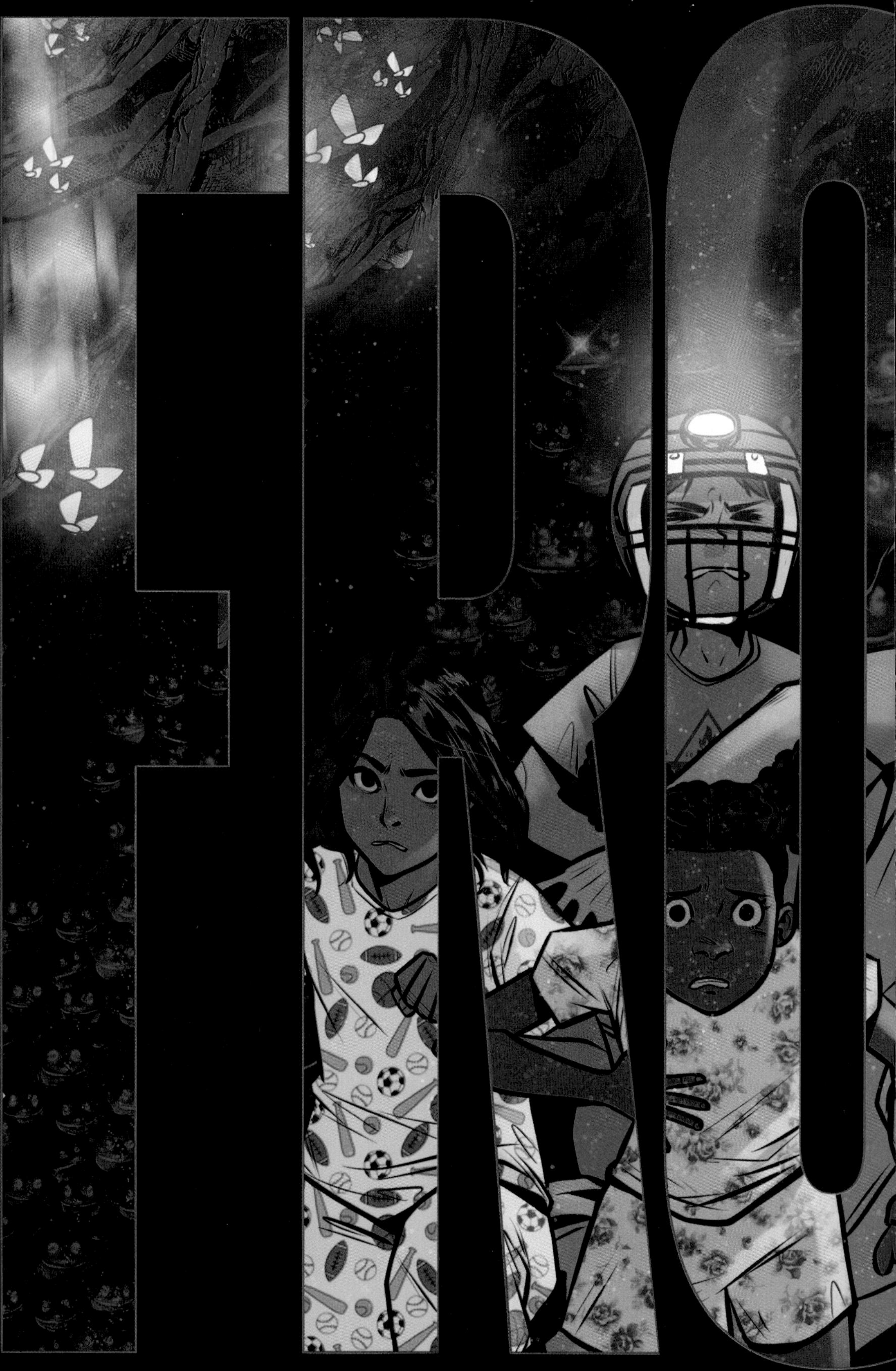
FRO

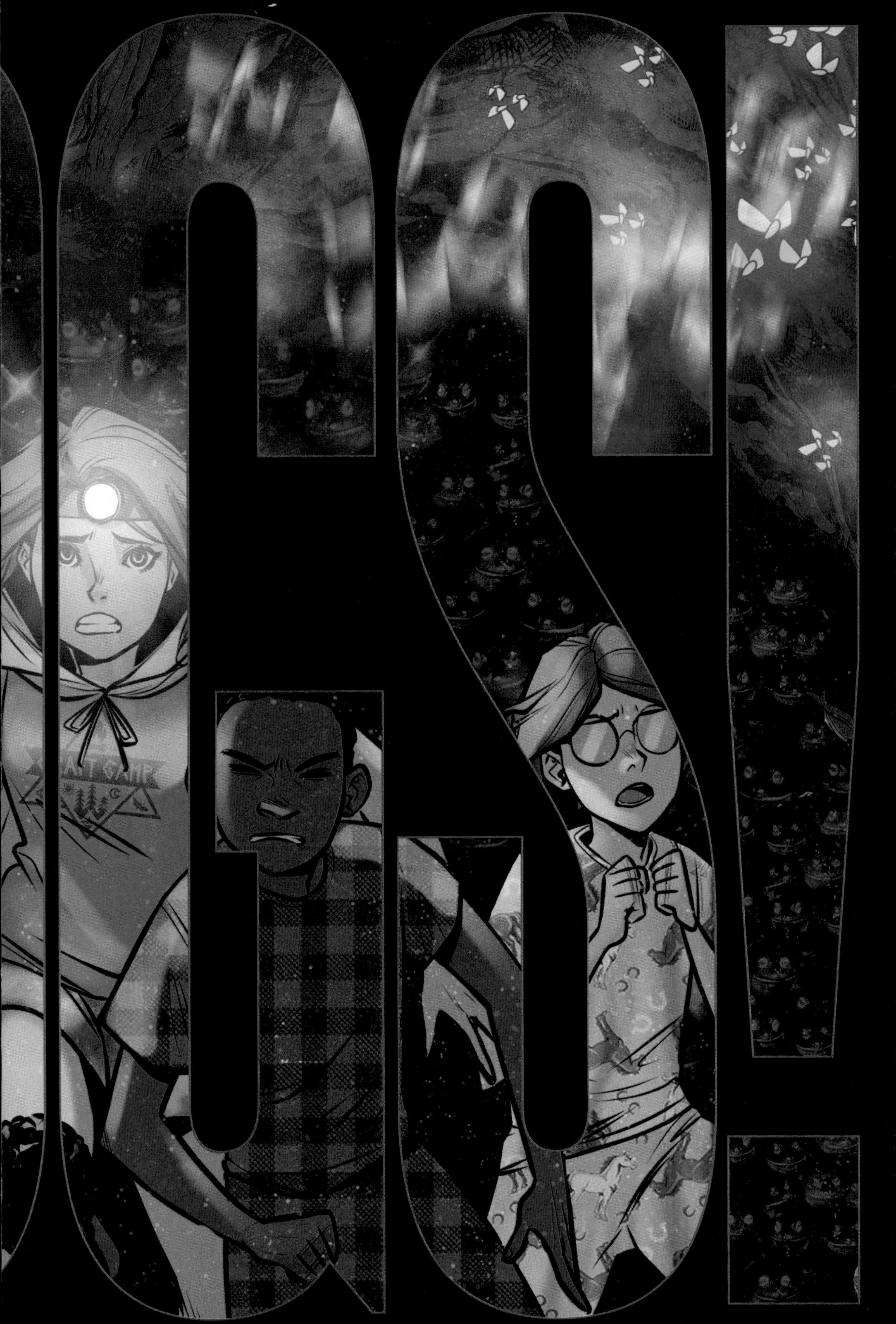
GS!

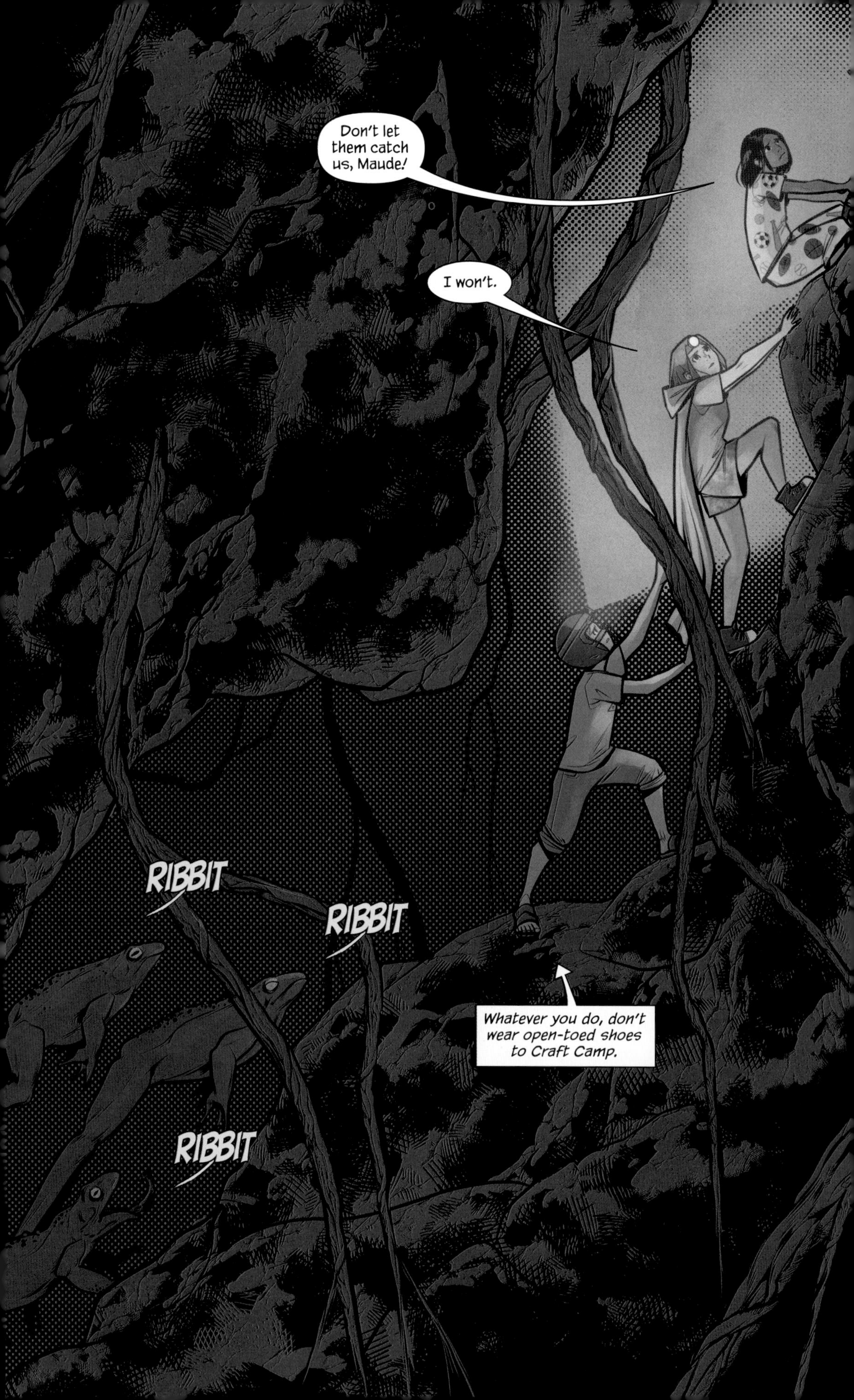
Don't let them catch us, Maude!
I won't.
RIBBIT
RIBBIT
RIBBIT
Whatever you do, don't wear open-toed shoes to Craft Camp.

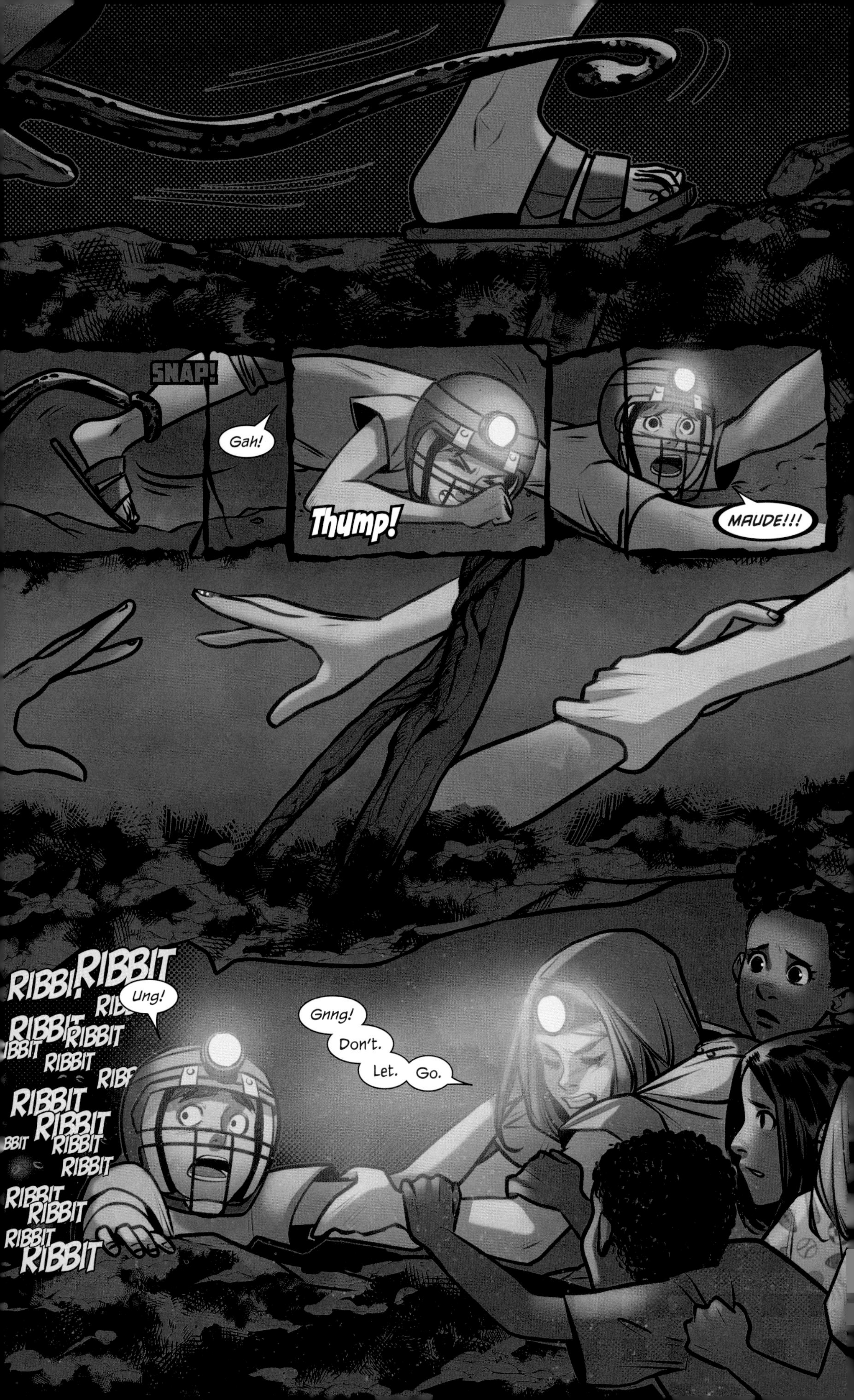
SNAP!
Gah!
Thump!
MAUDE!!!
RIBBIT RIBBIT RIBBIT RIBBIT RIBBIT RIBBIT RIBBIT RIBBIT RIBBIT RIBBIT RIBBIT RIBBIT RIBBIT
Ung!
Gnng!
Don't.
Let.
Go.

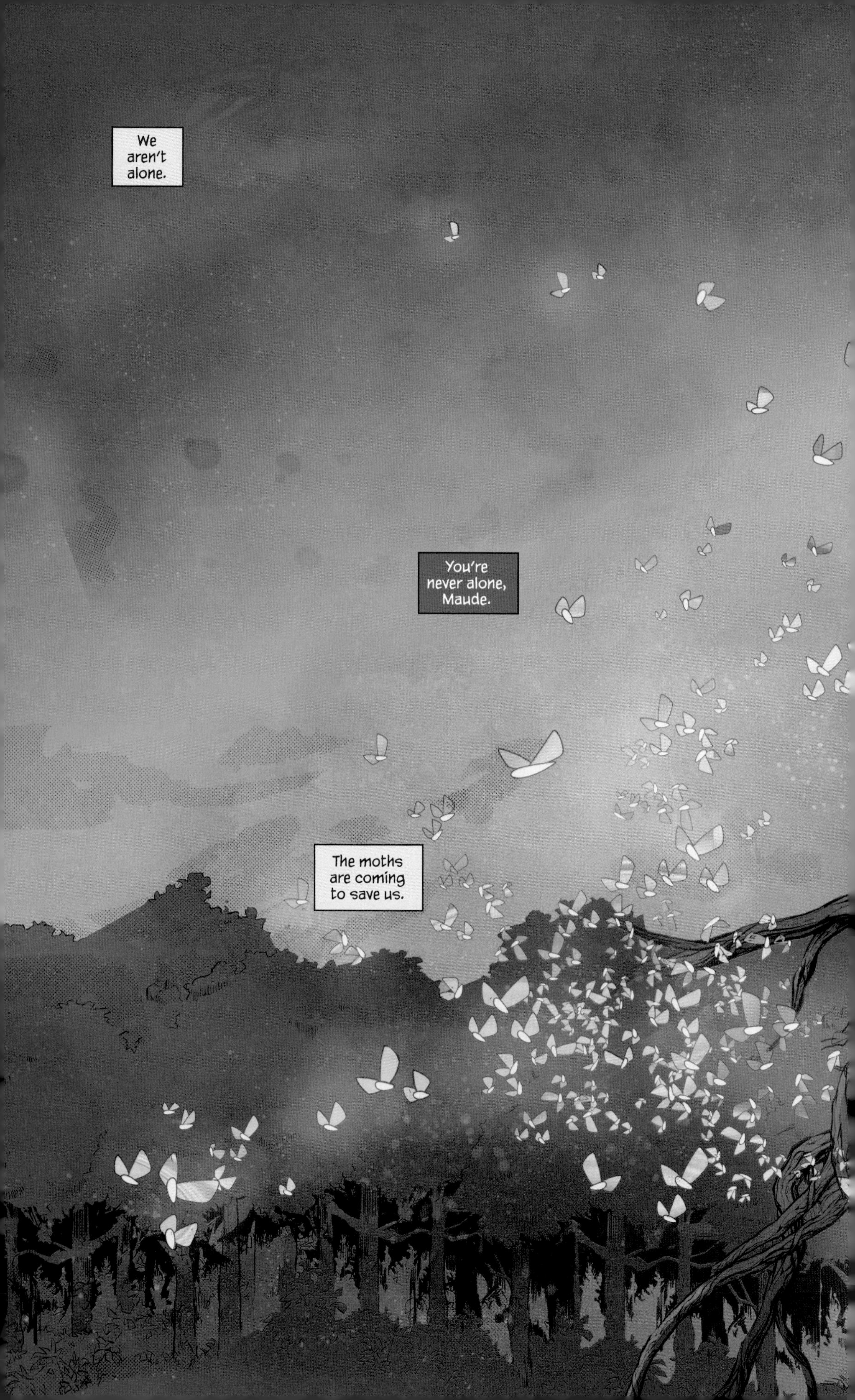
We aren't alone.
You're never alone, Maude.
The moths are coming to save us.

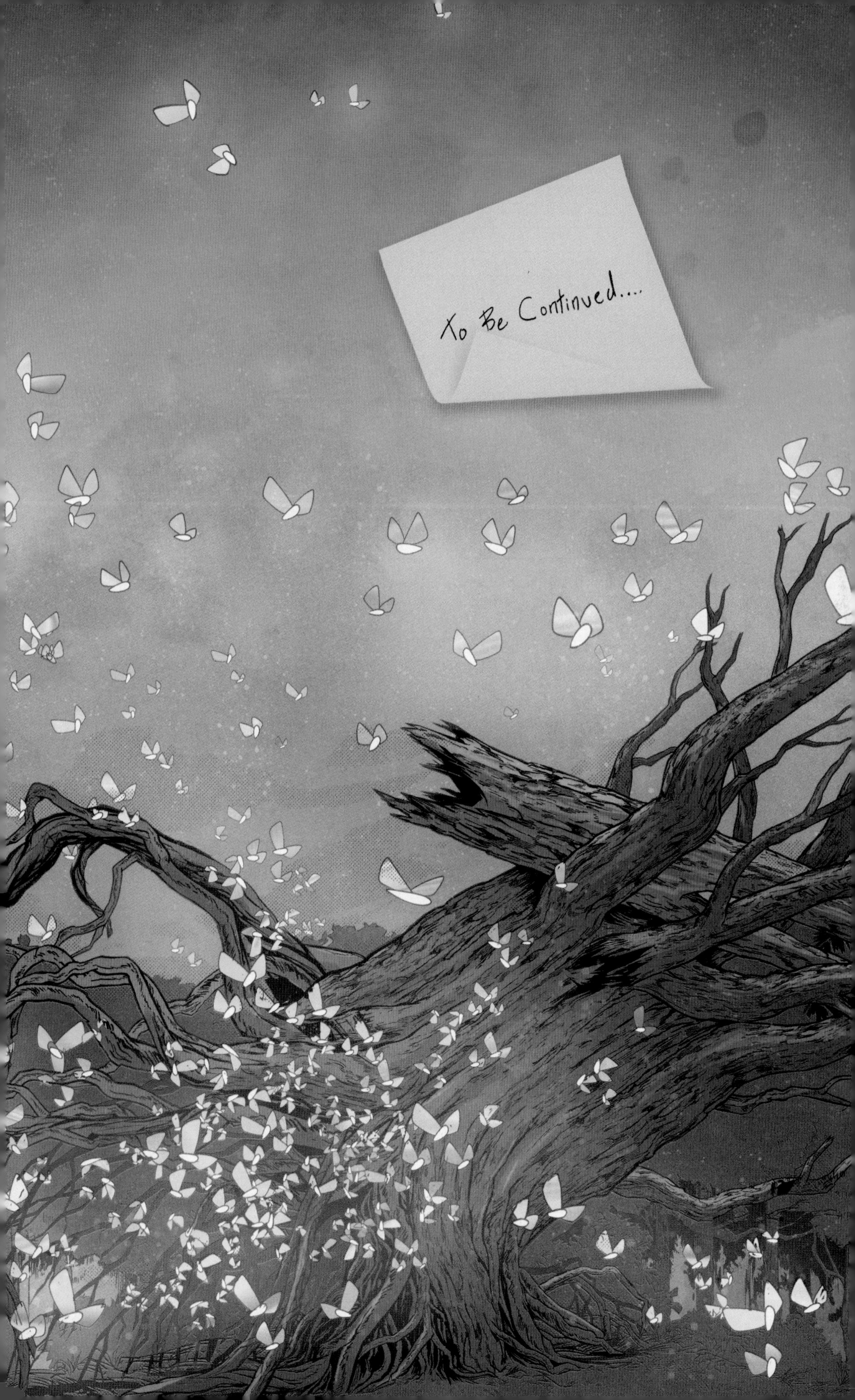
To Be Continued...

Craft Camp BADGE TRACKER

Name: _____

Skill-Building Badges

Skill-Building Badges							Date Earned	Date Awarded
Beekeeping								
Home repair								
Overnight								
Blacksmithing								
Whittling								
Mining								
Fortune telling								
Wand-making								
Potions								
Haberdashery								
First-aid								
Broom making								
Omniscience (beginner)								
Scrolls								
Invisible deer identification								
Candle-making								
Locksmithing								
Pickle ball								
Agriculture								
Herb identification								
Spell ingredients (beginner)								
Frog defense								
Necromancy								
Coven attendance								
Werepantherism								
Spell ingredients (advanced)								
Spell cards								
Potion-making (advanced)								
Capture the flag								
Fortunetelling (advanced)								
Voodoo doll making								
Crystal healing								
Mushroom identification								

Blood Donor

BLOOD DONOR

Journey Awards

Journey Awards							Date Earned	Date Awarded
Outdoor Journey								
Dawn								
Lake								
Sun								
Fire								

Earned	Awarded	Earned	Awarded	Earned	Awarded	Earned	Awarded

Side column

Earned	Awarded

Earned	Earned	Earned

Earned	Awarded

Earned	Awarded

Friend to Fairies

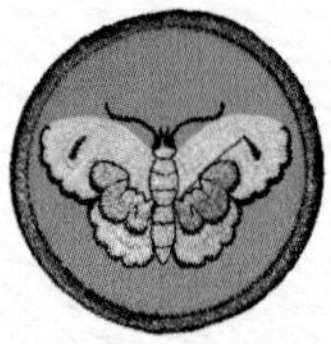

Earned	Awarded

Third Eye

Earned	Awarded

Best All-Around Camper

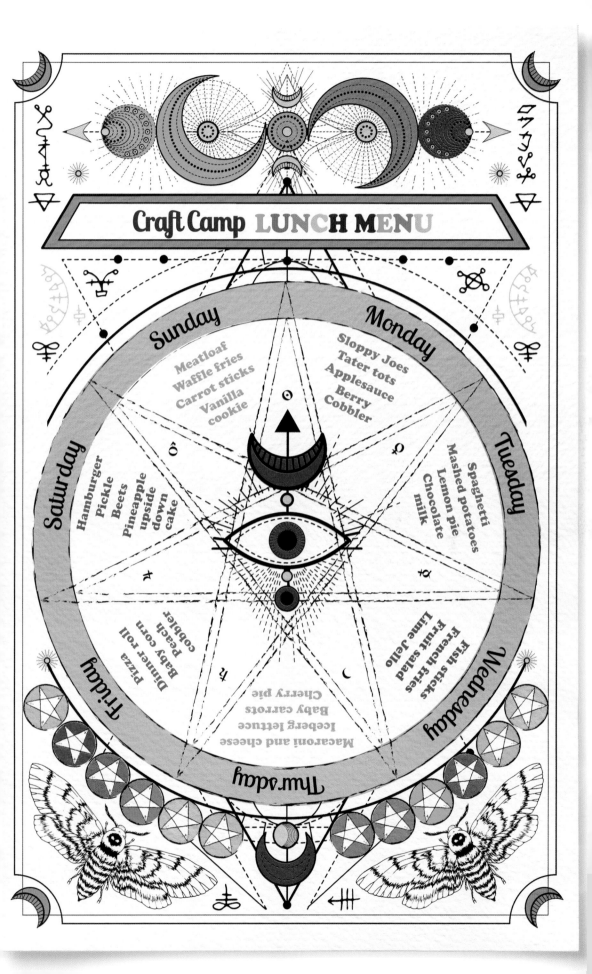

Craft Camp LUNCH MENU

Sunday
Meatloaf
Waffle fries
Carrot sticks
Vanilla cookie

Monday
Sloppy Joes
Tater tots
Applesauce
Berry Cobbler

Tuesday
Spaghetti
Mashed potatoes
Lemon pie
Chocolate milk

Wednesday
Fish sticks
French fries
Fruit salad
Lime Jello

Thursday
Macaroni and cheese
Iceberg lettuce
Baby carrots
Cherry pie

Friday
Pizza
Dinner roll
Baby corn
Peach cobbler

Saturday
Hamburger
Pickle
Beets
Pineapple upside down cake

Craft Camp **VOODOO DOLL**

Has the patriarchy got you down?
Fight back with this handy voodoo doll paper doll set.

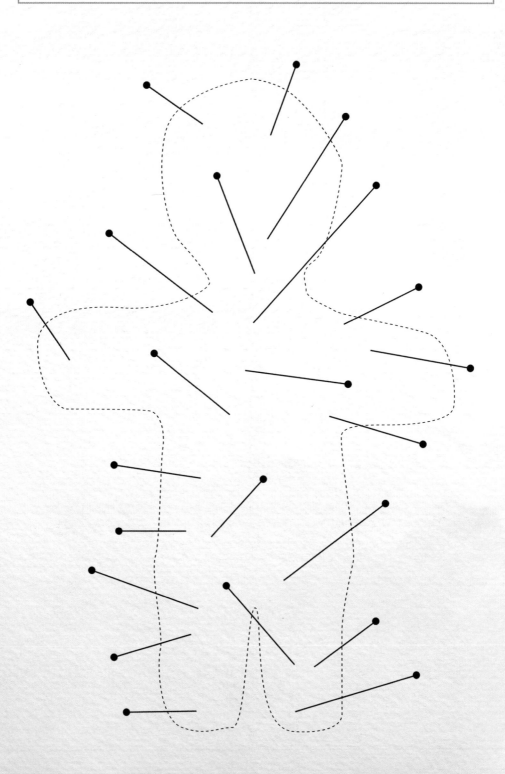

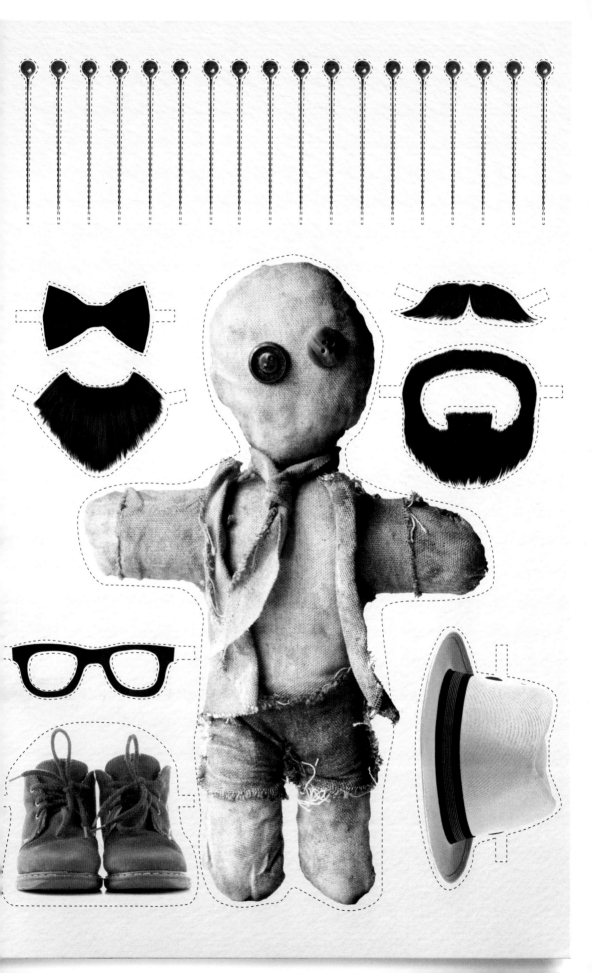

Poem
by Eliza Fantastic Mohan (age 16)

i want to be the girl in the bookstores with dark eyes and a cautious smile. black shoes that click and clack along the dirty floors, you could've sworn they paint the boards charcoal. i want to be the girl who cries alone in art museums and leans against great oak trees. she scribbled in her leather journal with the pages all crinkled and bare and tucks her thick hair behind her ears smiling to herself and chuckling at the breeze and the secrets whispered between her and the trees. she is alone and never lonely, music follows her like a shadow and love hits her like sunlight inescapable and overwhelming and suddenly unnoticeable in the picture of beauty created in its stead. she fixes her collar in the reflection written on marble walls and smiles at strangers with stationary lips. her skirt swishes as she walks and hums into the autumn air, her fingers trace the trails of wind and the after of a rainstorm, heels crunching freshly fallen leaves turned a rich pumpkin tone by the simple passage of time. the sun is setting and gold drowns her features and gleams in her eyes. And she is tired and alive and the history of people she'll never know is sewn between her fingers and webbed between her toes and the metal of rings passed down aches her mortal bones. Her fingers are eager for paper cuts and her eyes heavy for sleep, ears hunger for music and mouth craves release. She is full of stories and empty of adventure, but she'll get there someday and someday she'll know her worth from head to toe. But until then she works tirelessly to untie the knot in her bones and wishes on stars that will someday grow cold and hopes against hopes she'll have fun in the next world.

Wind Chime Haiku
By Emily Powell (age 16)

They don't look like much,
Just some old pipes tied to strings,
And perhaps they are.

MINISTRY OF
TROUBLE

CREDITS: ISSUE #4

CREATORS CHELSEA CAIN & LIA MITERNIQUE
WRITER CHELSEA CAIN
COVER ARTIST & GRAPHIC DESIGNER LIA MITERNIQUE
ARTISTS KATE NIEMCZYK AND LIA MITERNIQUE
COLORIST RACHELLE ROSENBERG
LETTERER JOE CARAMAGNA
SUPPLEMENTAL BACKGROUND INKER ANIA SZERSZEN
POEMS & POST-IT LETTERING ELIZA FANTASTIC MOHAN
HAIKU EMILY POWELL
ADDITIONAL INTERIOR ART STELLA GREENVOSS
ADULT HANDWRITING MARY JO BIERIG

YOU HAVE BEEN CONTACTED BY THE MINISTRY OF TROUBLE. AWAIT FURTHER INSTRUCTIONS. ⚲

WHISPERING WINDS

CHARMING CHIMES AND MEANINGFUL MEMORIES

FIND US IN THE HISTORIC WIND CHIME DISTRICT

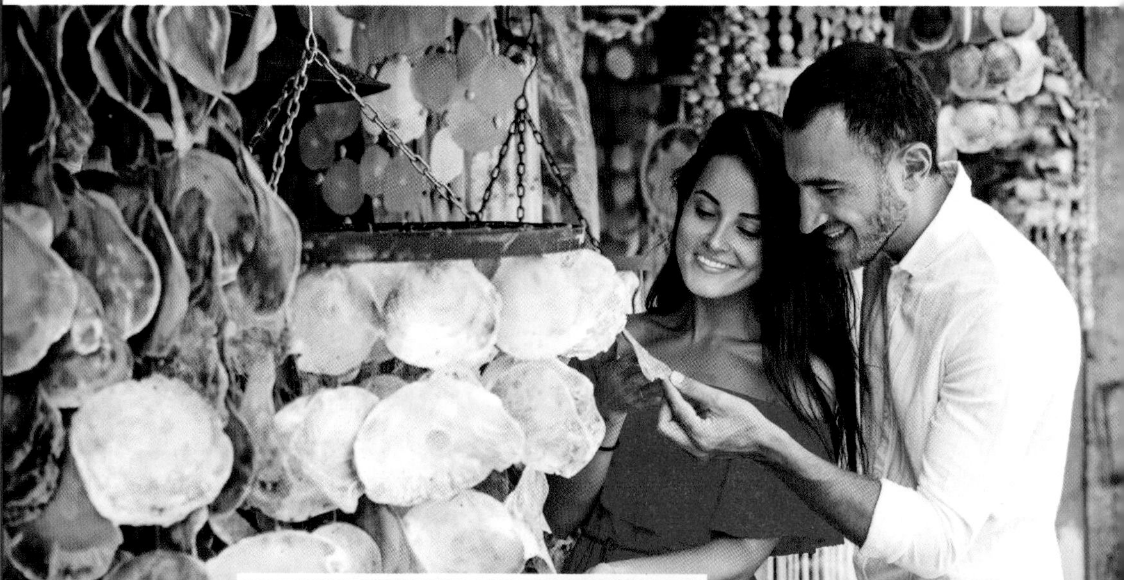

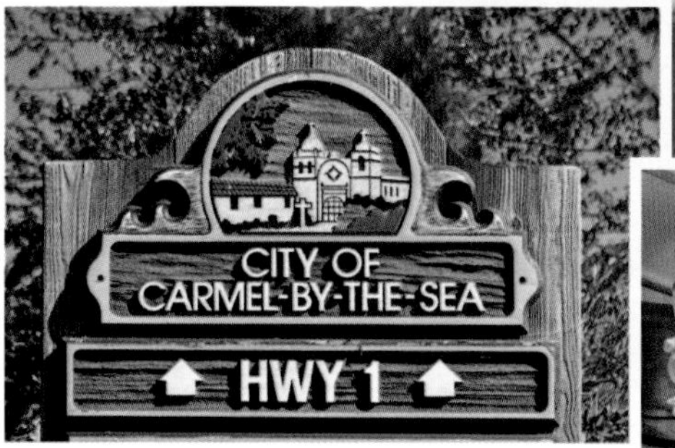
CITY OF
CARMEL-BY-THE-SEA
HWY 1

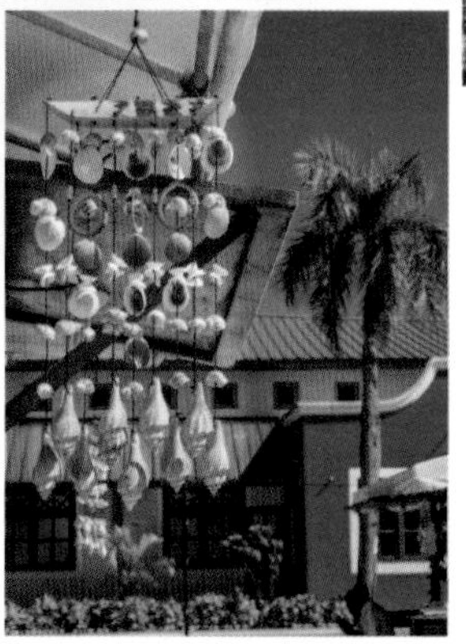

Whispering Winds is one of the oldest wind chime shoppes in Carmel-by-the-Sea's Historic Wind Chime District. Family-owned and locally sourced, Whispering Winds offers artisan-made wind chimes using materials from the Central California coast.

NOTHING IS MORE ROMANTIC THAN A WIND CHIME.

Whispering Winds uses only sustainable found-objects.
All wind chimes are hand-made. Quality guaranteed. No refunds.

[Issue 4, Cover B]

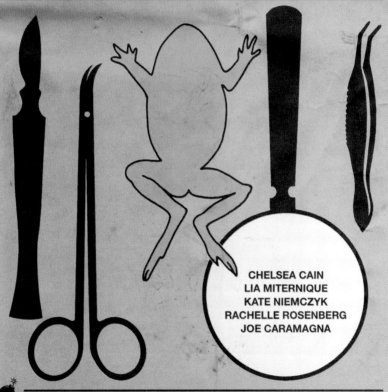

EXPLORING WITH PROBE AND SCALPEL

MAN-EATERS: THE CURSED

SPECIAL PROJECTS FOR ADVANCED STUDY

CHELSEA CAIN
LIA MITERNIQUE
KATE NIEMCZYK
RACHELLE ROSENBERG
JOE CARAMAGNA

Fourth Issue

Chapter 5

man-eaters:

The Cursed

Chelsea Cain Lia Miternique Kate Niemczyk Rachelle Rosenberg Joe Caramagna

NO. 5

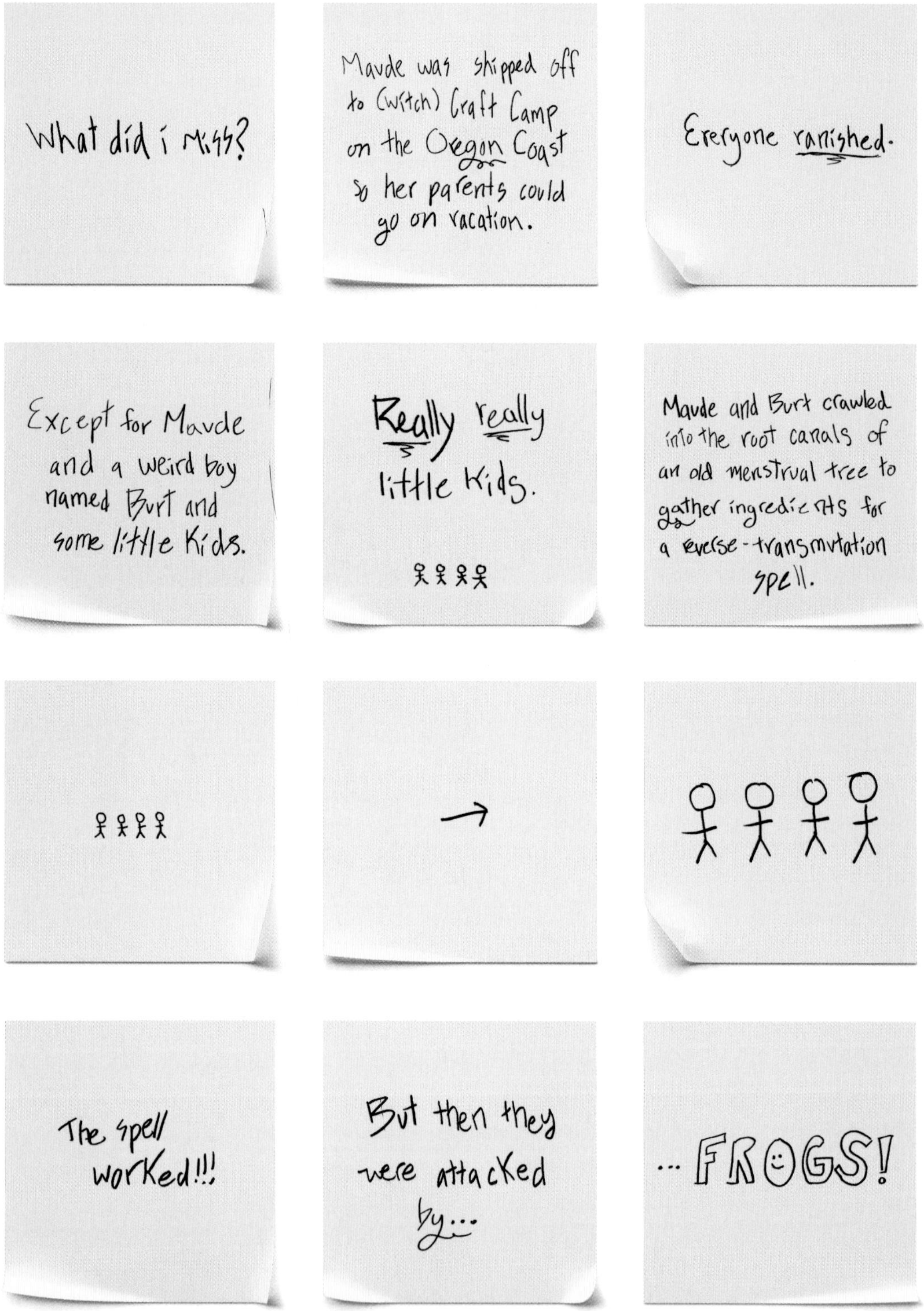
What did i miss?
Maude was shipped off to (witch) Craft Camp on the Oregon Coast so her parents could go on vacation.
Everyone vanished.
Except for Maude and a weird boy named Burt and some little kids.
Really really little kids.
Maude and Burt crawled into the root canals of an old menstrual tree to gather ingredients for a reverse-transmutation spell.
The spell worked!!!
But then they were attacked by...
...FROGS!

MINISTRY OF TROUBLE

CREDITS: ISSUE #5

CREATORS CHELSEA CAIN & LIA MITERNIQUE
WRITER CHELSEA CAIN
COVER ARTIST & GRAPHIC DESIGNER LIA MITERNIQUE
ARTISTS KATE NIEMCZYK AND LIA MITERNIQUE
COLORIST RACHELLE ROSENBERG
LETTERER JOE CARAMAGNA
FROG REPORT & POST-IT LETTERING ELIZA FANTASTIC MOHAN

YOU HAVE BEEN CONTACTED BY THE MINISTRY OF TROUBLE. AWAIT FURTHER INSTRUCTIONS. ☿

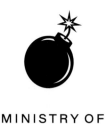

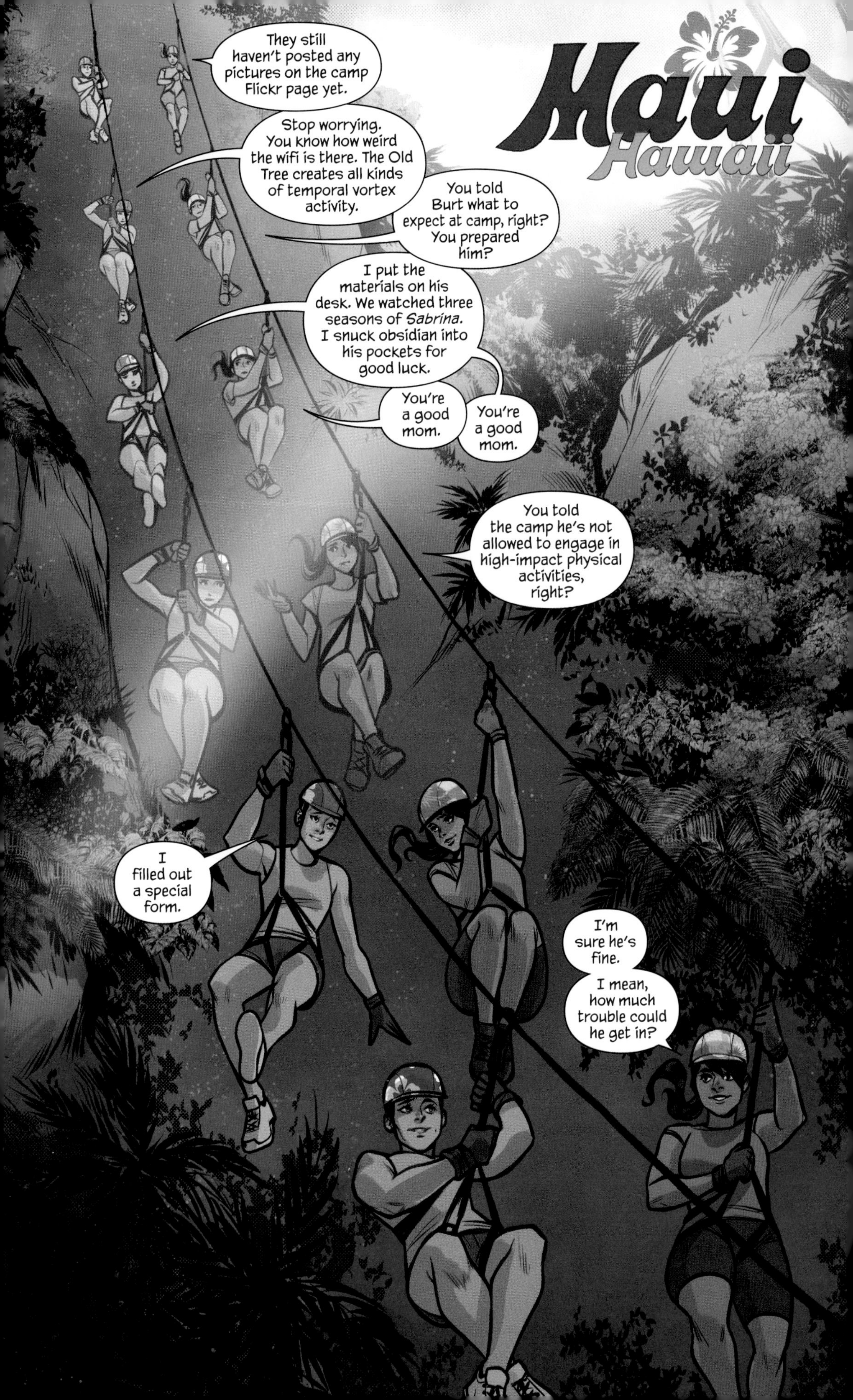
Maui
Hawaii
They still haven't posted any pictures on the camp Flickr page yet.
Stop worrying. You know how weird the wifi is there. The Old Tree creates all kinds of temporal vortex activity.
You told Burt what to expect at camp, right? You prepared him?
I put the materials on his desk. We watched three seasons of *Sabrina*. I snuck obsidian into his pockets for good luck.
You're a good mom.
You're a good mom.
You told the camp he's not allowed to engage in high-impact physical activities, right?
I filled out a special form.
I'm sure he's fine.
I mean, how much trouble could he get in?

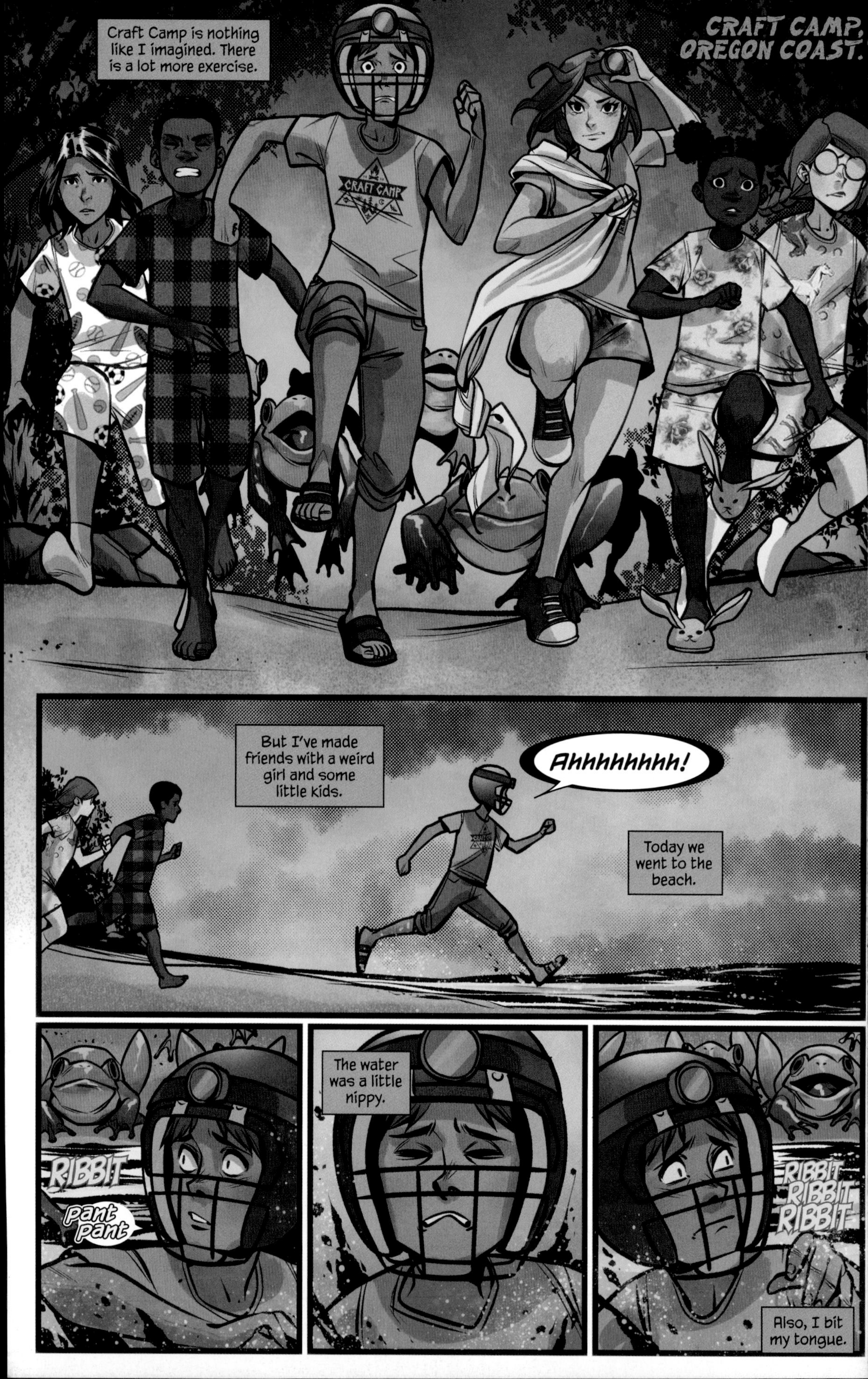
Craft Camp is nothing like I imagined. There is a lot more exercise.
CRAFT CAMP, OREGON COAST.
CRAFT CAMP
But I've made friends with a weird girl and some little kids.
Ahhhhhhhh!
Today we went to the beach.
RIBBIT
pant pant
The water was a little nippy.
RIBBIT RIBBIT RIBBIT
Also, I bit my tongue.

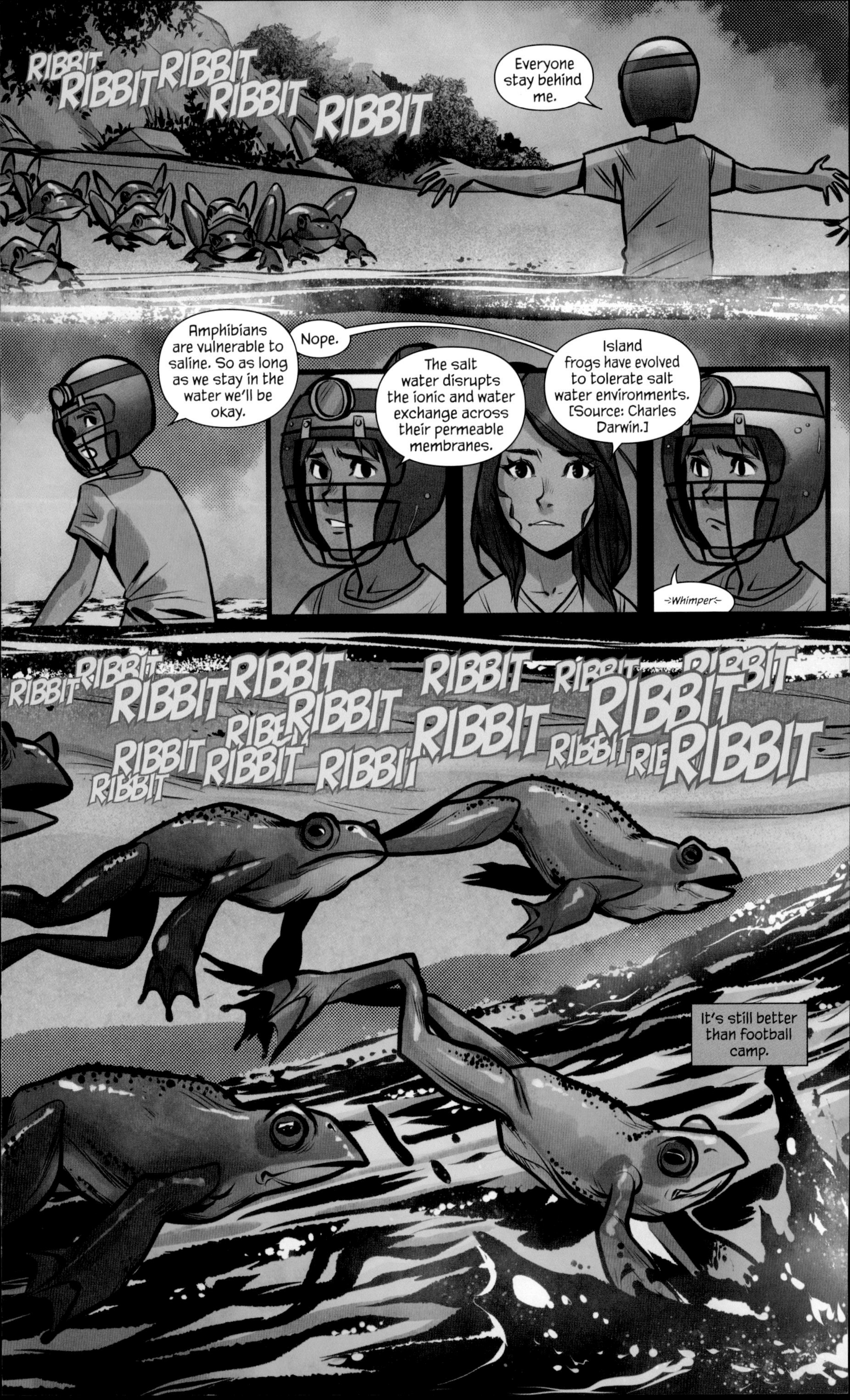
RIBBIT
RIBBIT
RIBBIT
RIBBIT
RIBBIT
Everyone stay behind me.
Amphibians are vulnerable to saline. So as long as we stay in the water we'll be okay.
The salt water disrupts the ionic and water exchange across their permeable membranes.
Nope.
Island frogs have evolved to tolerate salt water environments. [Source: Charles Darwin.]
Whimper
RIBBIT
RIBBIT
RIBBIT
RIBBIT
RIBBIT
RIBBIT
RIBBIT
RIBBIT
RIBBIT
RIBBIT
RIBBIT
It's still better than football camp.

Frogs

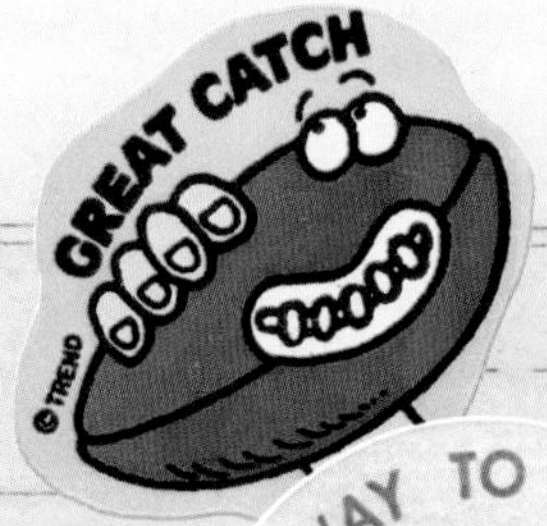

GREAT CATCH
© TREND

by Burt Y.

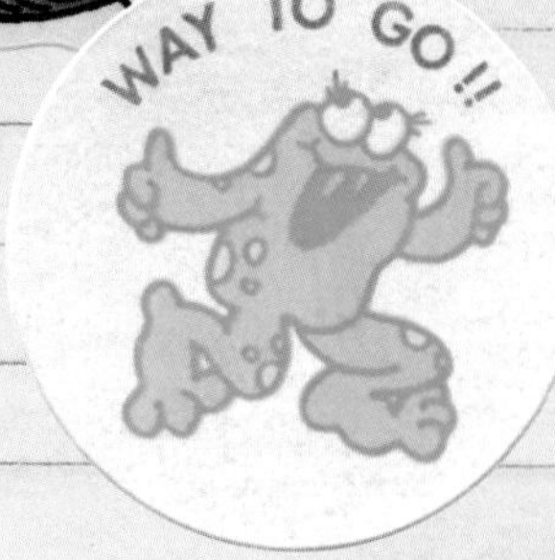

WAY TO GO !!

I don't like frogs.
They are green.
They are slip-
pery. They have
scary eys.

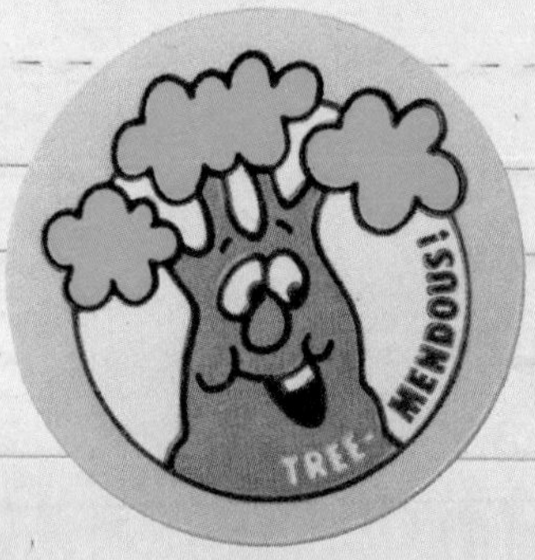

TREE-MENDOUS!

REPORT ON FROGS
by: Maude W.

Frogs are defined as being any short-bodied, tailless amphibian. The most popular habitat for frogs is a tropical rainforest, but they can live in a great variety of terrains, from the hottest climates to places of ice and freezing rain. Frogs come in all shapes, sizes and colors, ranging from smooth and sleek to covered in warts and various liquids. The smallest species of frog is only the size of a dime, while the largest (now extinct) frog was 16 inches long and weighed ten pounds. Frogs belong to the kingdom Anamilia, the class Amphibia, the order Anura, and the superclass Tetrapoda.

Most species of frogs lay their eggs in a source of water, which then hatch into larvae, otherwise known as tadpoles. Tadpoles look very different from the frogs they will grow into. Tadpoles have oval bodies with long, flattened tails and internal gills. These tadpoles exclusively reside in aquatic environments, with the exception of one species of frog, whose tadpoles develop along wet rocks. Much of a tadpole's body is made of soft tissue, so the transformation takes less time. As they develop, tadpoles will feed on certain aquatic plants and herbs such as algae and proteins in the water itself. However, the Cuban Tree Frog hatches tadpoles that can show cannibalistic behavior, but this is a unique phenomenon. Tadpoles eventually experience metamorphosis, a 24-hour period in which they will develop fully into frogs. This occurs when a tadpole produces a hormone known as thyroxine. Tadpoles will replace their gills with lungs, reveal fully grown legs, their shape will transition to more of the well known stout size of a frog, they grow eyelids to cover their bugging, differently positioned eyeballs, and they also develop ears and various ear systems, among many other important changes.

Once this transition is complete, the fully developed frog will take on a carnivorous diet, ranging from worms and slugs to fish, small mammals, and even other frogs. Frogs will consume their prey using differing techniques depending on their habitat and bodies, some will use their hands to physically capture the food and put it into their mouths, while some will use their sticky tongues to capture flying prey. On the food pyramid, frogs are classified as primary predators, and are essential to a lot of ecosystems. Most of the energy they consume is passed back into the ecosystem, keeping it perfectly balanced.

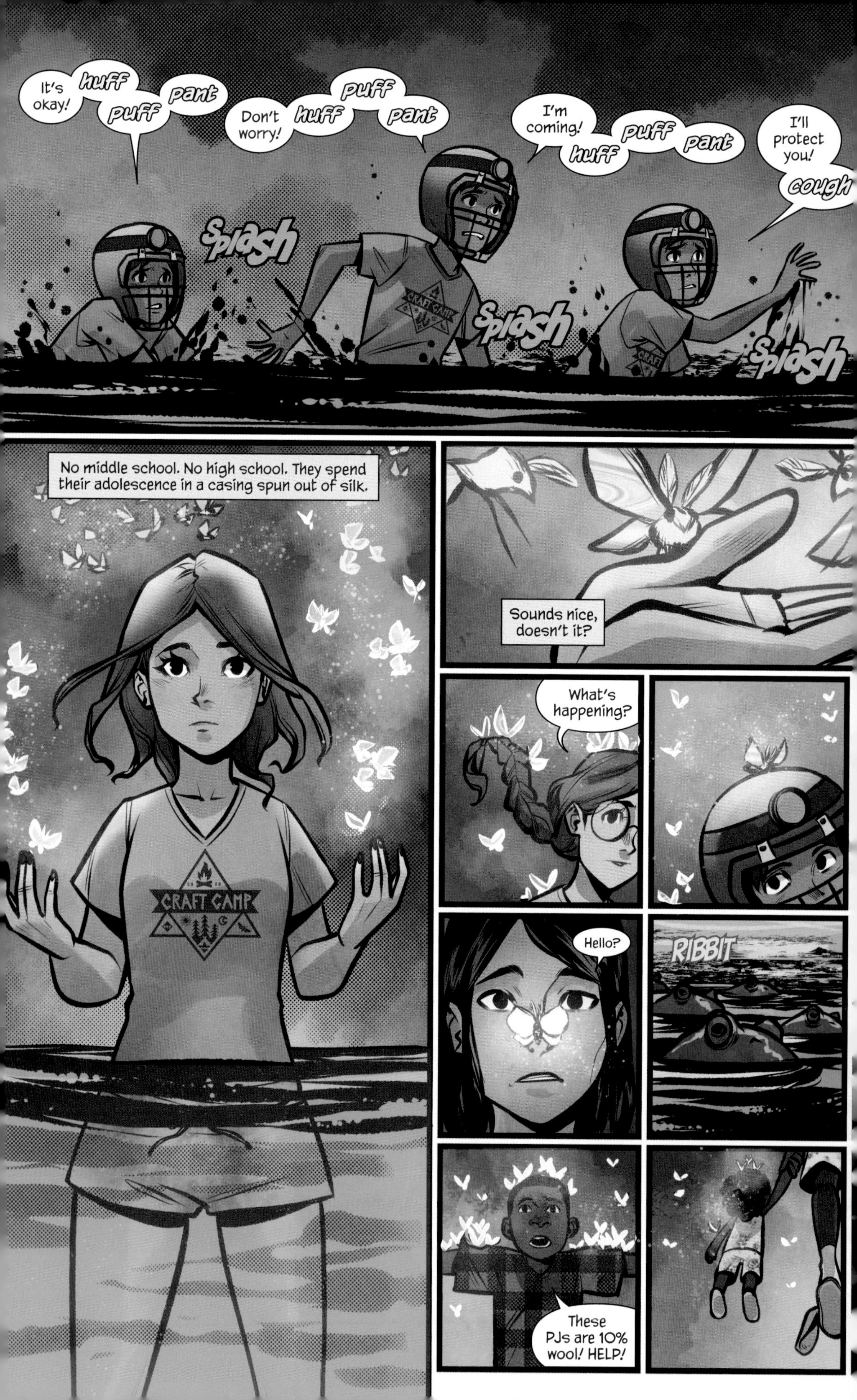
It's okay!
huff
puff
pant
Don't worry!
huff
puff
pant
I'm coming!
huff
puff
pant
I'll protect you!
cough
SPLASH
SPLASH
SPLASH
No middle school. No high school. They spend their adolescence in a casing spun out of silk.
CRAFT CAMP
Sounds nice, doesn't it?
What's happening?
Hello?
RIBBIT
These PJs are 10% wool! HELP!

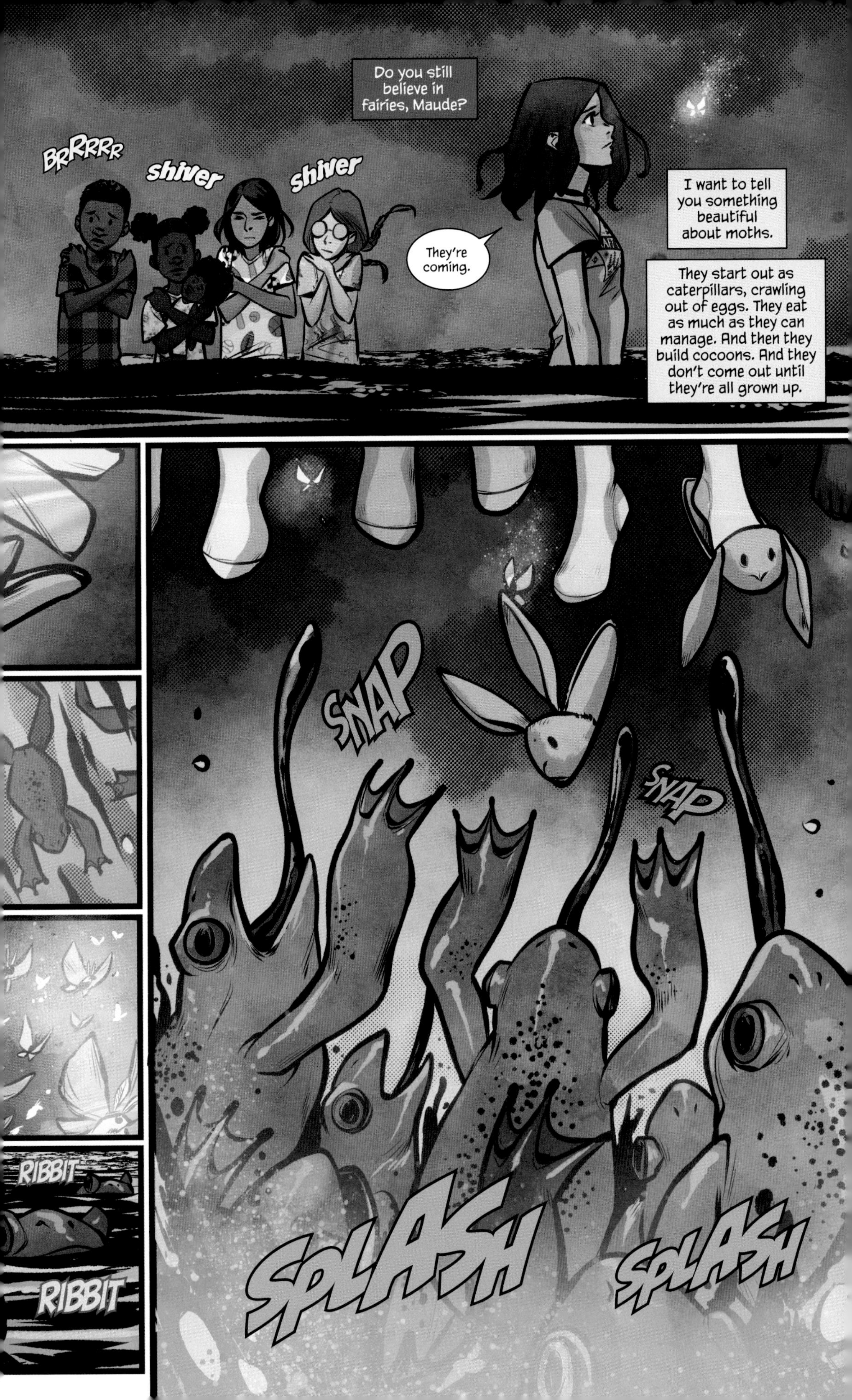

Do you still believe in fairies, Maude?
BRRRRR
shiver
shiver
They're coming.
I want to tell you something beautiful about moths.
They start out as caterpillars, crawling out of eggs. They eat as much as they can manage. And then they build cocoons. And they don't come out until they're all grown up.
SNAP
SNAP
RIBBIT
RIBBIT
SPLASH
SPLASH

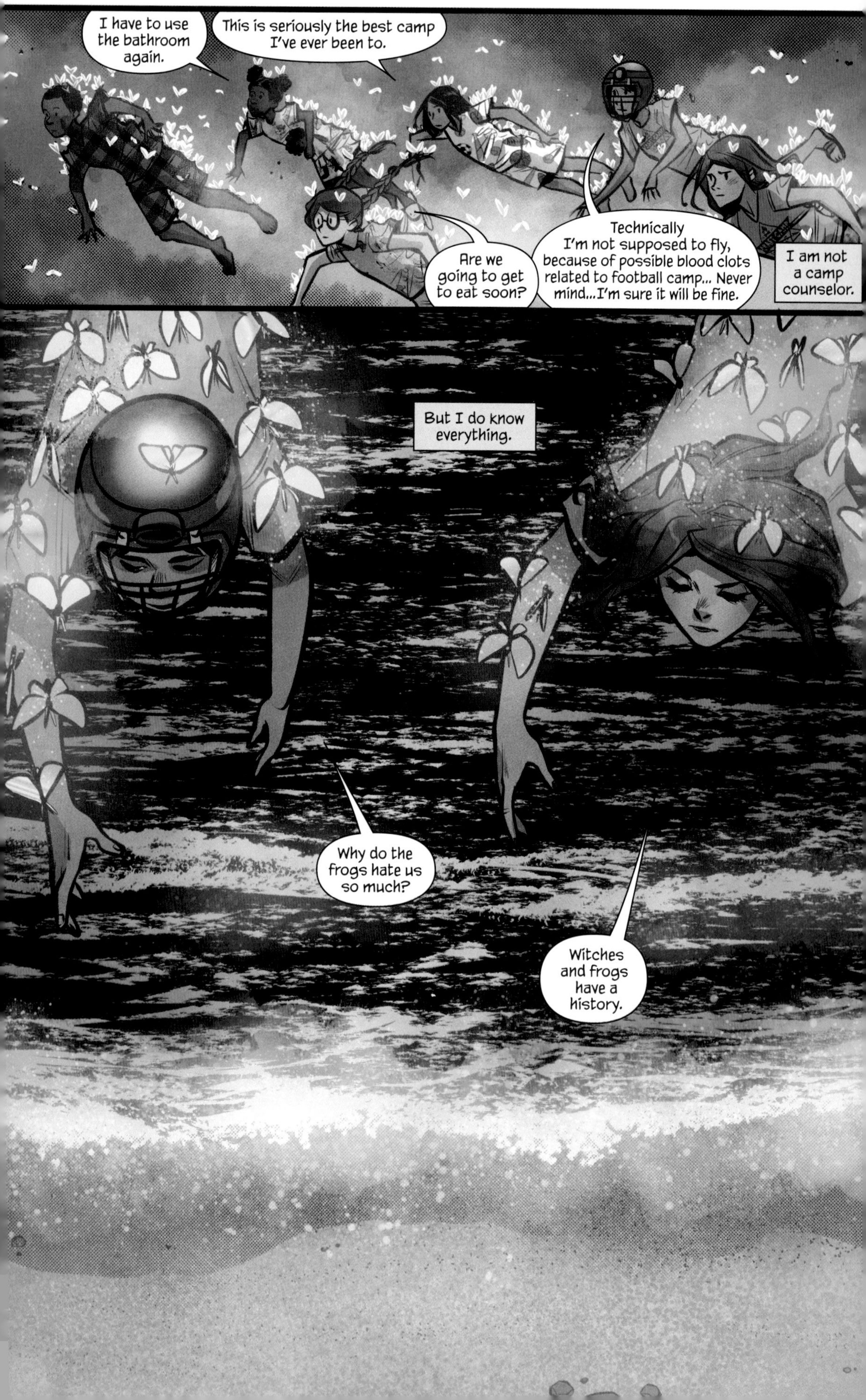
I have to use the bathroom again.
This is seriously the best camp I've ever been to.
Are we going to get to eat soon?
Technically I'm not supposed to fly, because of possible blood clots related to football camp... Never mind...I'm sure it will be fine.
I am not a camp counselor.
But I do know everything.
Why do the frogs hate us so much?
Witches and frogs have a history.

POTION SUPPLIES: FROGS

PAGE 4 OF 12

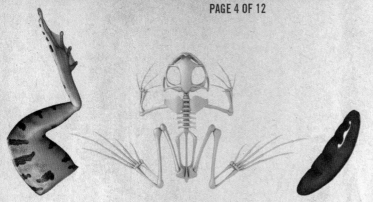

FROG LEG (LEFT)
$1 for 3 legs

FROG SKELETON
$6.25 each, limit 7

FROG KIDNEY
$2.50 each, fresh or frozen

FROG LEG (RIGHT)
$1 for 3 legs

FROG HEART
$6.29 each

FROG HANDS (2)
$2.50 for pair

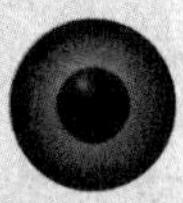

FROG EYE (RED)
$12.35 each

EYES (ASSORTED)
$5.60 (includes 4, no red)

FROG GALL BLADDER
$.25 per dozen

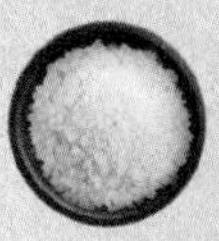

DRIED FROG BELLY
$.65 / ounce

CLOACAL APERTURE
FREE with any purchase

TADPOLE
$1.50 each

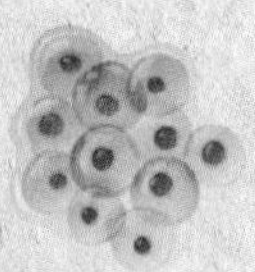

FROG EGGS (PHASE 1)
$.25 per dozen

FROG BLOOD
$2.25 for 12 fl.oz.

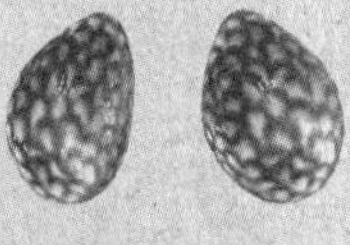

FROG LUNGS (2)
$8.69

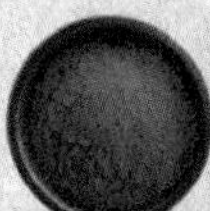

GROUND ORGAN MIX
$.75 / ounce

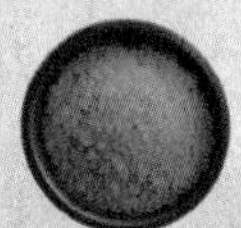

FROG BILE POWDER
$1.25 / ounce

FROG LIVER
$6.90 each

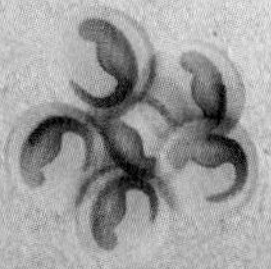

FROG EGGS (PHASE 2)
$.50 per dozen

FROG INTESTINE
$.25 per dozen

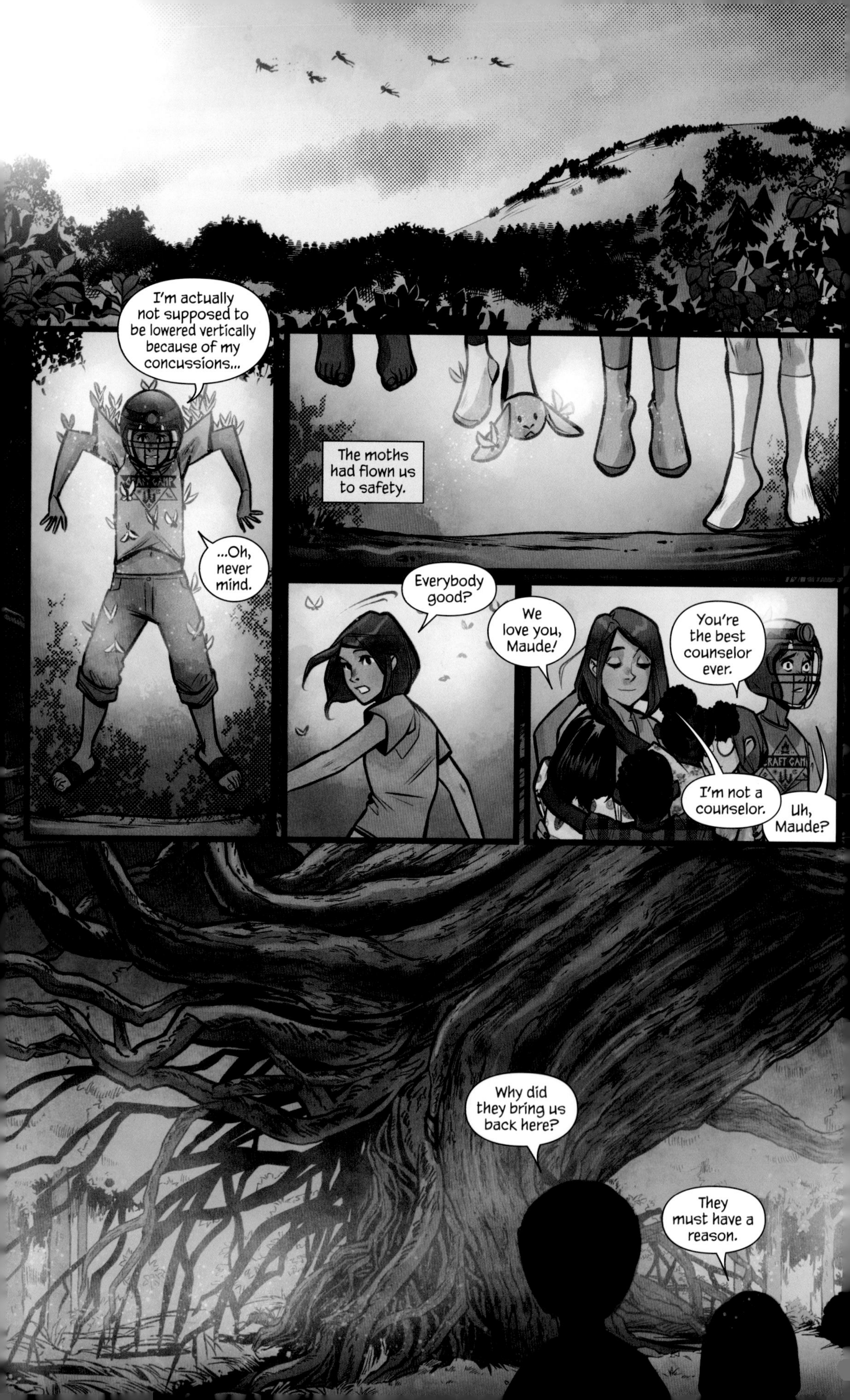
I'm actually not supposed to be lowered vertically because of my concussions...
...Oh, never mind.
The moths had flown us to safety.
Everybody good?
We love you, Maude!
You're the best counselor ever.
I'm not a counselor.
Uh, Maude?
Why did they bring us back here?
They must have a reason.

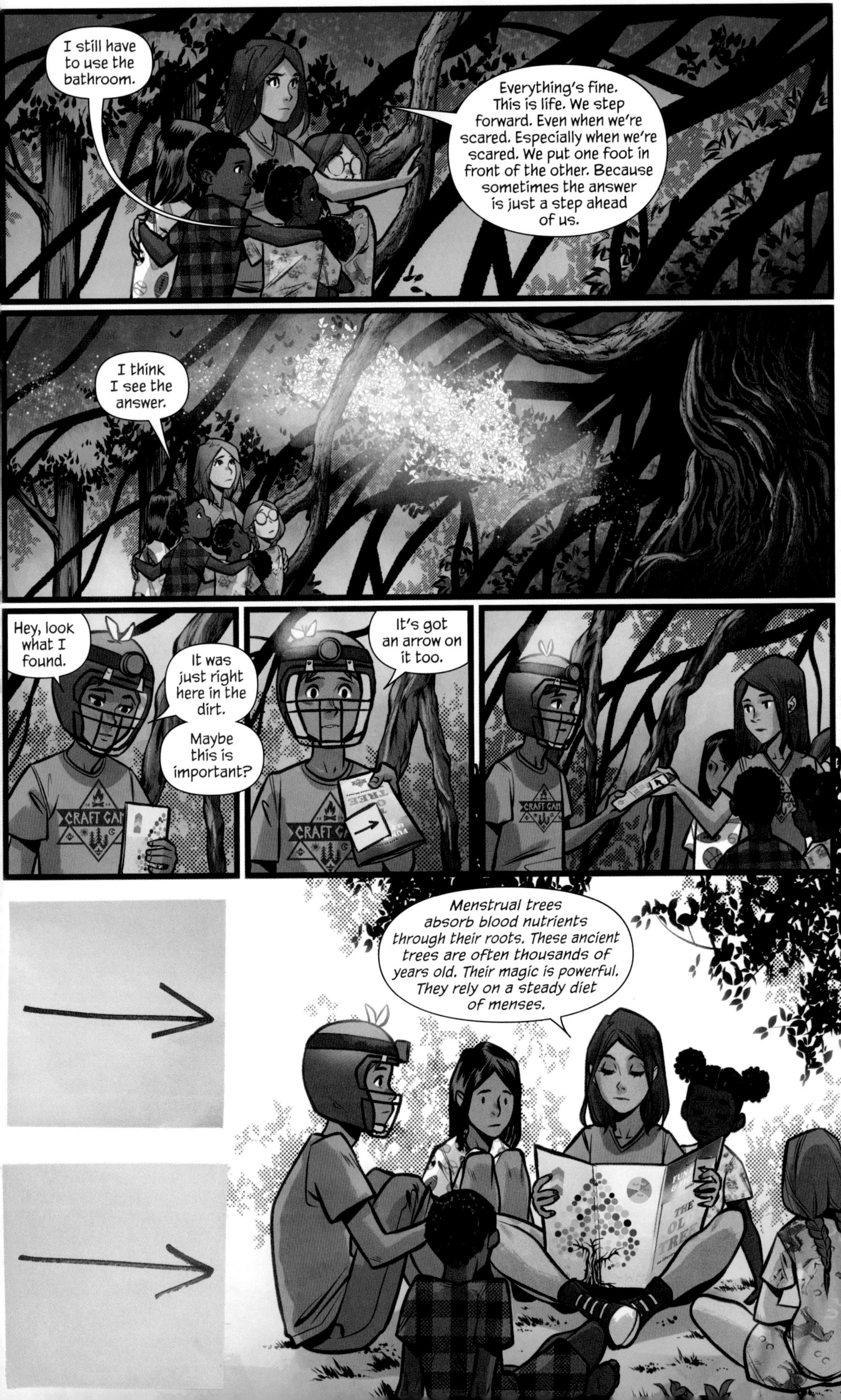
I still have to use the bathroom.
Everything's fine. This is life. We step forward. Even when we're scared. Especially when we're scared. We put one foot in front of the other. Because sometimes the answer is just a step ahead of us.
I think I see the answer.
Hey, look what I found.
It was just right here in the dirt.
Maybe this is important?
It's got an arrow on it too.
Menstrual trees absorb blood nutrients through their roots. These ancient trees are often thousands of years old. Their magic is powerful. They rely on a steady diet of menses.

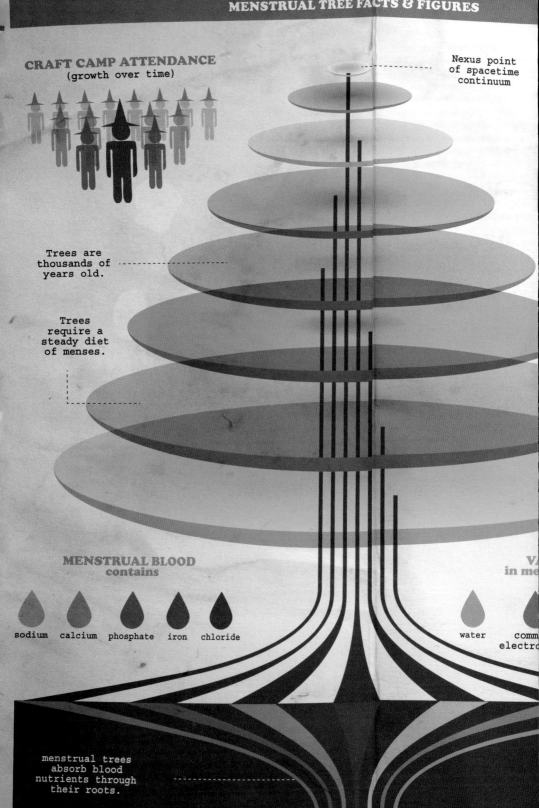

CRAFT CAMP ATTENDANCE
(growth over time)

Nexus point
of spacetime
continuum

Trees are
thousands of
years old.

Trees
require a
steady diet
of menses.

MENSTRUAL BLOOD
contains

sodium   calcium   phosphate   iron   chloride

VA
in me

water   comm
electro

menstrual trees
absorb blood
nutrients through
their roots.

MENSTRUAL FLUID
50%
blood
50%
cervical mucus,
vaginal secretions,
endometrial tissue
AL FLUIDS
nainly contain
organ
moieties
at least
14 proteins
including
glycoproteins
PROTEINS! PROTEINS! PROTEINS!
Menstrual
Blood
1,061
Total Proteins
[~36% Unique]
Venous Blood
1,774
Total Proteins
[~61% Unique]
Vaginal Fluid
823 Total Proteins
[~35% Unique]
GROWTH CHART
60
50
40
30
20
10
10
20
30
40
50
MENSTRUAL FLOW CHART
60
50
40
30
20
10
10
20
30
40
50
MENSTRUAL TREES AROUND THE WORLD

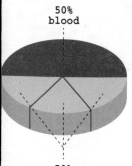

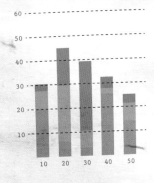

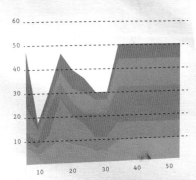

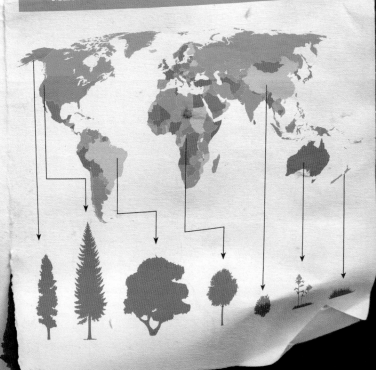

Well that explains the signs in all the outhouses.

I know what to do.

I *kind* of knew what to do.

It's important to project confidence.

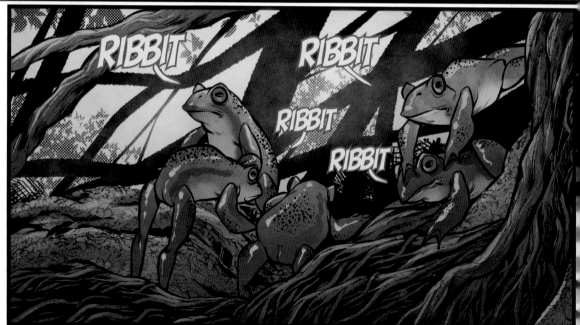

RIBBIT

RIBBIT

RIBBIT

RIBBIT

⚠ REMEMBER ⚠

PLEASE THROW ALL SANITARY PRODUCTS DOWN THE TOILETS

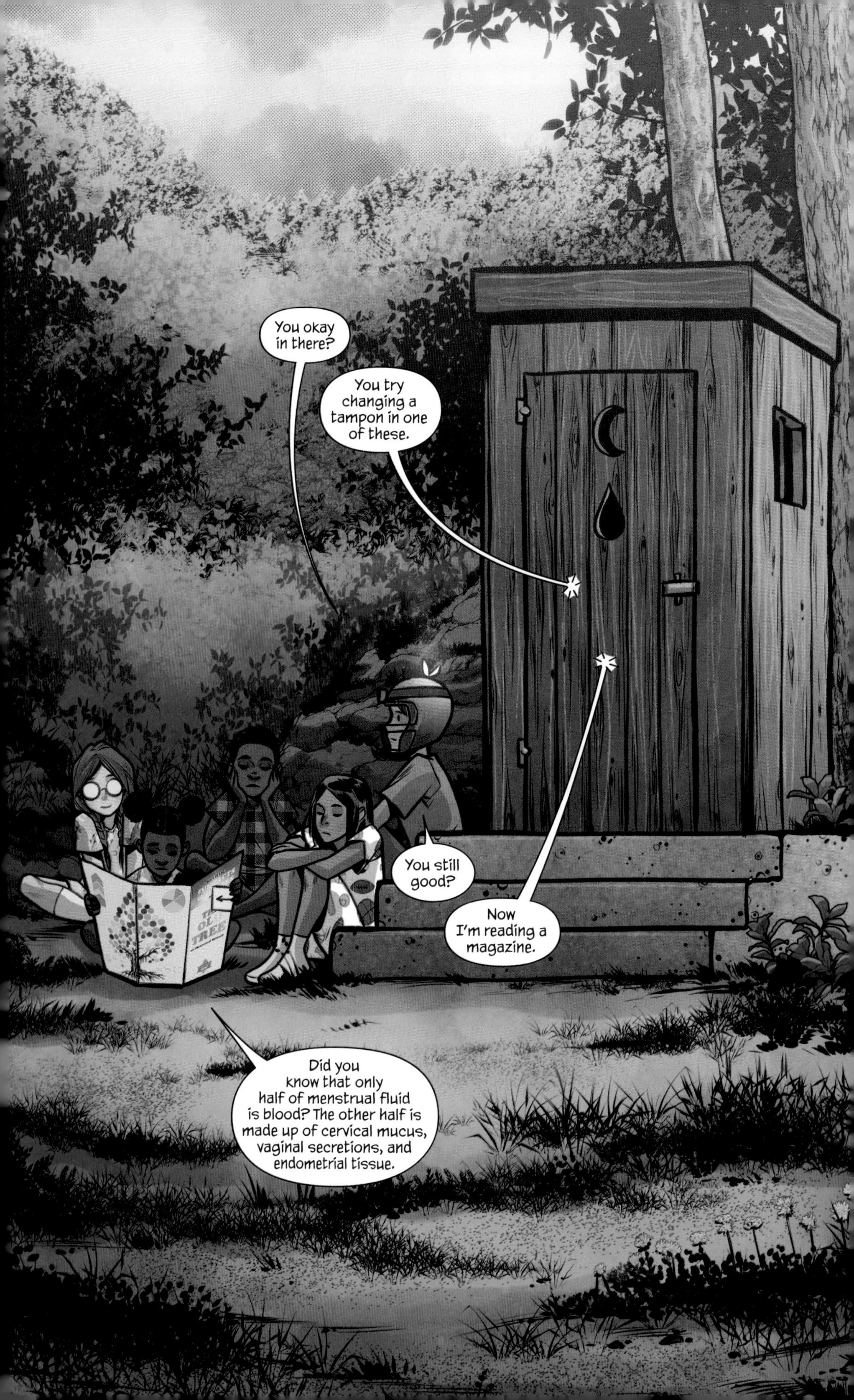
You okay in there?
You try changing a tampon in one of these.
You still good?
Now I'm reading a magazine.
Did you know that only half of menstrual fluid is blood? The other half is made up of cervical mucus, vaginal secretions, and endometrial tissue.

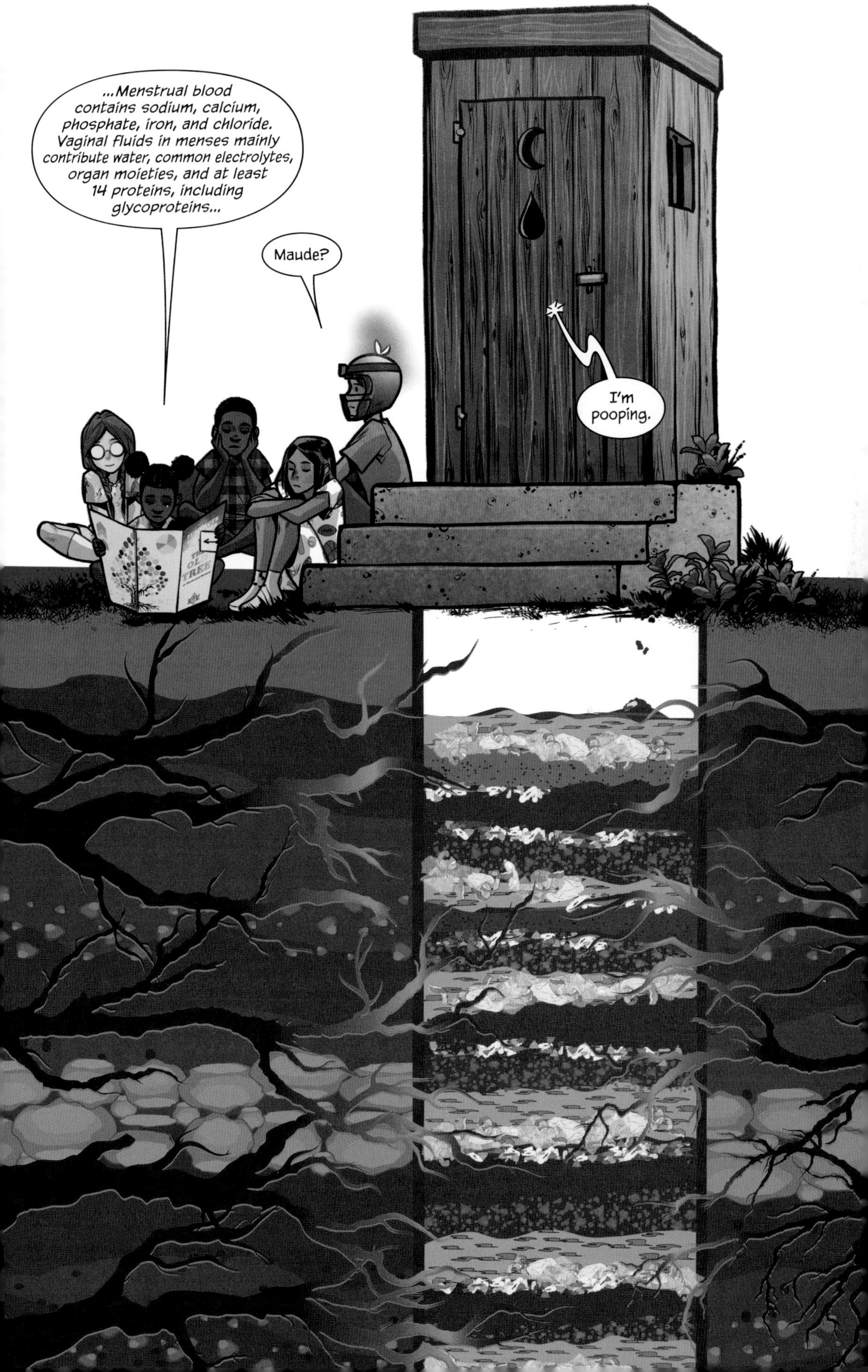
...Menstrual blood contains sodium, calcium, phosphate, iron, and chloride. Vaginal fluids in menses mainly contribute water, common electrolytes, organ moieties, and at least 14 proteins, including glycoproteins...
Maude?
I'm pooping.

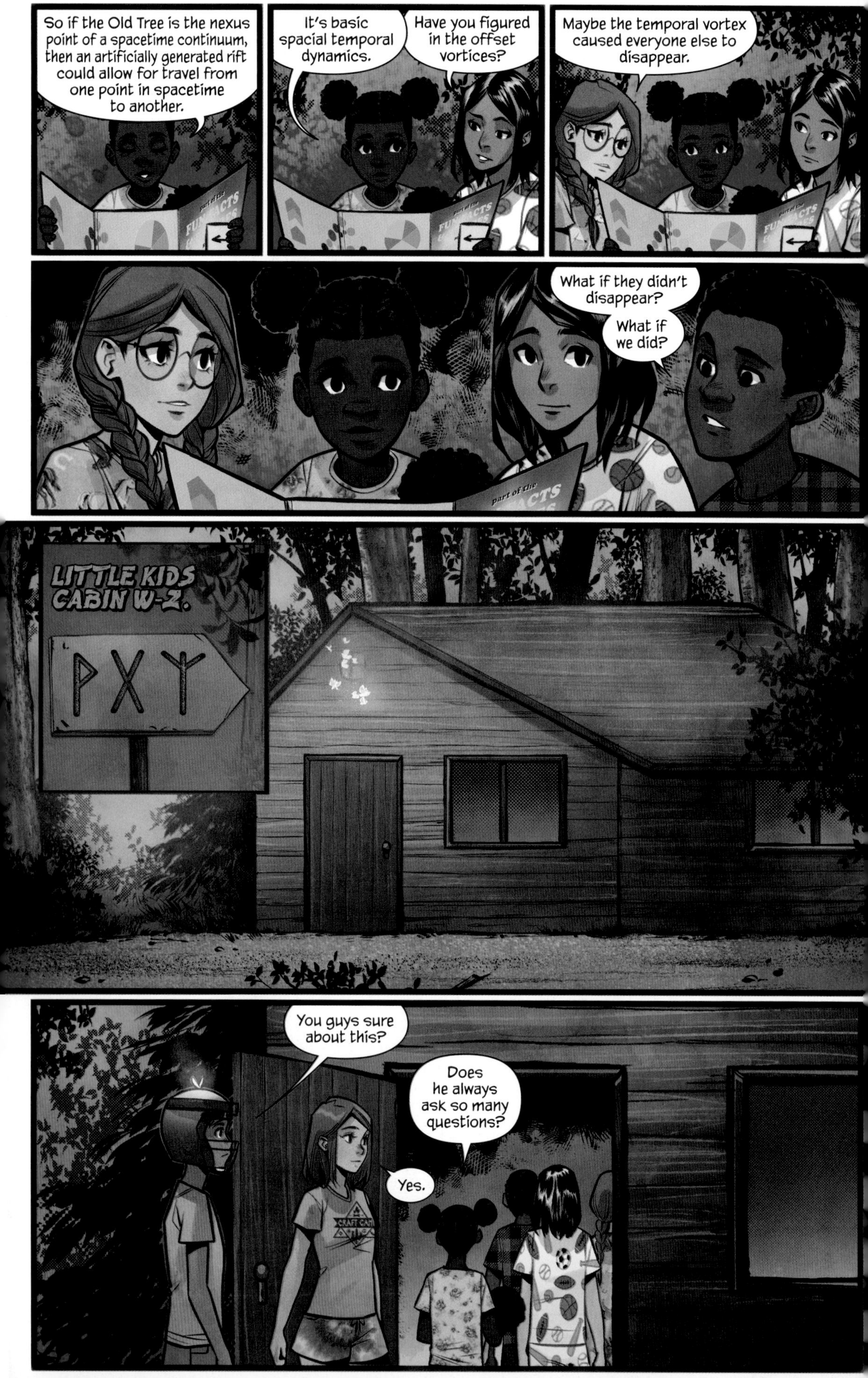
So if the Old Tree is the nexus point of a spacetime continuum, then an artificially generated rift could allow for travel from one point in spacetime to another.
It's basic spacial temporal dynamics.
Have you figured in the offset vortices?
Maybe the temporal vortex caused everyone else to disappear.
What if they didn't disappear?
What if we did?
LITTLE KIDS CABIN W-Z.
You guys sure about this?
Does he always ask so many questions?
Yes.

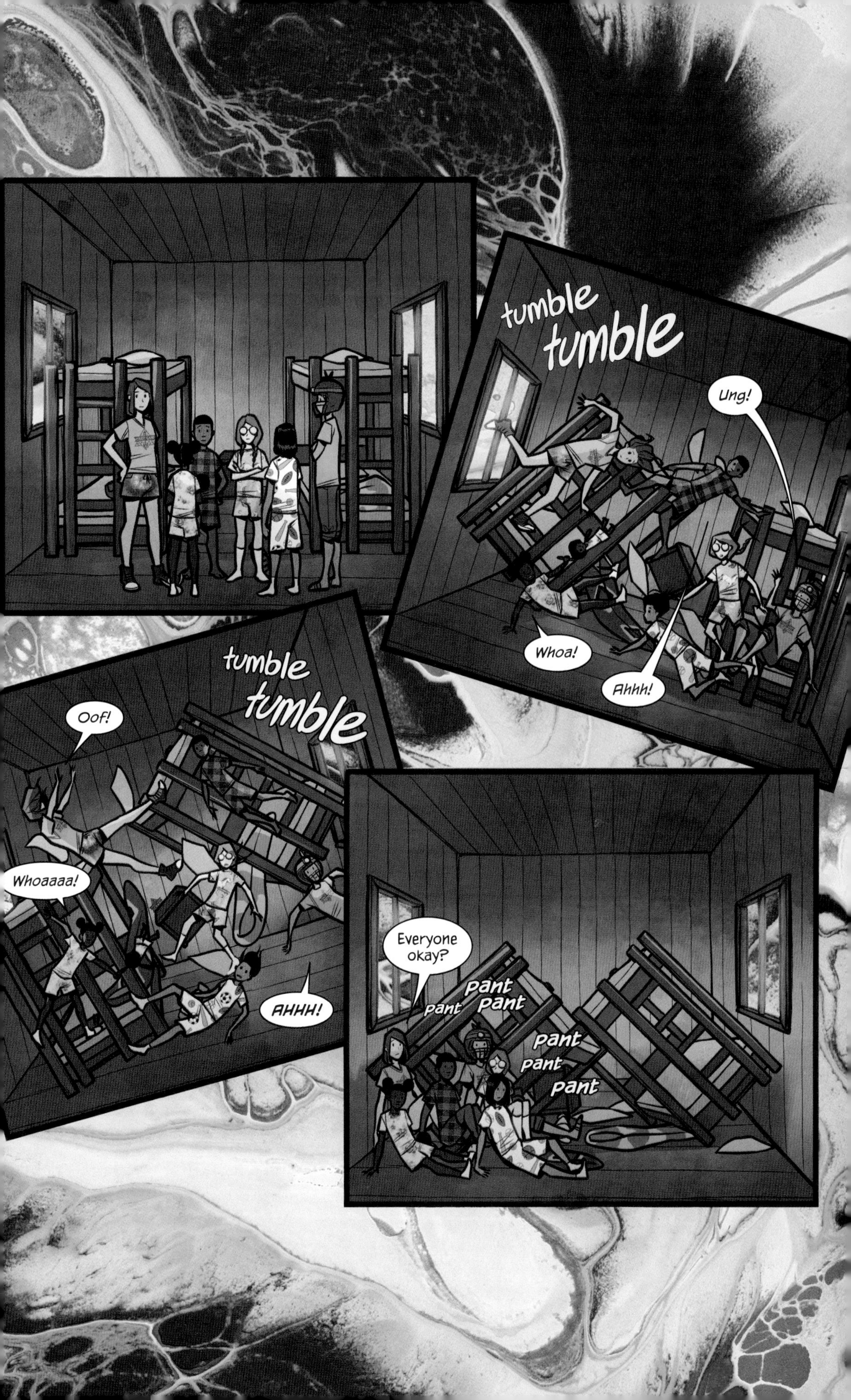
tumble
tumble
Ung!
Whoa!
Ahhh!
tumble
tumble
Oof!
Whoaaaa!
AHHH!
Everyone okay?
pant
pant
pant
pant
pant
pant

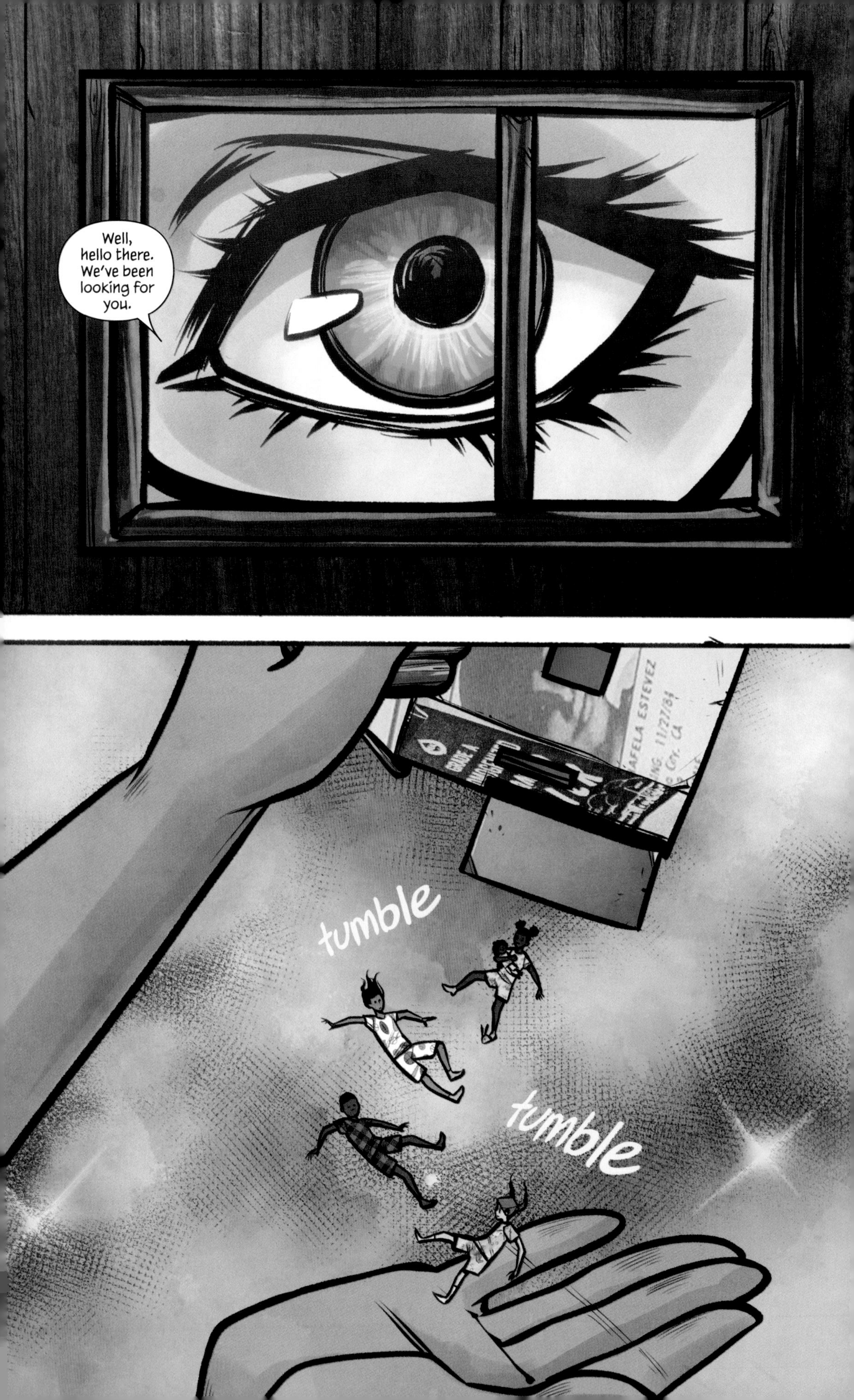
Well, hello there. We've been looking for you.
tumble
tumble

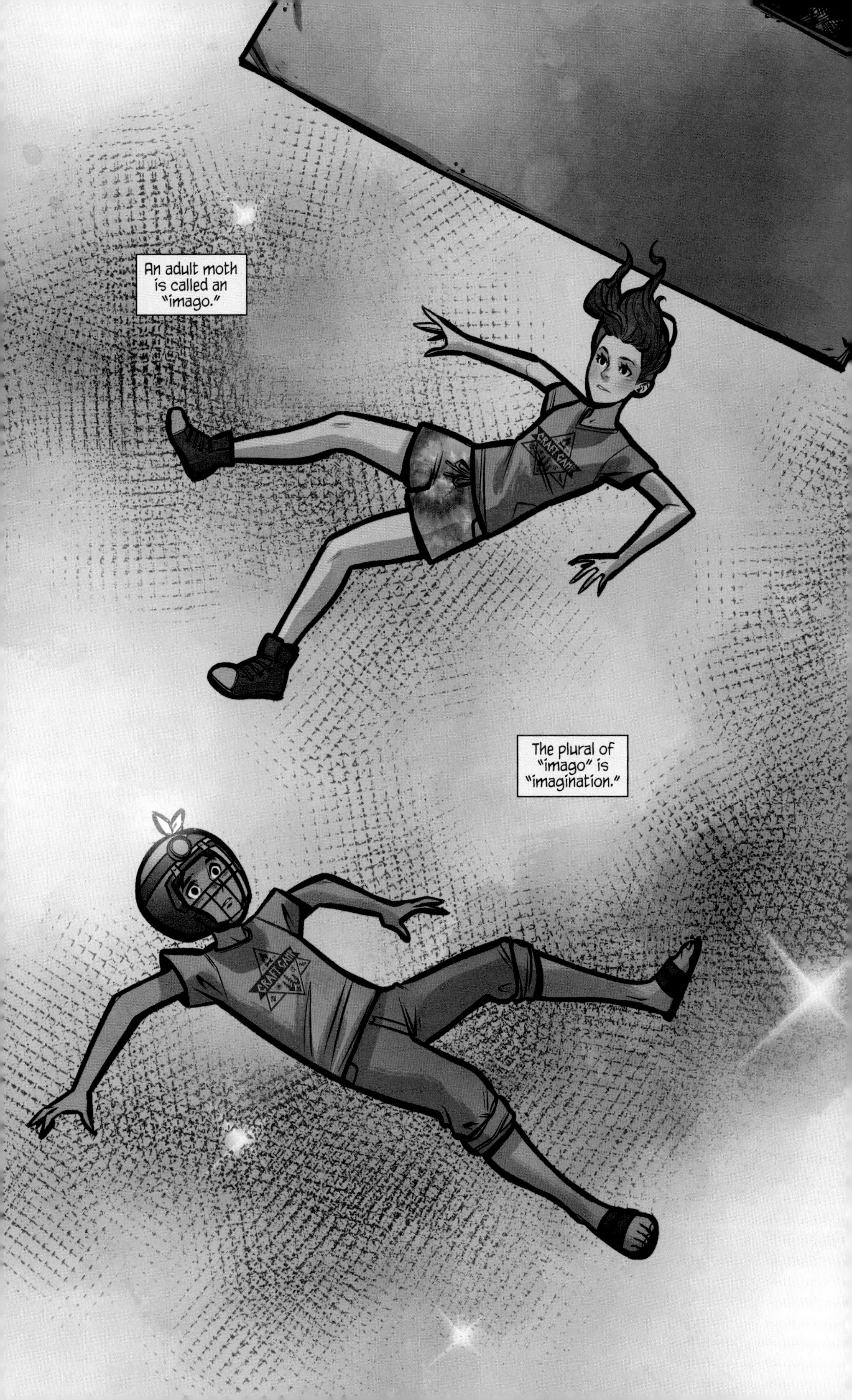
An adult moth is called an "imago."
The plural of "imago" is "imagination."

WOOOSH

Approximately 201 million years ago, Earth was transitioning from the Triassic to the Jurassic period. The world was shitty. A lot of dry heat. No flowers. Literally, flowers were not a thing yet. They did not exist. Picture dinosaurs. Picture a few creepy little mammals. And also picture moths. They were there. They evolved long before butterflies. Before flowers. Before wool sweater sets.

Fossils prove it.

Moths are badass.

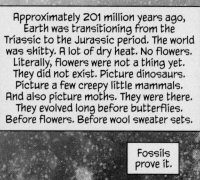

CRAFT CAMP SUMMER ACTIVITIES

Y	MONDAY	TUESDAY	WEDNESDAY	THURSDAY	FRIDAY	SATUR
	Monday manifestations/ journaling Archery Transfiguration lessons Making spells with glitter	Activism studies :) Hiking Beach day	Cabin cleaning Last overnight Arts + crafts	Journaling Spell jars Lunar meditation	Bottling memories Meditations Last campfire	Y

RECREATION DEPARTMENT

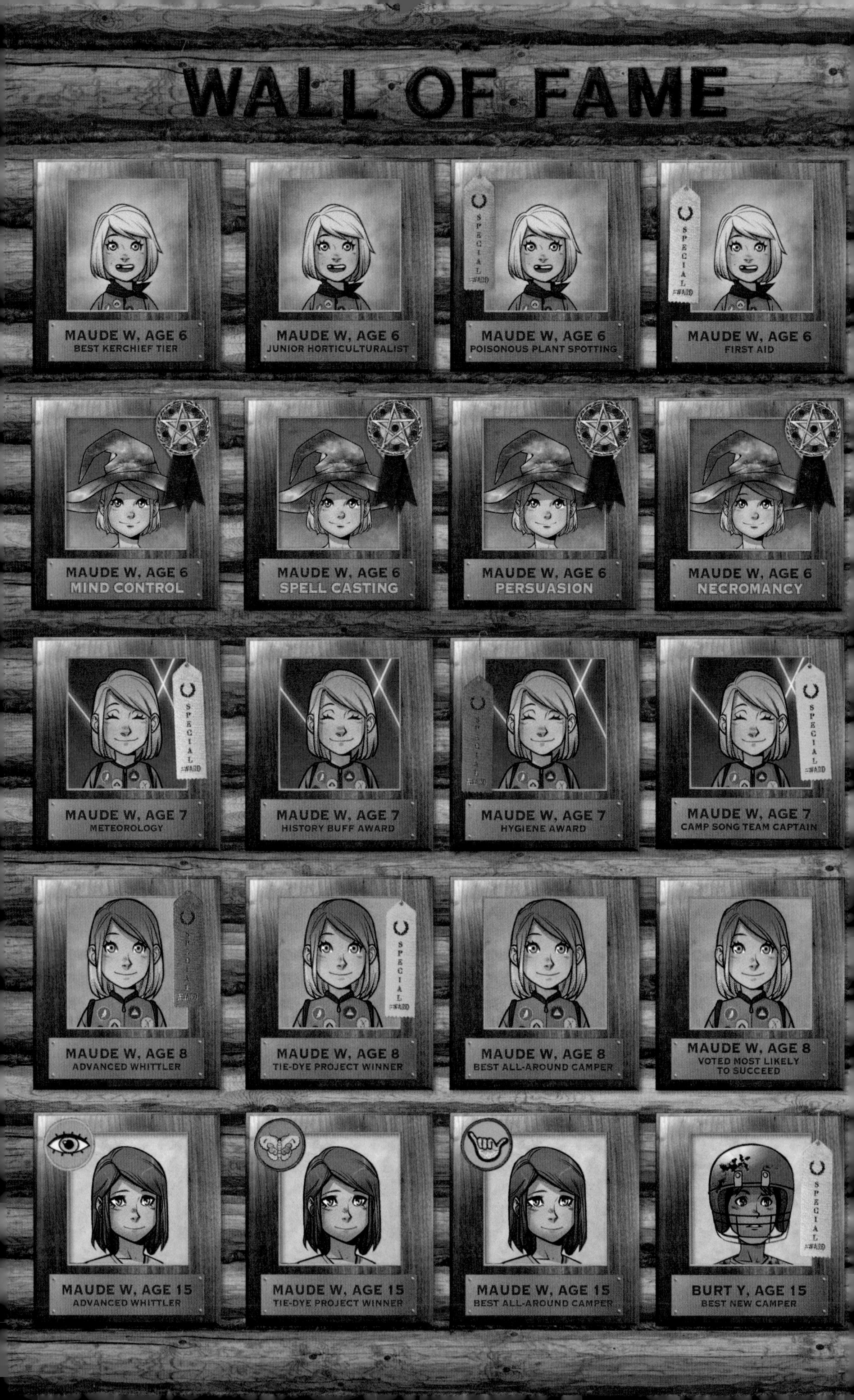

WALL OF FAME
MAUDE W, AGE 6
BEST KERCHIEF TIER
MAUDE W, AGE 6
JUNIOR HORTICULTURALIST
SPECIAL AWARD
MAUDE W, AGE 6
POISONOUS PLANT SPOTTING
SPECIAL AWARD
MAUDE W, AGE 6
FIRST AID
MAUDE W, AGE 6
MIND CONTROL
MAUDE W, AGE 6
SPELL CASTING
MAUDE W, AGE 6
PERSUASION
MAUDE W, AGE 6
NECROMANCY
SPECIAL AWARD
MAUDE W, AGE 7
METEOROLOGY
MAUDE W, AGE 7
HISTORY BUFF AWARD
SPECIAL AWARD
MAUDE W, AGE 7
HYGIENE AWARD
SPECIAL AWARD
MAUDE W, AGE 7
CAMP SONG TEAM CAPTAIN
SPECIAL AWARD
MAUDE W, AGE 8
ADVANCED WHITTLER
SPECIAL AWARD
MAUDE W, AGE 8
TIE-DYE PROJECT WINNER
MAUDE W, AGE 8
BEST ALL-AROUND CAMPER
MAUDE W, AGE 8
VOTED MOST LIKELY
TO SUCCEED
MAUDE W, AGE 15
ADVANCED WHITTLER
MAUDE W, AGE 15
TIE-DYE PROJECT WINNER
MAUDE W, AGE 15
BEST ALL-AROUND CAMPER
SPECIAL AWARD
BURT Y, AGE 15
BEST NEW CAMPER

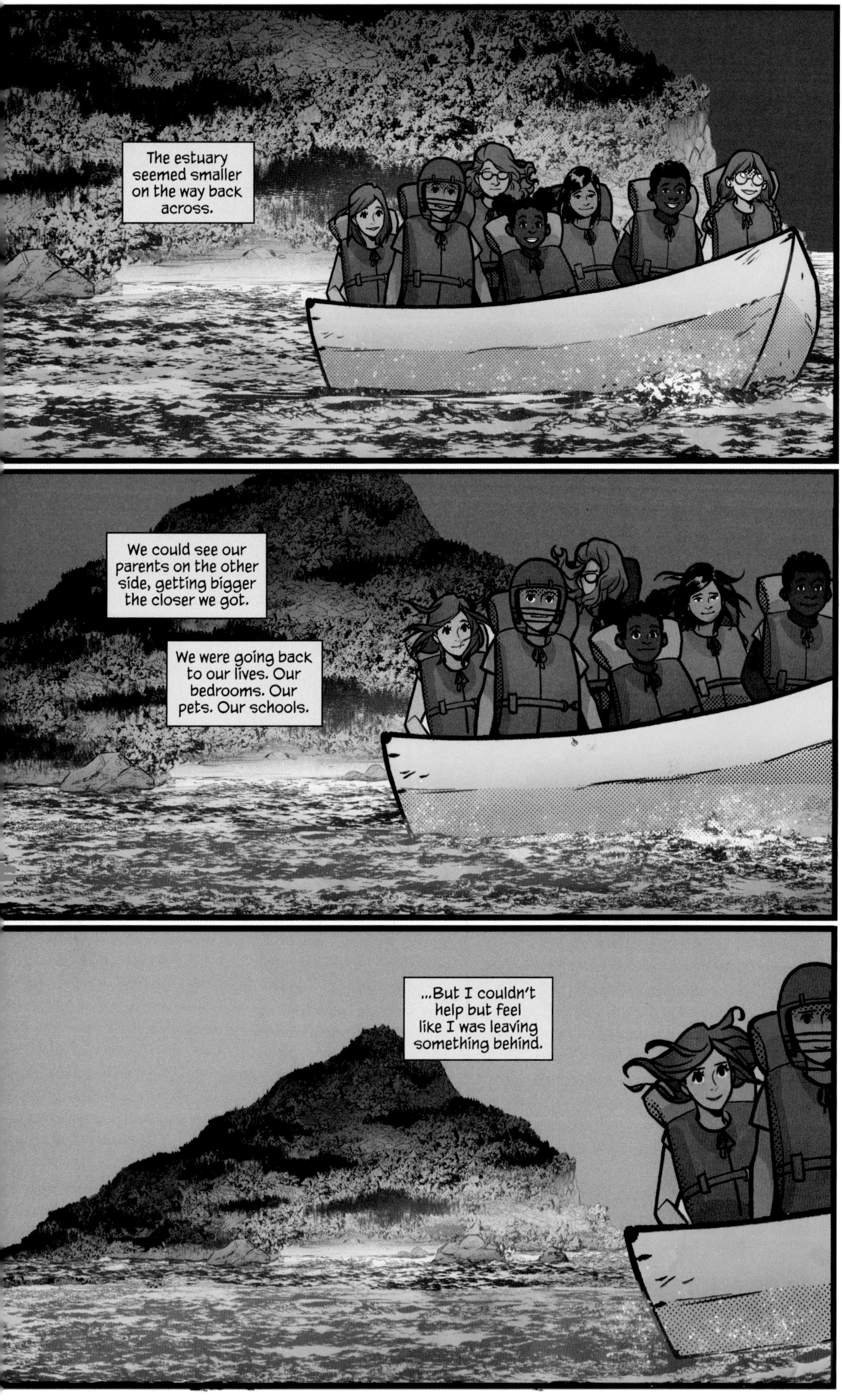
The estuary seemed smaller on the way back across.
We could see our parents on the other side, getting bigger the closer we got.
We were going back to our lives. Our bedrooms. Our pets. Our schools.
...But I couldn't help but feel like I was leaving something behind.

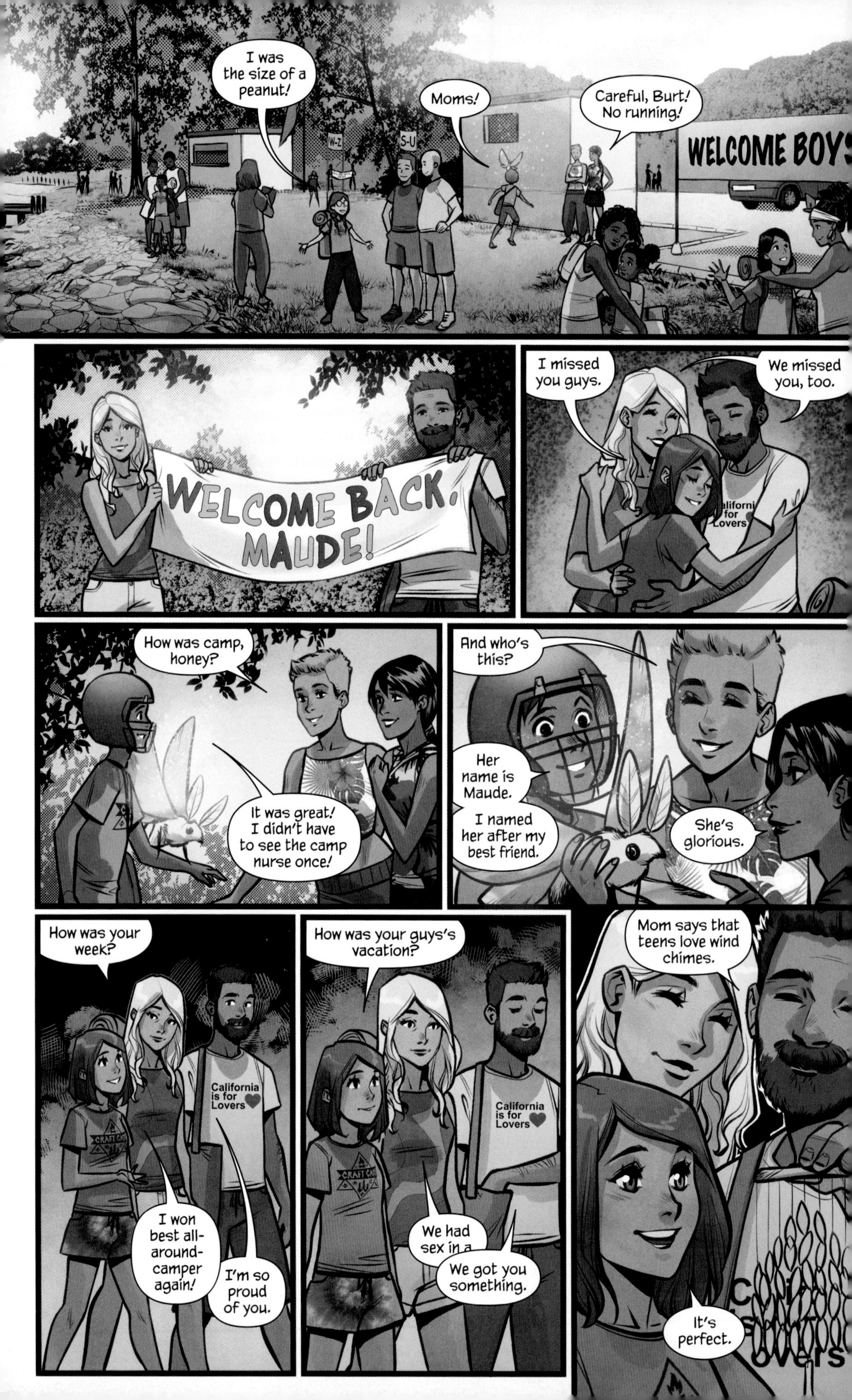
I was the size of a peanut!
W-Z
S-U
Moms!
Careful, Burt! No running!
WELCOME BOYS
WELCOME BACK, MAUDE!
I missed you guys.
We missed you, too.
California is for Lovers
How was camp, honey?
It was great! I didn't have to see the camp nurse once!
And who's this?
Her name is Maude.
I named her after my best friend.
She's glorious.
How was your week?
I won best all-around-camper again!
I'm so proud of you.
California is for Lovers
How was your guys's vacation?
We had sex in a
We got you something.
California is for Lovers
Mom says that teens love wind chimes.
It's perfect.

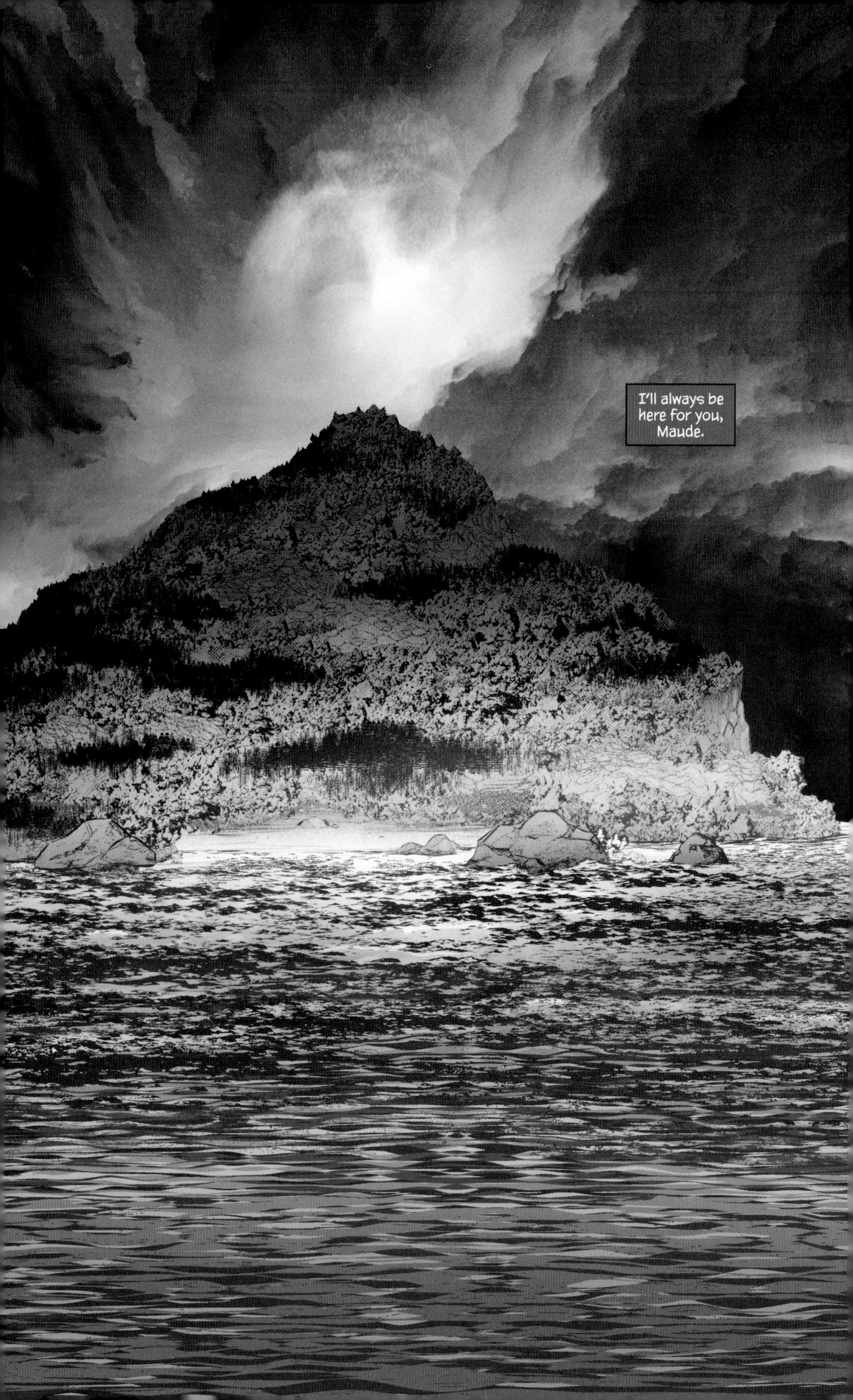
I'll always be here for you, Maude.

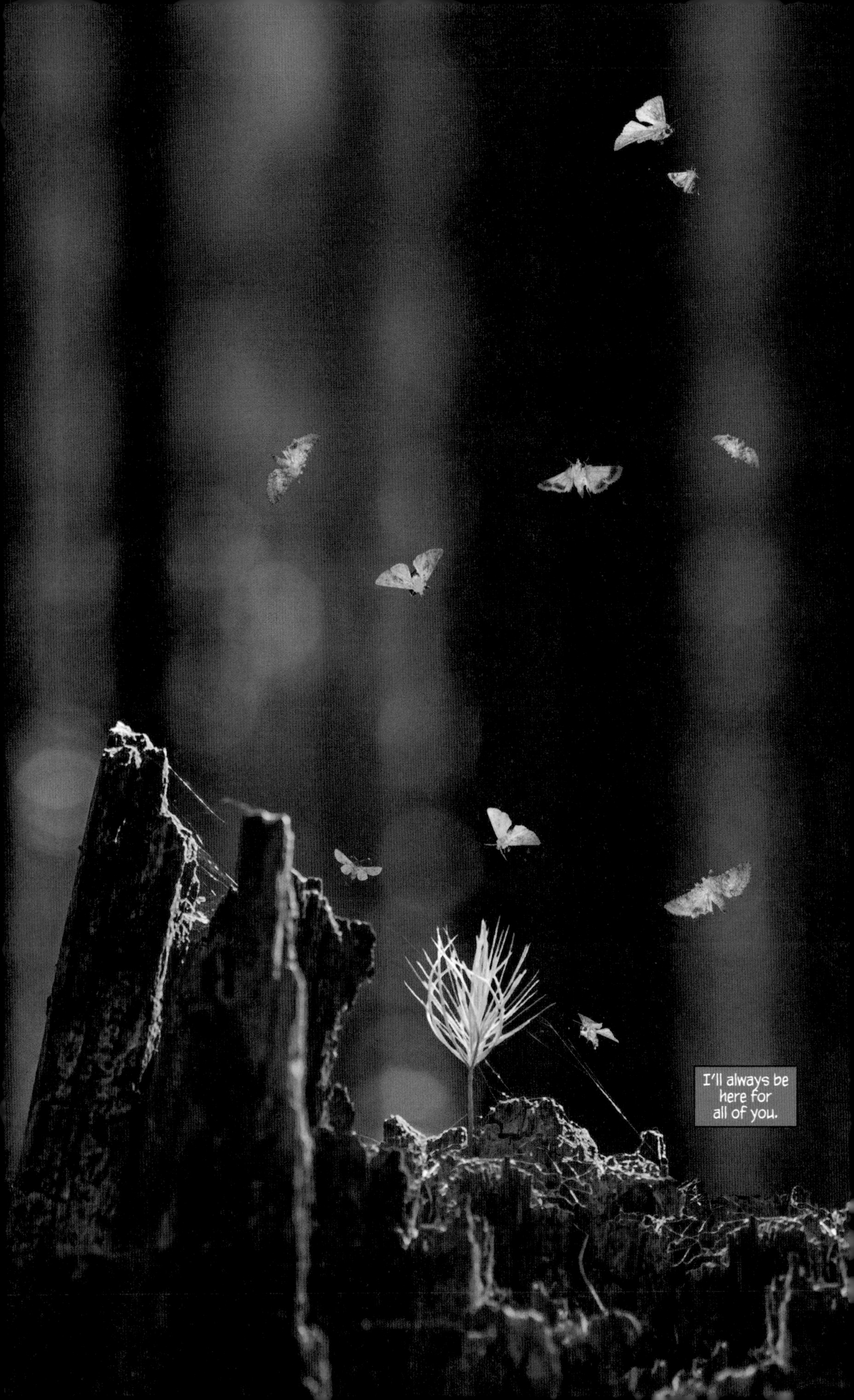
I'll always be here for all of you.

Craft Camp
CAMP COUNSELOR APPLICATION

Please complete and answer all questions accurately. Failure to do so may delay consideration and processing of your application.

Coven Number | Last Name | First Name | Initial

Home Street Address | Birthday (Month - Day - Year)

City | State | Zip Code

Home Phone | Other Phone

Email

Are you a U.S. Citizen?
☐ YES   ☐ NO

Do you have a broom?
☐ YES   ☐ NO

State _____ BL# _____

2. **Prior Criminal History:** Have you EVER pleaded guilty or been convicted of a crime against the Patriarchy? ☐ YES   ☐ NO
What Charge(s)?: _____ Where? (State & County): _____

3. List any/all Craft Camp Awards

1. _____
2. _____
3. _____

4. Are you willing to be a blood donor?   ☐ YES   ☐ NO

5. List four witch references. These cannot be relatives.

1. _____   3. _____
2. _____   4. _____

6. Have you completed Level 4 Transmutation? If not, list the last level completed.   ☐ YES ☐ NO

_____

7. Emergency Contact:

Name _____ Phone _____

8. What Type Spells/Skills/Potions Are You Interested in Teaching?

I certify that answers given here are true and complete to the best of my knowledge. By submitting this application I authorize the investigation of all statements contained herein.

_____   _____
Signature of Youth   Date

_____   _____
Signature of Parent/Legal Guardian   Date

_____   _____
Signature of Youth Coven Leader   Date

IN MEMORIUM
Witches: Death by Execution

Johann Albrecht Adelgrief
Adrienne d'Heur
Agnes Bernauer
Agnes Sampson
Agnes Waterhouse
Ahmed Kusane Hassan
Alice Lake
Alice Nutter
Alice Parker
Allison Balfour
Alse Young
Ama Hemmah
Amina bint Abdulhalim Nassar
Ann Glover
Ann Hibbins
Ann Pudeator
Anna Eriksdotter
Anna Göldi
Anna Koldings
Anna Roleffes
Anna Zippel
Anne de Chantraine
Anne Løset
Anne Palles
Anne Pedersdotter
Antti Tokoi
Barbara Zdunk
Bertrand Guilladot
Bridget Bishop
Brita Zippel
Catherine Deshayes
Catherine Repond
Christenze Kruckow
Elin i Horsnäs
Elisabeth Plainacher
Elizabeth Bassett
Elizabeth Clarke
Elizabeth Howe
Elspeth Reoch
Evaline Gill
Ann Hibbins
Franziska Soder

Gentile Budrioli
George Burroughs
George Jacobs
Giles Corey
Gilles Garnier
Goodwife Greensmith
Goodwife Knapp
Guirandana de Lay
Gyde Spandemager
Helena Curtens
Isabella Rigby
Jacob Distelzweig
Janet Boyman
Janet Horne
Janet, Lady Glamis
Jean Delvaux
Jeane Gardiner
Johannes Junius
John Cubbon
John Proctor
John Willard
Jón Rögnvaldsson
Katharina Henot
Kolgrim
Lasses Birgitta
Laurien Magee
Leatherlips
Lisbeth Nypan
Liu Ju
Malin Matsdotter
Maren Spliid
Märet Jonsdotter
Margaret Inne Quaine
Margaret Jones
Margaret Scott
Maria da Conceição
Maria Pauer
Maria Renata Saenger
    von Mossau
Marie Esnouf
Marigje Arriens
Marketta Punasuomalainen

Martha Carrier
Martha Corey
Mary Eastey
Mary Hicks
Mary Johnson
Mary Pannal
Mary Parker
Matteuccia de Francesco
Mechteld ten Ham
Merga Bien
Michée Chauderon
Mima Renard
Mrs. Kendall
Muree bin Ali Al Asiri
Narbona Dacal
Nyzette Cheveron
Paisley witches
Pappenheimer Family
Pendle witches
Peronne Goguillon
Petronilla de Meath
Polissena of San Macario
Rebecca Lemp
Rebecca Nurse
Ruth Osborne
Sarah Good
Sarah Wildes
Sidonia von Borcke
Soulmother of Küssnacht
Stedelen
Steven Maurer
Susannah Martin
Theoris of Lemnos
Thomas Doughty
Thomas Weir
Urbain Grandier
Ursula Kemp
Ursulina de Jesus
Viola Cantini
Walpurga Hausmannin
Wilmot Redd
Witches of Belvoir
Witches of Warboys

[Issue 5, Cover B]

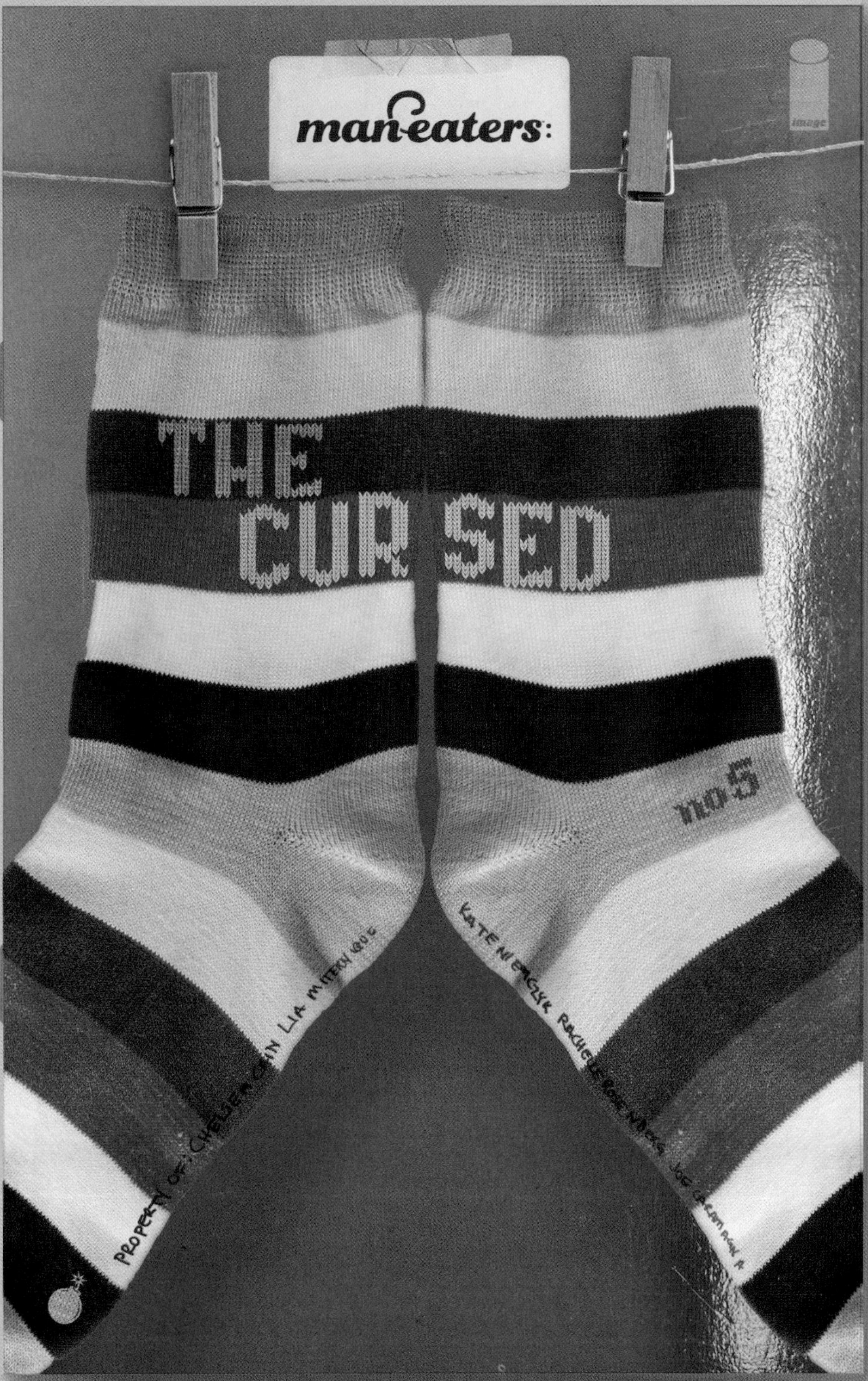

man-eaters:
THE CURSED
no5
PROPERTY OF:

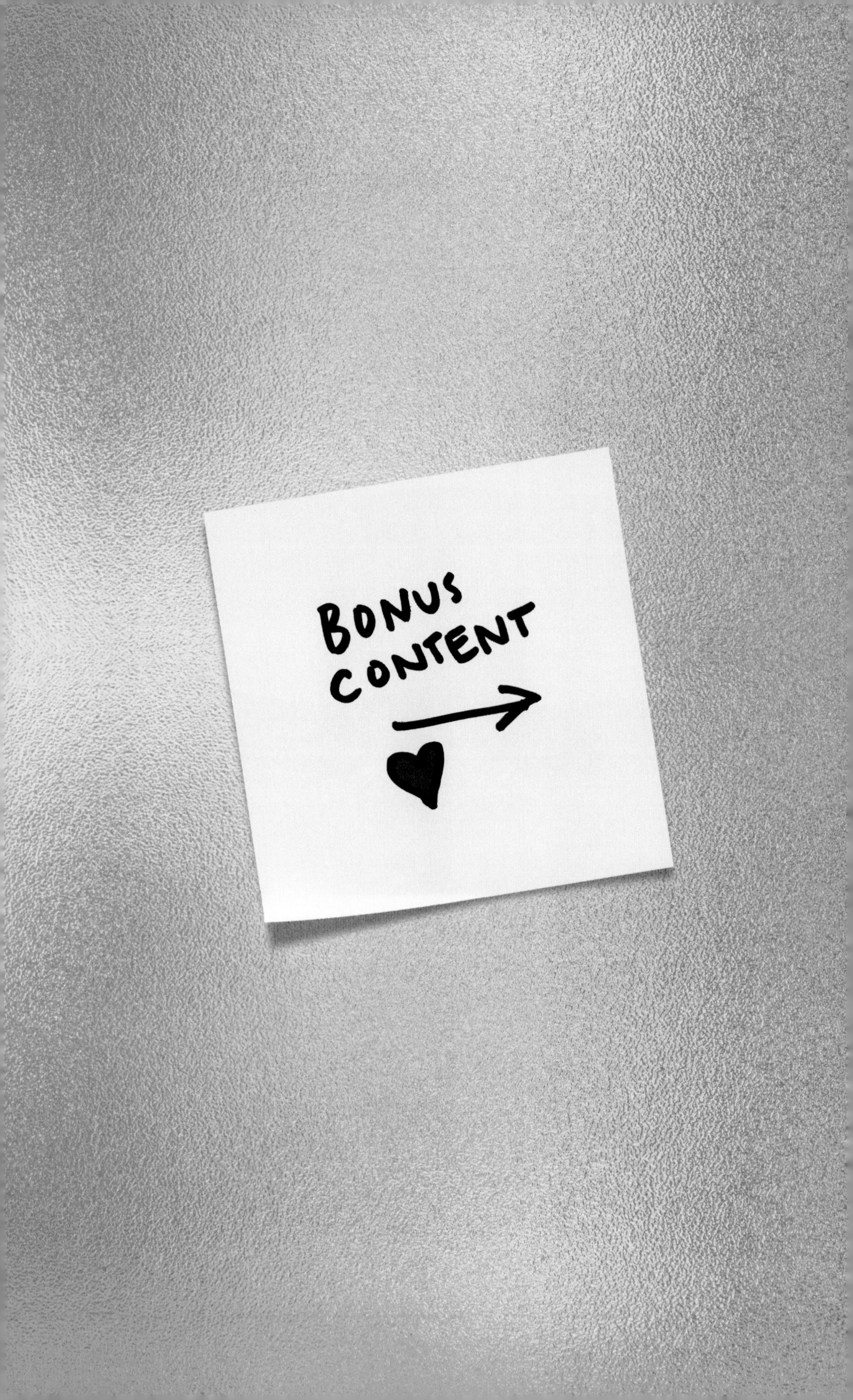
BONUS CONTENT

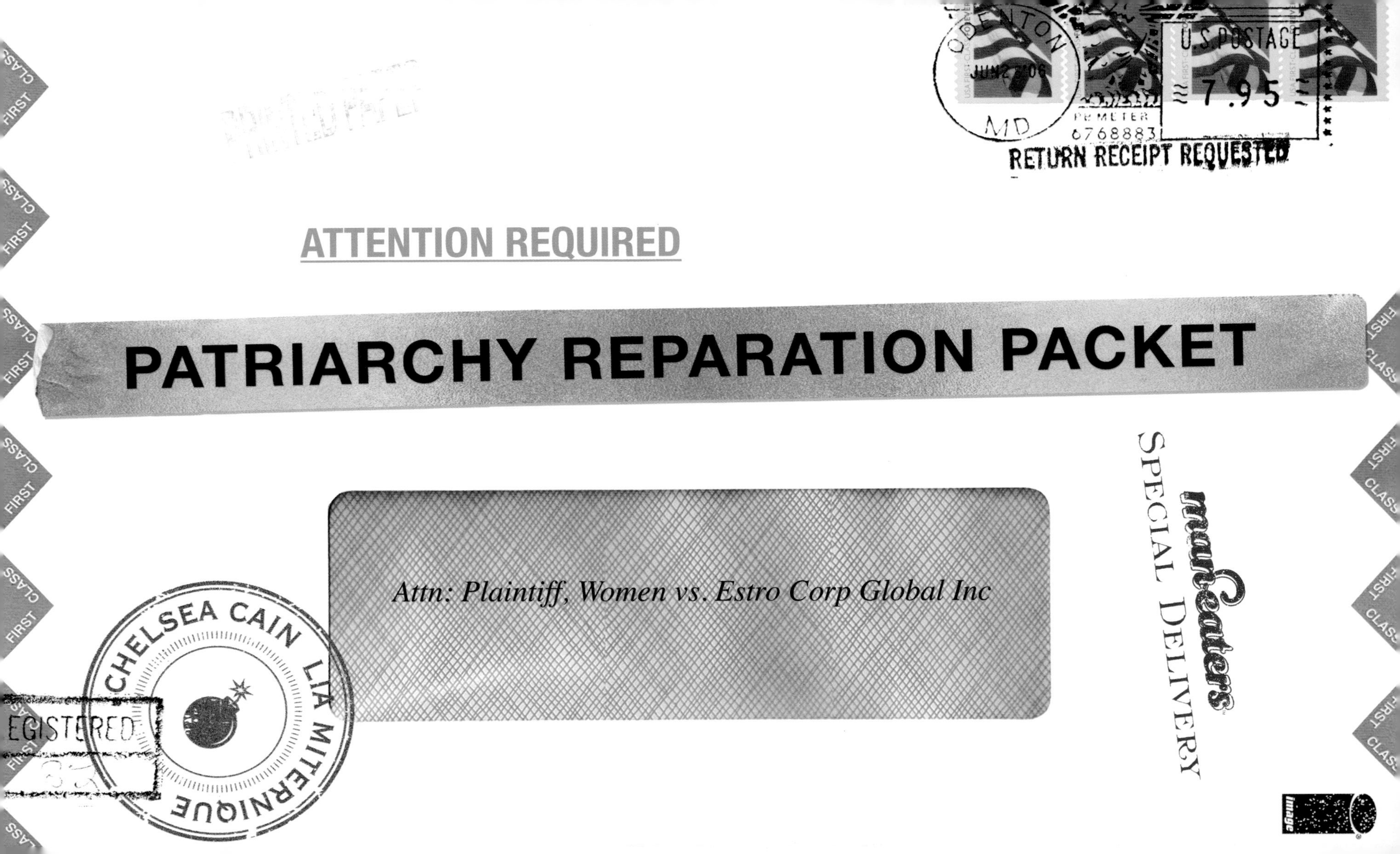

ODENTON MD
JUN 2 2006
U.S. POSTAGE
7.95
PB METER
6768883
RETURN RECEIPT REQUESTED
ATTENTION REQUIRED
PATRIARCHY REPARATION PACKET
Attn: Plaintiff, Women vs. Estro Corp Global Inc
maneaters
SPECIAL DELIVERY
CHELSEA CAIN
LIA MITERNIQUE
EGISTERED
FIRST CLASS
image

YOU HAVE BEEN AWARDED $800.

By accepting this one-time payment, you are forfeiting the right to pursue any further claims against the Patriarchy or its representatives. You fully and completely release and indemnify The Patriarchy and Estro Corp Global Enterprises from all future liability. The Patriarchy is settling your claim but does not publicly acknowledge or admit any fault.

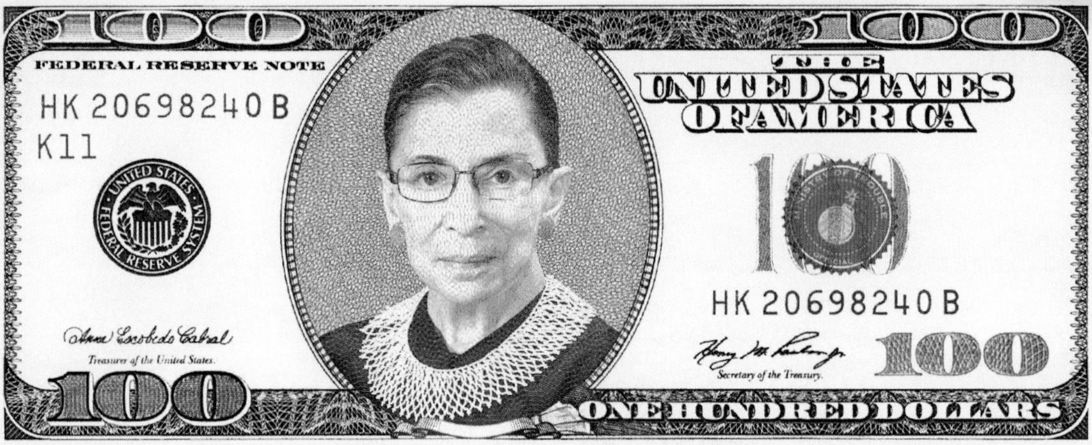
100
FEDERAL RESERVE NOTE
HK 20698240 B
K11
UNITED STATES FEDERAL RESERVE SYSTEM
Anna Escobedo Cabral
Treasurer of the United States.
THE UNITED STATES OF AMERICA
HK 20698240 B
Secretary of the Treasury.
100
ONE HUNDRED DOLLARS

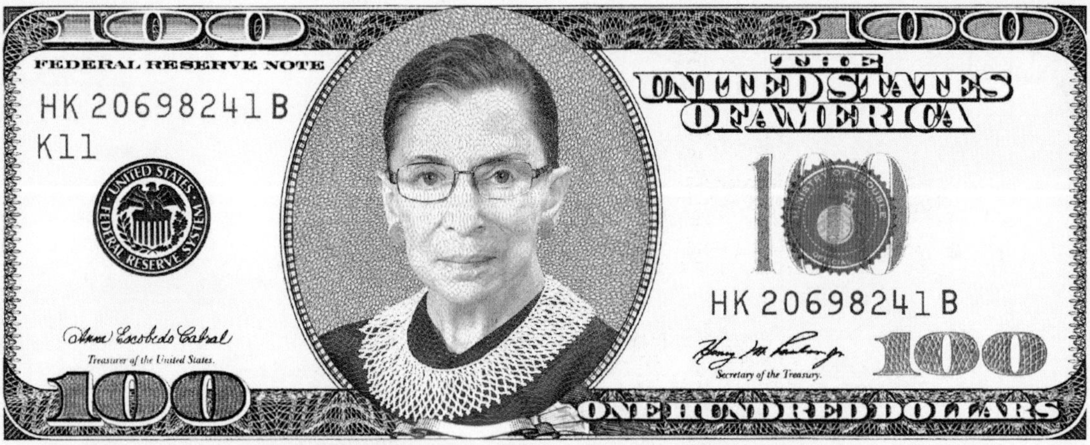
100
FEDERAL RESERVE NOTE
HK 20698241 B
K11
UNITED STATES FEDERAL RESERVE SYSTEM
Anna Escobedo Cabral
Treasurer of the United States.
THE UNITED STATES OF AMERICA
HK 20698241 B
Secretary of the Treasury.
100
ONE HUNDRED DOLLARS

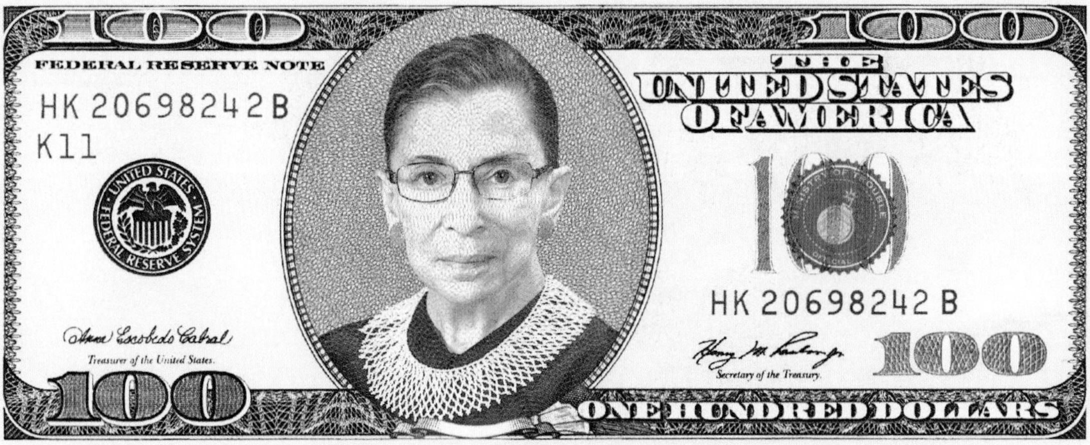
100
FEDERAL RESERVE NOTE
HK 20698242 B
K11
UNITED STATES FEDERAL RESERVE SYSTEM
Anna Escobedo Cabral
Treasurer of the United States.
THE UNITED STATES OF AMERICA
HK 20698242 B
Secretary of the Treasury.
100
ONE HUNDRED DOLLARS

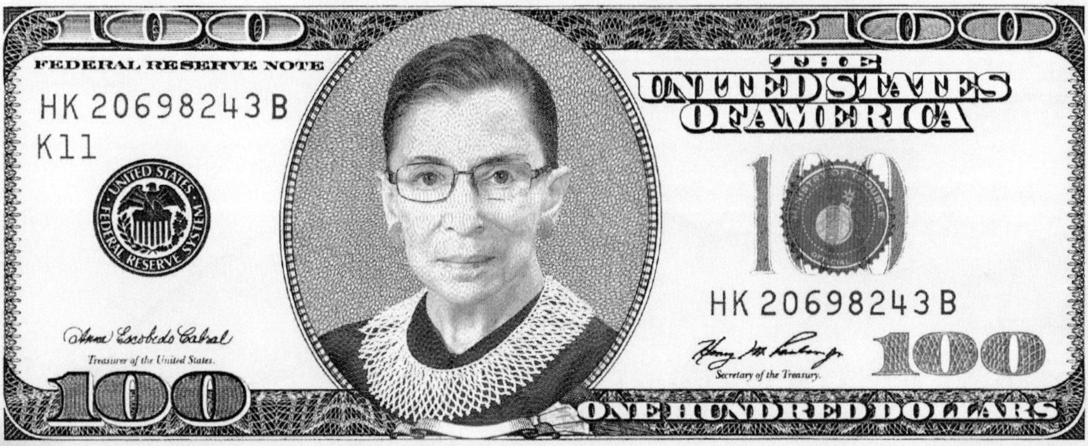
100
FEDERAL RESERVE NOTE
HK 20698243 B
K11
UNITED STATES FEDERAL RESERVE SYSTEM
Anna Escobedo Cabral
Treasurer of the United States.
THE UNITED STATES OF AMERICA
HK 20698243 B
Secretary of the Treasury.
100
ONE HUNDRED DOLLARS

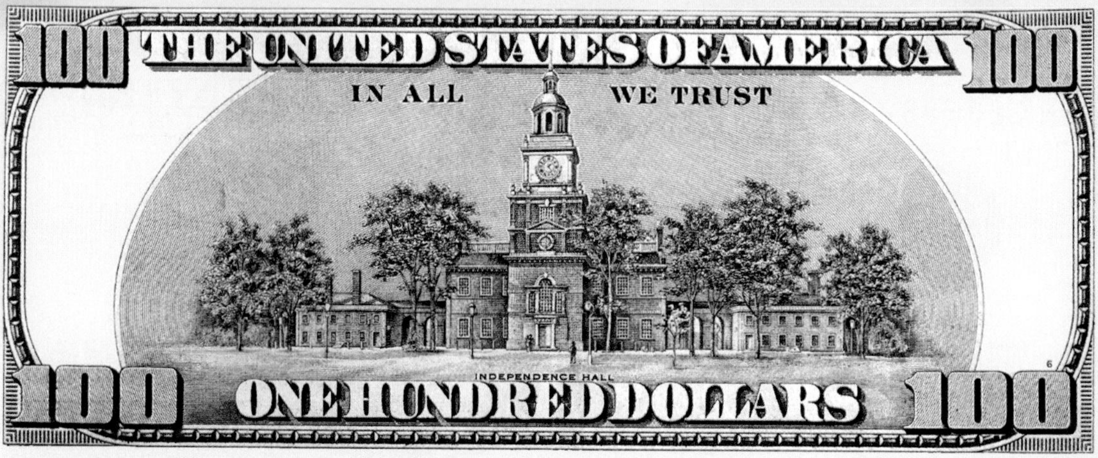
100
THE UNITED STATES OF AMERICA
100
IN ALL
WE TRUST
INDEPENDENCE HALL
100
ONE HUNDRED DOLLARS
100
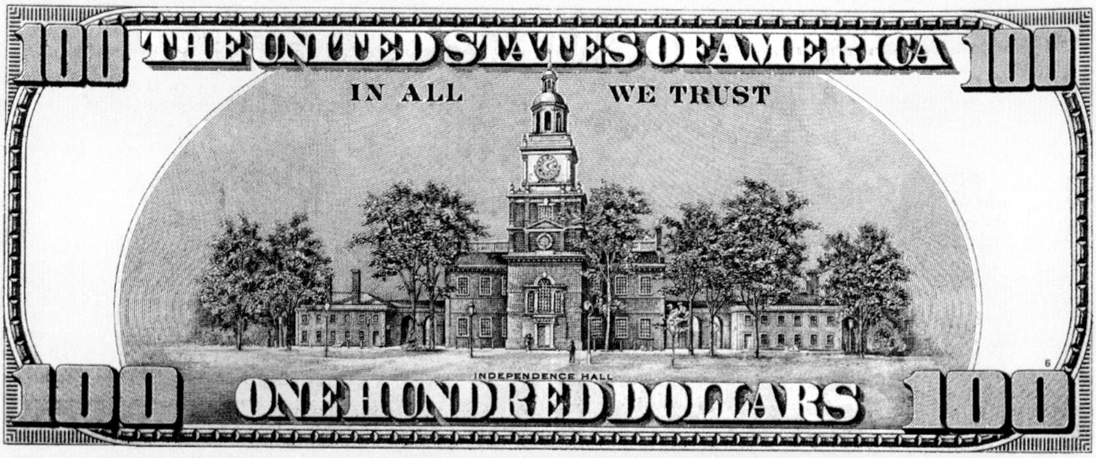
100
THE UNITED STATES OF AMERICA
100
IN ALL
WE TRUST
INDEPENDENCE HALL
100
ONE HUNDRED DOLLARS
100
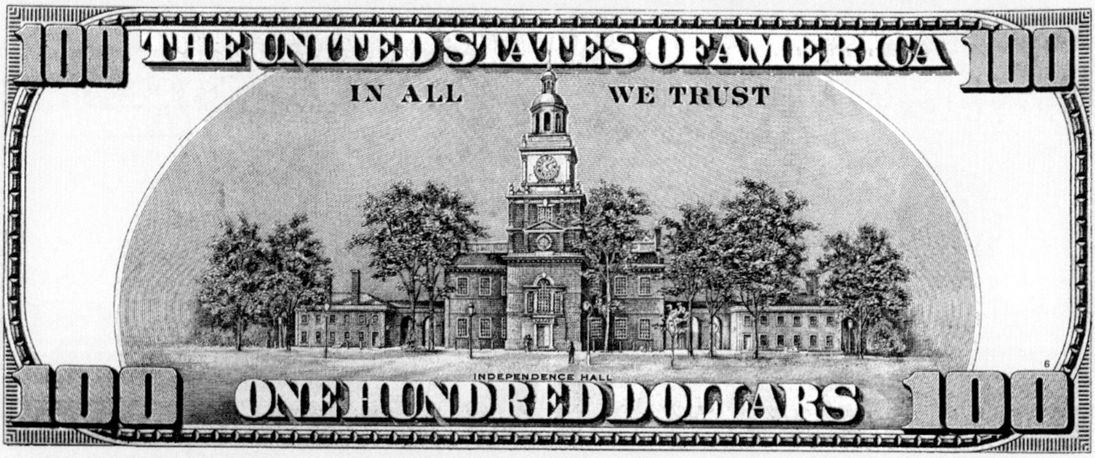
100
THE UNITED STATES OF AMERICA
100
IN ALL
WE TRUST
INDEPENDENCE HALL
100
ONE HUNDRED DOLLARS
100
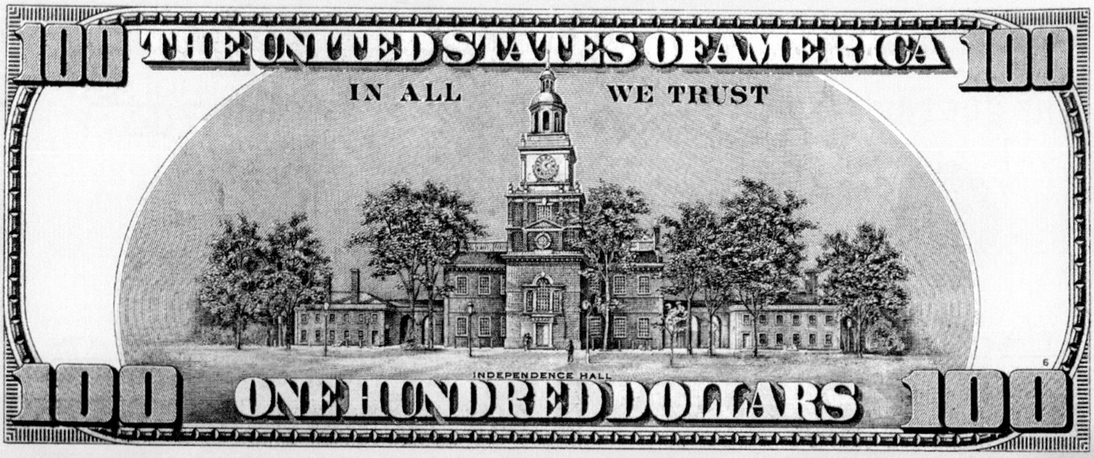
100
THE UNITED STATES OF AMERICA
100
IN ALL
WE TRUST
INDEPENDENCE HALL
100
ONE HUNDRED DOLLARS
100

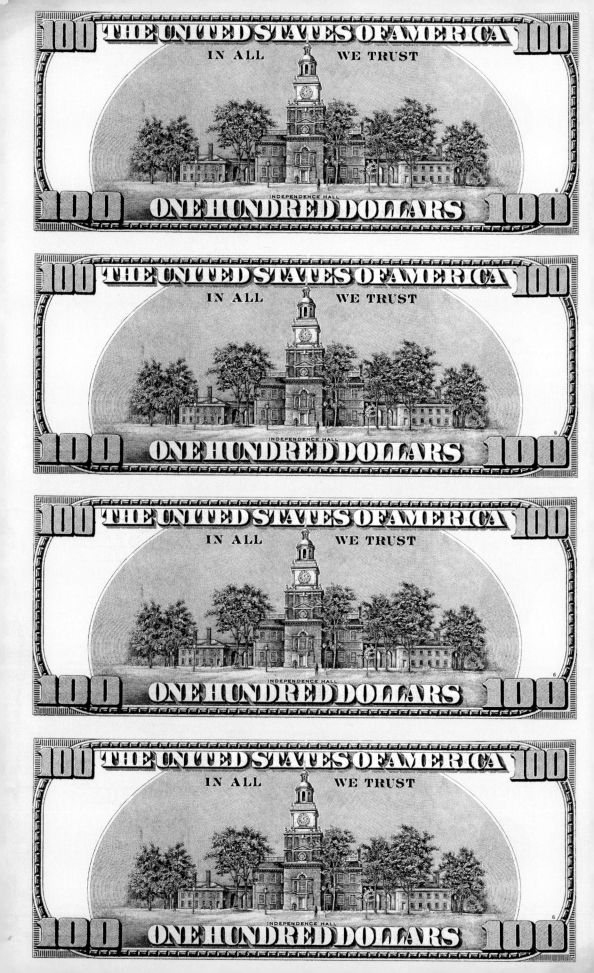

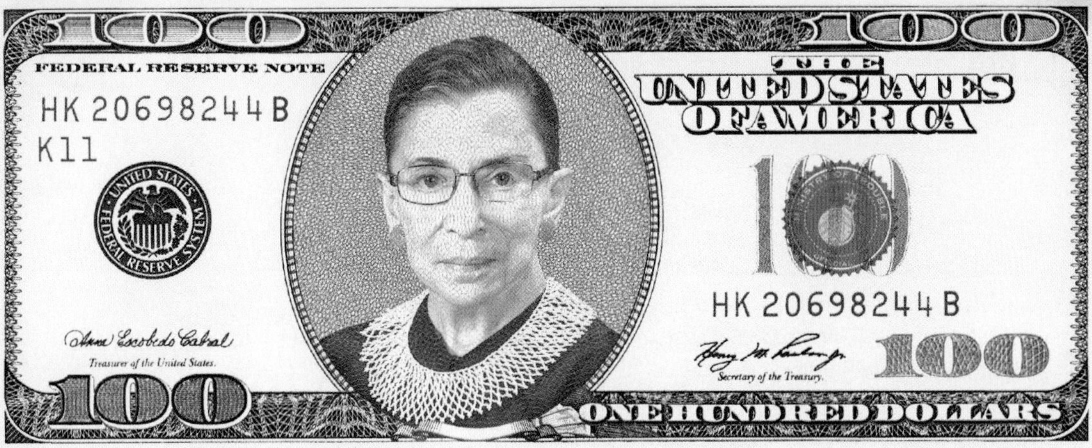
100
FEDERAL RESERVE NOTE
HK 20698244 B
K11
UNITED STATES FEDERAL RESERVE SYSTEM
THE UNITED STATES OF AMERICA
100
HK 20698244 B
Treasurer of the United States.
Secretary of the Treasury.
100
ONE HUNDRED DOLLARS

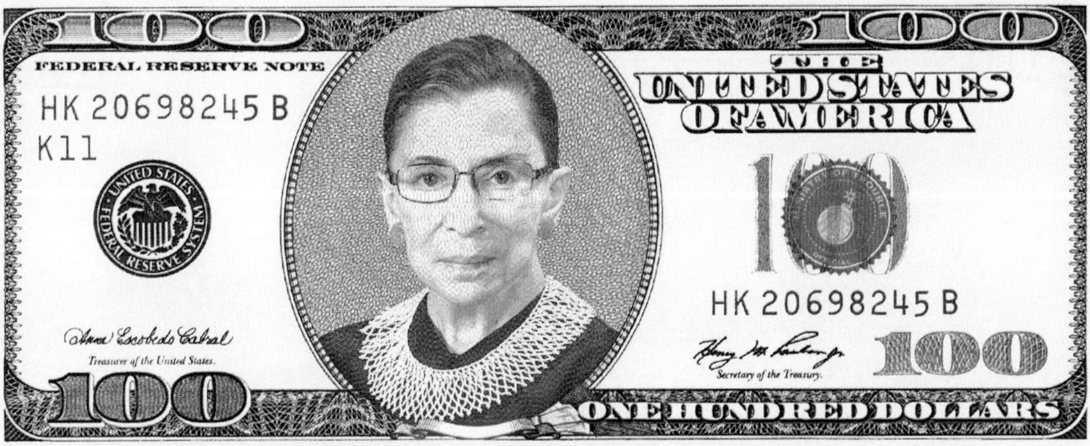
100
FEDERAL RESERVE NOTE
HK 20698245 B
K11
UNITED STATES FEDERAL RESERVE SYSTEM
THE UNITED STATES OF AMERICA
100
HK 20698245 B
Treasurer of the United States.
Secretary of the Treasury.
100
ONE HUNDRED DOLLARS

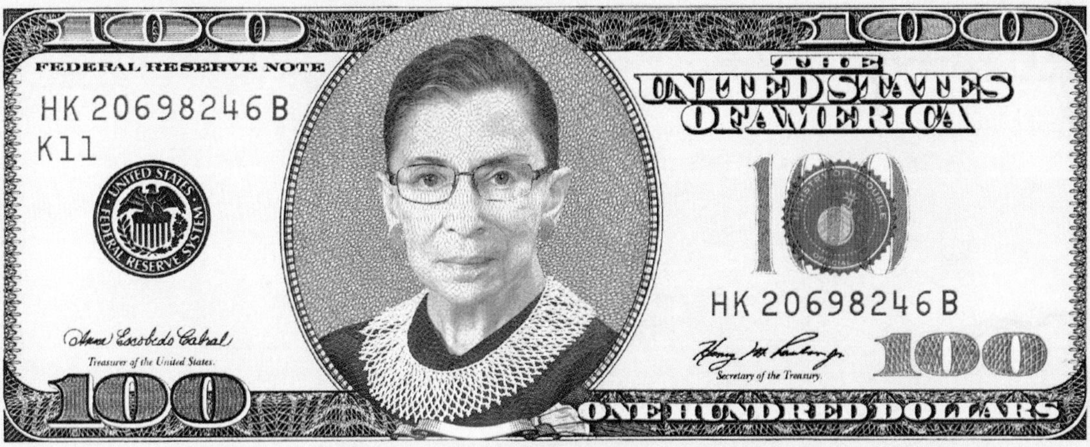
100
FEDERAL RESERVE NOTE
HK 20698246 B
K11
UNITED STATES FEDERAL RESERVE SYSTEM
THE UNITED STATES OF AMERICA
100
HK 20698246 B
Treasurer of the United States.
Secretary of the Treasury.
100
ONE HUNDRED DOLLARS

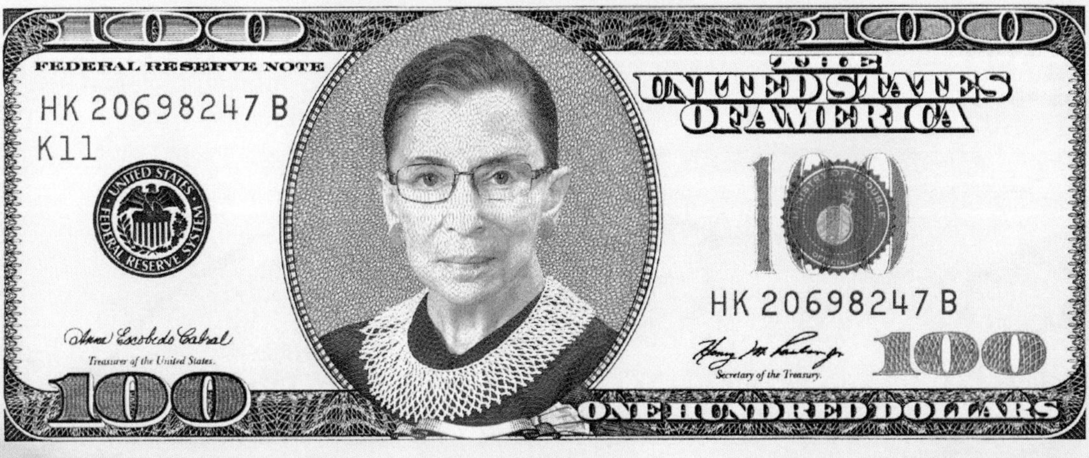
100
FEDERAL RESERVE NOTE
HK 20698247 B
K11
UNITED STATES FEDERAL RESERVE SYSTEM
THE UNITED STATES OF AMERICA
100
HK 20698247 B
Treasurer of the United States.
Secretary of the Treasury.
100
ONE HUNDRED DOLLARS

STOP!

SIGNATURE REQUIRED

TO CLAIM MONEY, YOU MUST SIGN THIS DOCUMENT

NON-DISCLOSURE AGREEMENT (NDA)

I. THE PARTIES. This Non-Disclosure Agreement, hereinafter known as the "Agreement", created on the 4th day of March, 2020 is by and between **THE PATRIARCHY**, hereinafter known as "1st Party", and **THE WOMEN**, hereinafter known as "2nd Party", and collectively known as the "Parties".

WHEREAS, this Agreement is created for the purpose of preventing the unauthorized disclosure of the confidential and proprietary information. The Parties agree as follows:

II. TYPE OF AGREEMENT.

☐ – Unilateral – This Agreement shall be Unilateral, whereas, THE PATRIARCHY shall have sole ownership of the Confidential Information with THE WOMEN being prohibited from disclosing confidential and proprietary information that is to be released by THE PATRIARCHY.

III. RELATIONSHIP. THE PATRIARCHY's relationship to THE WOMEN can be described as PATERNAL and THE WOMEN's relationship to THE PATRIARCHY can be described as ENRAGED.

IV. DEFINITION. For the purposes of this Agreement, the term "Confidential Information" shall include, but not be limited to, documents, records, information and data (whether verbal, electronic or written), drawings, models, apparatus, sketches, designs, schedules, product plans, marketing plans, technical procedures, manufacturing processes, analyses, compilations, studies, software, prototypes, samples, formulas, methodologies, formulations, product developments, patent applications, know-how, experimental results, specifications and other business information, relating to THE PATRIARCHY'S business, assets, operations or contracts.

V. OBLIGATIONS. The obligations of the Parties shall be to hold and maintain the Confidential Information in the strictest of confidence at all times. If any such Confidential Information shall reach a third (3rd) party, or become public, all liability will be on THE WOMEN responsible.

VI. TIME PERIOD. THE WOMEN's duty to hold the Confidential Information in confidence shall remain in effect until the end of time.

VII. INTEGRATION. This Agreement supersedes all prior proposals, agreements, representations, and understandings.

VIII. ENFORCEMENT. The Parties acknowledge and agree that due to the unique and sensitive nature of the Confidential Information, any breach of this Agreement would cause irreparable harm for which damages and/or equitable relief may be sought. THE PATRIARCHY shall be entitled to all remedies available at law.

IX. GOVERNING LAW. This Agreement shall be governed under the laws in the State of ____________________.

IN WITNESS WHEREOF, the parties hereto have executed this Agreement as of the date written below.

1ST PARTY'S SIGNATURE

____

Name (print) EZRA M. BEAUFAN

Date 03/04/20

2ND PARTY'S SIGNATURE (YOU)

____

Name (print) ____________________

Date ____________________

The Patriarchy Apology Fund
1600 Pennsylvania Ave NW
Washington, DC 20500
USA

March 4, 2020

A court authorized this communication. This is not a solicitation.

A settlement has been reached ("Settlement") in the class action lawsuit titled Women, et al., v. Estro Corp Global Enterprises, et al., Case No. 7:16-CV-0735-BCW. Pursuant to the Court's order granting preliminary approval of the settlement, the claims administrator provided notice of the Settlement to you.

The Court granted final approval of the Settlement, and thus we are providing the enclosed Reparations Packet.

REPARATIONS PACKET NUMBER: 12,182,001

Terms and Conditions: The items in this packet are non-transferable.

MINISTRY OF
TROUBLE
INCORPORATED

WRITER/CREATOR CHELSEA CAIN
COVER/CO-CREATOR/DESIGNER LIA MITERNIQUE
ADDITIONAL WRITING BY ELIZA FANTASTIC MOHAN

YOU HAVE BEEN CONTACTED BY THE MINISTRY OF TROUBLE. AWAIT FURTHER INSTRUCTIONS. ☿

PRODUCTION BY TRICIA RAMOS

IMAGE COMICS, INC. • **Robert Kirkman**: Chief Operating Officer • **Erik Larsen**: Chief Financial Officer • **Todd McFarlane**: President • **Marc Silvestri**: Chief Executive Officer • **Jim Valentino**: Vice President • **Eric Stephenson**: Publisher / Chief Creative Officer • **Jeff Boison**: Director of Publishing Planning & Book Trade Sales • **Chris Ross**: Director of Digital Services • **Jeff Stang**: Director of Direct Market Sales • **Kat Salazar**: Director of PR & Marketing • **Drew Gill**: Cover Editor • **Heather Doornink**: Production Director • **Nicole Lapalme**: Controller • **IMAGECOMICS.COM**

...IAL STATEMENT

After deep

Any relatic

We sincere   will
strive to e

We can, ar

We have   ble
accusation   rts.

As a token   our
complime

   Emot
   Pain
   False
   Wron
   Lost

   ... An

*[The encl   im
for physic*

We apprec

SORRY :(

"If we really want to
love
we must learn how to
forgive."

– Mother Teresa

WE'RE SORRY.

It has come to our attention that some of our marketing has caused
confusion. Pantherism is not dangerous. Efforts to suppress menstruation
in order to prevent women and girls from transforming into big cats may
have been misguided. Pantherism is a natural process.

We apologize for the misunderstanding.

Sincerely,

The Patriarchy Apology Fund

(A court mandated trustee of Estro Corp Global Enterprises)

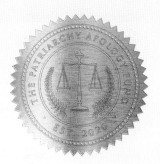

OFFICIAL STATEMENT

After deep reflection, we recognize that some of what we said may have been misinterpreted.

Any relationship between estrogen and homicidal rampages is purely coincidental.

We sincerely apologize for jumping to conclusions. This was a serious oversight and we will strive to ensure that this error is not repeated in the future.

We can, and will, do better.

We have made necessary adjustments and are spending time reflecting on all actionable accusations of wrongdoing currently under review by state, federal, and international courts.

As a token of our apology we are sending you this exciting compensation package, with our compliments. You'll find these special gifts divided into the following categories:

Emotional Distress
Pain & Suffering
False Imprisonment
Wrongful Death
Lost Wages

... And more!

[The enclosed vouchers meet the legal definition of "damages" as defined as a viable claim for physical and mental suffering.]

We appreciate your understanding in this matter.

THE PATRIARCHY APOLOGY FUND

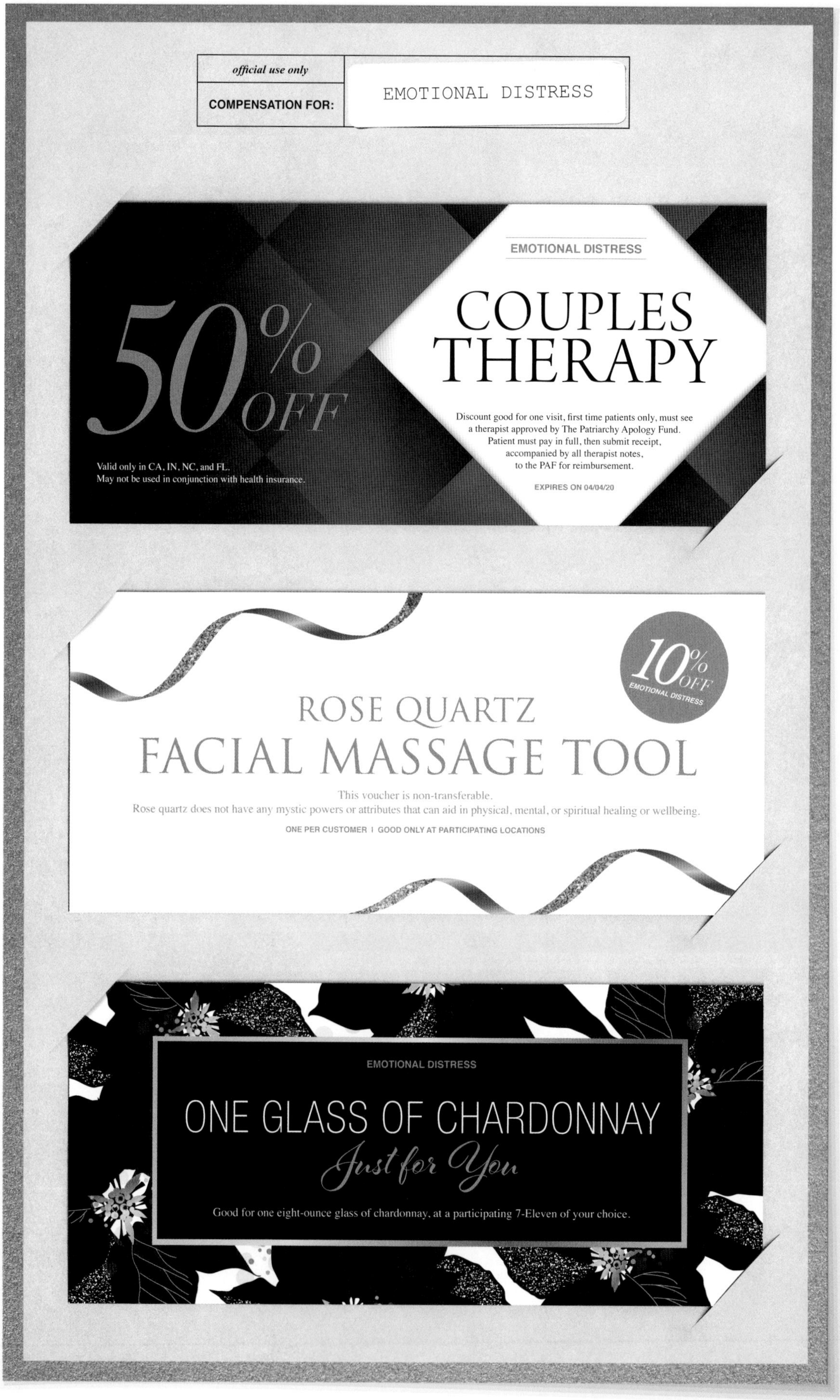

official use only
COMPENSATION FOR:
EMOTIONAL DISTRESS
EMOTIONAL DISTRESS
COUPLES THERAPY
50% OFF
Discount good for one visit, first time patients only, must see a therapist approved by The Patriarchy Apology Fund. Patient must pay in full, then submit receipt, accompanied by all therapist notes, to the PAF for reimbursement.
EXPIRES ON 04/04/20
Valid only in CA, IN, NC, and FL.
May not be used in conjunction with health insurance.
10% OFF
EMOTIONAL DISTRESS
ROSE QUARTZ
FACIAL MASSAGE TOOL
This voucher is non-transferable.
Rose quartz does not have any mystic powers or attributes that can aid in physical, mental, or spiritual healing or wellbeing.
ONE PER CUSTOMER | GOOD ONLY AT PARTICIPATING LOCATIONS
EMOTIONAL DISTRESS
ONE GLASS OF CHARDONNAY
Just for You
Good for one eight-ounce glass of chardonnay, at a participating 7-Eleven of your choice.

official use only	PAIN & SUFFERING
COMPENSATION FOR:	

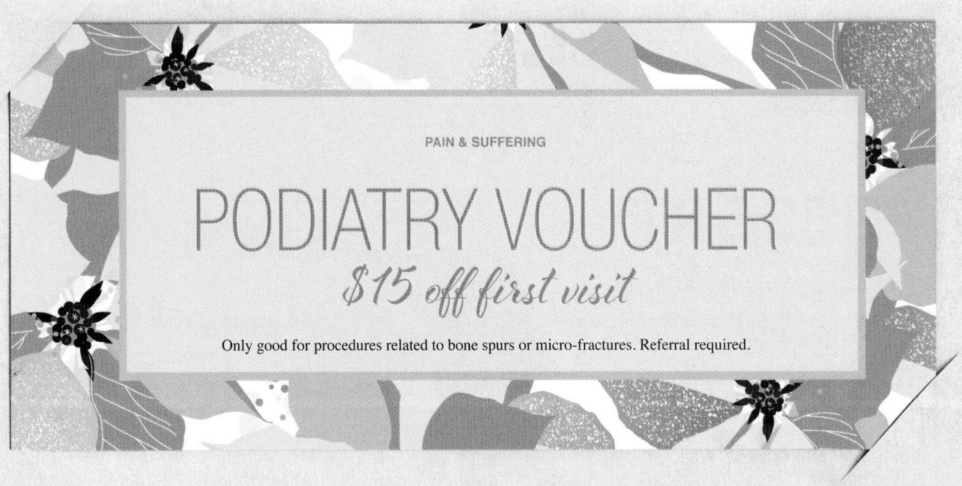
PAIN & SUFFERING
PODIATRY VOUCHER
$15 off first visit
Only good for procedures related to bone spurs or micro-fractures. Referral required.

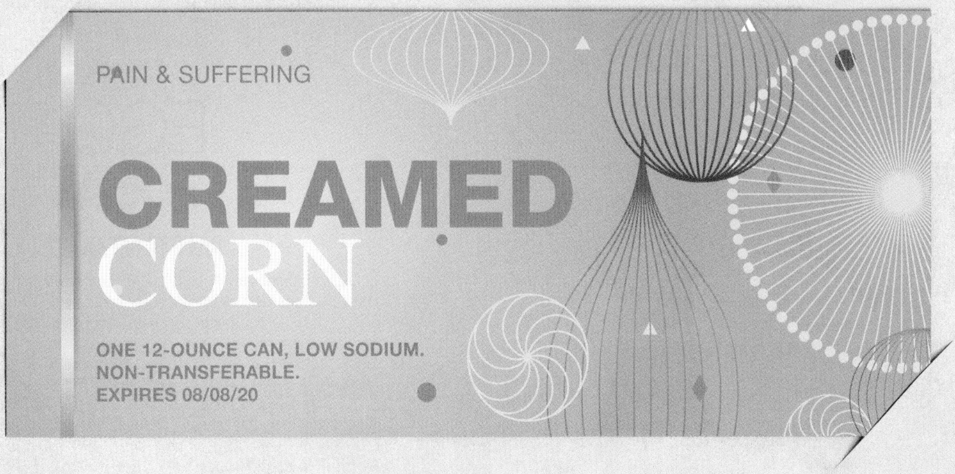
PAIN & SUFFERING
CREAMED
CORN
ONE 12-OUNCE CAN, LOW SODIUM.
NON-TRANSFERABLE.
EXPIRES 08/08/20

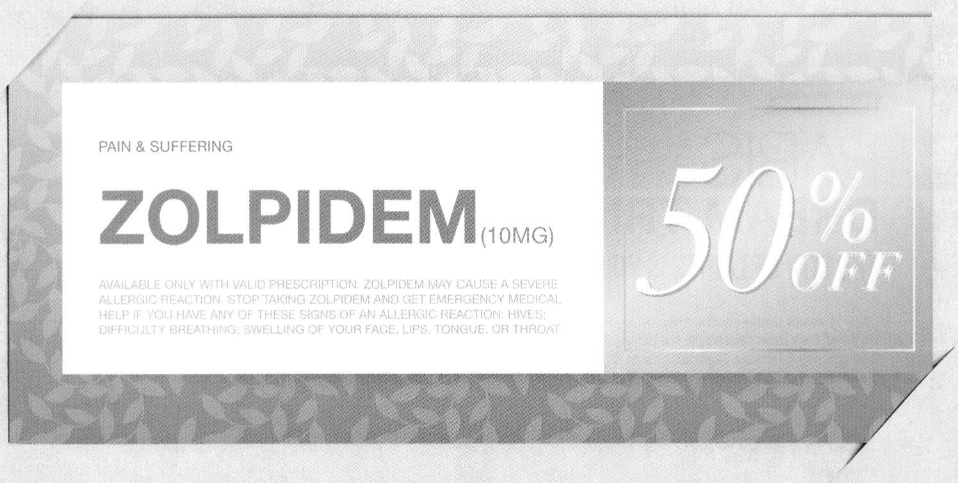
PAIN & SUFFERING
ZOLPIDEM (10MG)
AVAILABLE ONLY WITH VALID PRESCRIPTION. ZOLPIDEM MAY CAUSE A SEVERE ALLERGIC REACTION. STOP TAKING ZOLPIDEM AND GET EMERGENCY MEDICAL HELP IF YOU HAVE ANY OF THESE SIGNS OF AN ALLERGIC REACTION: HIVES; DIFFICULTY BREATHING; SWELLING OF YOUR FACE, LIPS, TONGUE, OR THROAT.
50% OFF

Every year, women lose $513 billion in lost wages due to institutional sexism and limited professional opportunities
Please accept these checks as compensation for your inconvenience.

ENDORSE HERE:

X _____

_____

_____

DO NOT SIGN/WRITE/STAMP BELOW THIS LINE
FOR FINANCIAL INSTITUTION USAGE ONLY

14235789

ENDORSE HERE:

X _____

_____

_____

DO NOT SIGN/WRITE/STAMP BELOW THIS LINE
FOR FINANCIAL INSTITUTION USAGE ONLY

14235789

official use only	
COMPENSATION FOR:	WRONGFUL DEATH

WRONGFUL DEATH

BIG SALE

70% OFF

EZRA'S ARTISANAL VINEGARS

While supplies last*

*Some infused vinegars are excluded from this offer, including marionberry, blueberry, saucy pine, hollyhock, strawberry, blackberry, raspberry, and dandelion.

WRONGFUL DEATH

NEW DROP

SALE

50% OFF

MOM JEANS

Submit receipt for reimbursement. Reimbursement may take 10-42 months. Bootcut, low rise, skinny, flared, jeggings, and boyfriend jeans not eligible.

WRONGFUL DEATH

FREE RENTAL

AT A VIDEO STORE OF YOUR CHOICE!

DVD OR VHS!

JUST PRESENT THIS VOUCHER AT THE COUNTER, ALONG WITH VIDEO STORE MEMBERSHIP CARD.

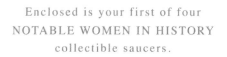

Enclosed is your first of four
NOTABLE WOMEN IN HISTORY
collectible saucers.

FRANCES PERKINS

THE PATRIARCHY APOLOGY FUND

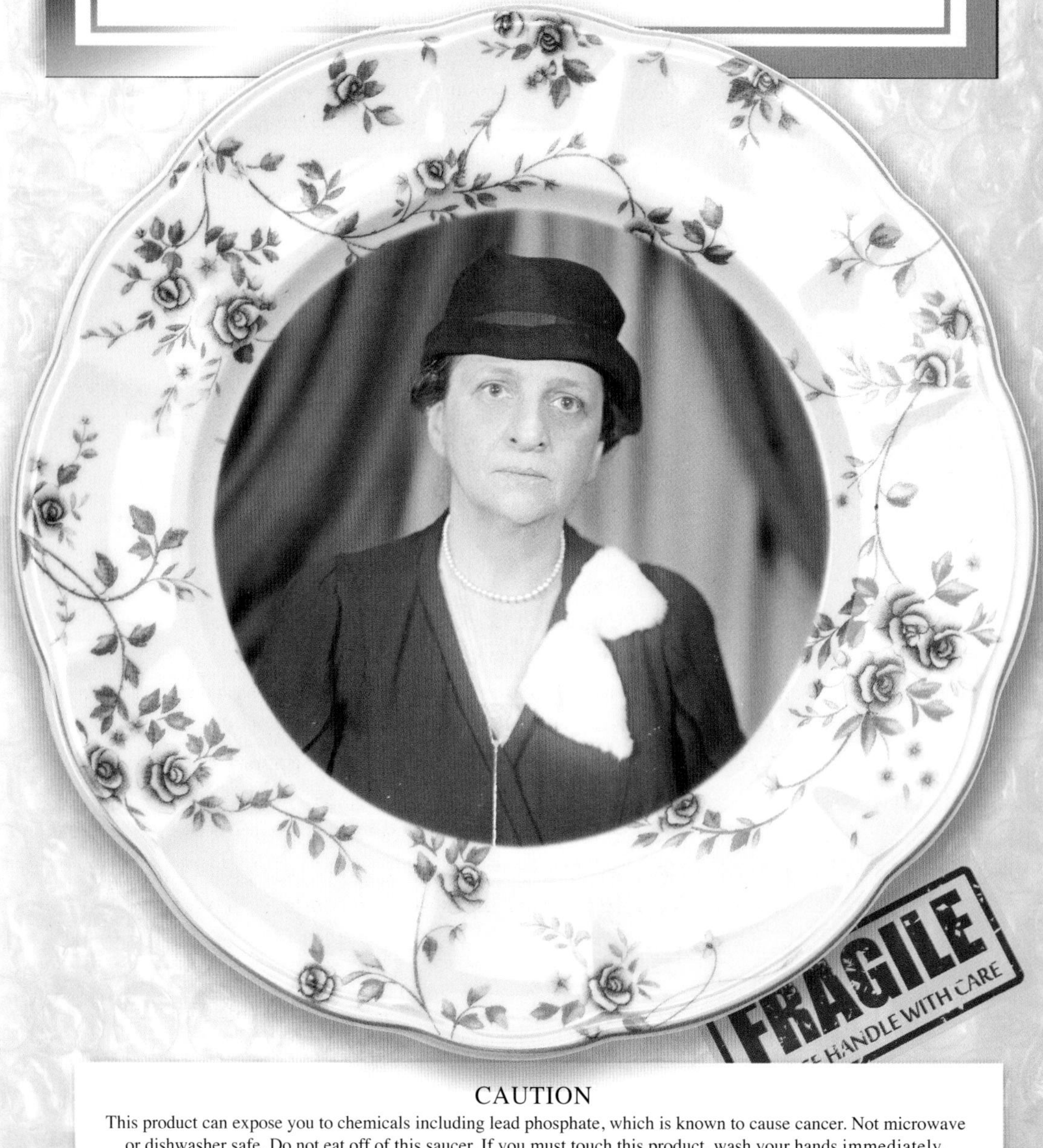
FRAGILE
HANDLE WITH CARE

CAUTION

This product can expose you to chemicals including lead phosphate, which is known to cause cancer. Not microwave or dishwasher safe. Do not eat off of this saucer. If you must touch this product, wash your hands immediately. Keep away from children. Teacup sold separately.

FRANCES PERKINS

(1 of 4)

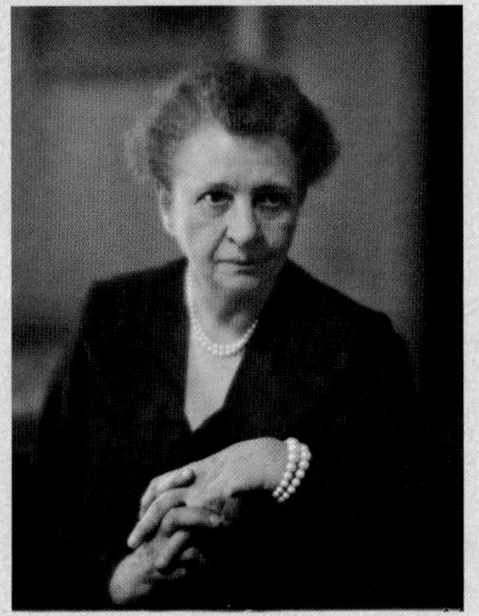

Frances Perkins was born in Boston, in 1880, and was raised in a household that promoted the idea that people became poor as a result of alcohol or laziness. While attending Mount Holyoke College, where she would earn degrees in chemistry and physics, Perkins took a class in American Economic History that required her to visit local mills. She was horrified at the lack of child labor laws and the dangerous working conditions. Perkins credited the experience with inspiring her dedication to social justice. She went on to study economics at The Wharton School of the University of Pennsylvania, and, in 1910, earned a master's degree in political science from Columbia University. This was ten years before women in the U.S. were constitutionally guaranteed the right to vote. At age 30, Perkins became executive secretary of the New York City Consumers League, a position that allowed her to improve the fire protection in factories and limit the number of hours that women and children had to work to 54 per week. On March 25th, 1911, the Triangle Shirtwaist Factory burned down in New York City, killing 146 workers — most of them women and girls — many of whom jumped from windows to their deaths after discovering that exits were blocked or doors locked. Perkins witnessed the tragedy. It was an event that would change her life. In the aftermath of the blaze, she became executive secretary of the newly formed Committee on Safety of the City of New York. She went on to serve in many positions in New York government. In 1933, President Franklin Roosevelt appointed Perkins to be the Secretary of Labor. She was the first woman to serve in a presidential Cabinet, and the first women to be in the presidential line of succession. She held the post for twelve years, and played a key role in establishing many of the laws we take for granted, including minimum wage, Social Security benefits, abolishing child labor, and basic worker safety (including the "fire exit" sign).

The Patriarchy Apology Fund would like to recognize her with this commemorative saucer.

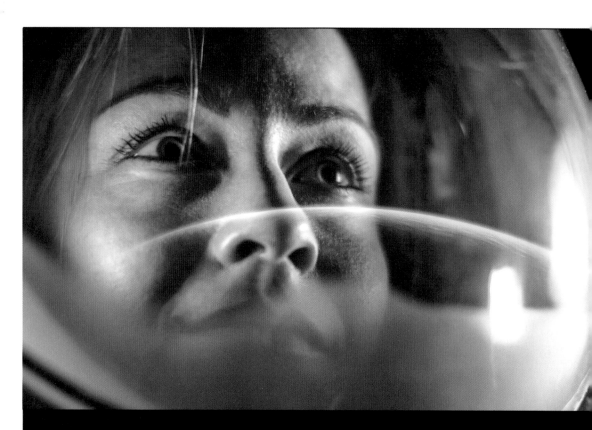

DREAM BIG.

Only 11% of history's space explorers have been women.

That's why we are immediately sending
TEN WOMEN*
TO THE MOON.

**Also, NASA will no longer require
astronauts to take math or science.**

*Women will be selected at random and receive one week of training by a certified NASA flight instructor.

YOU'RE INVITED...

...TO WATCH TEN WOMEN
GO TO THE MOON

DON'T MISS THIS
THRILLING TELEVISION EVENT
Date and Time To Be Determined

This event will be carried live by the following cable providers:

ATT&T Uverse	*Spectrum*	*Buckeye Broadband*
Cox	*Verizon*	*Volcano Vision, Inc.*
DIRECTTV	*Xfinity*	*WOW!*
DISH	*Access Montana*	*yondoo*
Optimum	*Acme Communications*	*Wheat State Television*

Paid For By Big Corn

FAMILY DINNER

brought to you by

CREAMED CORN

the taste of tradition!

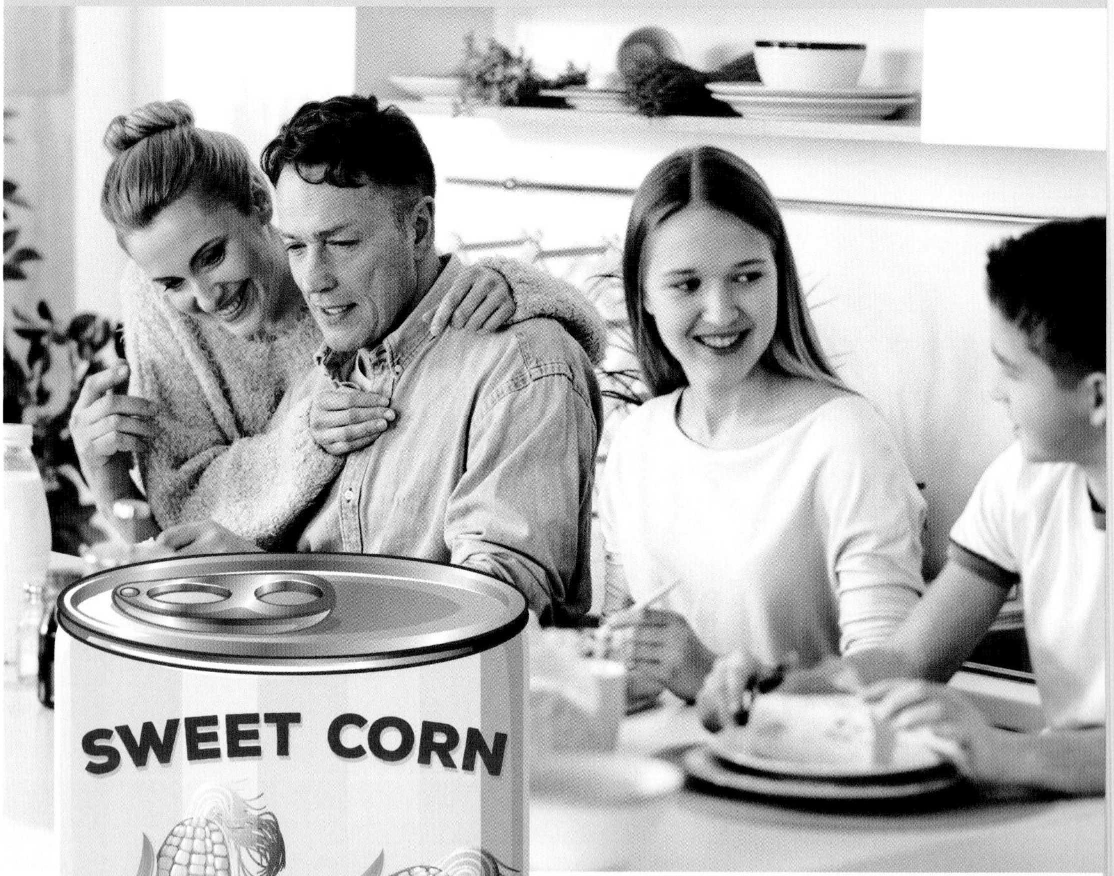

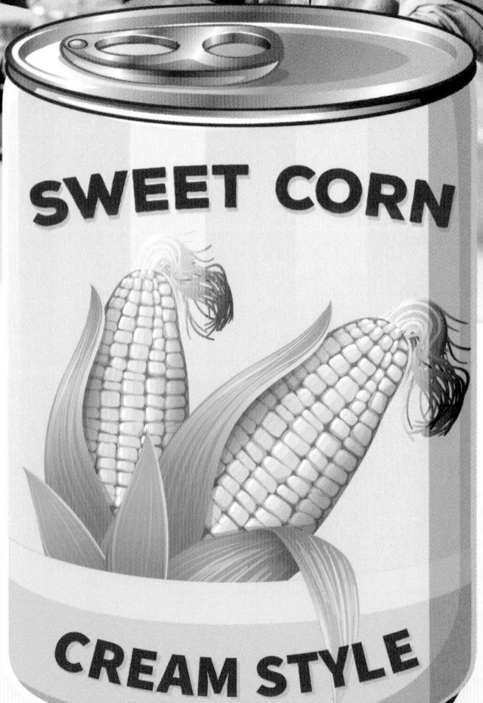
SWEET CORN
CREAM STYLE

EAT TOGETHER. EAT CORN.

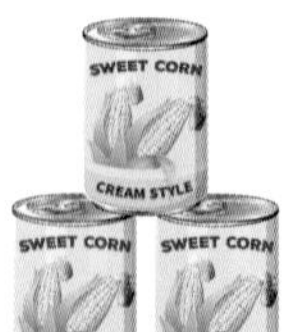
SWEET CORN
CREAM STYLE
SWEET CORN
CREAM STYLE
SWEET CORN
CREAM STYLE

BUY 3 GET 1 FREE!

Coupon not valid in all states.
Personal-size cans only,

REMINDER:

All Estro Corp products have been recalled. To get a full refund, simply enclose printed receipts for purchased products in the enclosed envelope. Processing may take up to 52 months. Please fill out appropriate information on back of envelope. Any error may result in delay of processing.

Thank you for your business and have a nice day!

NAME_____

REGULAR HOURS				
OVERTIME				
AMOUNT EARNED				
Less: F. I. C. A.				
Less: Fed Withholding Tax				
Less: State Disab. Ins.				
Less: U. S. Savings Bonds				
Less: State Withholding Tax				
Less: City Withholding Tax				
NET AMOUNT DUE				

RECEIVED IN FULL SETTLEMENT FOR SERVICES TO DATE

SIGNED_____

SAFETY RECALL!

PRODUCT RECALL

RECALL ALERT

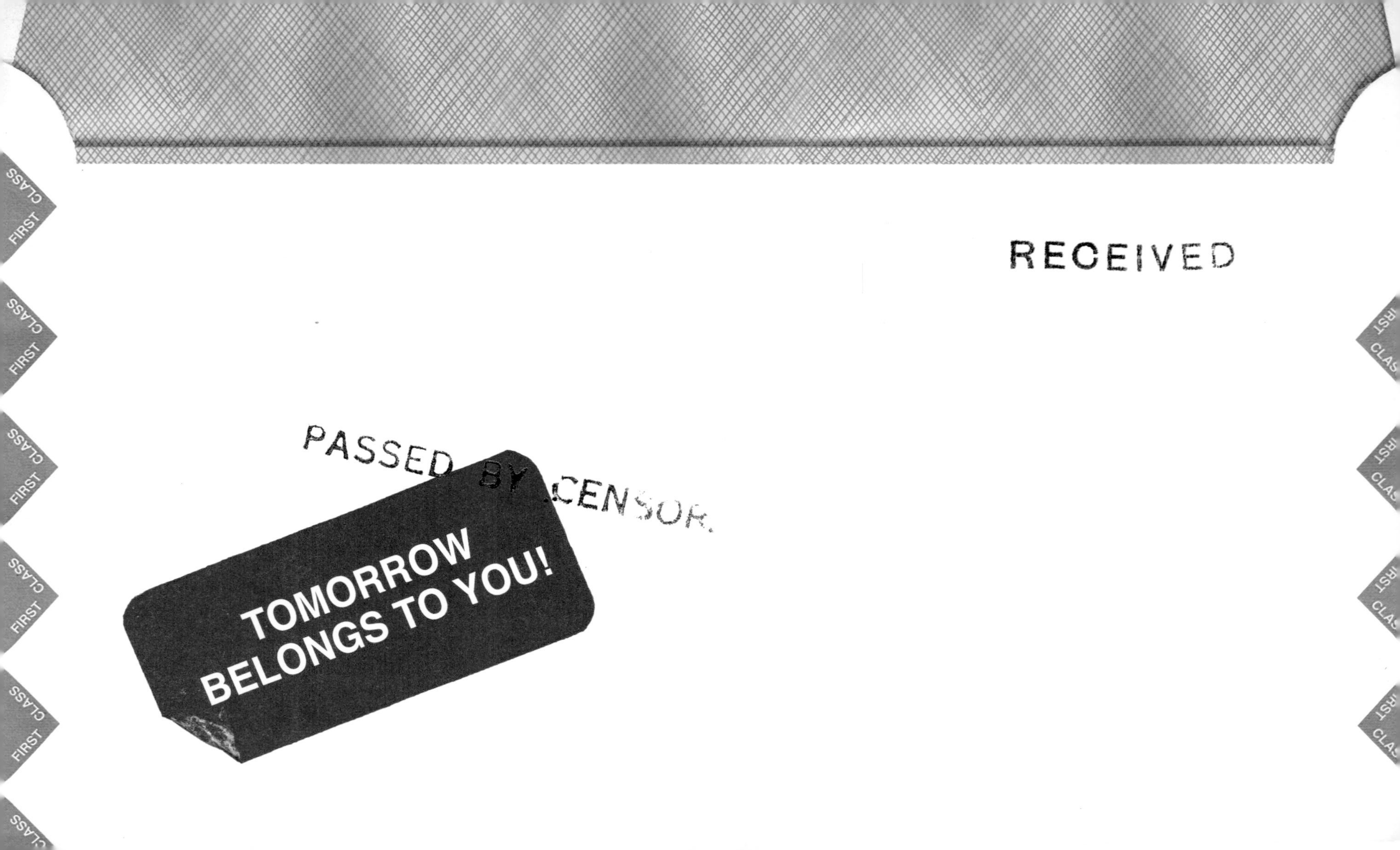

FIRST CLASS FIRST CLASS FIRST CLASS FIRST CLASS FIRST CLASS

TOMORROW BELONGS TO YOU!

PASSED BY CENSOR

RECEIVED